To ~~.,
Hope ~~ enjoy

Beverley Westwood.

TIME TRAIN

Beverley Jane Westwood

CROSSFIELD
PUBLISHING

Time Train

© Copyright by author, May 2012

Westwood, Beverley Jane

First Edition

ISBN-13: 978-0968664629 (Crossfield Publishing)

ISBN-10: 0968664628

Cataloguing in Publication Data

Fiction / Science Fiction / Adventure

1. time travel 2. quantum 3. SETI 4. artificial intelligence

5. aliens

Edited by E. Tina Crossfield

Cover design and layout by Harald Kunze

Illustration of Jake and Kiki by Larry Stilwell

font style Garamond

Manuscript prepared by Crossfield Publishing

502 Downey Place, Okotoks, AB, Canada

www.crossfieldpublishing.ca

Printed by Houghton Boston, Saskatoon, SK, Canada

See us on Facebook

To Henry: I love you all the way to the edge
of the universe and back again, which is a very very long way!
This book is for you.

Acknowledgements

My deepest appreciation to Tina Crossfield, my mentor, agent, publisher, and above all, wonderful friend. I would never have got this far without you.

Harald Kunze for his amazing interpretation of my vision into the artwork that covers this book and Larry Stillwell for illustrations of Jake and Kiki.

The members of my critique group who put me on the right track. Grant Coleman, Cam Geddes, Ron Ostafichuk, Kalder Pelkey-Muniz, Bethan Robson and Gail (Crossfield) Morrow.

Also special thanks to my friends who kept me going with plenty of humour and cappuccinos. Ruth Muniz, Monica Ostafichuk, Sasha Raimova, Kathie Betts-Geddes, Kim Regular, Amanda Butcher, Anne Morris, Jacqui Coen and Tammy Pelletier.

And much love to Stephen who has lived uncomplainingly with this book for over a year now! Also my parents John and Jacqueline Watson for the endless transatlantic phone calls they've endured listening to dialogue, plot development and computer woes.

My friends in England who have supported me my whole life in whatever endeavor I have undertaken. You know who you are...

Helen Johnston, Gillian Turnbull, Joanne Sharpe and Anne Emery. Thank you.

Chapter One

WORLD SING SONG 2085

*"A computer would deserve to be called intelligent if it could deceive
a human into believing it was a human."*
Alan Turing

Dad was a time travel engineer with the Future Project. I basked in the aura of coolness and mystique that this bestowed upon me among the inhabitants of our small village. The mysterious Site R where Dad worked was shrouded in secrecy. Any filming or taking photographs in the area were strictly and ruthlessly forbidden. Shots were sometimes heard and many people were frightened to even go near the heavily guarded perimeter fence. At school, all sorts of wild rumors circulated as to what really went on in the hidden, vast mountain caverns so tantalizingly near our village. Some kids speculated that a massive underground city had been built in case of a nuclear war. Others joked that Elvis, JFK and Michael Jackson were inside, and that covert government agencies had gone back in time and rescued them before their untimely demise. Many heated discussions were held in the school canteen about who else could be stashed away. Perhaps that old singing guy, Justin Bieber, trying to go back in time to relive his glory days!

As none of my classmates really understood what the Future Project was about, me included, it was easy just to make it up as I went along. I was constantly asked Hey Jake, what's the winning lottery numbers, bet you know! Hey Jake who's going to win World Sing Song tonight?

I smiled, shrugged my shoulders, and looked away. The truth was that no one knew any of that stuff. The Future Project was thought to have been set up by some top-secret government agency to investigate the possibility of time travel. Judging by Dad's late night sighing and work on his Pid Pad screen, I doubted whether the army of hidden underground scientists had worked it out yet or if they even could. Having said that, Dad would never tell me what went on at Site R, even when I questioned him relentlessly. He always said, "You know I can't talk about work," and would stick his fingers in his ears singing "La, La, La." All of the time travel engineers and scientists had taken an oath of honor to protect the future. This kept any information about the Future Project leaking out, that and the millions of guards, cameras, patrols and security checks! I wasn't about to let any of my classmates in on that though. I liked to act as if I might know something, nothing definite, and certainly nothing that I could ever reveal. Just enough, to keep them wondering if I'd really seen any of Dad's classified intelligence documents!

I kicked the autumn leaves out of my way as I trudged along the pavement, accidentally dragging my Personal Integrated Device Pad through the mud. I lifted it up, luckily it was in a case or Dad would have something to say! The Pid Pad was the latest in global web, knowledge and communications technology. Everything I needed to know in life was just a virtual finger flick away from me. I turned the case over, rubbing away mud with my index finger and peered at my reflection in the glass. Good looking or average I wondered. My reputation as a geek swung the pendulum more towards average. I'd inherited my Scandinavian mother's blond curls, and almost translucent skin which worked much better on my sister than me, or so she told me... frequently! I swung the case back over my shoulder and trudged on, my clumpy boots making the only sound on the deserted, misty street.

Kiki my robot dog ran ahead. He was a small, metal, vintage terrier model that I'd found at a robotics fair. Mom constantly badgered me to buy an upgraded more realistic pet, but I liked him, he was retro and quirky.

"Jake are you going to World Sing Song at Casey's house tonight?"

I jumped and almost tripped. "You scared me Emily; don't sneak up on me like that."

"I wasn't sneaking up on you and your Pid Pad case is filthy."

Emily went to my school and her Dad also worked at the Future Project. She spoke to me now and again but mainly hung out with her own crowd. The cool popular crowd!

"I don't know," I mumbled glancing sideways at her short red dress. "I'd forgotten about it." I hoped this made me seem more interesting.

"But it's Casey's fourteenth birthday, and he has a life-sized show arranged. He's invited everyone."

"I'll think about it," I replied casually looking down and still kicking leaves. Emily stared at me curiously with her luminous blue eyes, adjusting the collar on her black quilted Smart jacket.

"You should come over Jake; all your classmates are starting to whisper that you're a tweakie." My heart sank. Tweakies were kids that had been altered before birth to be super intelligent. They were also rumored to be really freaky. Most of the scientists at Site R had kids attending the special academy, which was more or less a genius college. The kids at my school shouted "freaky, tweakies," if they ever saw the academy bus.

"I'm not a tweakie," I said irritated. "My parents didn't have my genome tweaked for extra intelligence, and if they had, I'd know about it."

"Okay I'm sorry," she shrugged her shoulders nonchalantly, her dark hair framing her face, "but some of the guys in your class were saying anyone with amazing scores like yours must be a tweakie and that you should have gone to the academy."

I stopped kicking the leaves and looked at her. She was cool. I didn't want her to think I was some kind of weirdo. If I'd been tagged with the tweakie nickname then I had to disprove it fast!

"Those kids are geniuses, I'm just normal smart. You don't want to know how long my Dad made me revise for last week's math test." I hesitated. "I've heard tweakies have multiple tests every day!"

Emily smiled at me and slowed down fiddling with her Pid Pad strap. A cold burst of wind triggered our climate-controlled clothes and they glowed in unison.

"Well, be glad you're not a tweakie then! So who do you think will win World Sing Song?"

I thought about it for a second before saying "Tale." Emily looked at me and frowned.

"Tale? Really? I was surprised he got to the final."

I swallowed nervously, "Who do you think then?"

"I'm hoping Sugar will win. Have you heard his singing? It's amazing." Emily's enthusiasm was catching. I cleared my throat.

"Yeah, he's good, his singing is cool." By now we were almost at my house.

"Okay, so see you at Casey's tonight then?" She paused and looked at me, her head tilted to one side.

"Yeah," I said in an offhand way, glancing sideways at her. "I'll probably come over." She waved and carried on as I turned onto my driveway.

I waited a few seconds before I looked back. Light rain began to fall as she marched down the street, her dark shoulder length hair bouncing and her smart jacket changing color slightly to reflect the decreasing temperature. A black, heavily armored vehicle pulled in slowly opposite our house. I hesitated. The engine was still running. No one got out. The tinted windows remained closed. I shivered. The mist was getting worse. Kiki stood motionless by the door.

"Open!" I shouted and the door, recognizing my voice patterns, slid to the side. I threw down my Pid Pad and kicked off my boots. "Lights!" Nothing happened. "Lights!" I shouted louder feeling impatient and the room was suddenly flooded with a warm yellow glow. The food bot slid into view with a tray of munchies. I unrolled my cell phone from behind my ear. As I flopped on the sofa the wall opposite me lit up, indicating an incoming call. Dad's face suddenly appeared, his head floating forward in a holographic cube, three times its normal size.

"Finally, you're home."

"I walked. The school has a new health and fitness drive. They failed the fat quota again. Everyone within a two mile radius in the village has to walk home this week."

"Well that should keep you healthy," Dad smiled. "I'm going to be home soon. Your mother and I want to discuss something with you and Julia, so don't go anywhere."

I frowned. "Dad it won't take long, will it? I've already promised a friend I would meet her and some other guys at Casey's house. It's his birthday and he has big set up arranged for World Sing Song."

Dad nodded but looked at me strangely. His dark grey hair and distinguished wrinkles suddenly seemed more ageing than usual. "I'll try to keep it short, but I have to talk to you about..." he hesitated. "We'll talk when I get back. I won't be long." He seemed weird.

"I hope we aren't moving," I said quickly.

We hadn't ever moved before but I had the feeling that the Future Project, or Dad's involvement in it must be coming to an end. The sudden switch last month to late morning starts and early evening finishes seemed to indicate that the urgency at work wasn't there anymore. Maybe they had finished whatever they were supposed to do, or more likely ran out of money, while the World Council tried to control the oil crisis. Who would have thought years ago that we would actually run out of oil? Riots were going on everywhere and spreading. It was getting scary. I heard the door slam in the entrance.

"Hey Jake." A voice shouted down the hallway much louder than it needed to be.

"Hey Julia." My sister floated in, her long flowery dress billowing out behind her. She threw her Pid Pad on the table and flopped on the sofa opposite me, tucking her legs underneath the cushions. She looked at Dad's holograph, still floating in the air.

"Hey Dad, what's up"

"I'll be home soon. I'm on my way. Then we can talk. Don't go anywhere." Dad's distorted head leaned forward towards the sofa almost touching Julia. "And don't eat too many munchies!"

Julia laughed and stuck out her tongue. The screen went blank and the cube disappeared back into the wall. She yawned again, ran her hands through her long blonde hair examining the ends as she frequently did, then checked her nails and stretched out her legs.

"I saw you chatting with Emily." Her sharp blue eyes bored into me.

"Did you?" I glanced at her quickly.

"I got a lift home, I certainly wasn't walking." Julia groaned. "I don't care how many fatties are in the school."

"Weight challenged is the proper way to say it," I sighed. She ignored me.

"I think you really like Emily," she smirked looking me up and down and frowning when her eyes reached my old scuffed boots.

I shook my head. I knew better than to try and argue.

"You need to get some cooler clothes. Your khaki jumpsuit is so 2080." Julia stretched out further. "Put some music on will you, I can't get the house remote to work. I told Dad to have the circuitry checked last week."

I reached for the small square controller lying on the table and stood up waving it around. "Julia what do you think is going on with Dad's work? Have you noticed anything different lately?"

The door slammed again. I could hear the sound of Mom's heels clicking along the wooden floor.

"Jake, Julia," she shouted.

"In here," I yawned.

Mom hurried towards us looking flustered. Her usual immaculate blond bob was windswept and she seemed flushed and distracted.

"Is Dad back yet?" she asked in a tense voice.

"What's wrong Mom," asked Julia sitting up in surprise.

"Pack some clothes quickly," Mom replied throwing her work case on the table and tearing off her jacket.

"What?" said Julia. "What's going on? Where are we going?"

"Just pack," Mom repeated hurrying towards her bedroom. "Dad will explain," she shouted over her shoulder.

"Are we taking a last minute vacation?" I yelled after her, looking in confusion at Julia. Dad burst through the door before anyone had a chance to reply. He was still wearing his navy blue work overalls and his security ID swung around his chest. Two big burly guys in military uniform followed him.

"What's happening?" asked Julia in amazement.

Dad scooped up Kiki and handed him to me. "I'll explain in the car." I could hear a suitcase being dragged down the hallway.

"Jerry I've just got back, I'll throw some stuff in a case for the kids." Mom raced back down the hallway. One of the military guys stepped forward and picked up the suitcase.

"Who are they," I asked in astonishment.

"They're with the Future Project." Dad answered quietly taking me by the shoulders. We have to go with them, I'll explain in the car. He hustled us towards the door. Julia resisted Dad's firm guidance.

"I've just got a place at Fashion College with Helena. What's going on Dad."

"Julia, I'll explain in the car." Dad repeated. Mom pushed past us handing another case over to the military guy. He took it with a blank expression.

"Ready," she said breathlessly. Julia and I followed her through the door. She didn't bother to lock it behind her. The black armored vehicle was waiting on our driveway with the doors open. Clutching Kiki I almost fell inside. Mom jumped in quickly and Dad gently maneuvered Julia in, still protesting. The huge interior was fitted out in luxurious style and we faced one another on the soft, squashy leather seats. Virtual screens and holographic systems surrounded us. The doors slammed and the car immediately sped off. I clutched at a handle to steady myself as I tipped suddenly backwards.

"What's going on?" Julia turned on Dad furiously. "It's World Sing Song tonight, I'm going to a party."

Dad cleared his throat. "The World Council looks as if it won't survive the week. We have top secret projects linked to the government. It's been decided that we have to act now in the interests of mankind." Mom put her hand over Dad's and squeezed it tightly.

"We're leaving Pennsylvania," she sighed looking at me and Julia sadly.

"I knew it," I said excitedly, "It's a company transfer. Is it to another country?" Dad's face didn't change, "Are we staying in the States? Come on Dad give me a clue!" The car turned onto the misty highway. The military driver and his companion stared ahead impartially behind the glass partition.

"Okay, I'm not going anywhere; I just want to make that clear." Julia leaned forward pointing at Dad. "I'm fifteen and you need to talk to me first before you make any decisions about moving."

Dad looked up slowly and said, "What If you were given millions of dollars by the Future Project to travel somewhere else?"

"Yeah right because I'm so brainy and your company would really need my extensive knowledge and expertise in time travel," Julia snorted.

I interrupted, "What's going on?"

Mom glanced at Dad with an expression that was hard to read. Julia suddenly clapped her hands.

"Dad, you've won the company lottery, that's what this is about, how much, how much?" She jumped around excitedly on the black leather seat.

"Julia your Dad hasn't won the lottery so sit down and fasten your seatbelt." Julia's face settled into a sulky expression again and she folded her arms. Dad looked at us all.

"I suppose I have won the lottery in a manner of speaking, but just not the way that you kids could imagine." Everyone was silent. "I've... we've all been offered the chance to take a trip."

Julia jumped up again. "Paris, Rome?" she squealed.

"Julia," sighed Mom in exasperation.

"No," said Dad clearing his throat, "it's not that simple. The trip is through work, with the Future Project. It's highly confidential. Only a small group of people in the world have access to the information I'm about to tell you."

Julia sighed, "Okay, okay is this some freaky scene where we have to go to your office and visit someone from the past like Selena Gomez?"

"Trust you to think of some old vintage pop star," I said. "Why couldn't you think of someone like a scientist, for example, Albert Einstein or Stephen Hawking?" Julia looked at me blankly.

"Stephen Hawking the famous English guy, wheelchair, computer voice," I pinched my nose and began to talk like a bot. "Hello Julia, anyone home..."

Dad frowned and interrupted me quickly. "It's funny you should mention Hawking as he was one of the first serious scientists to put forward theories on time travel. We've expanded on much of his work in the Future Project, Julia, as in the science of the future." Dad emphasized.

Julia beamed, and said in her best sarcastic voice, "Dad you've found out I'm going to be a famous dress designer of the 22nd Century and make millions!"

"Julia shut up!" I was getting impatient. "Will you let Dad finish what he's trying to say?"

"What your Dad is trying to say Julia," said Mom very slowly, "is that we have been offered a trip to the future." There was a surprised silence as we all looked at one another. The car gathered speed as the mist cleared and we raced on through the night.

"I don't get it," said Julia looking at Dad blankly and switching on a heater by her seat.

"Dad, have you done it? Has the Future Project built a machine to travel through time," I said suddenly excited, "a real time machine?"

Dad smiled, "Yes we have Jake, although it's not quite that simple."

"What does it have to do with us though," asked Julia looking puzzled.

"Well Julia, the top engineers that have worked on the project these last ten years have been offered the first seats to go, along with their families, of course, because no one would go otherwise."

"Why?" said Julia slowly, now looking totally confused.

"Duh," I pulled a face, "because you won't be coming back."

"That's right Jake," said Dad, "although you could try to be a bit more polite in explaining that to your sister." Dad raised his eyebrows and I fiddled with my seatbelt. "Okay," he said, pointing at us. "Here's how it works. We have built an imaginary track in a far off orbit around the Earth and a rocket, which resembles a train, will run around it very fast at an unimaginable speed." Dad whirled his index finger around in a circular motion. "This will mean that time slows down for us, but it's still the same here. Hence, we won't age, but time will pass on Earth and we will arrive in the future." He paused looking at our stunned faces. "That's the really simple explanation. There is, of course, a far more complex system underpinning the whole endeavor which I'll go into with you when the time is right."

"So, what, do we reverse to get back?" asked Julia leaning forward, her brows knitted together in concentration.

"No," said Dad and I at the same time. "Julia, we haven't worked out exactly how to go backwards as it's a great deal more complicated than to move forwards. In fact until we figure out how to build and harness the power of a wormhole, we may never be able to go backwards in time." Julia looked baffled, squinting her eyes in total confusion.

"Wormhole?" she repeated.

"It's like a bridge in space from one time to another," Mom interrupted.

I looked at Dad in shock. "So you are saying go to the future and never come back?"

"Yes, Jake."

"How far into the future Dad? How do we know what will happen when we get there? Who else is going? When?"

"Whoa Jake, one question at a time." Dad held his hand up. "First of all, the project wants to travel five hundred years into the future, which will take about one week for us." Julia gasped.

"One week," I said in amazement, "how is that possible?"

"Because the train will go faster than the speed of light using antimatter energy, and pushing space time out in front and behind it. The same technology is now being developed to send a spaceship out beyond our solar system, so humans can expand both in space and time." Dad paused to let his words sink in for a moment. "Ten engineers and their families will go first. They are sending the most experienced staff so that all systems can be properly monitored on board the train, and who better to do the job than the people who have been closely involved with the Future Project right from the start."

"How about, like, astronauts!" Julia butted in sarcastically. "You know, those guys who go into space."

"Mom what do you think?" I asked incredulously.

"The way I see it, is that by the time we arrive in 2585, the world's oil crisis will have been resolved and it will be safer for you kids. Also, the advances in medicine will be enormous. I expect humans will be living long after today's average of 130 years. Wouldn't you want that, both of you?" Mom looked at Julia and me searchingly.

"Also," continued Dad, "the project will make a sizeable deposit of millions to a government account for all of us, so that when we arrive in the future we'll be set up financially for life."

"I just don't see the point of it though," I said. "I mean what use could we be to people in five hundred years from now? We'll be like a freak show, like medieval knights landing in our time."

"Yes and no," replied Dad hesitantly, "we can give our account of the project that will be more real than any history recording. Our engineers may be able to help with additional Future Projects, as they were the first humans to develop the systems and..." Dad paused, "we have other classified reasons for this venture, reasons which I can't tell you about now, but which I'll explain to you later. I wouldn't ask you to make this trip if it were not of the utmost importance for all of mankind." He looked around at us gravely.

"Yes, but Dad," I argued, "that's supposing everything stays the same. But we don't know what will have happened by 2585, and what if something goes wrong on the train?"

"It won't," said Dad firmly, "it's been subject to the most stringent tests, and has the most amazing advanced technology known to only a few. Even now it's being readied for launch on Moonbase, alongside the NASA space program, Starship One."

"Are we going there now?" asked Julia looking genuinely alarmed.

"Moonbase," I repeated my eyes open wide.

"Yes," Dad replied. "No one wants to risk word of what's happening getting out, for fear of protests and further unrest. As oil becomes scarcer, and countries are forced to choose an alternative energy source, the situation on Earth could remain in turmoil for many years to come."

"Who else will be on the train?" I asked, still in shock.

Dad looked thoughtful. "Well Adam is going, his daughter Emily is in your school," and another engineer, Simon, will make the trip with his two boys, Tom and Will, who are at the academy. The rest of the engineers are either single or have really small kids, and one guy who is a top quantum specialist is going to bring his mother!" Dad laughed and shook his head at this. I glanced at the military drivers through the glass partition. They were talking calmly to one another. I couldn't hear what was being discussed.

"So how does this train work Dad," I asked baffled, "I mean do we sleep the whole way or something?"

Dad shook his head. "It will be just like a normal train. We'll have our own cabins and a communal area. Our body movements may slow down and we may feel heavy, possibly even nauseous, similar to car sickness. But apart from that, we can read, walk around, and even fry your favorite sausages!"

I looked at Dad. "So you're asking me to take a 500 year trip into an unknown future on a train breaking the cosmic speed limit, while frying sausages. Dad, listen to what you're saying, it's crazy!"

"The whole thing is crazy," shouted Julia, "I want to go home right now."

"Well it may be, but it's possible," said Dad waving his hands at Julia, "don't you kids have any sense of adventure? Think about it, a world which will be far more technologically advanced than ours with all the money you need to enjoy it?"

"Dad, Julia can't even work the house remote," I said.

Julia flung herself back against the car seat. "You have no right to do this," she moaned.

"I have no choice Julia." Dad said quietly. "They need me, and given what's happening on earth I think it's best for you and Jake... and your future, if we go. Now," Dad continued, "let's have something to eat and switch on the TV. I know you both want to watch World Sing Song."

"Where is the car taking us?" I asked fearfully.

"To the airport," Dad replied. "There's a plane waiting to fly us directly to the spaceport in California."

"One more question" I asked, "will the people of the future know that we're coming?"

"Of course," said Dad confidently, "that's the whole point of the journey. Details of our trip will be stored as highly classified information, and the files will be preserved for future global governments. They'll probably be waiting for us when we arrive, like the kind of ceremony you have when you open a time capsule."

"But Dad," I pressed "What if they forget? Five hundred years is a long time."

Dad looked at me seriously. "I can assure you that an event of this magnitude will not be forgotten."

"Are they going to send any more Time Trains?" asked Julia, sullenly.

"First sensible thing you've asked all night," I said. Julia scowled at me.

"Well Dad?"

"No," he said quite definitely, "the World Council simply doesn't have the money. The Time Train and Starship One have cost trillions upon trillions of dollars. When they are launched, that's it as far as building anything else goes, although scientists will continue with research. They still want to try and figure out a way to time travel into the past."

"So someone could turn up soon from the future and tell us not to go," I laughed.

"You're hurting my brain," said Julia, annoyed, "just stop talking about it now before my head explodes."

"It can't because there's nothing in it," I hooted.

Julia pulled a face. "I'll go to the future if I can live in a different house from Jake."

"Make the remotes simple though," I chuckled.

"Anyway," said Julia slyly, "Jake will probably go if Emily is going."
Dad smiled and winked at me.

"So you know Emily?"

"Not that well," I mumbled. "She's in my year group. I know her because she's the only other girl in the entire school whose Dad works at the Future Project. How old are Tom and Will?" I asked quickly changing the subject and hoping they wouldn't notice the blush rising on my cheeks.

"Tom and Will are both fourteen, the same age as you and Emily. Can't you think what an amazing adventure it will be?" said Dad, dragging a case from under the seat.

"Well," said Julia, who had looked extremely doubtful up until this point. "If I have my own money to travel to Paris and start up a fashion business, it might be worth it. Perhaps I can design some kind of retro vintage fashion." She stared into space dreamily.

"Dad, what about our house, our clothes, everything we own?" I asked.

"Now who's asking dumb questions," said Julia.

"Everything will be left behind of course," Mom interrupted. "Don't worry Jake, the project will provide for us." Mom pushed her hair off her forehead and leaned back wearily. The case contained ready-made meals. Dad handed four across to Mom who began to heat them in the mini microwave behind her seat.

"Let's watch World Sing Song and try to relax," said Dad. "It will take another hour at least to reach the airport.

"You want me to relax." Julia exploded "After telling me we're going to fly 500 years into the future!"

Mom tried to calm Julia down. I was quiet, trying to take in the enormity of what Dad had just told us. Apart from holidays and school trips, I'd never left my hometown for any length of time. I wondered how it would look in five hundred years! Dad interrupted my thoughts.

"I think it goes without saying, Jake, that the Time Train is not to be talked about with anyone at any time." I nodded staring out of the window, as Joe's Pizza Palace flashed by.

"Here put this on." Dad coolly handed Julia and me a small black clip.

"You're bugging me?" I asked looking at him in astonishment.

Julia gave Dad a look of disgust and said, "They could at least have tried to make it look fashionable."

"It will only activate if certain words connected to the Future Project are mentioned." Dad continued soothingly, "It's just until we board the shuttle to Moonbase.

I sighed and discreetly clipped the tiny black pin onto my T- shirt.

"I hope you understand," continued Dad, "that we can't have a trillion dollar government investment jeopardized by our children." He glanced at me out of the corner of his eye. Julia folded her arms sulkily.

"Dad," I said uneasily, "how safe would this train be, I mean we're not like 'Ham the chimp' are we, you know, first little dude into space? Would we be in any danger as the first humans to travel into the future?"

"You'll be safe," Dad replied confidently. "I wouldn't take you if I wasn't sure of that." He smiled.

Mom handed us the meals on small trays, then switched on the TV. I looked at the virtual picture, which appeared floating in the air. I could already hear the World Sing Song intro tune. The maestro, in his yellow suit, stood waving at the global crowds. "We are here to celebrate the final round of World Sing Song 2085!" he screamed. Cameras flashed around the world and commentators began to speak in hundreds of languages. A hushed silence took over as the first bot appeared on the world stage. Tale bowed to the audience elegantly. His appearance was Asian, his face a flexible plastic. The suit he wore was bright red and a black silk tie completed his startling appearance. He had made it this far on the incredible emotion he was able to convey in his singing. The Chinese corporation that had backed his ambitious bid for World Sing Song Champion sat beaming in the Hong Kong studio. To have even made it to the finals would ensure their singing bots would be selling worldwide after the contest.

We were speeding along the freeway now. It was much quieter than usual. Everyone was at home, with friends or neighbors watching this most popular of all global transmissions.

"Who do you think will win?" I whispered to Julia.

"I like them both," Dad interrupted. "Tale is an Empathy Bot. He's going to win over Sugar. He's better at singing, it's as if he's real."

"Yes, but Sugar is a Newton Seven Series" said Mom eager to distract us. "He's got the most deluxe singing voice you have ever heard! He's been built using brand new quantum technology. It's not even available on Pid Pad yet."

I stared up at the picture mesmerized as Tale began to sing. I felt a sense of disbelief looking over at Dad. Was he really taking us 500 years into the future? Tale's voice reached a crescendo and everyone cheered and clapped on his finishing notes. The camera showed his Chinese backers shaking each other's hands and smiling. He took another bow and stiffly walked off the stage. Then Sugar was announced and entered the world arena to huge cheers. He looked breathtakingly human. I couldn't stop looking and wondering if he actually was. I stared again more closely at the TV and could soon see the immobility of his eyes and features compared to a human face. The strange glow and texture of his fake skin became more apparent under the studio lights. Still, it was pretty impressive. He moved better than Tale, and his American backers sat in the front row of the Los Angeles studio brimming with confidence.

Sugar was dressed in designer jeans, white T-shirt, and looked like a dude from a boy band. The maestro hesitated, unsure if he needed any guidance. Sugar held both hands up to acknowledge his audience, smiling, nodding, and swaying from side to side. He grabbed the microphone with both hands and then gestured for them to quiet down. This was such an unknown gesture from a bot that there was a shocked silence. The American team smiled at one another. They would all be rich by the time the next World Sing Song came along! If Sugar won, they would be making bots that could monopolize the contest indefinitely.

Sugar began his song, dancing around, and singing into the microphone now clipped onto his earlobe. He closed his eyes with feeling on the high notes and ended his song punching his fist into the air and bowing deeply. His plastic face stretched out in a wide smile as the audience roared their approval. I shivered, it gave me the creeps. Machines with human expressions!

The maestro appeared on the stage, encouraging a global audience he couldn't see. "Okay World, it's decision time," he shouted, "when the marker appears let's have a big show of eyeballs!"

"Might as well vote," said Julia grumpily, balancing her empty tray on the arm of her seat. Dad handed us a Pid Pad. We looked at the small, translucent, graphene screen. Lines of green data glowed as we logged on; a retinal scan identified and named us. Sugar's and Tale's names appeared in different corners. We both looked at Sugar's name and the Pid Pad noted our eye movement. Beside the announcer two columns began to rise in the air. At first, Tale's was ahead then Sugar took the lead. By now the global audience was shouting for their favorite and willing their column upwards. As they rose and fell, the shouts became louder. Finally, with what seemed like a massive surge, Sugar gained the lead and held it.

"Sugar is the winner of World Sing Song 2085," the maestro screamed. Cameras panned around the world to show billions of people looking shocked, happy, disappointed, many hugging one another and dancing around. Times Square, New York, was filled with thousands of residents and tourists beginning one huge party. The Americans had won for the third year in a row. World Sing Song was big money, and a lot of people would be celebrating tonight.

"I think Tale looks upset," Julia said as the camera flicked over his passive Asian features. Mom and Dad started to laugh.

"It's just a bot Julia." Dad said shaking his head. Then he continued more seriously, "Never be seduced into thinking that those machines are real. It's just an illusion made up of software."

Meanwhile Sugar stood motionless. His face retained an eerie, frozen, smiling expression as the American backers and software team jumped on stage whooping and slapping one another. They would receive $100,000,000 in prize money, a further development grant, and an automatic entry into next year's competition. The replays and analysis of the bot's performances began with far-flung commentators weighing in with their opinions.

I sipped a Coke and glanced over at our parents. Mom's eyes looked sleepy and Dad peered out of the car window. Anyone would think we were setting off on a normal family vacation. I wondered about Emily and how she might be feeling. Had the military been waiting for her as well tonight? Was she in a car even now on her way to the airport? I was no longer interested in World Sing Song, as for whether Newton bots would take over next year's event, what was it to me? I wouldn't be here. I might not even be alive!

The car lights on the opposite side of the road rushed by. Julia picked up a fashion magazine from the rack next to her seat and began flicking through the pages. It was doubtful whether she had even begun to grasp our situation. I leaned despondently against the window as we drove through the night, gathering speed, racing towards an unknown future.

Chapter Two

MOONBASE

"Here men from the planet earth first set foot upon the moon.
July 1969 AD. We came in peace for all mankind."
Neil Armstrong

As we flew out of the Mojave Desert on the Moonbase shuttle, Julia began to sob. Mom wrapped her arms around her and softly rubbed her back in an attempt to sooth her. Dad and I looked out the window. I watched the California Spaceport Headquarters shoot away from me and rapidly give way to blue sky. Clouds appeared and then disappeared as a growing darkness approached. All on board fell silent. I felt for my restraining harness and gently held onto it in anticipation for the moment of weightlessness that we would experience as the artificial gravity gradually kicked in. I listened to the whirr of the centrifugal force system clicking into place. Once it was switched on, the floating feeling would stop and our feet would sink to the floor again. I watched in disbelief as Earth began to move away in the distance. It was a view I thought I'd only ever see as a space tourist!

"Arrival time at Moonbase approximately 07:00 hours," a voice announced over the shuttle communications system. "Please remain seated. Refreshments will be served when the shuttle's centrifugal system has reached maximum capacity."

Our group sat in circles facing one another with a runway down the center. My seat reclined all the way back and was really squishy and warm. I looked around at the pristine white interior and chairs. Lights began to glow and a brand new Newton Bot glided towards us.

"Welcome to Moonbase service shuttle. What refreshments may I serve you?" It asked in a tinny metallic voice.

Julia looked up from Mom's shoulder. Lemonade," she sniffed. She was wearing her new white Chanel dress that Mom had bought as a bribe a few days before we left. I was still in my old khaki jumpsuit!

"Make that two," said Mom.

"Three," said Dad.

"Four," I chimed in and for the first time since Dad had dropped his bombshell announcement on us, it felt like we were a normal family again.

"Munchies?" enquired the Newton politely.

"Great," said Dad relaxing back into his chair.

"You will find a full meal waiting for you on Moonbase," the Newton continued.

"Will I have my own room?" asked Julia in a tragic voice.

"Of course," said Mom patting her arm.

Dad turned around to wave at a stern looking, grey-haired couple seated a few rows behind us. With them sat two smug looking teenage boys. They must be Tom and Will, the twins. I suspected that because they were at the academy, they must be tweakies, although Dad had already warned me that it would be impolite to enquire too much about it. They certainly looked clever. Their faces had that earnest, geeky look about them, accentuated by their side-parted, and neatly combed, dark brown hair. They looked so alike that I wondered how I would ever tell them apart. But then as I observed more closely, I realized that they both parted their hair on the opposite side. While I was wondering if this was deliberate or not, a white-haired, rather fierce looking woman came pitching down the aisle.

"Mrs. Henley, please take your seat! Artificial gravity is not yet at maximum capacity!"

The Newton hovered in the runway blocking her approach.

"Move your bot butt out of my way tin man!" she shouted.

I liked her already. A troublemaker on board was going to be great fun.

"Madam, we have not yet leveled out. For your own safety please take your seat!"

"Sonny, I've got washing machines with more circuitry than you and they don't tell me to sit down, so get out of my way. I'm old, and until they can build me a mechanical bladder with an on-and-off switch, I've got to go."

Mrs. Henley proceeded to wave her hand majestically in the air and the bot moved uncertainly to the side of the aisle. Everyone watched as she half-floated, half-ran towards the bathroom.

"I hope Mrs. Henley is going to wait until the gravity systems are fully operational before she does anything," Dad whispered and smiled.

"Why?" asked Julia sipping her lemonade.

"Zero gravity elimination is notoriously difficult." Dad was laughing now. Julia just looked puzzled.

"I don't get it."

"There's a mirror behind the toilet." Dad continued. "It's for checking."

"Checking what?" said Julia. By now I was desperately trying not to laugh.

"Popcorning," said Dad.

"Jerry!" Mom frowned at Dad. Julia still looked puzzled.

"Floaters in the air," I whispered.

"Oh gross!" said Julia and punched Dad in the arm.

I turned and looked around the room again. A huge hulk of a guy was laughing and winking at me. I could see from the resemblance and the seating plan that he must be Mrs. Henley's son, known as Henley. He was supposedly some kind of special quantum genius, but he looked reassuringly normal to me, sort of like a redheaded Santa Claus. He turned to talk to the man sitting opposite, a small, thin, nervous-looking Indian guy. That must be Previn, the other researcher that Dad had told me about. I settled back into my seat. No doubt I would get to know everyone extremely well very soon. Mrs. Henley eventually emerged huffing and panting and gave me a huge grin. She folded her arms in front of her ample figure and raised her bushy white eyebrows.

"Well, you must be Jake since you're not a twin or a girl."

"I am."

My father stood up. "So pleased to meet you Mrs. Henley, I'm Dr. Jerry Oakley, and this is my wife Evie, and Jake's sister Julia."

"Pleased to meet you all as well," said Mrs. Henley smiling mischievously. "You all seem very pleasant folks, which is just as well seeing as I have to spend the next 500 years with you," she chuckled, and I couldn't help laughing too, although Dad was probably horrified at her bluntness.

"I'm hoping I can get some new parts where we are headed, including perhaps a new bladder," she continued.

Julia snorted into her lemonade beside me.

"Well who knows what possibilities are in front of us," Dad said tactfully.

"I know that it will all work out just fine," said Mrs. Henley, and she smiled at Julia and I. "As long as no one snores," she added. With her feet now more firmly on the ground, she smoothed the creases from her dark green silk dress and began to slowly walk back to her seat.

"She's kind of old isn't she," whispered Julia. "I mean why would she want to go to the future?"

"To be with her son," Dad replied, "apart from which she's only ninety-three."

"Wow ninety-three," said Julia. "She's the oldest person that I've ever met in real life."

"Not all old people live in senior's towns you know," I said.

"Well they should," exclaimed Julia, "it's safer for them after eighty; they can get parts replaced and immediate medical attention."

"Julia, you are just repeating the lines from the senior's commercials," I replied, shaking my head in annoyance, "don't you ever think of anything original?"

"Have I got an eternity of you two squabbling?" whispered Mom.

"It's not me," replied Julia indignantly.

"Look out of the window both of you," said Dad tactfully. I craned my head; Earth was becoming smaller by the second.

"We will arrive at Moonbase on time at 07:00 hours," a voice announced over the intercom."

"That's another three hours, Dad," complained Julia.

"Think yourself lucky. Early astronauts took over three days to get here. They didn't have nuclear fusion rockets and they didn't have this kind of deluxe transportation ship to travel in. It was just a big tin tube fired up with rocket fuel and less circuitry than your Pid Pad charger."

I adjusted the virtual screen mounted on my seat. The news channel was showing images of the latest riots and protests. Cities burning, gas-powered vehicles overturned, people chanting in the streets while emergency crews struggled to rescue the injured. Meanwhile other parts of the world had been completely cut off by massive snowfall.

"This is why I know we are making the right decision," said Dad next to me, pointing at the military trying to control an angry crowd. I shrugged. I felt too tired to argue anymore and closed my eyes. I breathed deeply, sinking into my soft chair. Next thing I felt was a hand on my shoulder.

"Wake up Jake, we're almost at Moonbase." I felt Julia tugging at my sleeve.

"Look!" she shouted excitedly. "Can you see how close we are to the moon?"

"All passengers please fasten your seat belts and prepare for gravity deceleration."

"What's that?" asked Julia looking at me quizzically, "in normal speak please!"

"It means we will be weightless for a few minutes before we land." I rubbed my eyes sleepily.

"You mean they are turning off the swirly thing?"

"Yes, Julia, as you so scientifically put it they are indeed turning off the swirly thing."

Everyone was suddenly quiet as the whirring sound slowly stopped and the lights dimmed. All I could see now was the darkness of space and the glow of the lunar surface. The ship seemed to circle and turn and then I saw a mass of buildings, lights and some kind of super massive hanger. Still further out, I could see something white and shiny poking out of another crater. None of this could be seen from Earth as Moonbase had been built on the far side of the moon to guard its classified secrets from even the best telescopes. I craned my head to get a better view as we approached the white buildings. Glowing domes lay beneath us. We circled again, and I saw a landing strip illuminate the grey and dusty lunar surface. I held onto my restraining harness feeling quite light-headed.

"Fantastic," Dad whispered. "I can't even detect where they've hidden it."

"Hidden what?" I asked.

"The Time Train of course," he answered, pressing his face to the window intently.

The Moonbase service shuttle began to descend edging its way closer and closer to the surface. We touched down gently and sat swaying in our restraining harness.

"Please remain seated until the walkway has connected and we are able to disembark safely," the intercom pinged. Above the silence, I could hear Mrs. Henley in the background.

"I tell you I have to go!"

"Crikey," said Julia in my ear, "let's make sure she sits next to the bathroom on the train because I can't put up with that all week!"

The intercom pinged again. "Ready to disembark."

Two bots appeared through a door that had opened up further down the ship. They anchored themselves to the magnetic runway, which lit up two parallel lines in the ship's center, one on each side.

"Excuse me, would you mind taking my Mam off first?" Henley's deep voice called out from behind us. He had a weird English or perhaps Scottish accent going on. The bots slid up the runway, their white machine-like faces with huge blue eyes were unreadable.

Murmuring and the sounds of people shuffling and moving about, talking in low voices, slowly emerged. The bots approached the Henley's circle first. I turned around and saw them haul Mrs. Henley to her feet and fix straps to either side of her. They slid down the runway to the door. She was laughing as she passed me.

"Wheeeeee!" she cried out.

"Dad, I feel sick," said Julia flapping her hands in front of her face.

"It's the lack of gravity," said Dad patting her arm reassuringly. "Once we get you off here, you'll feel fine. The corridor is a short walk then the bots will take you through an airlock into Moonbase. The gravity is less than Earth's but a lot more tolerable than here." Dad motioned to the bots as they reappeared. "Please, can you take my daughter off next as she feels unwell?" There was a moment's silence as the bots stopped and processed Dad's request. They turned simultaneously and began to re-tether the straps on Julia's harness.

"Dad can't you come with me?" pleaded Julia.

"They can only take one at a time," he said, "but don't worry, Mrs. Henley is already outside."

"Yeah, that's what worries me," said Julia sarcastically. She stood up uncertainly.

"You'll be fine," Mom said looking up and rubbing her arm, "it's just like getting off any other plane."

"Yeah, except there's no gravity, I'm being dragged by two bots and this is the moon," Julia snapped back, looking very pale.

"She does have a point." I laughed as the bots approached us.

"You'd better be outside soon," Julia yelled at Dad as she was hauled along the runway.

By now everyone was talking, shuffling and getting restless. Another two bots appeared.

"About time," I heard Henley say. "Let's speed this thing up." The bots, as if sensing our impatience, began to move faster. Henley was the next to exit. He and Previn were wearing blue NASA overalls and looked comfortable in their flight uniforms. More bots appeared.

"When's it our turn?" I asked Dad restlessly.

"Just wait."

"Well they don't seem to be taking people off in any order," I said.

"Yes they are," replied Dad, "they are exiting the back circle first but Mrs. Henley and Julia got to go out of sequence because they felt sick. One of the main laws of robotics Jake is that a bot always helps a human in distress first.

"Well, can't you just say I feel sick as well?"

"No," said Dad shaking his head. "You can just wait."

I watched as the numerous engineers and quantum specialists were dragged past me. One of the tweakie twins turned and said hi as he made a rather undignified exit. He and his brother were much taller than me, and no doubt Julia would soon note, when she saw their smart pants and formal shirts, even less style conscious. The other twin passed me and just raised his eyebrows smiling with a rather mischievous grin. Finally the bots approached our seats.

"Jerry, let Jake go first," Mom said. Dad nodded and held my back tether as the bots fixed the belts in place. I half-stepped, half-floated onto the runway. The bots moved down the runway gathering speed and my legs drifted behind me as I was pulled quickly forward. The exit doors opened into a white airlock, and I passed through three identical interlocking chambers. Gradually I began to feel heavier as I moved down a narrow corridor, towards the main dome. I could feel the pressure of the gravity systems beginning to take effect on my body. A final door slid open, I stood up straight and walked through it.

"Got your sea legs Jake?" Mrs. Henley sat on a lounger facing the door. "I've appointed myself the welcoming committee," she smiled. Behind her Julia rolled her eyes and rotated her finger around her head. "I saw that young lady," laughed Mrs. Henley without looking around. "Glad to know you think I'm crazy, it always ensures a little more R.E.S.P.E.C.T."

"She didn't mean that," I said, gazing around at the large, white, circular reception area.

"I knew you were a gentleman," Mrs. Henley replied gently smiling at me. The door opened and Dad walked through.

"How are you feeling Julia?" he asked straightaway.

"A lot better," she replied, adjusting the straps on her high heel shoes, although she still looked pale.

Everyone was standing around now in groups. I could see that apart from Julia and me, some military staff were also waiting. The tweakies stood facing one another with their hands in their pockets talking quietly. The stark, almost clinical room was completely empty apart from some white leather loungers scattered around. Mom appeared from behind and put her arms around me.

"Alright Jake?"

I nodded and moved away. I didn't want the tweakies to think I was some sort of mommy's boy! A voice came over the intercom.

"Welcome to Moonbase, disembarkation is now complete. Your guide will be arriving shortly to take you to your quarters. Any luggage that you have brought will be delivered directly to your room within the next hour. Please remain seated until your name is called."

The doors at the back of the room slid open and two white-clad smiling Moonbase workers faced us with Pid Pads. They dealt with the military first who quickly left, then turned to us.

"Hi, I'm John," said the taller guy "this is Matt," he gestured to his colleague on his right. "It's our job to make you people comfortable and give you some do's and don'ts around here to keep you safe. Firstly, don't try and get out of any doors that don't automatically open," said Matt. "We say that because someone once managed to activate an outside door." There was a silence in the room.

"What happened?" whispered Julia when it became obvious that Matt had finished speaking. I heard Tom and Will begin to laugh behind us.

"Shh Julia, just listen."

"Secondly do not try to enter any restricted areas, you will be stopped and turned around," continued John and then paused to let his instructions sink in. "You will be housed in a dome specifically designated for the Future Project and your briefings will take place there. The bots are here to see to your domestic needs, any questions about anything else, then come to me or Matt and we will try to help out." John closed his Pid Pad.

"Okay," said Matt looking around at us. "I will take the first group out so listen up and we can get started."

"Did you get that kids?" Mrs. Henley appeared behind me. "No running around outside or playing with nuclear warheads," she chuckled to herself.

"Jake, Julia we are to go with John now, you too Mrs. Henley," said Dad ushering us together.

"Ah, why me!" whispered Julia in my ear. A small group gathered around John.

"Simon and Christy Howard," said John entering some information into his Pid Pad. The grey-haired couple nodded. They were dressed in white shirts and old fashioned pants just like their kids. "And these must be your sons Tom and Will." Will bowed elegantly and somewhat mockingly. His mother frowned. John continued, "Gavin Henley and Violet Henley."

"We are here and ready to board the big space choo choo," said Mrs. Henley grinning, and wiggling her white bushy eyebrows mischievously. Henley laughed and put his arm around his mother.

"Quite," said John clearing his throat.

"Previn," the small wiry Indian bowed his head.

"Okay," said John, waving us ahead. "That's everyone, follow me. I'm sure that you are all tired and hungry. You will be located in dome three; it has been booked for travelers with the Future Project."

John paused to press his eye to a retinal scan, the door slid open and we all followed him, the twins hanging on his every word. As he strode ahead we all struggled to match his pace. The walls and floors were white and everywhere had an almost hospital feel to it.

"When was dome three built?" asked Tom. I could hear Mrs. Henley puffing behind me.

"In the late sixties," replied John, still striding ahead, "to commemorate the first moon landings a century earlier. Most of the other domes were built in the forties and fifties... when the NASA Project Constellation finally got off the ground and construction on Moonbase began. Although you'll find that we have every nationality in the world working here."

"This place is enormous," said Julia who was surprisingly agile in her high heels! "When we landed it seemed to stretch out for miles."

Tom frowned, pushing himself further forward, he obviously thought that Julia should shut up and let him ask the questions.

"What are in the other domes?" he quickly asked.

"Some are used for construction and some for classified research and of course accommodation for the army of scientists, doctors, workers, military staff and astronauts." We turned a corner and entered yet another corridor. I was feeling tired again, the effects of the low gravity.

"Almost there now," said John as if he sensed how depleted we all were. The next corridor opened onto another huge, white circular area. Doors were set into all sides of it. John slid a key card into one and opened it. We all crowded around to peer inside.

"All of these rooms are identical," said John, and I shuffled forward to have a look. It reminded me of a hotel room, except for the white floors. There was a bed covered in white sheets, a desk, a Pid Pad with a docking station, a closet and another door leading to a white, ensuite, turbo, shower room. The only thing that was glaringly different was a kind of porthole in the outside wall. It looked like something you would see in a ship. The view was of the grey lunar surface spotted with a black sky full of stars. Will broke the silence.

"You probably don't want to be opening that window to let in any fresh air, Julia."

Then both Tom and Will laughed. Julia fixed them with the kind of glare that normally made me squirm.

"Quite right," said John quickly, "but even if anyone wanted to open a window, they would find themselves unable too. The glass is of the most durable reinforced quality and welded into the walls."

"Who does this room belong too," asked Julia looking around.

"It's yours if you want it," said John kindly. Julia flung herself on the bed.

"Heaven," she said closing her eyes.

"Okay, all the rooms are the same so I suggest you find some accommodation near your families and rest if you want too. The double doors at the bottom there," he pointed down the hallway, "open into a restaurant. The food is served continuously by bots and they will bring you pretty much anything that you want. If you would like to eat in your room, just shout in the bot box and a service bot will arrive. Any questions you can page me." He began to hand out small white pagers to everyone. Tom, Will and their parents began to move yawning towards the opposite doors.

"At last I can rest my aching bones," puffed Mrs. Henley as she took a pager. "Do you have some tea around here, John?"

"I'm sure that we can arrange something," John replied. As everyone keyed in and disappeared to rest, I followed John back down the corridor.

"John, can I ask you something... do you know where Emily Watson is? Her parents Adam and Ruby are also here with the Future Project. I think they may have come in on a different flight." John frowned in concentration and then smiled.

"Yes they arrived earlier today. Try to get some rest kid." John patted my shoulder. "The low gravity is really tiring."

"John, one more thing, can I ask you a personal question?" I said looking him straight in the eye.

"Sure," replied John in a flustered manner.

"If you were able to travel to the future would you?" John's face broke out into a huge grin.

"I sure would, that would be something worth seeing."

"Would you still want to go if you were my age?" I asked curiously. John's face looked a bit uneasy now; he sighed and stared at his Pid Pad.

"Listen Jake you will know soon enough that a lot of workers at Moonbase doubt the wisdom of letting the Future Project staff take their children with them on this journey. You and your friends are the only kids here in the domes so everyone knows who you are." John paused and looked around uncertainly. "Your Dad's colleague, Previn, campaigned against any children going on the train. He wanted only people that were willing to travel alone to make the trip. But he was overruled so you get to go. Having said all that, I think a wonderful future awaits you, and you are darn lucky to have a seat!" He smiled at me. "Now I have to get back to my other duties." He punched me lightly on the shoulder as he walked off. "Have the bots serve you some sticky toffee pudding. It's out of this world!"

I was alone in the huge hallway when Mom popped her head outside a door.

"I thought I heard footsteps, are you not settled in your room yet?"

"I'm hungry."

She peered down the corridor. "Let's just wait a while until our luggage is delivered, Jake, Dad's tired."

"I can go and get something myself; it's just through those doors."

Mom hesitated, "Alright then, knock on my door when you come back. I'll put your case in the room next to ours when it arrives." She closed her door quietly.

I approached the restaurant and the automatic doors slid open. The place was empty so I chose the nearest table. A bot approached me.

"Sticky toffee pudding," I said and the bot whizzed off to the kitchen. I was staring out the restaurant portholes when the door slid open. Tom and Will entered. They hesitated and whispered something to each other. One twin had his shirt tightly buttoned up around his neck, the other twin's shirt was loose and the buttons were undone halfway down his chest. They approached my table and without asking, both pulled out the white chairs facing me and sat down. Four identical brown eyes bored into me intensely. One of the twins with the tightly buttoned shirt spoke first in a quiet voice.

"We know you're Jake and presumably you know I'm Tom and this is my brother Will." They glanced at one another then Tom asked abruptly, "What do you know about the Time Train?"

The other twin, Will, leaned forward. "It makes sense for us to share anything and everything we know, if we are to have any say in what happens."

I stared at them both. "The fact that I'm sitting here seems to show that we have no say whatsoever in anything that happens."

Will smiled and raised his eyebrows. "Can't say I disagree with you at the moment, but if we stick together, we might be able to change that."

Just then the doors opened again and in came Julia.

"I wondered where you'd gone Jake. You could have asked me if I wanted anything to eat, and here I find you ordering food with tweedledum and tweedledee or should I say tweekiedum and tweekiedee," she snorted. Tom flashed an annoyed look at Will.

"My sister thinks that you could be tweakies as you were registered at the academy, or so we had heard," I mumbled awkwardly.

"Will and I are both part of the human genome project, so what, it's hardly new!" He leaned back in his chair and folded his arms casually behind his head.

"Well, don't think that means you can boss me around smarty-pants," Julia shot back, and gave them both a dirty look.

Tom put his hand up. "Look, it's in our best interests that we all trust one another and share any information that we have." Will nodded and pulled out a chair for Julia. She stared at him suspiciously. The bot returned. John was right; the sticky toffee pudding looked delicious.

Tom spoke next. "I think we need three more of those, that is assuming you want one too Julia?" She looked at him sulkily and sat down.

"Yes, okay, I do."

The bot whizzed off again and I started to shovel my food in quickly. I was starving now.

"Do either of you know anything about the classified reason for the Future Project mission?" Tom questioned us.

"What classified reason?" asked Julia eyeing my pudding hungrily.

"Don't you remember?" I said scraping the ice cream and toffee sauce around the bowl. "Dad said that there were other classified reasons for the Future Project but that we'd find out more on Moonbase. I remember thinking at the time that he was being very vague, but it was all so much to take in that I'd forgotten about it." Julia shook her head, a puzzled look on her face.

"We think it has something to do with Starship One," said Will looking at Tom, who nodded.

"What's Starship One?" asked Julia curiously.

I sighed. "It's the interstellar project that everyone on Earth was talking about. Don't you remember seeing it on the news before we left? Dad reminded us about it last week. It's been under construction for years. Now it's nearing completion and the launch date has been moved forward." I put my spoon down. "Julia, have you been living under a rock?"

"What's that got to do with us though?" Julia looked around.

"It has a rescheduled launch date the same as the Time Train," said Tom leaning forward, his voice very low.

"So what," said Julia loudly, "it could just be a coincidence?"

"Don't you guys think it's weird," I commented, "that the general public knows nothing about the Time Train, but everyone knows everything about Starship One?"

"Exactly," said Tom sitting back and nodding solemnly.

The bot came back with more sticky toffee pudding and everyone grabbed a spoon.

"So how do you guys feel about going," asked Will between mouthfuls?

"Not very happy but our parents couldn't leave without us so we had no choice," I sighed.

"It sucks," said Julia going straight to the point.

"We're really pleased to be going," said Tom looking a bit surprised.

"Are you?" replied Julia looking genuinely astonished. "Why?"

"Well for a start a lot more people in the future will have been born via the human genome project, so we'll be just like everyone else." Will nodded in agreement with Tom.

Julia put her spoon down. "What's the point if you're the same as everyone else? You won't be anything special then."

I looked at my older sister, her long blonde hair hanging over her toffee pudding, and wondered how she managed to be so clever and so stupid simultaneously. Tom looked a bit taken aback but quickly recovered.

"The point is Julia," and Tom began to talk pompously like he was giving a speech. "It was always left to nature to improve on herself, hence caveman Neanderthal was wiped out by Cro Magnon modern man because he was smarter. It took a long time though," Tom paused, "now we are smart enough to make humans super intelligent ourselves, which means the human race can advance at a much faster pace."

Julia twirled the toffee around her spoon. "Sometimes I think it's okay to be smart enough; being too smart can make things confusing. What will we be called then? Confused Cro-Magnons?" she snorted.

Before anyone had a chance to reply the doors slid open and Emily peeped through them.

"Jake!" She smiled anxiously at me, "I wondered when you would get here. Dad said you were coming. Never thought that the next time I saw you it would be on Moonbase!"

I hoped that I didn't have any ice cream around my mouth. I licked my lips discreetly.

"Yeah, we're all still trying to get our heads around that one!" I pushed a seat out for her. "Emily this is Tom and Will. Their parents work for the Future Project and you've probably seen my sister Julia around at school."

"Hi Julia, Hi Tom and Will." Emily sat down.

"This is good," I said pointing at my bowl with the spoon.

"Had four this morning" said Emily, "I can't even look at them now without feeling sick!"

"I'll have some Pizza," she shouted at the approaching bot.

"Actually bring enough for all of us," Tom added. The bot stopped, processed our request, turned and whizzed off again.

"I hate this place. I just want to go." Emily slumped forward across the table and ran her hands through her curls.

"Go home?" I asked.

"Go anywhere." Emily replied wearily, "I don't think home is an option at this point."

Julia gave Emily a sympathetic look.

"What have you found out since you arrived?" asked Tom quietly.

Emily looked around the table. "Has everyone got rid of their security pins?"

"Dad let us take them off on the flight over," I replied.

"We sabotaged the pins within hours," said Will smiling happily.

"Okay," said Emily in a resigned voice, "here's what I know. My Dad told me that Starship One launches as soon as the scientists here can get her ready, and we follow her out among the supply ships. Both ships take off simultaneously. I know that the Future Project remains classified to the highest level, with the World Council worried about the fallout. If the public finds out that a train to take people to the future was secretly built, they would be outraged. Especially as it was built without the knowledge of most Member States with money that came from who knows where."

"What's the big secret though?" asked Julia looking perplexed.

"The thought of time travel freaks people out," I replied. "Immediately everyone thinks you are going to shoot their grandfather or in some way alter the future and make it much worse."

"Whereas," continued Tom, "a starship sent out to explore and settle new worlds is much more news friendly."

"Have you heard how big Starship One is," said Emily, coming to life. "It's like a vast floating city, and get this," she gestured to Tom and Will. "The human genome project and the Defense Advanced Research Projects Agency, DARPA are here."

"Who?" asked Julia screwing up her face.

"That's tweakie makers and the department of mad scientists to you and me," replied Emily. I coughed. Emily looked at Tom and blushed.

"How do you know?" asked Tom ignoring her last comment..

"They were on our flight," said Emily picking up some pizza that the bot had delivered.

"My Dad told me that the canisters they were transporting contained millions of frozen embryos to be stored on the ship."

"What?" Will shot a stunned look at Tom.

"There's more," said Emily chewing quickly. "There are thousands of people in the outer domes. They are having full medicals and being boarded onto Starship One and put into suspended animation for the journey; I tell you thousands," Emily repeated looking around at us.

Julia looked worried. "We are going to be awake, right Jake? Dad would have said? I don't want to be frozen."

"We'll definitely be awake Julia," said Tom, surprisingly taking pity on Julia's panic. "The reason I know that is last semester I studied suspended animation and you have to be out for a minimum of six months. We are only travelling for a week."

"But we're really travelling 500 years," replied Julia, still not convinced.

"No our bodies will only experience a week. It's everyone else that will experience the 500 years."

"Oh," said Julia twirling the ends of her hair thoughtfully.

"Dad has been through this a thousand times already." I said impatiently.

"The Time Train has a hidden agenda that we don't yet know about," whispered Emily furtively, as she looked around. "There has to be a reason why it's such a secret."

"We've just been discussing that and I think at some point we'll find out," I said quietly. "Or we could ask John. He's already told me that Previn was against any kids going on the Time Train."

"Who's Previn?" asked Emily.

"The quantum specialist," replied Tom. "I was hoping I could learn a lot from him on our journey."

"Good that you picked him and not the other one," said Julia and she turned to Emily. "We met another quantum guy who was on our flight called Henley, and his mother Mrs. Henley is nuts!!! She's so old I can't even think how she passed a medical to travel here."

"Actually Mrs. Henley used to be Lucasian Professor of Math at Cambridge University in England. It's a very prestigious position and she also won the Noble Prize for her theories on Chaos." Tom looked smug at his possession of some inside knowledge.

I stared at him in complete surprise. Julia's face was a mirror image of my own. She shook her head.

"She's still a crazy old woman," Julia said to no one in particular, wiping away the cheese dribbling down her chin.

"Have you met Peter or Bronwyn yet?" asked Emily. Everyone shook their heads. "They came out on the same flight as us, they're both engineers with the Future Project and there is also a married couple, Jim and Faith. They have two small kids; Alex who is ten and Maya who is six."

"So that makes up the twenty passengers," I said, "it doesn't seem many compared to Starship One."

"Well Jake, Starship One has to colonize planets. We're just coming back to Earth," said Tom in a superior tone of voice.

"I know," I replied curtly. "Although I think that is a bit of an under-statement. I mean it's a huge deal to fly 500 years into the future."

Will glanced around the table. "You know that the two onboard quantum computers will make all the decisions and operate the flight. They're supposedly the most advanced quantums in existence. Even the robots, which built them, only understand parts of them. Apparently no one can figure out how the whole thing works when all the components are assembled. It's the spookiest physics ever! I've read that quantums function with qubits floating around in the subatomic particle world. They'll replace all electronics in the next century." He paused and shook his head, "That's far out isn't it?"

"Yeah, it's like that new Newton bot that won World Sing Song. Did you see how real that machine looked?" asked Julia looking around the table."

"Never watch such trashy TV," said Will smiling, but looking as if he might.

"It's entertainment for the masses," added Tom, who definitely looked as if he would never stoop so low as to watch World Sing Song.

"Crikey you two are uptight," said Julia folding her arms. "As if it wasn't hard enough just telling you both apart."

"Hair left and right partings," I said.

"Suppose they swap the partings around in the morning though," said Emily, narrowing her eyes. "Would any of us know who was who then?" The twins were finding it hard not to smile. Emily had obviously hit upon their plan.

"What would be the point of that though," asked Julia looking puzzled.

"Just to tease us," replied Emily looking at Tom and Will sweetly.

"Well I wouldn't find it funny," Julia replied sharply.

I glanced at my watch. "How about we meet up at eight, have breakfast, then take a look around Moonbase together?"

Tom frowned. I realized that as an academy student he probably thought that he should be making all the plans. But he said, "I agree." Will seemed more laid back. He just nodded and yawned.

"Don't go making too many plans," said Emily. "You have to fit in a couple of hours of exercise a day, in case the low gravity weakens your muscles."

"But surely there are opportunities for us to tour the domes and have a look at what's going on?" I asked tentatively.

"Maybe," Emily shrugged her shoulders. "It depends on when we're leaving. You need to check out the Buzz Bowledrome though, it's so cool. We should have a game if we get the chance."

"Emily do they have a spa here?" asked Julia looking at her nails.

The twins burst into laughter.

"I think most scientists have better things to do than worry if their pedicure is up to date," laughed Tom.

"Please trim my hairy toes," said Will in a gruff voice and even I began to laugh.

"Shall I have the red or the pink polish?" said Tom in a high-pitched voice and they began to laugh again.

Julia folded her arms. "Very funny, I must say."

"I think they have a hair salon, Julia," said Emily trying to be helpful.

"I'll find out from John tomorrow," said Julia frostily, "anyway, I'm too tired for this. I'll see you all in the morning." She pushed back her chair and flounced out of the room.

"We haven't offended her, have we?" asked Tom still laughing.

"No she'll be fine in the morning," I replied. "She has a short fuse and an even shorter memory."

"Well I think I'm going to bed as well," Tom yawned.

Will also stood up. "See you guys in the morning," and he slapped me on the back as he left.

Emily and I looked at each another in silence.

"I'm scared," she finally said. I examined her face; her blue eyes had matching blue shadows underneath them.

"I know," I replied consolingly, "we all are deep down."

"Those twin guys seem okay," she said.

"Well, that should make us feel better," I replied "because they're super smart. If they were scared then I would be really worried."

"What about Julia?" she asked curiously.

"Julia is Julia!" I sighed. "She's probably imagining herself in a world where she's a famous designer living a fabulous life with a closet full of shoes." We both laughed.

"We're lucky to be going I suppose," I said playing with my spoon, "given the oil crisis and the extreme weather patterns. It's going to be really tough on Earth in the foreseeable future and by the time we arrive back, the situation should have improved."

"I hope you're right Jake," said Emily still looking worried. "My Pid Pad has been downgraded to the most basic functions and my Global Connections and Me Time accounts have been closed. What do you think everyone will say at school when they see that we've gone and they can't contact us?"

I sighed, "Dad says it will be announced that the Future Project has been relocated elsewhere and we've all moved."

"I wouldn't believe that," replied Emily leaning back in her chair. "Not when people just up and leave in the night and don't even say goodbye to their best friends." There was a silence until she finally continued, "What do you make of the twins?"

"I thought at first, when I saw them on the shuttle, that they were a bit stuck up and arrogant, but then that's probably because they're so much cleverer than the rest of us."

Emily yawned, "I wouldn't be so sure. People who are often that clever have no common sense. Anyway," she continued, "I'm going to try and get some sleep now. I'm tired." She pulled back her chair. "See you in the morning."

I waited a few minutes before I finally left the restaurant and walked slowly to my room. I debated whether to knock at Mom's and Dad's door but hesitated as I could hear no sounds coming from their room. I should let them sleep. Julia being way less considerate than anyone else had probably woken them at least once already. My door unlocked easily with the key card. Mom had unpacked my clothes, and Kiki lay motionless on the floor. I looked out of the porthole at the vast domes. In the distance I could see space buggies being driven around. People were obviously still working and would continue to do so throughout the night. A blinking light caught my eye.

The Pid Pad in the corner of the room displayed an incoming message on the screen. I picked it up curiously and pressed receive. The glowing green lines asked for a retinal security scan. Strange! I completed the procedure and photographs of the nineteen passengers traveling on the time train flashed up one by one. Only my picture was missing. I stared in surprise. A message appeared on the screen.

"Nostradamus is a supercomputer, which exists to predict the future. One of these people is a traitor. This information is classified at the highest level."

Before I had time to react, the message deleted and to my dismay my entire Pid Pad wiped itself clean. I sat back on the bed holding it in shock. Was it a joke? A hoax? Some kind of game? Who had sent the message and why to me? I kicked off my shoes and lay down. Why would anyone be a traitor? A traitor to what? It didn't make any sense. I gazed through the porthole again tiredly. The domes glowed against the blackness of space and the stars seemed brighter and nearer, as if a short ride could take me to them. I pulled the blind down and switched off the light. The bed was incredibly comfortable and that was the last thing I knew.

Chapter Three

ASTEROID

*"This planet is 15 million years overdue for an asteroid strike
like the one that killed the dinosaurs."*
L. Neil Smith

I felt a tugging on my pajama sleeve and rolled over. I felt weird. Something just wasn't right. I wiggled my legs around and rolled back. "Holy crap" I screamed in fright. The white robotic face above me stared on undisturbed.

"It is time for you to rise Jake," the wakey wakey bot's mechanical voice maintained its even tone. It retracted the hand that had been held out. "Do you wish for me to bring you your breakfast in this room or would you prefer to eat in the restaurant?" The bot stood silently waiting for my reply.

It was tempting to lie there and have breakfast served to me, but I had already told everyone we should meet at eight. The bot had opened the blinds over the porthole. It made me feel a bit uneasy; black space and stars, it could still be last night. I decided to have a hot turbo shower and see who was up. "I'll go to the restaurant," I yawned, and began to haul myself sleepily out of bed. The bot bowed expressionless and shuffled out. Not for the first time did I wonder about those machines and what exactly went on in their mechanical heads!

I shouted commands at the room to increase the temperature, play some music and turn on some soothing green lights. By the time I was showered and dressed, I felt a lot better. The message from last night still played in my head, but I pushed it to the back of my mind. I looked in the mirror, ruffled up my short blonde curls and examined what I prayed was not a zit on my chin. Taking a deep breath I stepped outside. The doors to the restaurant were open and I could hear music and people talking. Emily sat at a table with Mrs. Henley, Tom and Will. It was getting easier to tell the twins apart. Mom and Dad were at another table nearby. I walked over to them. Mom got up and gave me a hug. "Sleep well?" she asked.

"Yes, I was really tired."

"I fell asleep right away," said Dad, "didn't even manage to get something to eat, that's why I'm so hungry now." I looked at his plate piled high with sausage, eggs, bacon, tomatoes and potatoes. He was shoveling it quickly into his mouth.

"Where's Julia?" I asked, hoping that she was in her room.

"Still doing her hair," replied Mom.

"I'm going to join Tom and Will then."

"Of course," replied Mom, "your Dad has a meeting at nine, and I'm going to spend some time with Emily's mom. If Julia isn't here soon, I'll tell her to join you."

"Thanks," I sighed, "You're too kind!"

"She's your sister Jake, and she's the only one you're likely to have."

"Thank goodness for that," I muttered under my breath. The thought of two Julia's would be too much for anyone to live with.

"Be nice," said Mom, wagging her finger at me but smiling playfully.

I smiled back at her and made my way over to Emily's table. She was laughing and looked happier. Her shoulder length, dark, curly hair had been tied back into a ponytail with a bright red band, and she wore an attractive matching sweater.

"Morning Jake," shouted Mrs. Henley, banging what looked like a cup of tea on the table.

"We're going exploring after we've eaten," said a twin, swinging on his chair, "so are you up for it?"

"Will, right?" I guessed. I'd already established he was the least tweakie of the two.

"Where's Julia?" interrupted Emily looking behind me.

"Apparently still doing her hair," I replied dryly.

"She'll break some hearts that one will," commented Mrs. Henley to no one in particular.

I looked at her in surprise. It had never occurred to me that anyone might actually find Julia attractive. I quickly shook the image out of my head. A food bot approached.

"I'll have the same as the others," I gestured to the half-eaten plates on the table, and the bot shuffled off again.

"What's the plan?" I asked pouring myself a glass of juice.

"We're going to take a look at the famous Starship One from a viewing point in dome six," replied Tom, "apparently because everyone is so busy preparing for the launch no one really has time to take kids on a tour. John says that if we don't get in the way or bother anyone he will give us some key passes and a bot guide to get there."

"It's too far for an old woman like me to walk," said Mrs. Henley, "but I'd really like to know what you have seen as soon as you get back. Ask questions," she continued, "always ask questions and plenty of them, and keep your eyes open."

"Does anyone know when we get to see the Time Train?" I asked. A bot placed my breakfast in front of me, lifted the lid off the steaming plate with a jerk and then whizzed away backwards.

"Soon," said Mrs. Henley and folded her hands.

"You're sure?" asked Tom looking doubtful. "Apparently it's not quite ready yet."

"Positive," replied Mrs. Henley. "Previn is already onboard."

"That's my Mom and Dad over there." Emily pointed out a tall, grey-haired man talking to my father and a much younger looking, dark haired woman.

"You look like your Mom," I said, though mouthfuls of food.. Emily pulled a face and smiled.

"Here comes the lovely Julia!" shouted Mrs. Henley. "Your hair is looking quite wonderful dearie."

Julia gave a quick half smile and sprinted over to our parent's table.

"Is Julia coming with us?" asked Tom, his eyes drawn to where Julia sat running her hands through her freshly blown, glistening, blond hair.

"I doubt it," I replied drily, "not unless there are any gift shops on the way."

"I'll go and ask her," said Tom moving his chair out and striding confidently towards their table.

"See, I told you," twinkled Mrs. Henley.

"Now you've just ruined my faith in the super intelligence of the human genome project," I said at which Mrs. Henley and Emily began to laugh. Will just looked puzzled.

"Well kids it's time for me to do a bit of reading," said Mrs. Henley pulling out her chair.

"Julia's going to have coffee with your parents then do some virtual shopping," said Tom as he wove his way through the chairs back to our table. "I mean here we are on the moon and she wants to go for coffee," he paused for emphasis, "on the moon!"

"Ying and Yang my dear," said Mrs. Henley kindly winking at me. "I'm off now, see you all later."

"What does that mean?" asked Tom, watching Mrs. Henley slowly depart.

"Ah, so you don't know everything," I said smugly.

"We never said we knew everything," Tom replied humorlessly, as if I really thought he might!

"Aren't you finished eating yet? And can we get going?" asked Emily looking at my plate.

"I'm done," I said, putting down my knife and fork, my mouth still full. "Lead on."

"Hang on a minute," said Will, "We need the guide bot." He pressed a number on his white pager. We hung around outside the door and a bot appeared. He approached and bowed his head, "6702 reporting for duty."

I'd always found it interesting the way that bots were given numbers. Dad told me it was to stop them from appearing too human. People began to have feelings for objects that had names, like Sam and Jack. Different bot shapes had been tried since the forties in an effort to stamp this out, but bots that were built with the most human like figures always made people feel most comfortable. However, there was a fine line between a human shape and a human appearance. Dad called it the 'uncanny valley' effect. If a bot looked too human people began to get very uncomfortable. The trick was to keep the bots appealing but not too realistic, as an almost human bot could provoke feelings of fear and revulsion. I wondered where this would leave the Sing Song bots?

"This way, follow me." 6702 began to glide along. We walked slowly behind. I resisted the urge to make conversation with the bot. Dad always said to me at home, would you talk to the coffee machine? Although I think with the coming of the new Newton bots he might have to rethink that argument! The guide bot led us out of our quarters and towards a huge vaulted door. Two slides of a security pass later the doors slid open onto a massive, white, cavernous area.

"It's a train station!" exclaimed Tom, looking at the magnetic railing in front of us.

"A train will arrive soon," said the bot in its even metallic tones.

"Over there" shouted Emily pointing. "Here it comes." A super sleek, white tube slid into view and we jumped onboard. Moonbase workers in their white overalls filled almost every spot. We squeezed into the corner seats.

"What do we do about the bot?" said Emily who was pushed up next to the window.

It's okay, it's hooked onto a floor tether to stop it sliding," I replied.

"You kids with the Future Project?" a tall bald guy shouted over the aisle.

"Yes," replied Tom proudly.

I could feel everyone looking at us and talking in low voices. Words like shame on the parents for taking their kids, floated over in our direction. Further murmurs of it's so dangerous, could also be heard. I was feeling a bit uncomfortable at this point so I was relieved when suddenly we shot out of the tunnel onto the moon's surface. Emily gasped and even Tom and Will looked impressed. The train sped along inches above the rocks following the magnetic tracks over a clear stretch of land. It turned around a massive crater, and Starship One came into view.

"It's huge," whispered Tom for once totally speechless.

"I don't believe it," said Emily her mouth slowly gaping open.

We were like ants crawling on the ground in comparison. It towered thousands of feet above us. On the sides, huge white domes stood out surrounded by the black sky of space. It was impossible to see much detail as they were so inconceivably high. The train sped into a station and workers began to push and shove as hundreds of people got on and off.

"Do we get off here?" questioned Will craning his head forward.

"The bot is moving," I replied uncertainly "I just don't think it can get to us."

"Let's push towards it!" shouted Tom who was already on his feet shoving the other passengers.

As I tried to make my way towards the door I felt Emily's hand holding onto my jacket sleeve. I jostled forward and finally made it onto the station. Our bot was waiting for us and we gathered around it.

"Inspection of Starship One from the viewing platform is permitted," it said in its tinny voice. "Please follow me." We moved with the crowds who were dispersing through a myriad of exit's and corridors. Smaller shuttles moved on an overhead rail. The place was teaming with activity.

"Watch out kid," shouted a worker brushing past us.

We walked behind the bot like chicks following a mother hen, slowly looking around and taking it all in. The bot stopped at an elevator and pressed a button.

"I kind of wish we were going on Starship One," Tom whispered.

"You would have to be frozen though," Emily whispered back, "possibly for centuries."

"I wouldn't mind that," said Tom confidently.

"Yes you would," Will added, "You know there is always a chance something can go wrong when they revive you," he turned to us all and said, "the academy wouldn't give us numbers but there is always a small percentage that don't make it. For some reason, their metabolisms just can't cope"

"I might be tempted to take the risk when I look at that ship," replied Tom.

Doors opened and the bot ushered us inside. The elevator quickly ascended about a hundred feet. The doors opened onto a shuttle.

"Please get in," said the bot. Emily went first, carefully buckling the seat belt, and once we were all inside, the bot manually closed the doors and sat down next to us. "Viewing station," it commanded and the shuttle gently slid away.

Looking down, we could see the huge station hall and another train pulling in. We were on a huge overhead track now whizzing past massive production lines and halls full of machinery and people. Suddenly we jolted forward onto a platform and the shuttle began to rocket upwards. It was a strange sensation and I began to worry that I might puke. I could tell that Emily felt the same way as she suddenly looked very pale. Then, just as I started to gag, we stopped, the shuttle docked and the doors opened. The enclosed viewing station was bigger than our house. We were looking down on the magnificence that was Starship One.

Its white surface shimmered with the beauty of a Michelangelo sculpture. Even the stars themselves seemed insignificant next to its overwhelming grandeur.

We floated out of the shuttle and into the enclosed translucent bubble. The sudden switch to zero gravity made me feel lightheaded.

"How high are we?" asked Emily, gliding gently towards the glass?

"10,000 feet," replied the bot, still tethered to the shuttle.

"What's inside the ship?" asked Tom in a quiet voice.

"Food, seeds, plants, animals, machinery and humans," replied the bot very matter of factly.

Emily whispered to herself, "Thousands of people are asleep inside, I wonder if they are dreaming?"

"That is one mother of a cool spaceship," said Will floating forward with his hands outstretched.

"How will it fly?" asked Tom, seemingly mesmerized by the white vision in front of him.

"It is an antimatter rocket," replied the bot. "It will travel through space using energy produced by the Moonbase particle accelerator."

"Where will it fly to?" I asked, swimming around the bubble.

"The first destination of Starship One is Alpha Centauri, a distance of 4 light years. This is the nearest star system to Earth."

"What will happen then?" asked Emily curiously.

"This is unknown," the bot replied. "A favorable planetary system could be colonized, but Starship One will ultimately travel to the Pleiades Cluster 400 light years away."

"How will she keep going so far?" I asked in wonder.

"The ship has a super massive reaction chamber on board that converts matter into energy." The bot froze as if processing more information.

"We must return now." The bot tightened its tether and we swam back towards the shuttle doors.

"How long will it take for the ship to reach the Pleiades Cluster," asked Emily, her eyes still glued to the ship.

"Possibly three hundred years," replied the bot, opening the shuttle doors. One by one we floated back inside.

"Jake, they could have reached other planets long before we return to Earth," Emily said, her eyes open wide.

"Weird," said Will unable to take his eyes off the ship.

"I agree," I said, fastening my seat belt, "although it would be pretty cool to see new planets and travel among the stars."

"It's not cool to have your blood explode when they defrost you though," replied Will, craning his neck to take a last look.

"Ouch," said Emily pulling a face.

The bot got into the vehicle and closed the door. The trip downwards was even worse than going up. My gut felt like it was falling out. Finally we were back on the shuttle rails again. "What happens if Starship One runs out of that antimatter stuff?" I asked the bot as it sat motionless in front of me.

"Starship One has harvesting capabilities. It will simply cast out its feelers for naturally occurring antimatter in space."

Tom and Will were thoughtful on the way back. I could tell that Tom was considering that Starship One was a better deal than the Time Train but Will still had doubts. Even Emily seemed quiet as if it was just too much to take in.

"What is antimatter exactly?" she asked at last.

"It's hard to explain, but it's like a kind of energy bubble that can be produced in any environment with a sufficiently high temperature," replied Tom in his know-it-all voice.

"Just that it's going to be the fuel source on the Time Train," said Emily. "I remember my Dad telling me."

"I'm aware of that," replied Tom condescendingly.

"This is too much for my brain to contain," I said, "I'm feeling like I need some quality Julia time." Everyone laughed. "Please tell me if and when you are going to explain any of this to her because I'd like to leave the room."

Tom and Will smirked at one another, and everyone leaned back in their seats lost in thought. Starship One was so unbelievably huge that I found it hard to grasp the idea that it could even get off the ground. I envied her sleeping passengers, and I knew Tom did too.

"Let's go to the Buzz Bowledrome when we get back," said Emily. "I have the feeling that security won't let us look in any off limit areas."

"I'm in agreement with that," said Will raising his eyebrows.

"How about we stop by Julia's room and check if she wants to have a game," Tom commented casually and I looked at him suspiciously. For such a genius he seemed very keen to include my bubble head sister in everything.

The shuttle came to a stop. We got off and joined the hundreds of Moonbase workers waiting for transport. The bot motioned us forward to join the line up.

"Get ready to push I shouted." We all struggled on and the doors closed behind us. I looked around. "The bot," I panicked, "Where's the bot?"

Emily looked out her window. "There it is, look, over there, it got left behind." We all pressed our faces to the window. The bot was in a frenzy. It was whirling around, its mouth opening and closing. I started to laugh first and soon we were clutching our sides. The train jolted forwards and we all fell against each other.

"Hey watch it kids," said an angry worker looking up from his Pid Pad.

"I hate to state the obvious," exclaimed Tom "but we are now officially lost on the moon."

This made us laugh even more. Emily wiped her eyes. "I think it's the low gravity but I feel really light-headed."

"Me too," I said, "it's the strangest feeling.

"What do we do now?" Emily asked Tom, "can you remember where we got on?"

"Haven't got a clue," said Tom looking blank. Will chuckled.

"Okay" I said, "what do you call a crazy moon?" I paused, "A lunatic." Emily giggled hanging on to the side of her seat.

Will rolled his eyes and groaned. "You know what I thought when I first got here?"

"What?" I shouted.

"That the food was good but that the place lacked atmosphere!"

Emily punched Will and we rolled into one another as the train took a sharp turn. More workers got on and we were gradually squashed further and further into a corner. I could hear different languages being spoken and Pid Pads constantly consulted. It was like being at the Superbowl.

"What do you think if we just tell one of the workers that we're lost. They can call the Future Project and have us returned to our quarters," I said, shouting to be heard.

"Or," Tom replied in a quieter voice, "we could just stay on the train for a while, investigate, and then tell someone we're lost."

"Won't any of these people realize that we're on our own and have no bot with us?" asked Emily leaning forward.

"I think they're too wrapped up in their own worlds to even notice us," I said. Emily looked around and it was true that most workers were either talking or working. They probably thought that we were accompanied by an adult somewhere nearby.

"Okay then, let's see the sights," Will said coolly and Tom nodded.

We sat on the train for another hour and watched the doors open and close. Workers got on and off at the different dome complexes until, at last, it seemed we'd reached the end of the service line. The doors opened and the remaining workers wearily stepped down. A bot on the platform was staring over at us.

"Okay time to go," I said trying to look casual.

"Let's make a run for it," replied Tom who had seen the bot as well. We raced towards the crowd waiting to get on the train, and pushed our way into the throngs of people. I could still see the bot, its head was swirling around searching for us. We slipped down a deserted side corridor. It was marked restricted personnel. All the doors were retinal scan activated. One of them opened. A tall guy in full military uniform came out and looked at us suspiciously.

"This is a classified sector. What are you doing here?"

"Our parents told us to wait here," Tom lied. "They've got some kind of meeting in this area."

The guy said "Stay here and don't move." He walked off, and disappeared around the corner at the bottom of the corridor.

"Why on earth did you say that?" I asked Tom angrily.

"Let's have a look in that room over there."

"What room?"

"The room that guy just came out of. He got so distracted when he saw us that he didn't close the door properly, come on."

"Are you sure?" I asked nervously, beginning to feel that things were going a bit too far now.

"Positive," said Tom arrogantly.

Even Will looked uncertain. "Might not be the best idea Tom."

"I don't want to get into any trouble," Emily said pleading with Tom.

"We'll just say we were looking for someone to help us and we got lost," said Tom impatiently. "Come on," he repeated and we followed him into the room.

"Shut the door so that it's almost closed," Tom said to Will behind him.

The lights in the room were quite dim and there were lots of seats arranged as if there had been, or was going to be, a meeting. What grabbed everyone's attention though, were the numerous huge space photos lit up on virtual screens all over the walls. Charts were strewn everywhere.

"What are these Tom? Do you know?" My nose pressed up against one of the photos and I moved it around with my fingertip. Tom stood in front of one of the charts.

"It's an asteroid," he said after studying it "apparently called 1999 RQ36. Its diameter is 2,896.819 kilometers." He continued to walk around the room squinting at the diagrams in the subdued light.

Emily whispered, "These are all the same asteroid too, that number you said is in the corner of all of the photos and charts."

"Tom!" Will shouted and I jumped. "Look at this one."

Tom walked over to where Will stood, and began to frown rubbing his eyes. He pulled a small Pid Pad from his pocket and began to move his finger around furiously.

"What's wrong?" asked Emily peering over Tom's shoulder

"According to the calculations on the chart, this asteroid has a likely chance of hitting Earth in 2182" said Tom, staring in surprise at his Pid Pad.

I looked at him stunned. "What, I mean how likely is likely?"

"See these charts," said Tom pointing at the wall. "They are all revisions of the asteroid's original orbit, which have begun to change since it was discovered. At first, in 1999 scientists calculated a 1/1000 chance of a hit, which was a tiny possibility, but that was almost a hundred years ago. They didn't have the technology available then to gather better data."

"So what does the data say now?" asked Emily

"It's at one in ten," whispered Will looking shocked.

"It's still almost another hundred years before it could possibly hit though, and we would be able to move it before then wouldn't we?" I asked, looking at the photos then back at Tom. He pointed to another chart.

"This seems to indicate that if it wasn't repositioned prior to 2081 then nothing further could be done, given today's technological capabilities."

"It's 2085," said Emily nervously licking her lips, "What does that mean?"

"It means you kids shouldn't be in here." The tall military guy stepped into the room. He was accompanied by two more men dressed in uniform plus a guide bot.

"The bot and I will escort you back to your quarters," said the tall guy. "Let's go, and I'll take that Pid Pad." He held his hand out to Tom who hesitated.

"Give it to me," he commanded. "I'm confiscating that Pad. It will be wiped and returned to you."

Tom looked furious, but we all sensed that Tall guy was not someone to mess with. He handed it over with a sneering look on his face.

"Does anyone else have a Pid Pad?" he asked. We glanced around at one another. "No matter," said Tall guy, his eyes narrowed, "the security system will have recorded everything."

He looked at us ominously. I felt nervous.

"I just wanted to ask..." said Tom imperiously, pointing to one of the photos. Tall guy held up his hand.

"No questions now follow me." The bot moved ahead and Tall guy waved us forward.

"This isn't the way to the trains," Tom said sharply.

"Who said we were going to the trains," replied Tall guy nastily.

"Where are we going?" asked Emily looking frightened.

"Back to your quarters via a lunar shuttle," he barked.

We walked on in silence until the bot activated a door into an aircraft hangar. A number of small, enclosed, helicopter-type machines stood there. The bot boarded first and the machine began to hum.

"Get in," said Tall guy menacingly. "I never want to see you in this quadrant again, do I make myself understood?"

"Yes," Emily whispered.

He leaned in closer and quietly said, "and I especially never want to hear that you have talked to anyone about asteroid 1999 or there will be serious consequences for your parents, do I make myself clear?" We all nodded in unison. He looked at Tom and said in a nasty voice, "Keep it shut." Then he drew a line in front of his lips.

The door slammed and he waved at the bot. The lunar copter rose up and the hangar roof slid open revealing the vastness of space. My heart was still pounding as we took off. I felt sick but realized that several hours had gone by since we'd last eaten, and the sudden weightlessness made my stomach lurch. I tightened my belt again, then I opened my mouth to say something but Tom pointed to the bot and put his fingers to his lips. Emily leaned back in her seat and closed her eyes. Will exchanged glances with Tom. We flew over the domes for fifteen minutes until we began to descend and hover over one of them. The roof slid open, the lunar copter descended and the bot at the controls set us down. Doors opened. We climbed out and walked behind it through a double set of doors. Suddenly Emily shouted.

"I've been here before, this is the lounge where our flight landed."

I looked around, "You're right," I replied. "Back to where we started." We accompanied the bot gloomily along the exit corridor. It stood at the door watching as we entered our quarters then it turned and slid away silently. No one was around, the silence was eerie.

"Okay," said Tom in a hushed voice, "I want to do some calculations, and change my shirt. Come to my quarters in about an hour." We all nodded wearily.

I returned to my room and lay down. Did this have anything to do with the message about the supercomputer? Could it be possible that an asteroid was really going to hit Earth? Starship One would make perfect sense if that was the case. The World Council must be working with the human genome project to preserve our species. I remembered my physics teacher quoting Stephen Hawking. He said that we were "a chemical scum on a moderate-sized planet, orbiting around a very average star in the outer suburb of one among a hundred billion galaxies," and soon we wouldn't even be that. No, I couldn't believe it would all end that way. I turned over on the bed burying my face in the pillow. Two minutes later there was a knock.

"Jake are you awake?" It was Julia. I lay perfectly still. "Jake I heard you come back a few minutes ago. I know you're awake so open the door."

I sighed and got up. Arguing was fruitless. Julia stormed past me and flung herself on a chair. "We have to persuade Mom and Dad out of this crazy time trip," she thundered.

"Julia what's happened?" I asked tiredly. She tightened the band around her hair.

"I've got a bad feeling about all of this. Why is the Time Train such a secret when everyone knows about Starship One, and why does everyone go quiet when I talk about being a designer in Paris when we arrive? I mean it's not like they've even seen my designs to think they're bad!" I lay back on the bed listening.

"I don't know," I hesitated. "If I tell you something will you promise me that you won't go blabbing to anyone?"

"Of course I won't. Is this a tweakiedum and tweakiedee secret?"

"Stop calling them that. They're okay once you get to know them."

"Okay," snapped Julia tapping her foot in agitation. "Just get on with it will you?"

"I mean it Julia, if you blab what I'm about to tell you, we'll all be in serious trouble and not just with Mom and Dad."

"I won't, I promise, now just tell me," She shouted in exasperation. I sat up on the bed.

"When we went on our tour this morning we slipped the bot and had a look in a classified room." I kept my voice low. "In the room there were loads of virtual space photos set up, all showing an asteroid that has a chance of hitting Earth in 2181."

"Is that it?" said Julia looking bored and flopping back onto my chair.

"Don't you get it?" I said urgently, "if the asteroid hits Earth, we will be arriving a few hundred years after the impact."

"They'll stop it before then though," Julia waved her hand around, "I mean look at all of this. If they can build this they, can do anything."

"I don't know," I sighed. "This looks a lot more difficult. The asteroid is huge and apparently they should have changed its orbit by 2081. Otherwise, it's going to be impossible to move such a massive rock far enough away from Earth in time."

"They'll just nuke it," she replied casually, examining her nails.

"This isn't the movies," I almost shouted, "everyone knows that nukes can actually make the problem worse; the asteroid will likely then be two giant rocks hitting Earth instead of one."

Julia looked thoughtful and breathed deeply. "So, we're like a rescue mission?" I mean if there's a disaster there's always a rescue mission right?" I looked at her stunned.

"Julia, you are wasted as a dress designer, that's it, that's it; we need to go and talk to Tom and Will right now."

"Why?"

"Because I think you may be on to something. Let's go."

Julia sighed and made a gag face, "Do we have too?"

"Yes, come on." I'd already opened the door. I glanced around. No one. I rapped on Tom's door. He looked surprised when he opened it and saw Julia standing there.

"We need to come in," I whispered. He motioned us inside. His floor was covered in charts and Will sat cross-legged with a Pid Pad in his hand. He frowned when he saw Julia. I sat down.

"Julia just came up with a great idea."

"Julia?" repeated Will, his eyebrows raised.

"Yes, listen, I told her about what happened this morning."

Tom immediately said, "You did what? At no time did we discuss you telling Julia, now she'll go and tell everyone."

"Hey, I can keep my mouth shut!" Julia glared at Tom.

"The point is we weren't supposed to tell anyone," insisted Tom.

"She's my sister and she has a right to know."

There was a knock at the door. Will opened it.

"What's going on with you guys. I can hear shouting next door," said Emily.

"Jake's told Julia about the asteroid and she has a theory," Will said, rolling his eyes.

"I've said I won't tell anyone," said Julia still angry but in a quieter voice.

"You'd better not," said Emily stepping inside. "The military guy that found us looking at the photos was as mad as hell and said there would be serious consequences for our parents if we let the cat out of the bag."

"Listen everyone," I waved my hands at them all to shut up. "Julia thinks we could be a rescue mission." Everyone looked at her in utter disbelief.

"How?" said Will. "It's only a small train with enough meds and food on board for us. It's hardly likely we can save the human race with a few packets of aspirin and some cheese sandwiches!" Tom began to laugh and shake his head.

"No," exclaimed Emily, "Julia could be right, not in that we have enough supplies on board to actually help anyone, but we do have one thing that will be needed if the asteroid has hit."

"Which is?" asked Tom scornfully.

"Information," replied Emily. "We have the quantum computers on board, the most advanced technology in existence. They are storing all kinds of data. In fact, the entire history and knowledge of everything the human race has accomplished so far."

Will looked at Tom and nodded, "You could be right. Perhaps if that asteroid hits Earth and destroys all kinds of infrastructure and networks, the quantum could be incredibly valuable to the survivors. Then along we come from the past, with all the information that people need to rebuild civilization."

"Is that an apology I hear?" asked Julia sarcastically. Will had the grace to look a bit bashful.

"Sorry Julia," said Tom coolly, "it was a great piece of lateral thinking from you."

Julia looked puzzled. "What's that mean?"

"That it was a really good idea," I said quickly.

"Then why didn't he just say so?" asked Julia sitting on Tom's chair and swinging her legs over the arm of it.

"Do you think many people know about this?" said Emily to no one in particular.

"I doubt it," replied Tom, still looking at Will's Pid Pad.

"Well I definitely don't want to go on that train now. It could be a total mess when we land," said Julia. "I'm telling Mom and Dad I want to take the next lunar shuttle back to Earth."

"And stay with who, Julia, you're fifteen!" I said exasperated.

"Maybe Helena and her mom," she replied uncertainly.

"They aren't going to let you do that," said Tom sneering "We are supposed to have moved and plus you know too much. How would you explain to this Helena where your parents are and why they aren't coming back for you?"

"The best you can hope for is a relative," agreed Will sympathetically.

"Mom and Dad are only children and we have no grandparents," I sighed.

Emily gasped, "That's the same with me."

"Spooky," said Will quietly "that's also our set up."

"So what does that mean?" asked Julia looking around at everyone.

"It means," said Tom thoughtfully, "it's not a coincidence that our parents were picked from the hundreds that worked on the Future Project. Having no relatives makes it much easier to disappear."

"I wonder," I said "if we still have registered social identification. Hey Will, give me your Pid Pad for a minute."

He handed it to me and said, "It's still connected up, it should work."

Everyone gathered round. I logged into the virtual screen to confirm my social ID with a retinal scan and looked into the sensor. "Retinal scan not confirmed please try again," came up on the screen; I tried again, nothing. I passed the Pid Pad to Will, who looked into the sensor. "Retinal scan not confirmed please try again." Tom tried next and after a couple of seconds shook his head and passed the Pid Pad to Emily. She tried three times, looked up and said no.

Julia grabbed the Pid Pad. "That's ridiculous let me see." She tried over and over then shook it. "That's impossible; there must be something wrong with the sensor. I'm going to get mine, I know it works. I was shopping this morning. I'll be back in a minute."

The door closed. We all looked at one another in silence. Julia burst back through the door again in a matter of seconds and sat down. "Okay this will work." She looked into the sensor again trying frantically to get it to register.

"It's no good Julia they've cut our connections and erased us from the system," I said.

Julia twisted her hair in agitation. "But I mean how can we do our schooling, take a taxi, access healthcare, shop?"

"We don't need to Julia," Tom looked exasperated now, "because we won't be going back."

"So I'm really stuck here!" said Julia looking horrified.

"You always knew that," I said gently, "right from when we decided to come."

"But I always thought I might be able to change my mind," she persisted. "Won't they be able to put me back into the system?"

"How?" asked Tom, "when you can't prove who you are."

Julia flopped back on the chair her hands covering her eyes, finally grasping the situation.

"What about telling Dad what's happened?" Will looked at Tom.

"No way," said Tom tersely, "do you know how much trouble we'll be in?"

"What about your Dad?" Will asked me. "He seems okay."

I shook my head sadly, "No, he's been totally brainwashed by the Future Project. He won't question anything they tell him."

"I didn't sign up for this deal," said Julia angrily, "I was promised money and Paris."

"You want to travel 500 years into the future to become a trust fund babe?" Will raised his eyebrows.

"You need to look at the bigger picture, there's far more at stake than we can possibly realize." Tom looked at Julia intently.

"Okay" replied Emily quickly. "I know the one person we can ask about all of this."

"Who?" I asked.

"Mrs. Henley," she replied brightly.

Julia snorted. "Things are really bad when the only person we can talk to is the crazy lady. Can you imagine, why don't we go and say to her, here's some more crazy for you, we believe an asteroid may be headed for Earth, there is some creepy military guy after us and no one has any online connections or social ID. Do you have any ideas about what we can do as teenagers stranded on the moon, oh, and please don't worry, we can wait for an answer while you use the bathroom."

"I wouldn't have put it quite like that," I said calmly.

"Which part would you change Jake? Let me know when you've decided." Julia shot me a dirty look and stomped out of the room slamming the door hard behind her. Emily got up.

"She'll be okay," I said "just leave her for a while to cool down. I think it's a good idea to speak to Mrs. Henley, but we'll have to get her alone first."

"Leave it to me," replied Tom confidently, closing his Pid Pad. "Let's go and get something to eat. She's probably in the restaurant by now."

We followed Tom out into the white corridor. The restaurant doors were open, and a soft synthesized tune wafted towards us. Mom and Dad were playing cards with Henley and Mrs. Henley. The other scientists, Jim and Faith, sat nearby with their kids, Alex and Maya, who were doing some kind of IQ puzzle. Emily's parents were hunched over a Pid Pad deep in conversation. I pulled out a chair next to my parents as Tom and Will hovered around the table.

"Have a good tour?" asked Dad examining his deck of cards.

"Yes." I said awkwardly.

"See anything interesting?" asked Mrs. Henley, peering over the top of her glasses.

"A few things," I said wondering how on earth I was supposed to ask Mrs. Henley if we could talk to her without arousing suspicions.

"Maybe I'll have to chat to you about your discoveries," she answered perceptively.

Henley laughed, looking up from his cards. "I know your distraction tactics, Mam," he waved his finger at her. I nodded and rolled my eyes around like crazy while Mom and Dad concentrated on their cards.

"You got something in your eye, Jake?" asked Mrs. Henley smiling.

"I think they are just a bit dry," I replied still rolling them.

"I know the feeling," she said with empathy. "I couldn't sleep yesterday and came down here late at night for a cup of hot cocoa. I think the powers that be must have turned down the air purifier. Hope it doesn't happen again tonight," she paused, "I'm always blinking so much." She winked at me slyly and looked down at her cards again.

"Mrs. Henley is an excellent poker player," commented Dad, still deep in thought looking at his hand. I nodded and joined Tom, Will and Emily who were busy pouring some Coke from the dispenser.

"Well?" whispered Tom glancing around cautiously.

"She comes here on her own late at night."

"Okay let's say that we're off to bed now and set our alarms to wake us up at midnight," said Tom as we drew closer to him.

"How do you know that she'll be here then?" I questioned.

"Trust me," said Tom, "the others won't leave until ten at the earliest so let's aim for twelve."

"Okay, shall I tell Julia our plan?" There was a silence.

"It's up to you," Tom finally said, "she's your sister, you know if you can trust her and if she can hold her mouth and her temper."

"She's always had trouble with that," I replied honestly. I had visions of Julia as a child, screaming and kicking the walls, having a meltdown.

"Tell her," whispered Emily, "it's only fair, then it's her decision if she wants to come or not." I nodded.

"Let's go then, I'll drop by and see her."

"I'm going to hang around and catch up with Mom and Dad first," said Emily looking over at her parents.

We all said our good byes, and I knocked on Julia's door. Her eyes were red and swollen. She was wearing her new silk robe; one of Mom's many bribes.

"What?" she said in a resigned voice, standing with her arms stiffly folded.

"We're all going at midnight for a chat with Mrs. Henley if you want to come," I said, pushing past her and sitting on a chair.

"Why would I want to come?" she said, sulkily looking at the floor.

"Because it's your future too," I replied, "and you should hear what's being discussed. It's important."

"Fine," she said quietly.

"Fine, as in you're coming?" I asked trying to read her expression.

"Just fine," she replied, still in a huff.

I got up and she closed the door softly behind me. With that I crossed the hall to my own room and set my alarm.

Chapter Four

THE TIME TRAIN

"Once confined to fantasy and science fiction, time travel
is now simply an engineering problem."
Michio Kaku

I heard the beep beep beep in my ear, turned over, and tried to ignore it. A soft insistent knocking stirred me awake. I opened the door to see Julia standing there.

"You look like hell," she said frostily, pushing past me, "hurry up and have a wash."

"Not everyone can look as immaculate as you do all the time." I yawned and stumbled towards the bathroom.

"I make an effort," she replied and sat down, calling through the door as I splashed some cold water on my face.

"I still can't believe we're asking advice from the crazy lady."

"I think she's the only one that's likely to give us any answers," I replied, shuffling tiredly towards the dresser with a towel still in my hand.

"Well Mom and Dad certainly don't," grumbled Julia. "I tried talking to them again but it was the same old, oh everything will be fine Julia, don't worry Julia, you have a great future Julia!"

"You didn't say anything?" I asked, suddenly worried.

"No," she snapped. "What's the point?"

I hopped back into the bathroom and quickly pulled on some jeans and a sweater.

"It's really cold at this time of night," I said shivering.

"They probably turn down the heating to save on the bills," replied Julia drily examining her nails.

The thought of someone looking at the Moonbase heating bills struck me as funny. I smiled.

"Come on," said Julia impatiently, "Let's go."

We slipped out quietly. I could see the restaurant lights were on low. The door creaked open. There sat Mrs. Henley in a pink fluffy dressing gown.

"Cocoa dears?" she asked, as if it were the most normal thing for us to see her like this in the middle of the night."

Tom and Will entered silently and Emily followed behind. We huddled around the table.

"I knew you had something to tell me," she said calmly, stirring the chocolate in five more cups. She passed them around. Tom began.

"We found a classified room with details of a future asteroid strike, in approximately a hundred years from now." He paused and said in a hushed voice, "Some military guy found us and said there would be trouble if we told anyone."

"We have no online connections or social IDs anymore," Julia butted in, leaning forward. "We've all done a retinal scan and came up with a negative identification."

Mrs. Henley looked around the table and sighed. "This is a lot for you to take in, I can imagine."

"Aren't you surprised?" I asked, wondering at her tranquil expression.

"When you get to my age dearie there are few surprises left. Henley did tell me that the Time Train had classified reasons for its run and that the variables would be calculated and assessed during the journey."

"What are the classified reasons?" I asked directly.

Mrs. Henley shook her head and sighed, "I honestly don't know Jake. Apparently we will be briefed once we begin our journey."

"But what about our ID?" asked Julia thumping the table with her fist.

"You can't take a trip of this magnitude and still be in the system," replied Mrs. Henley, sipping on her chocolate. "You are now as classified as the Time Train, and as such, you will only exist at the highest level of government information." She stopped and took another sip. "Tell me about this asteroid Tom."

He cleared his throat. "Well, it originally had a 1/1000 chance of a strike back in 1999. The data seems to have been recalculated to 1/10 with zero chance of stopping an extinction level event due to the asteroid's complicated orbital path."

"So," said Mrs. Henley, "I have dealt with probability in maths a lot in my career and what this means is we still have nine chances that when we land, the asteroid will not have hit and only one chance that it will. I maintain that's still pretty good odds," she added calmly. "As for moving the asteroid, what's impossible today may always be possible tomorrow. Look at how far we have come this century alone. When I was born, none of this existed." She waved her hand around the room. "In fact, we barely had a space program back then."

"That's exactly what I said," Julia replied firmly, looking more relaxed and licking her chocolate spoon. "I told Jake not to worry."

"That's not how I remember it," I replied annoyed.

"Well the quantum on board will calculate everything we need to know and hopefully find the best answers to our questions," said Mrs. Henley, completely composed.

"So will it know if the asteroid has hit?" asked Emily anxiously.

"No." Mrs. Henley put her mug down. "We'll be travelling through space and time so until we stop we won't know what has occurred on Earth during our absence."

"What about Starship One?" I asked. "How come everyone knows about the space program and no one knows about the Future Project?"

"Well, I would think that's because people are a bit funny about time travel. The government might not want the information that we are traveling on the train to be common knowledge in case our trip could somehow alter decisions that future generations might make." She cast her eyes around us all. "Is everyone feeling better now"? Silence flooded the room.

"So we shouldn't worry?" Julia asked hesitantly.

"No, I'm not worried dearie," said Mrs. Henley patting Julia's hand. "Even in the unlikely event of an asteroid strike, the government of the day will make plans. Somehow we humans will survive and don't forget we will be arriving hundreds of years after a possible impact, and I repeat possible, it's not by any means certain."

"Okay," said Julia satisfied, "information overload. I'm going back to bed." She drank the last of her cocoa and pushed out her chair. "See you all in the morning."

"What about the rest of you?" asked Mrs. Henley as the doors slid shut behind Julia.

"I feel better," I responded looking around. "I just wish my parents would talk to me."

"They are nervous themselves and don't want to worry you," said Mrs. Henley kindly. "Now you just point out the military guy that tried to bully you, and I'll sort him out." She drew herself up to her full height on the chair and smiled. "You would be amazed at how crazy old women can frighten men in uniforms," her eyes twinkled. "Off to bed all of you. I want you bright eyed and bushy tailed for whatever the morning may bring!"

"What?" asked Tom, a puzzled look on his face.

"That's an old saying," she replied. "Now get off to bed, all of you." She started to clear the mugs. We were yawning now as a bot brought Mrs. Henley a second cup. She picked up her book on quantums and peered again over the rim of her glasses. "I'll be doing a bit more reading before I turn in."

"Good night then," I yawned again wearily. I opened the doors and everyone followed tiptoeing back to their rooms.

In the morning I felt a violent shaking of my arm as the wakey wakey bot stood over me. There was a soft knock on the door and Mom peeked through. I pulled back the blankets and leapt off the bed.

"What's wrong?" I asked immediately, looking at her worried face.

"Protesters. Europe has had three major floods overnight. It has been reported on the news as a class two catastrophe. The World Council is meeting as we speak."

"How does that affect us?"

"Obviously the money spent here is being questioned because of the needs of the people on Earth. The ongoing costs of this place are enormous." She sighed and sat down on the chair. "It looks as if this is it. The World Council can't last Jake. It's all falling apart." I chewed this over in silence.

"Does that mean we're going home?" I asked finally, feeling apprehensive but relieved at the same time. I sat back down on the bed.

"Moonbase military are meeting now," Mom replied, "they have thousands of people on Starship One in suspended animation all ready to go. They can't just reanimate them if the take-off is cancelled. It will take months, perhaps years."

There was a sharp knock at the door. Mom sighed again, rose quickly, and opened it. A man in military uniform stood in front of two others similarly dressed.

"Please pack all of your personal possessions and assemble in the main hanger immediately." I could hear him knocking on Emily's door repeating the same message.

"Well it seems we'll know soon enough what's happening?" Mom said. "Get everything together quickly." She left abruptly.

I raced around throwing clothes into a bag. The bot watched me in silence. I picked up Kiki and stuffed his remote in my pocket. Dad had laughed at my insistence on taking him, saying that in the future I would be able to get a dog so real I wouldn't even be able to tell it was a bot dog. I felt peculiarly attached to Kiki. He'd been with me since I was a child and I wasn't about to leave him now, even though Dad said he would be a museum piece by 2585.

Dad appeared in the doorway. "Are you ready yet?" His face was tight with tension.

"Yes, what's happening?"

"Just hurry up and come with me." The shadows looked deeper under his eyes, and his expression was distant.

"Jerry, I'm ready." Mom was breathless. She had changed into her blue traveling smart suit and was carrying a small bag.

"I haven't finished doing my hair," Julia moaned trailing behind her, with a brush in her hand, clothes spilling out of her case.

We followed Dad half-walking, half-running down the corridor into the huge hanger. Thousands of scientists, workers and the military were assembled. It seemed that every possible nationality was represented. One of the older military guys mounted a small lectern.

Dad whispered, "That's General Hall. He's in charge of Moon-base."

Everyone was quiet and looked at him expectantly. He fiddled with the microphone and stood up straight. He was silent for a few seconds as if composing himself. He moved closer towards the microphone and took a deep breath.

"As you all may know a class two catastrophe has occurred on Earth, with more upheaval predicted in weather patterns. The energy crisis continues to worsen and the World Council is under attack from many countries. We have been advised that a vote of 'no confidence' is being tabled and an overthrow of the present delegates is imminent. In order to protect our projects here, command at Moonbase has decided to launch within the next few hours. If we do not leave soon we may receive instructions from a new World Council to abandon our countdown and hand over all our supplies to struggling countries." The General paused and looked at the assembly. "Our science teams and engineers have worked through the night to place Starship One into orbit. Final preparations can take place on board as we head out to our final launch positions. This is the best that we can accomplish with so little time left. I want to thank you all for your loyalty and support."

The General stepped down and everyone loudly applauded. Then it seemed as if people were running in a hundred different directions. I saw Emily with Mrs. Henley. Previn was talking excitedly to a military guy and two other engineers. They were clad in NASA suits and I guessed they must be Bronwyn and Peter. She was very masculine looking with short dark hair and he seemed very surly with long straggly locks. A voice came over the loudspeaker: Prepare for lunar shuttle arrivals.

I could hear the doors being air locked and attached as a swarm of lunar copters approached. Dad took Julia and me by the hand. A sense of urgency crackled in the air. Everywhere thousands of people were yelling and scuttling around, like mice in a warehouse. Doors slammed, machinery and equipment were thrown on the floor and people collided in a frantic race to board copters and reach work stations. Julia and I stuck close to Dad as we were pushed around in the chaos. I saw John, our guide, getting on a lunar copter with some military personnel. He hung out of the door, gave me a thumbs-up and smiled before he rose up to the transit area.

Dad was now racing us towards one of the exit tunnels. "This way, quickly!" We panted behind him.

Mrs. Henley, Emily and her parents were close on our heels. We entered the airlock, falling over one another, and were soon tethered and hustled down the gangway. Inside the lunar copter we nervously buckled our belts. Previn, Peter and Bronwyn squeezed in. One of the bots slammed the doors shut and signaled to an invisible pilot. We shot up into the dark starry sky and sped across the lunar surface.

"Dad, I'm going to be sick!" screamed Julia.

"No you won't" shouted Dad above the roar of the thrusters. "It's all in your head." Seconds later, Julia threw up all over her legs and hit Mrs. Henley sitting opposite.

"I'm sorry, I'm so sorry," she moaned.

"No worries dearie," said Mrs. Henley. "When you've raised children you get used to lots of vomit."

Mom fumbled in her backpack for some wipes. Julia cleaned herself up and Mrs. Henley wiped herself down.

"Such a rush," she grumbled, "no time even for a proper cup of tea, most inconvenient."

We rounded another crater and began to fly higher. The moon's surface became smaller and smaller. Many ships were docked at various heights above Starship One, which was now in orbit. It hung in space silently like a huge queen bee with all the worker bees gathered round it. We wove in and out of the ships and then finally I saw it. It looked exactly like a train. It was a long silver tube with a pointed front and rear, and it had some sort of concertina part in the centre, like an accordion squeeze box connecting the second carriage. Both carriages were long, slim and windowless. Other shuttles cloaked it, and I could see that one was already attaching. We flew in nearer and slowed down.

"Amazing," whispered Dad in awe, "they have her in orbit already."

The train glowed with a translucent lustre. Only by parking other ships nearby could they hope to disguise it behind the supply and transport shuttles stationed on the far side of the moon. Even so, I puzzled over how they had kept the train hidden from the inquisitive telescopes on Earth. Everyone working here must have wondered about it. How could they hope to keep it a secret. Surely someone would talk?

Julia leaned her head despondently against Mom's shoulder. Dad looked silently out of the window. We flew around the train while the first lunar copter deboarded its passengers. Once it had taken off it was our turn.

"I wish they would hurry up," complained the guy called Peter "This is taking too long."

"We're lucky we made it," replied Bronwyn, the other engineer. "There's no way Moonbase can defy a World Council. We need to get out of here quickly before new orders and troops arrive."

"I'm as anxious as you are." Peter's face had a worried expression. "I'm going to need at least an hour for the systems start-up and checklist."

"We can do it in half that time if we all pull together," interrupted Dad.

"It's not how I imagined we would set off," Bronwyn said irritably. "Damn that Tsunami."

"I expect the people caught up in its path are saying pretty much the same thing," Mrs. Henley chimed in. Bronwyn looked over at Mrs. Henley in surprise. Just then the copter jolted and came to a standstill.

"Prepare for deboarding," the bot's voice came over the intercom.

At least this was a lunar copter with a direct entrance to the train I thought. It wouldn't take as long to get everyone off. Peter leapt through the exit tunnel pushing everyone aside. "Slow down," Bronwyn exclaimed.

"Ten years I've worked for this, I'm not letting it all go for the sake of sixty minutes!" Peter shouted, as he bounced through the low gravity.

"After you Mrs. Henley," Dad said courteously, reigning in his obvious impatience, as she walked slowly through the exit tunnel. "Kids," said Dad, and I took hold of the handrail with Julia following me through a rear door.

I gasped as I entered the train. It was the most sparkling silver I'd ever seen, reflecting light off every surface. Even Julia was impressed.

"Wow," I heard her say, "this is so cool."

I crept down the train tentatively. I still felt like I was floating, so I know the centrifugal force wasn't yet at full capacity and probably wouldn't be until we got underway. The aisle was wide with silver seats grouped together. Virtual computational screens were pressed into the walls. I could hear Peter and Bronwyn in a room behind a large door. Henley pushed past me.

"Excuse me young man," he said pleasantly. The door slid open. I followed Henley through into what seemed to be a control room. Peter and Bronwyn were working furiously. A young couple stood consulting with their Pid Pads. I took them to be Faith and Jim. Their height and general demeanor led me to believe they must be tweakies. Her blond hair was tied up in a ponytail, which swung around when she moved. He looked a bit nervous, constantly tucking his short brown hair behind his ears. Both were wearing the same overalls as Peter and Bronwyn.

Peter motioned to Henley, "Okay, we are ready to start up the quantum systems. Henley moved towards some glowing tubes and began to make light sweeping motions with his hands.

"Previn has already started on the quantum at the rear," he said cheerfully, and leaned over what looked like a metal container with a series of pins. "All connected," he said, "the antimatter is also stable and sweet."

Dad pushed open the doors. "Okay, Jake, I need you to go to the communal room with Julia, Emily and the twins. We are preparing for take-off. Your mom is needed in engineering."

"What will happen now?" I asked, starting to feel worried.

Dad steered me firmly down the corridor, his hands on my shoulders. "We are just positioning ourselves to get into our final orbiting path. We will be half way between Earth and Mars on our track."

Julia, Emily, Tom and Will lounged around a large table littered with graphene files and Styrofoam coffee cups.

"Dad I don't like it, there's no windows, it's creepy," moaned Julia.

"You'll get used to it. I'll give you the full tour once we get started, but for now, I have to leave you and get busy." He disappeared, leaving us alone.

"Do you think this train will really work?" Emily asked Tom fearfully. She was gripping the table tightly.

"No reason why not," replied Tom positively, "and the way things are going on Earth, I hope it does."

"Where's everyone else?" I asked softly.

Will began to tick off his fingers, "Peter, Bronwyn and Henley are in the front quantum room or Front Q as they call it on this side, and Previn, Jim and Faith have gone down to the Rear Q. Mrs. Henley is watching the two small kids, Alex and Maya. Our parents are in the engineering rooms."

I surveyed the scene. Plenty of storage cupboards, a lot of refrigeration units, huge deep sinks and what sounded like running water. A fountain tinkled away peacefully in the centre. Everything glowed like a prism reflecting a rainbow of colors. After so much white it was all a bit overwhelming.

"I think we are moving," whispered Julia. I sensed a low vibrating hum. Emily buried her head in her hands. The floor seemed to glow and move beneath my feet.

"Trippy!" Will said, stretching his hands out to steady himself.

"Hey the table is moving," cried Julia.

Will said in a solemn voice, "Knock three times if there's anybody there."

"Very funny," replied Julia clutching her stomach.

"This is cool," gasped Tom, his hands grasping the dancing table.

Will glanced over at Julia who had turned deathly white. "Tom," he whispered "I think she's gonna blow!"

Julia pulled back her chair and puked all over the floor.

"Get a towel or something," I shouted at Tom, leaning over Julia, but he was transfixed by the glowing colors and the moving floor. I stood up tentatively like a foal that's just been born, wobbling to its feet. I put my arms out and suddenly felt ridiculous. The floor looked as if it was shifting but once I was actually standing it felt perfectly normal. In fact as long as I didn't look down, and focused on the cupboards in front of me, I could shake it off. I opened one of the doors. It was packed with piles of powdered packet food. I opened another and saw plastic food bags, drinks, powdered bags of different substances and hundreds of NASA's dreaded ready-made meals. Finally, I found a cupboard stacked with some linen and medical supplies. Julia was groaning, kneeling on the floor clutching her stomach. I ran over to her and held a damp cloth to her face. She took it gratefully. I then dropped a towel on the floor, ran back, grabbed an armful and laid them all around her.

"It's okay Julia if you don't look at the floor." The walls were swirling around now.

"I hope this isn't going to go on all week," retched Julia, bringing up what looked like a half-eaten cheese bagel.

"Gross," said Will, but he had also leaned forward and covered his eyes. Even Tom looked pale. No one wanted to talk. Emily's eyes were closed. She was muttering beneath her breath. The colors, movement and the hum had made everyone sick and dizzy. Moments went by and we sat frozen by the sensations beating up our bodies until suddenly it stopped. Everything was quiet and the walls and floor glowed but no longer danced and spun. Dad flung the door open.

"You all okay in there?" No one answered.

"Julia, are you alright?" He knelt where she sat in a pile of towels covered in puke.

"I've been sick again," she said in her extremely tragic voice, "and I think some of it went in my hair!"

"You can take a shower soon," said Dad gently rubbing her arm. "It's extreme motion sickness, but we've taxied to our starting position now near Mars."

"We are near Mars?" exclaimed Tom astonished, "already?"

Henley burst through the door. "Starship One is good to go, they've started their countdown," he said breathlessly. "We've just had news that the World Council has fallen. There's been a massive terrorist attack. We have to be ready to leave before a new government gives orders to stop us. They want all our supplies and equipment. Troops are boarding at the spaceport as we speak." He paused and looked first at Dad, and then at us.

"They'll be okay, we have to go." His voice was low and urgent, "now!"

Dad ran out of the room with him, the door slid shut. A strange hum started to build.

"Why don't we lie on the floor?" I suggested nervously, "and close our eyes."

"Watch out for Julia's puke," Will said, sitting as far away as possible from the acidic stench.

I swished the towels out of the way as the swirling began. Julia and Emily were squeezing my hands tightly. I felt as if my body were spinning and floating all at once. I wasn't sure if I was even lying on the floor anymore. I couldn't feel anyone's hands now, but I was too terrified to open my eyes. I was half-floating, my hands grasping at the air. Terror overwhelmed me. I couldn't open my eyes. I couldn't breathe. The next thing that happened, I can't be sure, but I think I must have fainted.

When I came around I was lying on a comfortable bed. Dad was kneeling on the floor with a cool towel pressed against my forehead.

Previn had a heart monitor in his hands. He murmured, "Thank God," and began to pack up the medical case.

"What happened?" My voice was croaky and my lips were dry. "Where's Mom?"

"She's with Julia," replied Dad gently. "She's been sick although nowhere near as bad as you."

I looked around. The room was glowing but nothing was moving or spinning. The blankets were soft and fluffy. I turned on my side. I felt so relaxed. My clothes hung in a closet opposite the bed. Kiki lay on the floor.

"We didn't make it did we," I rasped.

"What? No." Dad's face looked surprised. "We're on our way."

"But I can't hear anything." I managed to say.

"That's because we have reached maximum capacity. Jake, we are now traveling faster than the speed of light, tearing through the fabric of space and time as we speak."

Mom appeared at the doorway. "Jake," she said tearfully bending over me. "I'm so sorry I wasn't there with you. We took off in such a hurry. How are you feeling?"

"Better," I whispered. "How's Julia?"

"She's doing fine. Emily is with her." Mom glanced over at Dad.

"What about Tom and Will?" I felt so weak.

Dad put his hand on my shoulder. "They are in the Front Q room with Henley, Bronwyn and Peter. Now get some rest. Everyone else is fine. Mrs. Henley had rather a hard time of it, as did Alex and Maya, but the main thing is that we are on our way."

Previn cleared his throat. "Evie, I've given him a mild sedative just to let his body rest and recover. He should sleep for a few hours."

"Thanks for everything you've done," I heard Mom say, "I know you didn't approve of kids making the trip."

Previn sighed. "Given the tight security restrictions Evie, it was perhaps inevitable. I hope for their sakes, that when we land all our dreams are fully realized."

"I hope so too," Mom said softly.

"The important thing is that both the Future Project and Starship One have set off and the last minute attempts to sabotage both programs failed... Previn's voice began to fade. I don't know how long I slept, but a familiar voice was getting louder.

"Jake, Jake," I could hear Julia's voice in the distance.

"Go away," I mumbled. I was back at home cuddling an old teddy bear. It felt warm and soft.

"Jake," she persisted. I opened my eyes. The teddy became a wad of bunched up blankets. Julia sat on the bed looking at me. She'd curled her hair and put on a long red robe with a sash around the middle.

"You look just like you did when we were kids, probably seventy years ago now." She gave a wry smile.

I yawned. "What time is it?"

"That's a strange question given our present circumstances," she said still smiling and smoothing my linen bedcover.

"Sometimes, just sometimes Julia you astonish me with your insight."

She laughed. "Well, don't get too proud of me just yet," she continued. "You and I share the dubious honour of being the sickest on the train. I puked the most, you passed out the most!"

"No doubt Will and Tom will trumpet their superior genome," I said tiredly.

"Actually they have been really good about it all. They looked in on you while you were sleeping, and helped me sort out my shower."

"Shower?" I queried.

"Yes, my hair was a mess." She checked the ends of her long blonde hair absentmindedly.

"Good to see that some things always stay the same," I chuckled.

"Are you ready to get up now because if you are, I can show you around, not that I can explain much," Julia hastened to add. "Mom told me I absolutely wasn't to touch anything." She paused, "You will never guess who once lived in Paris!"

"Who?" I asked rubbing my eyes.

"Henley," smiled Julia, "He was at university right in the heart of the city, and he's promised to tell me all about it."

"Great," I smiled, "You do realize it was astrophysics not dress design that he studied. I can't imagine he was over at Chanel much."

"Ha, ha," Julia pulled the covers off me. I swung my legs over the side of the bed. I felt a bit wobbly but otherwise okay.

"Where's the shower?" I asked, looking around the silver room.

"That door there," pointed Julia. "Everyone has their own. They're tiny but I guess they'll do for a week. I'll just tell the others that you're up and then I'll be back." She slammed the door behind her. The shower was the same as in any hotel, and after five minutes and a change of clothes, I felt a lot better. Julia reappeared with Mom who hugged me.

"We're almost ready to eat," said Mom brushing the hair off my face. "Are you hungry?"

"Starving," I replied, "feels like I haven't eaten in a 100 years."

"Come on," said Mom, smiling and putting her arm around me, "let's get you something."

In the common room, I could hear a heated discussion going on between Previn and Peter.

"We should at least have found out what the political situation was before we left," Previn was saying.

"What does it matter," shouted Peter. "They were going to stop us and Starship One. It would have been a tragedy for mankind."

"Well it's now just a tragedy for us," replied Previn grimly. "We've taken off without being fully briefed or prepared, and we don't have the proposed landing site specs or codes. We don't even know if the outgoing government destroyed all files relating to the Future Project in order to protect themselves."

"Once we approach 2585 we will be able to assess the situation better." Peter shoveled food in his mouth, chewing loudly.

"I hope that you're right," replied Previn irritably.

"I just want to go to Paris," chimed in Julia from the Coke dispenser.

Previn refilled his glass and tousled the top of her head as if she was a really small kid. Julia frowned.

"We'll do our best," he said kindly.

"Let's all have something to eat now," Mom said quickly. "Julia, go and knock on Mrs. Henley door."

"Do I have too?" sighed Julia pulling a chair out.

"Yes," said Mom firmly pushing the chair back in.

"I'm going back to the rear Q room." Peter stood up sliding his dirty dishes to the side of the table. "I'll send Henley over and let him get a bite to eat," he shouted on his way out.

Previn picked at his food delicately. I sat down next to him as Mom began to rummage in the cupboards. "Won't the quantum be able to land us properly?" I asked, pulling a plate towards myself.

"The train was intended to be parked in Earth's orbit on arrival," Previn explained. "But should the need arise it can convert into two landing crafts and come down on the surface. The quantum on board will work it out." He paused. "Quantums are strange Jake," he continued staring ahead. "They can be a bit unpredictable, rather like humans which is why they are so wonderful and also why they are so hard to understand."

Mrs. Henley came puffing through the door with Julia trailing behind her. "Tom, Will and Emily are with Henley in the Front Q room before you ask me," she said looking at Mom. "Heard you had it rough," she added, sitting down next to me.

I nodded, "I'm back to normal now."

"Glad to hear it."

Mom handed us some food bags; they were hot and a bit mushy.

"Hope the food's better in the future," said Mrs. Henley tipping the mush out on the plate.

"There is some fresh food in the refrigerator," Mom said, "but I thought we could have it for our evening meal tonight."

"That's fine Evie," said Mrs. Henley "don't take any notice of me. I'm still a bit disorientated."

Tom, Will and Emily burst through the door with Henley laughing behind them. They had obviously raided the storage cupboards, as they were now wearing NASA overalls as well.

"You okay now?" asked Tom, looking at me uncertainly.

"Dude, you totally freaked out," said Will.

"I'm fine," I replied wanting to avoid any more fuss. "Where's everyone else."

"Our parents are in the Rear Q doing some calculations," replied Will. "Thanks." Mom put a plate down in front of him. Emily pulled up a chair on the other side of me.

"How far have we traveled now?" I asked Henley.

"They're still calculating," interrupted Will, stirring the mush on his plate.

"It's over seventy years for sure," said Henley's booming voice. "I'd better get back to my work, thanks Evie, see you later Mam." He left and squeezed Mrs. Henley's shoulder on the way out. Mom followed him with a tray of munchies to hand around.

"Well," said Mrs. Henley looking around at us all, "here we are again."

"I think we should ask Previn and our parents about the asteroid, and find out if they know anything." I put my knife and fork down.

"Why worry them now Jake," said Emily gently, "let's wait."

"Suppose it was part of the brief that they missed," I insisted. "Suppose they should have been informed about it."

"I think Jake's right," said Tom unexpectedly. "If we at least tell Henley, he can enter details into the quantum and it can calculate possible outcomes."

"Ah, but it can only calculate outcomes based on the data that we input," said Mrs. Henley.

"We don't know if the asteroid's orbital pattern has changed. So anything we calculate will only be based on what we knew when we left Moonbase. Until we slow down and re-enter the time line again, we won't have access to any new information about what is happening on Earth."

"That sucks," said Julia drily.

"Totally," replied Mrs. Henley calmly taking a spoonful of mush. "Henley is in the loop now about the asteroid." She slurped the hot liquid. "Naturally I let him know after we left Moonbase. I gave him a short and whispered version in the lunar copter, didn't want any military chasing us before we had the chance to give them the slip!" She winked. "Go talk to him. I'm off now for my nap." She hobbled out and we could hear her tapping down the corridor. There was silence as everyone ate the mush on their plates.

I leaned back on my chair. "I want to go and have a look around the train. I think I'm the only one that hasn't had a tour."

Tom looked at me, "I'll go with you." Will was dishing out ice cream.

"See you guys later," I said, and we left them eating.

Out in the corridor we walked slowly down the glowing hallway. I ran my finger lightly along the walls.

"This isn't like any material I've ever seen before."

"It's made out of atomic particles and carbon nanotubes tightly compacted." Tom shook his head, "The technology is so advanced only a handful of people in the entire world understand it, although it may be commonplace by the time we land."

"That take off was so freaky when everything was spinning around. I can't remember much about it."

"Everyone had their eyes shut Jake."

"But not you?" I asked.

"No" replied Tom. "I don't know exactly what happened but it seemed like there was two of everyone, one version lying on the floor and one hovering above. Perhaps that's a normal occurrence when you enter the time line." He paused, "We don't know enough about it yet."

"I wish I'd asked my Dad more questions," I sighed.

"It wouldn't matter if you had," said Tom shaking his head. "He wouldn't have been allowed to talk about it anyway." We stopped.

"All the cabins are located on this side of the train. It's divided into ten at the rear and ten at the front, although I think the two small kids are probably in their parent's rooms. Two mini particle accelerator rooms are on either side of the train and, of course, two Q rooms. The concertina corridor connects both sides."

"Wonder why they did that." I asked.

"Did what?" queried Tom.

"Put this concertina corridor in." I replied touching the grooved and bent walls.

"It's so the train can bend around the track as we're running in a circle. It can squeeze in and expand out again." Tom said, as if he was explaining something to a small child.

"Yes but we're not really running on a track, I mean we're in space somewhere between Mars and Earth," I replied frostily.

"Yes," replied Tom in exasperation. "But the time line is laid out like a circular track so that the anti-matter rockets can follow a specific path."

"Okay, whatever, you're making my head spin." I held my hands up to my forehead. "What if we hit any space debris?"

Tom looked unconcerned. "Won't happen, we're ripping through time as well as space, everything gets pushed out of the way." He waved his hand at a door. "The particle accelerator rooms are off limits. The anti-matter is way too delicate for people to go traipsing around in there. Only Previn and Henley go in." He yawned. "Let's go and check on Henley, he's always in the Front Q."

I could feel a slight motion beneath my feet as if I were moving, but it was so subtle that I had to concentrate to be aware of it. "It's pretty amazing," I said.

"The technology is way beyond anything I've ever read about," replied Tom. "It must be top secret." Emily's parents passed us in the corridor carrying cups of coffee.

"Feeling better Jake?" asked Emily's dad.

"Yes thanks."

We finally came to the Front Q doors. Tom didn't knock and Henley didn't seem at all bothered when we sat ourselves down on some seats next to him. He was eating munchies from a huge plate balanced on a long tube in front of him.

"How does this thing work?" I said, looking at all of the tubes and the translucent box in front of me.

Henley laughed. "I think we'd need longer than a few days on this train for me to explain that to you," he replied. "But I can give you a short and simple version. This quantum here," he pointed at the crystals and pins, "is the most powerful one ever built. It uses light and atoms to process billions of computations at the same time. They're performed in collaboration between parallel universes. In fact the quantum could be said to be conscious in the way that it thinks on multiple entangled levels just like a human brain."

"So it thinks it's real," I said surprised.

"No sonny, it really is real," Henley replied, crunching on some crackers.

"What do you have to do with it?" Tom asked, peering at the cube.

"Keep the gates in check and watch that the atoms remain stable."

"But how do you know it's real?" I asked confused. "Isn't it just a glorified bigger and better computer?"

"Oh no," said Henley. "Not this baby. This is something altogether different, this is actually thinking as we speak. Whereas your Pid Pad can perform one calculation at a time my baby here can perform over a million computations at once, and it stores the entire knowledge of mankind in its memory banks. In fact it's grown even as we have been on board very much the way a child develops its own personality."

Julia and Will appeared behind me. I hadn't even heard them come in I was so engrossed in the quantum.

"Isn't that a bit dangerous?" Julia asked.

"How?" replied Tom smirking "How can a computer be dangerous?"

"I'm just thinking," said Julia looking at Henley. "If it has a personality like a child what if it throws a tantrum?"

"Julia's thinking about herself now," I laughed.

"Actually Julia, you could be onto something there. We have to be very careful of quantums. There is an element of chaos in these machines caused by identical universes becoming different."

Julia stared at Henley quizzically. "Oh, okay, got that."

"How far have we come now?" I asked, looking around at the crystals.

"The quantum has calculated over 200 years," replied Henley.

"So if an asteroid had hit Earth it would now be done and over with." Julia didn't mince her words and looked Henley straight in the eye.

Henley shifted in his seat. "My Mam told me about asteroid 1999, I had the quantum examine it and it definitely had some inexplicable data coming through the logic gates."

"Such as?" asked Tom moving nearer to Henley.

"Well," Henley sighed leaning back and playing with a piece of tubing in his fingers.

"The orbit was shifting but it almost seemed as if it was being moved rather than anything that obeyed the laws of physics. The quantum's ultimate outcome was that an unknown force was acting upon it. That puzzles me." Henley rubbed his eyes, "Very puzzling," he repeated.

"I'm sure they will have found a way to fix it," said Julia cheerfully.

Henley shook his head. "I hope so, because it might have made one big mess if it landed. I mean you would be looking at centuries before any survivors could even come above ground again."

"Are we a rescue mission Henley?" I asked. "Julia thought we might be taking the quantum to help the people of the future."

"The mission wasn't sold to me on those terms," replied Henley, "but so much happened in the week before we left that hearing about the classified room at Moonbase and what you all saw has left me wondering. Anyway I have some checks to run now. Have a look around, but don't touch anything," he said, and started to wave his hands about in the air.

We wandered around the tubes and the virtual glowing screens.

I whispered in a creepy voice, "Wonder if it's watching us?"

"Stop it," laughed Julia.

Will continued in a high-pitched robotic voice, "Your hair is looking messy Julia."

Julia pretended to hit him. "I'm going back to the others now, this is boring. I only came to tell you that we were going to watch a movie."

"What movie?" I asked.

"The quantum chose it for us earlier," she said. "It's a vintage piece, called Back to the Future."

I could hear Henley laughing behind me. "Oh my baby has a sense of humour."

"I think he's becoming as crazy as his mother," whispered Julia. "See you later." She left with Will and the door slid shut.

"Do you think the quantum can really think?" I asked Tom.

"I don't know what the definition of think is when it comes to quantums," replied Tom.

"Well said," shouted Henley behind us. "At least it didn't pick 2001 a Space Odyssey, I might have been worried if it had it picked that movie."

"Never heard of it," I replied.

"It's about a computer that takes over a spaceship and kills all the crew," Henley said. "Don't they give any cultural lessons in school now?"

"You're right," I replied. "That would be tricky, I'd be really scared."

"Could it do that though?" asked Tom curiously.

"In theory yes," replied Henley. "Although in practice its systems will only override a human decision in an emergency."

"Why?" I asked sharply.

"Because it can see every possibility in a split second and also weigh all outcomes. No humans are capable of anything near that amount of processing in their brains. It may even be, Jake, that when we arrive in the future, humans will have joined with machines in order to increase their strength."

"I hope not," said Tom. "We wouldn't be human anymore."

"It depends," I replied. "If you have enhanced biological systems you are still human. Look at people now, a replacement arm here, a replacement leg there. As long as you still have it all up here," I tapped my head. "That's what counts; I mean what would you be otherwise?"

"A singularity" replied Henley. "The most perfect combination of man and machine."

"Don't agree," I said, shaking my head. "You would just be a machine then."

"I'll have to argue about that some other time with you," laughed Henley. "I've got work to do boys." He turned back to the colored crystals as Tom and I wandered around the room.

"What do you think will be waiting for us when the train stops?" I asked Tom.

"I don't know," replied Tom gloomily. "I'm trying to remain hopeful but let's be honest, we didn't exactly leave under the best circumstances. A failing global government, a massive terrorist attack, floods, climate change, an energy crisis and a potential asteroid strike."

"You need to talk to Julia," I laughed. "She'll tell you about her plans to be a Paris fashion designer and not even an asteroid is going to get in the way of that."

"Post apocalypse chic," grinned Tom. "I shall look forward to it."

"I keep wondering about Starship One; do you think they've reached other star systems yet?"

Tom looked thoughtful. "Probably, that's if nothing has gone wrong on board," he sighed. "Now that would have been the ship to be on. You sleep and wake up in a new world."

"Or explode if your metabolism has a meltdown. It's a bigger risk," I said.

"What do you want to do on Earth 2585?" Tom suddenly asked me.

"I don't know," I scratched my chin and thought hard. "Obviously before Dad dragged us along on this trip, I had thought that I would finish school, go to university and maybe go into time engineering like him. What about you?"

"I always wanted to be an astrophysicist," replied Tom pompously, "and find out more about the universe. Will and I had plans to achieve big discoveries together."

"You still can," I replied.

"Well, we'll have so much to relearn," he paused. "But we are confident given our superior intelligence, that we can work in any field of scientific research."

I smiled, "Don't say that around Julia, or she'll be reminded that you're tweakies and I think she may have just about forgotten."

"Let's go and see what this movie is about," said Tom changing the subject.

"Bye Henley," I shouted over my shoulder as we left the room.

Henley waved his hand behind his back and wiggled his fingers at us. As I walked down the corridor with Tom behind me, I suddenly felt a strange sensation. My stomach heaved and I turned to say something to Tom, or should I say Toms as there were now two ghostly apparitions on either side of him. He opened his mouth to say something and merged into one Tom again.

"What happened there?" he asked astonished, examining his hands.

"Haven't got a clue," I replied feeling uneasy, "but there were three of you."

"You too" he said staring at me.

Henley came out of the Q room wiping perspiration from his face.

"The quantum has just made a huge push through time. We are now roughly 300 years from where we started."

"Can you ask the quantum to give us some warning if that's going to happen again because it was a little freaky and a lot scary?" I said catching my breath.

Henley pushed past us. "I'm going to find Previn if anyone needs me," he shouted.

Emily and Julia came running down the corridor towards us. "Did you feel that?" Emily gasped.

"It was a big time shift," sighed Tom uneasily.

Will followed. He didn't look so good. His face was white. "Man I can't wait to be off this thing," he muttered.

"Well if the quantum and the anti-matter keep pushing this fast, we may arrive a lot more quickly than anticipated," said Tom looking calmer.

"Do you want to go and play Galaxy Explore?" Will asked Tom. "I'm a bit bored and the movie the quantum picked is so old and the quality so bad you can barely understand it."

"It's funny," insisted Emily. "I want to watch the rest of it."

"A guy goes back in time using an old fashioned gas car," Will glanced at Tom, and raised his eyebrows. "He has no wormholes, no proper physics or science, nothing. It's totally unbelievable!"

"It's just a story," said Emily.

"If I'm going to watch a vintage movie," Will interrupted, "as a movie buff, I prefer the old vampire twilight films, at least they don't have any fake science in them."

"Yeah because vampires are so real aren't they, Will?" Julia snorted and tossed her hair. "I'll watch the rest of the movie with you, Emily," Julia continued and made her way back to the communal room. Emily followed.

"Go on, play some games," I said to Tom and Will. "I'm going to read for a while."

I headed for my room waving to Henley and Previn further down the corridor. They didn't seem to notice as they were so deep in conversation. I sat down on my bed wearily and picked up my Pid Pad. What was waiting for us in 2585?

Chapter Five

CRASH, BANG, NOTHING

"We all know that UFO's are real. All we need to ask is where they come from, and what do they want?"
Apollo 14 Astronaut Captain Edgar Mitchell

I turned over and heard the door slide open. Mom gently pulled back the covers to reveal my tired face.

"I've prepared some food when you're ready," she said softly. "Dad is going to have a chat with everyone."

"Um okay," I yawned. "I'll be there in a few minutes." Mom nodded, and I listened to the rustle of her Smart suit as the door slid shut behind her. I ran my fingers lightly along the glowing walls. It was hard to think of what year it was now, somehow it just didn't matter. We were living outside of time, rushing towards the future at unimaginable speeds. What did it matter when you slept or ate or did anything at all? I hauled myself out of my comfy bed and washed quickly. Everyone was seated and serving themselves as I activated the communal door. For the first time I saw all of us together, even Alex and Maya. They looked like miniature versions of their parents. Their Lego was strewn all over the floor and they concentrated on building their spaceship, oblivious to the fact that as they played, the centuries were hurtling past. The message about the supercomputer flashed through my mind again. One of these people could be a traitor, but who and why. This continued to baffle me as I looked around for a seat.

"You're late," smirked Tom. "We almost postponed this meal to yesterday!"

"I'm glad you didn't because I'm really hungry," I replied with a dead-pan face. "I haven't eaten since tomorrow morning!"

Will laughed and said, "Who's there? The time traveler; the time traveler who? Knock Knock."

"Who's there?" asked Julia smiling and leaning forward.

"Oh Julia!" I slapped my forehead.

"What?" she said looking around. "What?"

Tom pulled out a chair for me and I sat down between him and Julia as Dad began to speak.

"I think it's time we talked about what we know about the Time Train and put some rumors to rest regarding asteroids." Dad looked in Tom's direction and then mine. "First," he said, holding his hand up when it looked as if Tom was going to speak. "There has never been any hard evidence that the Earth would be hit by an asteroid."

"But Dad!" I started to protest.

"Henley has told me everything," he said. "But it doesn't add up with what we already know and," he paused to let his words take effect, "what we already know is that we do make it to the future. This is why I knew we had to make this trip. It was the classified information that I couldn't tell you earlier." There was a silence as everyone around the table looked at one another.

"I don't understand," said Tom frowning, "there's no way that you can know that."

"There is," said Peter, "it was one of the information briefs that was supposed to take place before we set off."

"Twenty years ago," continued Dad, "a message was received at the Large Hadron Collider in Switzerland, Europe."

"What's that Dad?" asked Julia looking around the table, "for those of us that did more art than science in school." Will smirked and looked at Tom.

"It was a machine that was built in late the 20th Century in order to find out more about the universe through different unique experiments," Dad paused. "At the time people were worried that potentially the collider could create a black hole that would swallow up the Earth."

"Which obviously didn't happen," said Will, looking at Julia.

"You don't say," replied Julia sarcastically, raising her eyebrows.

"Instead," said Dad raising his voice, "it created the most miniscule wormholes called Higgs singlets that opened for a split second before they collapsed again."

"And this is the really interesting part," said Peter, looking at Julia who had pushed her empty plate to the middle of the table. "A message was received via one of those singlet wormholes from another dimension in time. It was thought to have originated in the year 2585." Julia sat up.

"What did it say?" she blurted out before anyone else had a chance to speak.

"One word," said Peter, "Wow!"

"That's it?" asked Julia sharply.

"What does that mean to us though?" Emily looked around the table.

"It means we are a people of few words in 2585," laughed Mrs. Henley still eating.

"No," said Dad, "we couldn't receive the whole message. We believe it was part of a sentence, but it was enough for us to know that the Time Train would succeed. Our research group surmised that not only would we make it to the future, but that we would finally find a way to communicate with the people still living on another time line; that of the past."

"What does that have to do with the asteroid?" I asked puzzled.

"Don't you see," said Dad banging his fist on the table decisively. "Everything in the future is safe. No one would send a message saying, 'Wow!' if an asteroid had hit, and if civilization was struggling."

"Maybe they wanted to say wow it sure is a mess down here," Julia snorted. Mrs. Henley tried to hide a smile with the back of her hand.

"It's significant that the message came from 2585, our approximate landing time," said Bronwyn coolly. "It seems to indicate that someone wanted to reassure the Future Project in whatever way they could that we had all made it safely through the time line."

"So you are saying that someone from the future sent it, or perhaps someone who knew about our trip?" asked Emily looking puzzled.

"Spooky," said Will. His parents, who appeared stern and serious, frowned at him. Their glance seemed to say, all that genome tweaking and that's the best he can do. I looked around the table. Previn was quietly attacking his food while shaking his head.

"I took it as a very positive sign," Jim exclaimed, smiling at his wife Faith and the two small kids. "It's the reason we made the trip, knowing that we were more or less assured of a happy outcome."

"Based on what?" said Previn incredulously, putting down his knife and fork loudly. "There's no evidence that the message was meant for us and there's no way to conclude from a three letter word, which was part of a whole transmission not received, that all is well in 2585, or that it even came from 2585!" He looked at Dad in exasperation and continued, "Some of the findings of that investigation were deeply flawed and possibly falsified. The more we learn about quantums the more we realize that past, present and future events are entangled. There is no way that we can be sure the message was aimed at us."

Dad shook his head stubbornly, "It's the logical explanation Previn."

"There is no logic to quantum." Previn leaned forward. "What you do on this train today could influence whether the Egyptians build the pyramids, or whether Buzz Aldrin decides to join NASA, or if King Henry VIII will chop a head off one of his wives! It's not all decided at this point in time. Undiscovered places in the universe may not even exist until a human being sees them. Everything is to some extent uncertain."

"Well it's a riot in here tonight," sighed Julia loudly scraping some ice cream out of her dessert bowl.

"Furthermore," Previn continued intensely, "having reviewed the asteroid data with the quantum I find it most disturbing. The course changes can't be accounted for by the laws of physics as we know them, and this supposed message from the past only proves one thing; that if the asteroid did hit, there were survivors."

"With technological capabilities, Previn," said Dad excitedly banging his fist on the table. "This means that humans did more than just survive."

"I wonder what they meant to say with Wow!?" said Henley. His eyes were half closed thinking.

"Perhaps wow it's wonderful here," suggested Emily.

"It seems a bit of a childish even old fashioned kind of thing to say," I added. "I mean who really says wow a lot now anyway?"

"Perhaps it's back in vogue in 2585," said Julia. "They may be wearing long dresses as every day wear, who knows." Her face took on a dreamy look as she was no doubt imagining herself at a future virtual fashion show with lots of long flowing skirts.

"I could do with a long dress dearie to hide my varicose veins," said Mrs. Henley. "So if you are bored and would like to whip up something for me then feel free to do so!" Julia shifted uncomfortably in her chair and simply smiled politely.

"Did the collider find anything else at all?" asked Previn, sarcastically, who obviously knew the answer to his question.

"No, the researchers at the Hadron Collider have been looking for decades to find the rest of the message," replied Dad quietly, "and as far as I know they continue to search."

"How could they have sent the message in the first place," asked Tom with a puzzled look on his face.

"That's still a mystery to us," sighed Dad.

"I thought you always said we couldn't travel back in time." Julia looked at him accusingly.

"There is so much we still don't know," replied Dad shifting around uncomfortably, "but it seems that a Higgs singlet, which is an invisible particle, can pass through other dimensions and transmit information. Somehow, someone managed to get that one word back to us."

"Does anyone here know any space history?" asked Tom. He looked around the table.

"What's that got to do with anything?" Previn said sharply.

"It strikes me as odd that the message would say wow," replied Tom "because there was a signal from space received in 1977 from an unknown origin that became known as the Wow! signal."

"What was that?" I asked curiously.

Previn frowned, "I vaguely remember what you're talking about from some of my academy space history lessons."

"The wow! signal was received by an old fashioned radio telescope in 1977 called Big Ear," continued Tom. "By an organization called Search for Extraterrestrial Intelligence. Early SETI astronomers were looking for alien signals in outer space. One night they ran a paper print out from a really primitive computer scanning different star systems in the cosmos. A scientist saw a strange anomaly in the data. It showed an inexplicable transmission. He was so surprised that he wrote Wow! next to it on the printout. No one could ever explain where the transmission had come from. Hence it became known as the Wow! signal."

"And your point is?" asked Dad impatiently.

"That you've received a wow signal as well," I replied before Tom could say anything.

Dad looked at us exasperated but his expression was uneasy. He replied, "No, we received a signal that said Wow! We didn't write it anywhere."

"I know that," said Tom sounding annoyed, but isn't it funny that it's the same word.

"Okay," said Julia. "I'll say wow a lot more from now on seeing that it's so popular, who knew!" She took another drink of juice, looked at Will and mouthed the word "Wow!"

"It's an interesting coincidence but nothing more," said Tom's father gently.

"Anyway," Dad said sternly, "my point is that we can be confident that no asteroid strike is likely and we can land safely." Previn sighed, and began to clean up his plates shaking his head.

"Who sent the first signal?" persisted Julia.

"It came from the constellation of Sagittarius many light years away. Scientists couldn't find the source. It never repeated itself, and I think in the end, everyone just gave up looking." Tom replied.

"Little green men!" Mrs. Henley leaned forward as she spoke, "aliens!"

"There's no such thing," said Julia looking at Dad wide-eyed.

"We can't be sure of that." I spoke with my mouth full and saw Mom frowning at me. "We haven't explored enough of the galaxy or logged enough 'extra solar planets' yet to know for sure."

"Oh they exist," said Mrs. Henley. I could see Julia rolling her eyes at me. Emily's mouth was twitching.

"There's no data to support that statement," said Tom firmly. "Astronomers have searched thousands of 'extra solar planets' and not one has been found to be capable of supporting life."

"Ah, but absence of proof isn't proof of absence," continued Mrs. Henley. "What about UFOs?"

"Ach Mam, leave the kids alone," laughed Henley.

"Most UFOs can be explained," said Tom stiffly, "and those that can't are just a tiny percentage of all sightings. They all probably have a natural explanation that we just haven't thought of yet."

"Okay," said Dad sternly. "We are getting off topic. I wanted to inform everyone that we will be landing back in the States. The quantum onboard will pick the best site. This is due to the fact that we don't know which places will be built up and which will provide us with a clear landing area. So we will have to get nearer before we decide. The Time Train will stop orbiting at the correct point in the time line and will scan the US topography for a put down point. The future World Council may even guide us to whatever landing spot they have chosen for us."

"Might we be on a world broadcast?" asked Julia brightly, sitting up and fluffing her hair. Dad ignored her.

"Can we pick up satellite signals by then?" asked Emily.

"We should be able to," answered Dad. "This will help us prepare for what to expect."

By now Previn and Henley were talking with Peter and Bronwyn. Tom's and Will's parents were discussing the landing with Emily's parents. Alex and Maya were playing on the floor with their Lego and the atmosphere felt relaxed. I looked around the room, and like Julia, I just wished that there was a window or something else to feast my eyes on, other than the glowing walls.

Emily leaned over to me. "It hasn't been as bad as I expected. Moonbase was actually far worse than this. In fact, apart from the scary take off it's really been okay."

"We still have to land!" I said playing with my fork.

"I know, but at least now we know about the message. It makes me feel like everything will be okay, don't you think so?"

"I'm not so sure," I replied. "I mean it's good that the collider picked up a message, but it doesn't really tell us anything other than someone is alive in 2585 to send it."

"And that somewhere a collider is operational," said Emily happily. "Surely that has to count for something, that's a huge piece of equipment to operate. It must take a ton of people to get it going."

"I haven't got a clue Emily. I know very little about it other than what we learned in school." I glanced over at Tom. He was lost in thought. I knew he wasn't convinced by Dad's arguments either and that disturbed me.

Emily shifted around on her chair picking at her food.

"Do you know how long we've been traveling now?" she asked.

"It's funny, but I'm not sure," I replied. "I think for a couple of days."

"It could actually be more," Emily said. "Dad thinks that we've been sleeping longer and that our watches and measurements of Earth time are unreliable now."

"I just wish I could see outside," I sighed.

"There wouldn't be anything to see," replied Emily between mouthfuls of pasta, "we're in a sort of time vacuum so it would just be blackness, no stars, planets, nothing."

"I know, but even to see nothing would be better than...." I trailed off looking around me.

"What, you don't enjoy seeing my gorgeous wrinkled face every day?" said Mrs. Henley leaning across the table and helping herself to some more food.

"You can get some really good treatments for that you know," Julia said evenly. "There's no reason for anyone to let themselves go."

"My dear, at ninety-three I've given myself full permission to let myself go, and unless the future can provide me with a completely new body, I shall continue to do so." Julia rolled her eyes at me as usual. Suddenly Faith spoke up. She was normally so quiet that everyone stopped to hear what she had to say.

"It's Alex's tenth birthday tomorrow, and we'd like to hold a celebration, a birthday party for him. I know it may not be the exact day now, but we told him that we'd do something for him on the train," she paused. Alex clapped his hands and his little sister Maya shouted, "A party, a party," jumping up and down.

"I think that's a fabulous idea," said Mrs. Henley cheerfully. "Why don't we use the other communal room in the rear carriage? We can set it up and make it look great while people are still using this room for meals. I love a party!" She added, smiling broadly at everyone. Then she winked at young Alex who beamed back at her.

"Good idea," replied Faith. "I'll clear the kid's toys away, and we'll set it up in the morning." Mom rose and began to move the plates. I helped her stack everything neatly under UV lights to be sterilized.

"I think I'm going to use my Pid Pad in my room," I said thoughtfully.

"I don't want to appear anti-social, but I'd like to read up on that odd signal that Tom was talking about and also, the old Hadron Collider."

Mom smiled at me and patted my arm. "You do that Jake."

"I'll be back later," I shouted at everyone and ran down the corridor to my room. Once I was settled on the bed I began to search on my Pid Pad's stored data banks and started to read. I felt agitated by Dad's spooked face when the Wow! signal was mentioned, Previn's explanation of quantum and Tom's obvious dissatisfaction with the whole topic. I don't know what happened next. I felt as if I was floating through the air. The Pid Pad drifted out of my hands, then nothing. Who knows how long I had been unconscious when I awoke with a start. Something was different. I stretched out my legs and looked down. My trousers were much shorter; they were up around my ankles. I rubbed my eyes; what was that? I then ran my hands over my face and it felt different. I jumped out of bed and dashed to the mirror. I'd grown! My face looked curiously different. It was the same me, but subtly older. There was an urgent knocking at the door. Still feeling like I was dreaming, I opened it, my mouth hanging slack in shock. Dad burst through and grabbed me by the shoulders looking at me intensely. His hair had turned much greyer and his fine distinguished lines were now deep wrinkles. I was speechless.

"It's okay, it's okay," he said looking at me. "It's happened to all of us, we've all aged slightly, the adults more than you kids."

"But how?" I managed to whisper. "Was this supposed to happen?"

"No one as far as we know has ever traveled the time line before, so it's impossible to predict." Dad fumbled in his pocket pulling out a pager. "Yes he's okay Evie."

I continued to stare at him. He smiled. "It's not so bad. I'm sure I can get some hair dye in 2585. It's the women that are taking this the hardest, without all their beauty and anti-ageing treatments, they're feeling pretty hard done by. They wanted to look their best when we arrived so... well you can imagine. Best to be tactful when talking to them Jake, you know, tell them they still look good." I nodded still amazed. Dad patted my shoulder,

"Always knew you'd grow up to be a looker!" We both burst out laughing, the absurdity of the situation was overwhelming. Julia stuck her head around the door.

"Can anyone join this party?" she twirled into my room. She was wearing one of Mom's dresses. Her face looked only slightly older, her hair was longer and she was definitely at least two inches taller.

"You should see Alex," she laughed. "It's going to be the weirdest thing ever, celebrating the birthday of a ten year old that looks about twenty!"

"Really?" I said shocked. "I don't think that's something to laugh about Julia."

"No one knows why the latest time shift has affected Alex the most, but I'd appreciate it if you didn't go on about it." Dad shot Julia a warning look. "Faith is understandably upset and worried about him."

"What about Mrs. Henley?" I asked.

"Oh, she couldn't possibly look any older," said Julia dismissively. "I don't even think she has room for any more wrinkles."

"She is fine," said Dad. "Older, but still able to manage. Although if this happens again, I'd be concerned."

"Will it happen again Dad?" asked Julia, suddenly looking at him apprehensively.

"I don't know Julia," he replied.

"Everyone's going to be afraid to go to sleep at this rate," I muttered under my breath.

"I'll be in the Rear Q if you need me," Dad said awkwardly, ignoring my last comment, "and Jake, feel free to go to my room and get yourself some pants that fit." Julia and I looked at each other as he disappeared down the corridor.

"This is so weird," I shivered.

"Totally, wait until you see the others," she shook her head.

"I'll be in Mom's room, see you later," I said quietly.

"I'm doing party preparations," sighed Julia. "However, I think we need to scrap the teddy bear plans!" She took off laughing down the corridor while I groaned inwardly at her insensitivity.

Mom was in her room sitting on the bed. Her hair had some serious grey in it and she seemed maybe five years older. She looked at me sadly, "Hey Jake, do you need some bigger pants?"

"You still look great Mom," I said, remembering Dads words.

She sighed, "I look old."

"Once we arrive you can fix your hair and anything else you don't like." I sat down next to her and took a deep breath.

She smiled, "You're right, it's only a bit of grey. I shouldn't let it ruin my big adventure. I just wish I'd thought to bring some hair dye."

"You'll look more distinguished when we arrive," I said opening the closet and pulling on a pair of Dad's jeans. They were still too long for me, but much better than the 'high water pants' that exposed my ankles. I rolled the sleeves up on one of his sweaters, hoping that it wouldn't fit me by tomorrow!"

"Okay," said Mom, appearing to cheer up. "I'm not going to mope. We have a party to prepare for an extremely tall, ten year old who needs to have a shave!" We both looked at one another and started to laugh.

"It's not fair," I exclaimed. "I don't think I need to shave yet, although..." I stroked my face feeling the slightly stiffer hairs beginning to develop.

"That's because you're so fair," Mom said, "let's go," and she pushed me gently." We walked down to the communal room arm in arm. When I saw Alex sitting at the table I struggled to contain my shock. He was a man. A very tall blond man! The last time I had seen him, what seemed like just hours ago he had been a child playing with a toy spaceship. Faith stood nearby talking with Previn.

"I just want you to consult with the quantum," I could hear her saying.

"It's probable that his particular metabolism hasn't coped as well with the time shift."

"But what if we have another big push?" she insisted, "can't we slow it down?" Previn looked unhappy.

"I don't think we can Faith. The systems are going at nominal speed. I don't know what the effects would be on anyone if we tried to taper it. We are traveling in the time line at the optimal calculations that have been very carefully worked out for over 20 years. We can't just throw that all to one side because Alex has some facial hair."

"Has some facial hair!" Faith just about exploded. "Can you even begin to imagine what it's like for him?" she continued angrily. "To go to bed a child and wake up," she waved her arm at him, "like this?"

"Calm down," said Previn sternly. "We all knew the risks when we signed on for this, which is why I was so opposed to children making this journey."

"Saying I told you so isn't really helping the situation." Faith folded her arms and glared at Previn. The strain showed on his face. For all his genius and technological wizardry, Previn was out of his depth now, and it seemed to me that he knew it.

"I will go and try out some calculations with the quantum," he muttered, and strode off in the direction of the rear Q Room, almost colliding with Tom and Will as they opened the door. Like me, they appeared to have aged slightly but nowhere near as drastically as Alex.

"Phew," said Tom scrutinizing my face. "We were worried you would look years older than us and have grown a beard!"

"I think it's more Alex you have to worry about on that score," I whispered. They looked around the room until their eyes found him at the table munching his cereal. Tom's mouth opened wide. Will spoke first.

"Holy crap, that can't possibly be Alex?"

"Keep your voice down," I whispered. "Faith is really upset."

"What if it happens to us?" Tom said quietly. "What if we wake up and suddenly find that we look our Dad's age?" There was an ominous silence.

"It won't," said Will anxiously. "If it was going to, it would have happened already, plus I'm sure we don't have that much longer to go."

"I hope you're right," I said. Mrs. Henley came in leaning heavily on some kind of balancing stick. It looked like a spare lever from the Q Room. She was puffing more than ever.

"I just keep getting better with age boys!" she quipped and sat down. Then she looked around the table. "My, my, Alex, I think I'm going to have to change that present I had in mind for you. It could be a bit age inappropriate now." Alex looked up.

"A present?" he said excitedly in an amazingly, deep man's voice.

"That just sounds so wrong," whispered Will. Tom nodded.

"Well, it wouldn't be a birthday without one, would it?" smiled Mrs. Henley showing no surprise at all.

"Goody," said Alex, and clapped his hands in delight.

"I have to get out of here," said Will quietly. "This is freaking me out." We stepped into the corridor. Emily walked towards us. Like Julia she'd grown taller and more graceful. She was even lovelier then before.

"I know, I know," she said as we all stared at her "I saw Alex earlier. Maya is just a bit older like the rest of us. I'm glad we all seem to have aged at the same rate. It would be awful if one of us had made a huge jump like poor Alex did. Where are you going?" she continued.

"Anywhere but the com room," said Will. "It's just too weird with Alex. I need some time to get to grips with his beard before we celebrate his tenth birthday!"

"Have you seen Julia?" I asked.

"She's in the Front Q with Henley," replied Emily sensing my concern.

"There's a first," said Tom smiling.

"No, she's been in there before bugging Henley about Paris," Will yawned.

"She's concerned about how much she could age before we arrive," said Emily gently.

"She's not the only one," Tom frowned.

"Perhaps Henley has an explanation," I suggested, making my way towards the Q Room. Julia was hanging over Henley's seat when we opened the doors.

"Can't you just ask it to give us its best guess?" I could hear her saying.

"Quantums don't guess Julia," Henley sighed.

"Well, I think you should make something up then to tell Faith," she replied, "because she's going to want some kind of answer about what's happened." I heard a tapping on the door. Mrs. Henley walked slowly through with a cup of tea that she handed to Henley.

"We're just talking about Alex," I said worriedly.

"Well," Mrs. Henley sighed. "We have a saying from earlier in my youth, 'Bleep happens,' and I'll leave it to you to fill in the bleep!" Henley roared with laughter.

"You're right Mam, although I think Faith will be looking for a more technical explanation than that." He pulled a face. "What! No sugar in my tea?"

"Ah, I forgot," said Mrs. Henley. "This is what age does to you." She made a move to get up.

"No trouble Mam," Henley swung himself out of his chair. "You watch the quantum, I'll get the sugar." The doors slid shut behind him.

"Where's everyone else?" I asked Mrs. Henley.

"Faith and your Mom are at the rear carriage preparing a party room for a very hairy ten year old! Have you seen that kid's legs? Previn is working in the rear Q Room with everyone else, running through different scenarios of what can happen next."

"What do you think might happen next?" I asked.

"We are outside of anyone's knowledge on that, sonny," she replied. "We've entered chaos now, and there's no telling what will happen. All the quantums in the world can't change the fact that we don't know didley squat."

"That's ridiculous," said Julia sharply. "Dad knows perfectly well what he's doing."

"What's that?" I asked straining my ears.

"What's what?" said Julia impatiently turning around.

"That sort of grinding noise." I listened and everyone else fell quiet.

"I can't hear anything," said Tom.

"I must have imagined it." I sat back. "No wait, can't you hear it?" A low hum rumbled, increasing in intensity and then the floor began to shake.

"Dad" shouted Julia hysterically, "Dad." She ran towards the door but before she had a chance to open it the walls suddenly started spinning. The glow increased and colors danced around the room. Emily screamed. I grabbed a chair, but as the train tipped sideways, it slid towards the wall with me hanging onto it. I looked over at Tom. He had slipped on the floor and his face was pale. Mrs. Henley began to speak, surprisingly clear and strong.

"Quantum voice activation, explain present movement," she shouted, and hung onto the crystals in front of her.

"Unknown attack," a calm woman's voice replied. "Evasive action taken."

"What action?" shouted Mrs. Henley, as the train, still tilting heavily to one side, began to shake violently.

"Emergency separation, time shift completed." The floor spun and I could hear Julia vomiting behind me. Will was shouting for Tom and my ears popped. I let go of the chair and slid to the ground. We were moving unbearably fast now. The train righted itself, scattering everyone once more. Furniture crashed around and the lights dimmed. I could feel the G forces pinning me to the ground, my face flattening and my lips wobbling. The last words I heard were Julia shouting for Dad.

When I came to, everything was quiet. I cautiously moved my head. Everyone was moaning and trying to get up off the floor. Will staggered to his feet in front of me. The hum had stopped, the colors had gone and I couldn't see the glow on the walls or floor anymore. The emergency back-up lights were on dim. Apart from Julia being sick and Emily sobbing, not a sound could be heard.

"What just happened?" gasped Will, his face a picture of shock. "What just happened?"

"It's what they call a crash landing sonny," came a croaky voice from the corner. I pulled myself up. Mrs. Henley was lying perfectly still by the wall. She was still holding a crystal in her hand.

"Are you alright?" I asked shivering. She didn't reply. "Are you alright Mrs. Henley?" I repeated crawling over to her.

"I have broken some bones and the pain is pretty bad Jake," she whispered. "Don't move me, wait and see if anyone arrives. I'll need some medical help sooner rather than later."

"Where's Dad," screamed Julia wiping her mouth and trying to stand. "Go and get him Jake, bring him here!" I pulled myself up and leaned against the wall trying to comprehend the scene. Will was bending over Tom. He lay crumpled on his side.

"Is he okay?" I breathed, staggering over to them.

"He's coming round," Will croaked, gently repeating Tom's name over and over.

Julia screamed again, "Just get Dad will you, my foot hurts. Get Dad! Get Dad!"

Emily stood up shivering, holding her arms around her stomach, "Why aren't they coming to help us?"

"Are you okay?" I asked. She had stopped crying and was taking deep breaths.

"Yes, have we landed?"

"I'm not sure, I think so... It felt like we were dropping," I replied, rubbing my head. The door was closed. I dragged myself towards it. My body ached all over. I barely had the strength to activate it. The corridor looked scary in the dim light, but I staggered along trying to remind myself of how it used to look. I passed the com room. It was empty. My mind raced, the party! They were all in the rear, that's why they hadn't come straight away. I paused and looked around. The corridor ended! I ran my hands over the smooth metal, my mind trying to comprehend the wall in front of me. Where was the concertina corridor? Where was the rear connection? I whirled around and scanned the interior. It wasn't possible, it couldn't be. It simply had to be there. With a growing sense of horror I hammered on the wall.

"Dad, Dad!" I shouted frantically. I slumped down onto my knees, dazed. What was going on? I heard footsteps. Will stood panting behind me.

"Tom is okay, where's everyone else?"

"I don't know."

"What do you mean you don't know?" Will pressed his hands against the wall in disbelief and turned to me, "What's happened? Where's the concertina?"

"I don't know," I whispered at him, horrified, "It's gone!"

"It can't be gone," said Will, his face incredulous. "It can't just have disappeared." He hurled himself against the wall.

"Stop it, Will, you'll hurt yourself." Tom came limping towards us rubbing his forehead. "There was an emergency separation," he said calmly. "Those were the last words that the quantum said."

"I didn't hear that," said Will breathing heavily. "So what, we open the doors and the rear part of the train will be somewhere nearby, is that what you're saying Tom?"

"Let's go back to the Q Room and decide what to do next," said Tom seemingly unflustered. "Perhaps the quantum can figure out how to help us."

"We boarded via the rear side of the train Tom," said Will his voice rising with panic. "I haven't seen any other doors, have you Jake?" He whirled around.

I shook my head. "There would be another way out Will, I'm sure of it, some kind of emergency exit that we just don't know about."

"Let's go back," said Tom, running his hands through his hair. The girls looked stunned as we walked through the doors.

Emily was bending over Mrs. Henley, "She's unconscious," she said, tears running down her shocked face.

"Where's Dad?" Julia asked immediately. I knelt down to where she was sitting on the floor and took her hands in mine. It was such a rare gesture from me that she was instantly silent.

"Julia, the concertina broke away at some point in the landing and the ship separated. There is just a wall now where the connection used to be. It's possible that the rear ship landed nearby, so we're going to consult the quantum and ask it what we should do next." Tears rolled silently down Julia's face.

"Mom and Dad are gone?" she whispered.

"We'll find them," I said, still holding her hands.

"Oh Jake," she cried and flung herself at me wrapping her arms around my neck sobbing. Tom knelt down beside me.

"Julia, we'll find the others, we just have to work out how to open the doors and what to do next." Julia sat back and dried her eyes. Her nose was running and being so distressed, she wiped it with her sleeve.

"Tom, what do we do about Mrs. Henley?" asked Emily in a trembling voice. Tom got up and limped slowly over to where Mrs. Henley lay. He knelt down next to her and checked the pulse point in her neck.

"I don't have enough medical knowledge to know what to do."

"She said to me before she passed out that she thought she'd broken some bones," I said.

"She's done more than that," replied Tom. "Perhaps it's a concussion or it could be an internal injury, either way she needs help. We have to get her out of here."

"The real problem," I said, "is that she's the only one who has any idea how to operate the quantum, unless either of you know?" I looked at Tom and Will. Will shook his head.

"We have the latest in Pid Pad technology, but because quantum was new and so experimental, they weren't widely available. I mean they were used in research, the military and those mega rich entertainment corporations that built the Sing Song bots." Julia sniffed and pointed her finger at Will accusingly.

"I knew it, I knew you watched Sing Song."

"The point is," said Will exasperated, "is that quantum wasn't mainstream enough for a regular person to have access to quantum technology."

"Can't we hang on for someone to rescue us?" asked Emily shakily. "I mean surely we must have been detected entering Earth's atmosphere, suppose we just sit tight and wait."

"I want to get out of this thing now," I said.

"I agree," Tom added, his face unreadable.

"I may be able to help," Julia said unexpectedly, wiping her eyes.

"You may be able to help?" repeated Tom, looking at Julia as if she'd gone mad.

"I've sat and talked to Henley about Paris the last few days," she sniffed. "He always listened and never laughed at me," she glared accusingly at Tom. "He had studied there when he was younger."

"Er, so how exactly does that help us?" queried Will. "Memories of Henley's visits to the Louvre and coffee on the Champs Elysees don't really seem all that relevant in our present situation."

Julia glared at Will. "While I was talking, he was always fiddling with those crystal things. It was quite hypnotic. I watched him over and over while we were chatting."

"So you think you might be able to work the quantum?" I said excitedly. She looked doubtful.

"Well I could try," she said slowly. "You'll need that crystal on the floor over there." Julia pointed to the tube that had fallen from Mrs. Henley's hands. I knelt down. I could hear Mrs. Henley's slow breathing. I handed the crystal over. Julia pulled herself up and moved stiffly over to the central port.

"You place them in like this," her face wore a look of pure concentration and she closed her eyes. "Then the cube needs to go here, and these pins need to line up."

"Who knew," said Tom in amazement. "Who knew that Julia was leading a secret life as a quantum operator?"

"Shut up Tom, I'm trying to visualize how this works," snapped Julia. Finally she seemed to decide, and swapped a few of the crystals around.

"That's it," she said triumphantly, "well at least I think so," she hesitated.

"Now what?" asked Will.

"Well you need Henley's security codes to open it."

"But we don't have them Julia" I said exasperated.

"I do," she replied.

"How do you know Henley's security codes?" asked Emily in astonishment. Julia looked a bit bashful and hesitated.

"It was just, well I only wanted to look up dress designs, I wasn't doing any harm," she insisted while we all continued to stare at her. "I hid behind the door and listened in."

"Julia you are brilliant," Tom shook his head. "Totally mad but brilliant."

"Man." Will shook his head. "Who would have thought it; saved by Christian Dior!"

Julia stretched and leaned over to reach the quantum. Then she quickly reeled off a string of numbers and began to wave her hands in the air. We all stood open mouthed in amazement. The crystals and the cube began to glow. "That's the qubits interacting," she said proudly. "You just have to wait a bit, okay now you can ask."

Tom cleared his throat, and in his best captain's voice asked "Can you confirm what has happened to the ship?"

"Star date unknown. The ship was attacked from a source of unknown origin, unable to identify," the calm voice of the quantum continued. "Emergency action and separation invoked. Time shift to an approximate 2635 sequence was considered best course of action."

"We've overshot the time line by 50 years," gasped Will.

"Did the rear ship do the same," Tom asked the quantum, seemingly unruffled.

"Unable to confirm" the quantum continued, "separation severed contact." I thought rapidly.

"Is it possible Tom?" I asked holding my head, "that the others still landed in 2585?" Tom stared ahead.

"I don't know, I just don't know, I'm not even sure if the quantum has the right time line, look at the cracks in it over here." Tom ran his fingers over the crystals.

"Quantum where are we?" I asked. The voice hesitated.

"Adjusting systems, damage sustained on impact." It glowed more brightly and then faded out again.

"North America, specifically in the foothills of the Olympic Mountains."

"Where's that? Where are we?" asked Emily, looking at Tom to provide an explanation.

Tom answered, "It's on the pacific coastline, near Seattle."

"Well that's got to be good news," Will said hopefully. "We're back in the US."

"Quantum why did you select this area?" I asked again. The next words sent a chill through everyone. "No evidence of human activity observed on re-entry."

I shook my head. "What, nothing?" I questioned it, astounded. "That can't be possible."

"No satellites in orbit, no evidence of populated areas, no communication signals," the quantum continued.

"The asteroid did hit then," Julia whispered her eyes huge.

"Quantum what are the radiation levels outside?" I felt sick now.

"Atmosphere is within a normal range."

"Are there any signs of a catastrophic event on Earth's surface?" I asked, my heart pounding.

"Unable to confirm. Radiation levels are normal."

I took a deep breath. "Why have you selected this location?"

"Microsoft headquarters were located in Seattle. The underground silo could be used in an emergency."

"What does that mean?" asked Emily her eyes darting wildly between Tom and me. "What kind of emergency?"

"It's where the quantum was first constructed, I believe," said Tom shaking his head. "Microsoft made the Pid Pads, in fact they were a mega billion dollar computing corporation," he paused. "They must have built some kind of bunker underneath their head office."

"That was hundreds of years ago Tom," said Emily confused. "Everything will have changed since that time."

"Well if the quantum thinks we should go there, then let's head for Seattle and hope we find help along the way," I said, looking at Tom for approval.

"No," cried Julia "We have to stay here and wait for Dad."

"They might even be outside." I looked at everyone. "Let's get the doors open and decide. Quantum," I began again, "where are the exit doors located?"

The calm voice replied, "Material will dissolve to create an exit on command."

"What's it saying?" asked Julia, her hand on my sleeve.

"I think we have to just tell it where we want to get out," replied Will looking at Tom. I walked around the room.

"What about here Tom?" I said pointing to the far wall.

He nodded. "It's as good a place as any!"

"Quantum open a door for us here," I commanded and pounded the side of the wall.

A burning smell began to fill the room. Julia stepped back alarmed. Slowly the train's wall began to melt away. A small hole appeared that began to grow until it was big enough for a person to get through. Blue sky was visible and the sun cast its rays inside. We looked out onto a green field of high grass surrounded by tall fir trees with snow-capped mountains in the distance.

"We made it!" breathed Julia pushing past everyone. She cautiously stepped through the hole. We all climbed out carefully, glad to be on firm ground again, and cast our eyes around our new surroundings. It was a breezy, beautiful, summer's day. I squinted in the bright sunlight and shielded my eyes. Once I'd inhaled a lung full of fresh air, I slowly explored the side of the train. The concertina corridor and rear section were severed. The back of the vehicle was now sealed as if a second carriage had never existed. Emily followed behind me swishing the grass absent-mindedly with her hand. She scanned the horizon in bewilderment.

"I don't believe an asteroid hit Earth," I said examining the landscape. "Even if centuries have passed I can't see how it would look like this." I motioned to the wild flowers growing nearby.

"What should we do now then?" asked Emily tearfully.

"I think we should start walking and get out of here" I replied firmly.

"Are you mad?" said Tom who joined us, "we haven't a clue what is happening. We should stay where we are and wait to be rescued, that's apart from the fact that we can't leave Mrs. Henley."

"I think we should go," I argued. "Remember the quantum only took emergency action in the first place because we were under attack. The country could be at war, we should hide."

"Hide!" shouted Julia "Hide! I haven't travelled 500 years to hide."

"What does everyone else think?" I asked.

Unexpectedly Will suddenly said, "I agree with Jake, something weird is going on here. Why are there no planes in the sky?" We all looked up. "I mean isn't this place near a major city? We must have been detected at least thirty minutes ago and nothing." He waved his hand at the sky. I turned around and stared at the silver train sitting so out of place in the tall grass. A blackened trail behind it showed our skid on landing.

"Let's vote on it," I suggested.

"Tom and I want to stay," shouted Julia.

Will glanced at Tom apologetically. "I'm sorry Tom but on this one I agree with Jake, there's definitely something wrong here. The place looks totally deserted."

"What about you Emily?" I asked.

She scanned the horizon with her hands shading her eyes. "I agree with you Jake," she said quietly wiping her tear stained face. "I don't understand what's happened, but the others definitely didn't land in this area. We should do as the quantum said and head for Seattle, perhaps everyone else is already there waiting for us."

"Are you crazy?" said Julia angrily. "Head for Seattle, how? We don't have any kind of transport."

"We'll walk," said Emily simply. "It can't be that far, a few days at the most."

Tom sighed. "Okay, let's do it."

Julia turned on him, "I can't believe you would cave in that easily, I'm staying put."

"Then you can look after Mrs. Henley," I said.

Julia looked furious. "You are not leaving me alone here with Mrs. Henley. I'm coming with you."

"What are we going to do about her though?" asked Emily "Julia's right, we can't just leave her here."

"Let's see if there's anything we can use in the medical supplies store," I said climbing back into the train. I rummaged through the unlocked units with Emily standing behind me.

"Here," I said pulling folded bags off the shelves. "Smart suits for everyone, so we will be climate protected." I handed them over. "Smart boots as well."

"Over there in the corner," Emily pointed, "is that a stretcher?"

I followed the direction of her finger. "Yes, let's move it into the Q Room then we can figure out how to set it up, and look," I added "booster shots, they will give us at least a week's worth of nutrients. We can take them before we leave. We'll pack up some of the food bars and water too."

Emily and I made a few trips back and forth to the Q Room until everyone was suited up. Julia made a fuss about wearing the blue astronaut's suit as she called it. The sight of the black all terrain boots sent her off into a ten-minute rant! It was only after we all pointed out to her repeatedly, that a silk gown and gold high heel shoes weren't suitable for a forest hike, that she relented and changed. Tom and Will wisely said nothing when she packed a TV interview outfit! While they discussed what else to take, I ran along the corridor to my old room. Kiki lay on the floor. Even though I knew it was ridiculous to carry the extra weight of a toy dog, I stuffed him in my backpack anyway. No one would notice. Back in the Q Room we regrouped. Julia had a face that could kill at ten paces. I avoided any eye contact with her.

"Okay," I looked at Tom. "Have you any idea how this stretcher works?"

Tom knelt down. "I inflated one of these in a first aid class last year. We need to activate the all-terrain capacity. It will use environmental sensor rollers to travel over any surface."

"Do we need to lift it?" I asked.

"Just out of the train," replied Tom. "One of us will have to wear this tracker band." He threw a bracelet at me. "The small quantum engines inside can power the stretcher up to 100 kilometers per hour. It will follow the remote signal."

"Still no sign of anyone," said Will gazing out of the open hole in the wall of the train. "Man, this is weird."

Tom and Emily rolled Mrs. Henley carefully onto the smart stretcher. I hooked her arm up to the vital intravenous fluids kit, thankful that I had paid attention in my human systems lecture back at school. At the time, I never thought I would actually have to do this. She lay there quietly, unmoving.

"That's the best I can do for her," I said sadly, wrapping her in the smart bag. "I hope she wakes up, we could do with her more than ever now." Emily nodded miserably.

Julia sulked. "I never walk anywhere, I always take stay thin pills."

"Well you'll be thin by the time we get to Seattle," said Tom grimly.

"Are you sure that we shouldn't stay here and wait," pleaded Julia.

"Look," I said firmly. "We have been here now for two hours, not one single plane has gone overhead. The quantum has found no satellites, phones or any kind of other communications devices. It's unable to connect to the Internet. That alone tells me something is seriously wrong. We need to leave."

"It's the no Internet that's really freaking me out," said Will. "How can we not connect? What's going on?" He shaded his eyes with his hands, and stared at the horizon through the hole in the wall.

"Are we taking the quantum?" asked Tom.

I sighed and looked at him. "We have our Pid Pads, but yes, even though it's extra weight to carry I think we should. The quantum probably has enough power to last a few weeks without online connections."

"Will it work outside the train?" asked Emily. Her eyes searched my face for a crumb of comfort.

"I'm not sure," I sighed. "But I don't want to leave it behind in case someone else can access it and find out about the Future Project."

"Listen to yourself," said Julia shouting. "You've gone all freaky and paranoid, who would access it, and wouldn't we want them to know about the Future Project? I mean why else would we come all this way, I just don't get it."

"Listen to me Julia." I took her by the shoulders. "We may have stumbled into some kind of war zone, we just don't know what's happening, and I think until we do, we should be very careful." I let go of her. "Now seeing as you seem to understand the quantum better than anyone owing to your secret midnight dress discussions, I think you should take the first turn in carrying it! I'll put it in a backpack for you."

"Great," said Julia looking thoroughly miserable. "Just what I traveled to the future for, a mountain hike with a computer on my back and an old granny on a stretcher. Just great."

"I hope the others are alright," said Emily anxiously. "I mean shouldn't we leave them a message in case they find the train and wonder where we've gone?"

"No, I don't think that's a good idea," I replied as I stuffed the crystals and the quantum cube into a backpack. "Someone else could find it."

"Oh here we go again," said Julia. "I think you need to lay off the secret agent Pid Pad games Jake."

"Let's leave a clue that only they would understand." Tom looked around at us all.

"I despair," said Julia placing the backside of her hand on her forehead. She was acting like a drama queen.

"What kind of clue?" I asked Tom.

"Well it has to be something to let them know that we are headed to Microsoft in Seattle." We all sat in silence thinking.

"I know," said Tom suddenly. "We'll simply draw a window on the wall."

"Why a window?" asked Emily. "What does that mean?"

"It's the old operating system that Microsoft used prior to the Pid Pads, called Windows. The others would know that but by now it would surely be too obscure for anyone else to figure out, especially if we draw a window."

"You think they would get that?" I asked doubtfully.

"It's the best I can think of," said Tom. "Previn would surely have used, or at least studied, Windows in his lifetime and hopefully the rear quantum will have offered them the same advice as ours. So they'll know we're headed to Microsoft in Seattle."

"Okay, let's do it and go," I said. Emily drew a childlike window with a grey marker from the console on the side of the Q Room wall.

"Shall I add drapes?" she asked wearily, her pale face glancing around at us.

"No, let's just keep it simple," I replied. She laid the marker down and turned to face us. Everyone watched in silent contemplation. It was almost too much for us to comprehend.

"Let's just hope that our parents overshot the time line as well," said Will uneasily, "or man we really are in trouble."

"Well that's it," said Tom taking a last look around the wrecked interior. "Let's get the stretcher outside and start moving." We hauled Mrs. Henley carefully through the opening.

"Which way?" moaned Julia. Tom and I looked at one another.

"Straight ahead into the trees, what do you think?" I asked.

Tom's eyes scoured the area in front of us. "I was thinking the same thing myself." He glanced at me with a worried expression.

I took several deep breaths and said "Let's go."

Chapter Six

FUGITIVES AND CITONS

*"Sometimes I think we're alone in the universe and sometimes
I think that we're not. In either case the idea is quite staggering."*
Arthur C. Clarke

We half jogged, half ran towards the forest. Everyone was spooked by the eerie silence and wanted to quickly take cover. Our inbuilt, pre-civilization survival instincts kicked in, and adrenaline pushed us forward at an astonishing rate. Out of breath, we finally reached the tree line and our panic subsided. I slowed down and relaxed slightly. Julia leaned forward panting, her hands grasping her knees. Emily was flushed. Will, who was breathing heavily, had his head tipped back still scanning the skies, looking for a rescue plane. Tom knelt down and checked the stretcher, which had followed behind me. Its shock absorbers protected Mrs. Henley from any sudden bumps or knocks. The bracelet, which I wore on my wrist, indicated her condition was stable. I sank to the ground wondering where our parents could be and what they would be thinking right now. Tom stood up and wiped his arm across his forehead.

"We need to keep moving," he said quietly.

"Now?" complained Julia, "Can't we rest?"

"No!" Tom replied. "Let's get further away from the train."

"Further away?" cried Will "But what if a..."

Tom interrupted him. "Something weird is going on; no satellites, no planes, no one around. We should be careful until we can establish contact with the US government."

"Not you as well." Julia moaned

"Come on." Tom strode forward and we meekly followed him, pushing branches out of the way and moving deeper through the trees into the shade. Hours passed with Julia still complaining and Emily walking beside her in stoic silence.

"Where is everyone?" asked Will again and again swishing a branch in frustration.

"Maybe this is just an uninhabited part of the country now," suggested Emily anxiously behind us.

"But that still doesn't explain the lack of satellites!" added Will in a puzzled voice, "and the absence of a rescue team. I mean we crash through the atmosphere at an unimaginable speed, and no one comes to see who, or what, we are. That's weird."

"You think that's the strange part of this situation," groaned Julia. "I haven't walked this far ever, not even on the last school fitness drive."

"What time of the day do you think it is Tom?" I asked.

He looked up at the sky, using his fingers as a venetian blind. "I'd say from the position of the sun it must be late afternoon." This whole mess could have been worse, I thought, at least we didn't land in the dark.

"Any ideas where we should sleep tonight?" I peered through the overgrown and tangled bushes.

"Let's pitch the thermal tent somewhere safe," shouted Will from behind.

"Who will keep watch?" asked Emily apprehensively.

"Keep watch for what?" asked Julia moodily.

"Well anything, wildlife or a rescue team," answered Emily quietly, trying not to betray her fears.

"Actually that's a good idea," replied Tom. "Why don't we take turns that two people watch, while three sleep, then switch over?"

"You can borrow my gun," said Julia sulkily. Everyone stopped in surprise.

"You have a gun?" I asked, stunned. We all stood open-mouthed staring at her.

"Duh, of course," replied Julia. "You didn't think I'd come out wandering around without some kind of protection did you? Even I know forests have wild animals in them."

"But where did you get a gun from?" I asked again, still astonished that Julia could actually be carrying a weapon.

"Henley must have smuggled it on board. He kept it under the quantum console. I saw him check it once when I was listening to the security codes."

"But why would Henley have a gun on the train?" I asked, totally flabbergasted.

"How do I know!" said Julia impatiently. "I'm just glad, given our present situation, that he did."

"What kind of a gun is it?" asked Tom looking at Julia incredulously.

"A small laser thing," she replied, and pulled a compact silver pistol from her pocket. Then she turned it over in her hand. "I think it's basically a simple point and shoot."

I had to laugh. "Bet you never thought you'd ever be hiking in mountains with a gun Julia."

"Only in my very worst nightmares," she sighed, and returned the gun to her pocket.

"I think we should keep going for a few more hours before we stop," I said to no one in particular. "Let's get deeper into the forest and see if we can find a covered area to set up."

Tom dragged his finger over his Pid Pad. "I can access some old maps in the memory banks. Even though we can't connect online, the stored data is available as long as the power holds out. We can make it to Seattle from nearby trails if they still exist." He turned and glanced up, "It will take us a couple of days on foot though."

"You don't have a few horses or a car stashed away somewhere Julia, do you?" asked Will sarcastically. "You know, something that you just happened to find under a quantum while you were spying on Henley."

Julia pulled a face at Will and ignored him. We trudged on and suddenly I remembered the message, 'One of these people is a traitor.' Of course, it had to have been Henley. My stomach lurched. I didn't want to believe it, but what other explanation could there be for him having a weapon? After a few more hours tramping through the woods racking my brains for a reason as to why Henley had a gun, we stopped to rest. I checked on Mrs. Henley. She looked deeply unconscious. "How's she doing?" asked Emily kneeling down beside me.

"Well she's still alive," I replied. "But I don't have a clue what's wrong with her. I suspect she's in a coma, but as to if and when she'll ever wake up..." My voice trailed off.

"Can't believe I'm saying this, but I wish she would just wake up," groaned Julia, kneeling down next to us. "I'm exhausted Jake, can't we stop now?"

"Julia, let's just press on for one more hour." I answered, "We should try to keep walking until the light fades. The quicker we can get to Seattle, the sooner we can find everyone else." She nodded, too tired to argue.

"Man, feels like we're the only humans on the planet," said Will looking around.

"Ah shut up Will," I said, and rolled my eyes over at Emily. We stumbled on further through the trees until we entered a meadow.

"Look, over there," cried Emily, and she pointed straight ahead. A small, derelict house stood before us. I saw Julia's hand go to her pocket as we glanced at each other nervously.

"It seems like it was abandoned a long time ago," I whispered, but we still hovered around the tree line.

"Then why are you whispering?" asked Julia in an equally low voice.

I cleared my throat, and gave it my best effort. "Hey, anyone there?" Apart from the slight rustle of leaves behind us, there was only silence. Julia pointed the gun straight head and armed the trigger with her index finger.

"Quite a warrior woman aren't you!" said Will, creeping next to her.

"I have a good survival instinct," she answered. "Nothing wrong with that."

"Er, no," replied Will. "But since you've never fired a gun before can you just be careful. We don't want to blast a potential rescue team to dust before they've even said hello!"

"I don't think anyone's around," said Emily quietly, her head turning from side to side.

"Tom and I will take a look," said Julia still pointing the gun.

"Now who's been playing too many Pid Pad action games?" I said sarcastically. She ignored me and I activated a small button on the bracelet, which gently laid the stretcher down under a tree. Tom's sense of superiority broke through and he strode towards the cabin with Julia trailing behind him.

She bent her knees and jerkily pointed her gun from side to side as if she was in a police show. It would have been hilarious if it weren't so scary.

Tom approached the door cautiously shouting, "Hello, anyone home?" He hesitated. Julia kicked the door lightly, it opened and they disappeared inside. After a few nail-biting moments she came out.

"Totally empty," she called and beckoned us over.

"Well, I guess we've found a place for the night," I said, as we approached the crumbling building. Will helped me maneuver the stretcher through the door. I took off the bracelet, and laid it safely on top of Mrs. Henley. Inside, the house was coated in dirt and leaves, with vines obscuring part of the walls. Dry sticks crackled underfoot.

"Whoever lived here left a long time ago," I said, noticing the broken screens on the wall.

"This was built after 2085," said Tom. "Look over here! I don't know what this screen does, or that one there," he pointed at some sort of machine. I looked at the strange contraption and walked over to it, blowing off the dust.

"You know what this looks like Tom," I said thoughtfully, "some kind of quantum console, a different more complex version of the one on the train."

"You could be right," answered Tom looking doubtful. "Even if it was, it's dropping to pieces. This place wasn't abandoned recently. I think it was vacated decades ago."

"Well, at least it's a shelter of sorts for tonight. We can pitch the thermal tent inside and warm up some nutrients."

"What's in the other rooms?" asked Emily, shuffling her feet through the leaves on the floor.

"Some kind of weird looking beds," replied Julia tossing her bag on the floor.

"Who would have lived here?" I wondered aloud, sweeping debris aside with my boots to expose the rotting hardwood beneath.

"It looks like a vacation home to me," replied Emily. "I mean, stuck out here, miles away from the nearest town or city."

"It gives me the creeps," said Will, kicking his boots on the floor. "I think I'd almost rather sleep outside than in here."

"Was this the food prep area do you think?" I asked, stepping over pieces of glass and crockery on the floor. Emily followed me through the door, and we stood gazing at all of the strange implements and trying to make sense of the queer looking machines hanging off the walls. A rustling outside the window startled me, and I felt my heart beat faster. I backed out of the room slowly, motioning Emily to come with me. She followed with a look of pure terror on her face.

"Julia," I whispered out loud, "Julia."

"What now?" she looked up from where she was sitting on the floor chewing an energy bar

"Julia, I think there's something outside!" She sprang to her feet, the gun already in her hands.

"It's probably just some wildlife, maybe a rabbit?" said Will nervously. We stood looking at one another in silence.

"Let's open the door and check it out," said Tom, in a voice that was calmer than I knew he felt.

"I'll cover you," said Julia getting up behind him and pointing her gun over his shoulder. Tom moved towards the door and pulled it open quickly, like ripping a plaster off a scab. Emily screamed and Tom stood rooted to the spot in shock. Julia held the gun firmly, and pointed it at the young girl standing in the doorway. She looked to be about fourteen or fifteen with a mass of long blue hair. She had the most perfect pale skin, and was dressed in a dark, green, all-in-one body suit. Her expression was a mixture of wonder and fear. She put up her hand. Tom took a step backwards. She cautiously moved her hand slowly towards Tom's face and gently stroked it with her fingertips.

"Are you human?" she asked in a low voice.

"Of course," Tom whispered in amazement.

She looked at us all. "Don't be frightened, I would never harm you."

"Who are you?" asked Tom brusquely.

"My name is Seffie," she replied softly. "May we come in?"

"We?" Tom repeated. Another girl about the same age and a boy perhaps a bit older appeared on either side of her.

"This is my sister, Sookie, and my brother, Chin." Sookie, who resembled Seffie except for her blonde hair, put her arms around Tom and held him close.

"Are you sure?" asked the boy Chin, who was tall and muscular with long black hair "are you absolutely sure?"

"I'm sure," replied Seffie. Sookie still hadn't let go of Tom, and was running her hands through his hair, gently caressing him, no doubt to his acute embarrassment.

"He's real!" she breathed. "He's real!"

"They're all real," said Seffie. "I can't believe it, that they are all actually real."

Chin cautiously stepped into the room. "Put your weapon down, we would never harm you," he said to Julia gently. She slowly lowered the gun, still eyeing him suspiciously. Chin edged his way up to her, and touched her blonde tousled hair. Julia backed away.

"Okay, quit with the funny stuff, who are you?" she said. They had all moved into the room now, and my heart began to return to its normal pace.

"More important is, who are you? And how did you get here?" asked Chin folding his arms. Tom had managed to free himself from Sookie, who stood with her arm around him gazing at his face adoringly.

"Er, I think I'm going to let you explain this one Tom!" Will raised his eyebrows.

Tom cleared his throat. "We came on a train travelling through time from the year 2085. We crash-landed in the foothills of this region not far from here. The other part of our ship, with our parents and friends, is still missing."

"Have you seen them?" asked Julia directly.

"Is it possible?" said Seffie looking at Chin.

"There's no other logical explanation," replied Chin looking thoughtful. "I can't think of any other way that they could have gotten here, and in such good condition."

"I take it that's a no then," said Julia sarcastically.

"Why are you so surprised to see us?" I asked. "Don't people live in this area anymore?" Sookie, Seffie and Chin silently looked at one another. They all had the same bright blue eyes, that seemed to stare right through you.

"I'm Tom," he said, holding his hand out to Sookie. "My brother over there is Will. My friend Jake, and his older sister Julia." He waved his hand towards us, "And our other friend Emily."

"Look, just give us a phone, get us online, or take us to the authorities," said Julia exasperated. "We can give them the location of the train, they can find our parents and we can change and do some interviews for TV if needed." She smoothed her hair down. Seffie looked at Chin and Sookie. Her expression was unreadable.

"Where is your train?" asked Chin, looking concerned.

"It's a few miles from here, so don't expect us to walk back," said Julia, "because my feet are killing me."

Sookie clutched Tom's arm really tightly and said in a voice filled with panic, "We have to hide them immediately, they're not even sprayed."

"Why should we hide?" asked Tom puzzled. "Are we in some kind of war zone? Are the States occupied? What's going on here? Where is everyone?"

"The States?" repeated Sookie in wonder, gazing up at Tom's face.

"Yeah, the United States of America, like where we are now?" said Will uncertainly.

"Much has changed since your time on Earth," said Chin. "We must leave here immediately."

"And go where?" I asked.

"We will ensure your safety first, then answer all of your questions later," said Chin.

"Hang on a second," Tom looked puzzled. "We have just told you that we came from 2085 and you believe us, just like that, without having any evidence."

"Your being here is evidence enough," replied Chin enigmatically.

"Your clothes are really strange," said Sookie fingering Tom's sleeve. "Nice strange though," she hastened to add.

Julia sighed, "I was hoping for dresses but obviously it's military wear this season!" She stared at Sookie and Sookie stared back at her.

"What about Mrs. Henley?" asked Emily. "One of our travelers was injured," she turned to Chin and pointed at the stretcher on the floor. "We can't leave her."

"Absolutely not," said Chin. "We will take her with us."

"Do you have some means of transport?" asked Will, looking out of the window.

"No, we came on foot," Chin replied.

"On foot," Julia squealed. "We have to walk somewhere else again?"

"Of course," Chin looked puzzled. "Let's go."

122

"Now?" said Tom. "We just got here, can't we rest? We've been walking all day and it's going to get dark soon."

"No we have to leave now," insisted Chin.

"Well is it far?" I asked.

"I demand to know what's going on," stormed Julia.

Chin put his hands firmly on her shoulders, "You are in grave danger. We have to leave right now." Something, in his voice silenced Julia and she felt for her gun again.

"Will, let's get the stretcher out of the door," I said, pulling the sensor band onto my wrist.

Chin bent over the stretcher, peeled back the cover, and saw Mrs. Henley's face. He gasped, "So old."

"Tell us about it," said Julia drily. "I told her she should have some rejuvenating work done."

"Let's go," Chin repeated urgently and we gathered up our backpacks. Everyone quickly jogged back into the trees. Sookie and Seffie followed behind us, constantly peering backward over their shoulders. Chin led the way, almost at a running pace. I frequently glanced at the stretcher behind me. It kept rising and falling with the uneven ground.

"Slow down," Julia wheezed. "I'll be putting in for the next Olympics if we keep this pace up!" Chin pressed on ahead. We stumbled through an old trail of tangled branches, mud and leaves, stopping only to check on Mrs. Henley. By now it was dark. Chin had a dim flashlight that barely lit the way. No one talked much, just shouted left, right or watch out for logs and ditches. Julia and Emily grasped onto one another panting and disheveled. We had been walking for three hours, with no breath left to talk. I had to say I was frightened. The urgency of Chin's pace worried me. Where were Mom and Dad? What had happened? My mind went over and over all the possibilities,

Finally Chin said, "Wait here," and disappeared into the trees.

"What now?" moaned Julia, "all I want to do is sit down with something to drink and have a hot shower." A look passed between Sookie and Seffie that was hard to read. Maybe they thought that having rescued us, we should be more grateful. Clearly we had a lot to learn. After a few minutes Chin reappeared.

"Over here," he waved us forwards.

"Here we go again," Julia hissed through gritted teeth. "Isn't anyone going to ask where they are taking us and what is going on?"

Will panted, "Whatever happened while we were on that train, wasn't good by the looks of things!"

"We have arrived," said Sookie gently. Chin motioned us over to what appeared to be a rock shear. He tapped on a flat surface and pressed his hand on it. A small hole slid open in the side of the rock, near the forest floor. Sookie got down and crawled through it.

"Go," said Chin, "now!" One by one everyone began to crawl through the opening.

"Is it wide enough for the stretcher?" I whispered.

"We'll have to deflate it to pull Mrs. Henley through," said Tom, "We can fix it once we're inside."

Will assisted and we dragged the still comatosed Mrs. Henley into the entrance of the hole. We emerged in a huge dark cavern. Sookie raced up to us holding what looked like a can of spray paint.

"I must spray you, stand still," she ordered. The spray was clear and odorless.

"What's that?" asked Will.

"Particle spray," said Sookie. "It will disguise your human signature, and protect you from detection by thermal imaging."

"What?" asked Tom, in total bewilderment.

"We will explain later," said Sookie in her sweet gentle voice.

Once we'd all turned around and been sprayed, we followed Chin further into the cave. An elevator door opened and Sookie motioned us inside. Will and I re-inflated the stretcher and everyone squeezed in. The doors closed and we began our descent. I felt somewhat claustrophobic. The shaft seemed ancient, not the high tech futuristic set up that I had been anticipating. Emily glanced around looking jittery.

"Don't worry you're safe now," said Sookie. "We will protect you."

"It's what I need protecting from that worries me!" said Will.

"Are your parents here?" asked Emily anxiously. Tears began to slide down Sookie's face.

"They are gone," said Seffie sadly and wrapped her arm around Sookie.

"What!" exploded Julia. "You've brought us all the way here and there's no one to even help us? You have got to be kidding me, I've walked miles..."

"We live with an old man who goes by the name of Odo," interrupted Chin. "He will help us decide what to do." Julia shook her head at me, raising her eyes to the ceiling. The elevator stopped and the doors opened into a dull grey passage. We followed them to the door at the bottom. It swung open to reveal a large dimly lit room. Bits of machinery lay stacked in piles. The walls were made out of some kind of reinforced concrete and the floor was covered in dusty threadbare cushions. A white-haired man struggled to get out of an ancient recliner chair. A long, loose, brown smock robed his portly figure. He stretched out his hands towards us, his eyes brimming with tears.

"You are most welcome here. Everything that we have we will share with you."

I walked over and took his shaky hands in mine. "Thank you," I said gently. "We've become separated from our parents and friends and we need to know what's happening. Why do we need to be rescued and hidden? Is the US at war?"

"All in good time," replied the old man breathing heavily. "My name is Odo, and I will do everything I can to help you, but first you must sit down, eat, and refresh yourselves."

Sookie took me by the hand. "Come to the food prep area. I don't know what you would like to eat, but maybe you can help me? Odo will examine your injured companion while we sort out places for you to sleep."

"Look this is really kind of you," said Julia her hands on her hips. "But I would like to know why we can't go to Seattle, stay in a hotel, use a phone, or contact the authorities. I mean, are you even online down here?"

Tom nodded, "We appreciate your hospitality but it's vital we let the government know we've arrived and let our parents know we're safe."

"Eat first then we will explain," said Chin. He motioned us out of the room as Odo bent down slowly to examine Mrs. Henley. Julia looked around exasperated and shook her head. We followed Sookie down the hallway into another room decorated in military style.

Tom, who had been studying his surroundings, said "This is an old silo, I mean centuries old."

"What's a silo?" I asked.

"They are old nuclear war bunkers; this one has to be hundreds of years old!"

"Over here," said Chin. We followed him towards the primitive cooking equipment. The walls were painted white, which was just as well given the dim lights. Carbon steel storage units lined the walls and a table made from the same material stood in the center of the room.

Will held up a funny, old, rusty pot and looked at Chin, "Seriously Dude, is this a kettle?"

"See," said Tom, running his fingers over a rustic stove. "I was right, this is an old silo." He looked at Chin. "Was there a nuclear war? Did an asteroid hit Earth?"

"No," said Chin offering no further explanation.

"Then why on earth would you be living in a bunker?"

"It's safe," said Chin looking at the floor.

"Er, so are you expecting a nuclear war anytime soon," Will asked nervously. Tom frowned at Will, "Hey just asking."

"I've made some soup," interrupted Sookie, "from vegetables we grow in the forest." She took some containers out of a storage unit and quickly heated them. Chin ladled some of the green-colored liquid into large cups, which he handed to us.

"Aren't you having any?" asked Emily taking a cup and warming her hands on it.

"No," replied Sookie, glancing at Chin. "You'll find that we don't eat much at all, our bodies have slowed down and we take a lot of powdered food and nutrient pills."

Julia slurped at the soup and pulled a face, "What's in this stuff?"

"It's lovely," Emily interrupted, obviously eager to be polite and stop Julia from making any more complaints. I slowly took a sip. It certainly wasn't the most flavorful soup I'd ever eaten but Sookie's face looked at me expectantly so I said,

"Delicious!" Julia rolled her eyes. Sookie smiled and looked pleased.

"Let's take some into Odo," said Seffie filling another cup. Will sat at the table, his head resting on his arms yawning. It had been a long day walking and everyone was tired. We had to stay awake a bit longer to find out what had happened on Earth since our departure. One by one we followed Sookie back into Odo's room, where she handed him the soup. I sank cross legged on an old floor cushion. Julia lowered herself down, sniffing loudly and soon everyone was slumped in a circle. Odo sat in his rag-tag chair. I marveled that it was still in one piece. He slurped from his cup and we waited.

"Your companion, the lady on the stretcher, has a very bad head injury. There's some swelling on her brain due to trauma. It's called an epidural hematoma; often fatal if complicated by other injuries."

"How do you know that?" asked Tom perplexed.

Odo took a small device out of his pocket and handed it to Tom. "It's a hand held medical scanner."

"Clever," said Tom turning it over. "It's like a mini MRI machine," he continued to study it.

"Will she get better?" asked Emily timidly.

"I don't know," replied Odo. "We have no medical facilities here to treat her, so all we can do is wait."

"Why can't we take her to a hospital?" asked Julia astonished.

"Because there are none," replied Odo.

"What, no hospitals nearby?" said Julia looking stunned.

"No hospitals at all," said Odo quietly. We all looked at one another struggling to understand what he meant. He put down his soup, folded his arms and sighed.

"Chin has told me about your Time Train, and while it's quite an unbelievable story, I agree that it's the only logical explanation as to how you are here." Sookie and Seffie stretched out on the cushions eager to add their observations.

"Look at their clothes Odo, I've never seen anything like them before," said Seffie.

"Oh I remember seeing old movies with clothes like that, but it was such a long time ago." Odo shook his head and for a second, seemed as if in a trance.

"How old are you?" I asked curiously.

"I'm two hundred and ten, give or take a year or two," he chuckled. "It doesn't matter now. I've lost count. I could even be older." He tapped his head. "Memory's not what it used to be."

"No one is that old," said Julia leaning forward. "That's impossible."

"Perhaps there have been new advances in medicine that we don't know about yet," said Emily tactfully.

"Let him tell us what's happening," said Tom, impatiently.

"Two hundred and ten," repeated Will. "Man, that's amazing!"

"What's happened since we left earth in 2085? And what's the situation in the US now?" I asked. "It's important that we know."

"I'm trying to remember my history." Odo closed his eyes, and we fell quiet.

"After the fall of the World Council in your century, there was a period of chaos. I remember reading in my history downloads about a Starship that was supposed to be carrying thousands of humans into the stars, but I never heard of any Time Train."

"We saw the Starship," I said. "What happened to her?" Odo shook his head.

"No one knows anything about that. She ceased contact immediately and given what happened afterwards, it's probably just as well." Odo sighed. "In this time humans struggled along with climate change and much less food and resources. People fought over water and many countries collapsed and became areas of desolation and despair. Then as new technologies were developed, and people began to see an end to their struggles, a strange asteroid began to approach the planet."

"We knew about that," I said immediately. "It was predicted even in our time."

Odo stroked his chin thoughtfully and continued. "Well, the scientists tried hard to move the asteroid's course so that it would pass harmlessly by Earth, but it couldn't be done. Eventually people accepted that the asteroid would hit and that we had all better prepare for the worst, and I mean the very worst. One by one countries, fractured apart as people abandoned their homes and fled looking for shelter in mountainous areas. I know some of this from the archive files, which I was able to download. It seemed that humanity would not survive this great monster in the sky.

Then a miracle occurred! As the asteroid grew closer and closer a huge spaceship appeared in the sky filled with creatures from another planet. They used their advanced technology to nudge the asteroid's orbital direction. The aliens then flew alongside it, heating the surface and generating a jet stream that re-directed the monster rock. This saved humanity from certain destruction."

"Aliens?" whispered Julia, her eyes enormous. "Real live aliens?"

"You are so apologizing to Mrs. Henley if she wakes up," said Will, shifting around on his cushion.

"What happened next?" I asked astounded.

"What did they look like?" interrupted Tom.

"Are they still here now?" Emily looked around anxiously.

"Look," said Julia standing up. "Thanks for the soup and the story but we need to go to some kind of government office and report in, you know, tell them what's happening and find our parents."

"Sit down Julia," I said pulling her back onto the cushions.

"There are no government offices," said Odo looking at me calmly.

"Just let him tell us what's been happening." Tom shook his head impatiently. "Be quiet, the aliens, what happened next?"

"Well, at first they didn't give us much information about themselves," continued Odo, "and everyone was so grateful to be saved that no real questions were asked until later. The Citons, as they came to be known, helped all governments to restore order to Earth. They gave us many new technologies to improve our lives, assisted our medical scientists and lived among us in peace. The energy crisis that had caused so much conflict was resolved when the Citons showed us how to manage controlled nuclear fusion. That's harnessing energy from the Sun." Odo looked at Julia who had already opened her mouth to speak.

"The Citons had fled their home, a water planet many light years from us when an exploding supernova had made it uninhabitable. At that time they numbered only a few hundred, and given how they had saved humanity from extinction, no one felt really threatened by them. As to what they looked like," and here Odo paused and looked at Tom. "They were long, slim and hairless, but that was not how we saw them. They developed exoskeletons in order to adapt to life on Earth."

"What's that?" asked Julia fascinated.

"It was a sort of biomechanical body suit much like armor. It was designed to give them a more human appearance. That made it easier for us to accept and work with them. The suit was filled with gel, as their normal habitat was sea water. They asked us if they could set up a small colony in our ocean and, well, who was going to say no after what they had done for us. The few that dared to speak against them, were rounded up and they disappeared. Afterwards, it was discovered that the Citons had bred into thousands underwater. They built magnificent cities, where they conducted many experiments to alter their biology so that they could become more adapted to life on land. But all that meddling with nature and two intelligent species living side by side was bound to end in disaster."

"Are you telling us the Earth has had some kind of alien invasion while we've been gone?" Julia looked incredulous. "Like in the movies?"

"Oh, shut up about the movies Julia," I said impatiently. Odo ignored Julia and carried on with his story.

"Eventually the Citons retreated into our oceans and had less contact with humans. People rarely saw them. Submarines and ships found it impossible to cross where they lived, without huge storms arising, and the deep seas became a place where no human ever ventured Still, no one wanted to do anything about this. Memories of the chaos before the Citons arrival guaranteed them our good will. The years turned into decades. Human lives had improved beyond all imagining, but a new World Council formed, one that was more powerful than anything seen before. They decided to rid the seas of these creatures. The Great Alien War began soon afterwards, with massive attacks on their ocean cities. During this time though, the Citons had developed new sciences, grown stronger and began to reveal their true nature. They hit back at us with a strange genetic weapon that no one understood. People fell asleep and, simply didn't wake up. Doctors struggled to find the cause."

"So okay, the aliens weren't the good guys that everyone thought they were," Julia stared hard at me, "exactly like the movies!"

"Let him finish," I frowned.

"This sounds like it's headed for a bad ending," groaned Will, cradling his head. Odo sighed and continued.

"The cities under the ocean flourished like an algae bloom. Our weapons couldn't touch them, and our downfall had begun. Scientists discovered that the nanobots used in our medicine had somehow combined with the strange genetic infection that the Citons had unleashed. It became known as Micro Virus. Nothing could stop the spread of it. We didn't have enough scientists left to do the research. The virus was airborne in robotic micro particles. It spread around the globe slowly. Cities became deserted and human civilization began to crumble. I only know this from recorded history on an ancient quantum. I cannot verify the truth of it all." Odo's head sank forward on his chest. For a moment I thought he'd fallen asleep.

"What are nanobots?" whispered Julia looking scared

"They were robotic microscopic particles given to the population in a mass vaccination program, decades before the alien war. They floated around the body and at the first sign of illness sprang into action. Disease was totally eradicated and every human thereafter was born with them." Odo stopped and looked around at us all slowly.

"You're telling us everyone has gone?" said Will, incredulously, "The whole population? All of civilization? That some robot plague developed by aliens has wiped out humanity? Billions and billions of people? Will stumbled over his words, "That, that, surely can't be true?"

Odo nodded sadly. "I believe so, although I cannot be certain. I don't know what is happening in other parts of the world."

Julia covered her mouth in horror, "Paris!" she whispered.

Odo just looked at her puzzled. "Humans may possibly exist in small settlements, much as they would have done many thousands of years ago at the dawn of civilization."

"How many humans and where?" asked Tom, looking shell-shocked.

Odo paused, "I don't know, but I would be surprised if there are more than 1,000 humans in total living on the entire planet. We are almost completely wiped out. According to my old quantum, the virus also destroyed dolphins, whales and primates. It didn't seem to affect any other species though."

"And the Citons?" I asked, feeling a horrible plummeting sensation spreading through my gut. Odo spread his fingers.

"Still in their underwater cities, probably millions by now."

"You talked about keeping us safe," I said. "Safe from what?" I had to ask, just as I knew what the answer would be.

"The Citons," said Sookie gently. "They will probably kill everyone here if they find us."

"Is that what happened to your parents?" asked Emily, stammering over her words fearfully. Sookie and Seffie gazed at each other sorrowfully. Odo shifted uncomfortably in his chair and Chin stared at the floor.

"Oh crap!" I heard Will mutter softly to himself.

"The particle spray will stop the Citons detecting your body heat," said Odo hurriedly. "I assume that they must have observed your Time Train enter Earth's atmosphere. I don't think that they will hurry to find the cause. Humans have not been in space for so many years that they will likely assume it's stray space debris, or a small meteorite. Sooner or later though, they will come and investigate. When they do, they will find your train and start to look for you."

"I don't understand," Tom looked at Will in confusion, "at the academy when the possibility of alien life was discussed, everyone agreed that an advanced civilization would behave with empathy and compassion."

Will shook his head, "Man, you just have to look at how humans behave to know that one was pure fantasy!"

Julia snorted, "Even I knew aliens would be baddies Tom!"

Tom looked angry and his face flushed a deep red. "They can't be allowed to get away with what they've done."

"Er, reality check," said Will. "Eight kids, a comatosed granny, and one incredibly old guy versus a planet full of gun-wielding fish. That movie does not have a happy ending for ten people!"

"Even though they live in the ocean do they still fly into space?" I asked wearily.

"We have no way of knowing," replied Odo. "But they were a space faring race at one point in their history, so it could be that they still travel outside the planet."

"I'm thinking about the attack on the Time Train," I said turning to Tom. "Remember that the quantum said it was of unknown origin. Could it have been them?"

"It looks as if it might be," replied Tom in dismay.

"Do you think they've killed our parents?" asked Emily, her face white.

Julia sat with her head in her hands. "So much for our amazing life in the future with a full bank account and unlimited opportunities," she said bitterly.

Odo opened his arms and looked at our shattered faces. His eyes filled with sadness. "All I can offer you is a life here with us, and a share in what we have."

"How long have you been living here?" I asked quietly.

Odo stroked his beard. "I'm not entirely sure, a very long time and then the young ones came and joined me."

"How were you not affected by the virus?"

Odo shook his head. "I don't know. I'm not sure why we survived, perhaps it's safer here in the forest, or perhaps the bunker sealed us off from the airborne particles."

"We have to find out what has happened to our parents," interrupted Julia fiercely.

"I agree," said Tom firmly, looking at Odo. "We have to get to a city that used to be called Seattle, to a place where our quantum instructed us to go."

"But the quantum didn't know about any of this Tom," argued Will. "It gave us that plan based on centuries old information. It doesn't matter now."

"Why did the Citons turn against us?" I asked Odo abruptly, "why save us then try to destroy us? Was it the bombardment of their cities?"

Odo replied. "No one knows for sure if the Citons always had our best interests at heart. After they had helped us and retreated to their ocean cities, a famous scientist put forward a new theory about them and their species. He thought their arrival at the time of the asteroid, when humanity was facing extinction, was too great a coincidence. He studied the signals from their space ships for many years and found a startling similarity to a signal received by a primitive telescope in transition times. It was discovered in the year 1977 and ignored."

"The Wow signal!" gasped Tom. He and I looked at one another.

"Remember how Henley told us that the asteroid was moving and he didn't know how?" I said excitedly.

Now it was Odo's turn to look astonished. "You know about this?" he asked.

"Yes" I said quickly. "What did the scientist say about the signal?"

Odo scratched his head and frowned in concentration. "If I'm remembering rightly, I read that the Citons were advancing in the direction of our solar system at this time. They set the asteroid on a collision course with Earth in order to rescue us all at the last moment. This gave them an excuse to move into the oceans. Without any protest from humans, they could then slowly destroy us. This theory, which could not be fully proven, determined the course of action that the World Council took to dismantle the ocean cities."

"What about the warning sent to the Hadron Collider. It must have had something to do with the signal," said Emily in surprise, looking around at everyone.

"Well that obviously worked," added Julia sarcastically.

"What warning," asked Odo leaning forwards in his chair.

"There was a warning sent possibly from this time to the past. To the Future Project which sent us here," I paused struggling to explain. "It said one word, Wow."

"Which the Future Project interpreted as being a sign that things were okay in this time, that they were wow, which in our time meant really terrific," continued Tom. "But of course whoever sent the message wanted to say more than that. They probably said something like 'look at the Wow signal, aliens are out there.' But the rest of the message was never received."

"Who sent the message though Tom?" I asked stunned. "Who now would have access and knowledge to machinery so powerful that they could send a message through time, especially if there are so few people left?"

"Us," whispered Tom in shock, "we sent the message."

"Are you crazy?" said Julia heatedly. "How can we have sent the message, we've just got here."

"We sent it before," repeated Tom looking dazed.

"What do yoy mean before?" asked Emily. "Before when?"

"This is seriously freaky Tom. What you are saying is seriously freaky." Will shook his head, and looked confused.

"What is he saying?" asked Sookie curiously. She sat with Seffie and

Chin, all of them regarding our conversation with fascination.

"I'm thinking that perhaps time runs in a circle not a straight line, and perhaps we have been here before. That perhaps Previn was right after all when he told us that all time is entangled."

"I don't understand a word that you are saying Tom," said Julia impatiently. "How can we have sent the message?"

"I don't know," replied Tom frowning and holding his head.

"So it means that we must reach Microsoft headquarters in Seattle," I said, looking around the room optimistically.

"Why?" shouted Julia throwing her hands up and flinging herself back against the cushions. Chin watched her in amazement with an expression that almost looked like admiration.

"Because if we sent the message we must have made it there," shouted Tom loudly.

"Well this time around I'm choosing the word to send," shouted back Julia, "and my word is crap!"

At this Will began to smile. "You have to admit, Tom, Julia's word does make more sense in a totally nonscientific way."

Tom sat down and turned to Odo. "We have to go to Seattle. I know I speak for all of us when I say that we're more than grateful for your offer to look after us. However, we need to look for answers to help us find our families, and contact the Future Project."

Odo nodded. "It's a strange tale that you are telling. I have to say though, that Seattle has been in ruins for longer than I can remember." Odo shifted in his old creaky chair, deep in thought. "I don't know what you will discover there, but if you must go, I hope you will find your answers."

"How can you say that Odo?" Seffie stood up, her voice shaking. "How can they be safe from the Citons if they make this trip? They will be too near to the ocean."

"Why do you live so near the ocean?" asked Emily. "Surely it's safer to move further inland."

"And if any humans are left they will probably have done just that," replied Odo. "Get as far away from any marine environment as possible. But I'm an old man, too old to move now. My family has always lived here and when my time comes, the young ones will go further inland in search of a settlement to join."

"Don't say such things Odo" said Sookie reaching out for his veiny hand. "You are not so old."

Will looked up at us all and coughed.

Odo smiled at Sookie tenderly. "We fugitives all have to go sometime!"

Chin spoke next. "If you want to go to Seattle we must go with you."

"No," said Emily with a worried expression on her face. "We can't put you in danger."

"You won't find your way, you will need help," replied Seffie.

"What if those Citon alien things come out of the sea," said Julia shuddering. "What will they do to us?" Everyone was silent for a moment.

"Well I'd be very suspicious if they offer to teach you front crawl!" Will remarked, still holding his head in his hands.

"We must take great care not to be captured," Chin spoke calmly.

"Are the Citons so bad?" I asked Odo tentatively.

Odo spread his hands out. "They are like humans and probably similar to us in that there are good Citons and bad Citons. Who is to say that given the same situation, humans would have behaved any better. But you should never make the mistake of thinking that you can speak to them. As a species they wished to rid the planet of all of humanity and that will now include you."

"If the Citons were so much more advanced than humans, then why not just destroy us immediately?" Tom wondered aloud.

"They were only hundreds when they landed and we were billions," replied Odo. "Also, if they wanted our oceans then they wouldn't have wanted to risk a nuclear war that could damage the water with radioactive fallout."

"Couldn't they find a planet with lots of water somewhere else?" asked Julia angrily.

Odo spread his hands again. "Apparently not."

"We can't leave you here when we go to Seattle," I said. "Suppose the Citons find the train and then come looking for us. They may locate you instead."

"Why don't we all go," suggested Tom. "If you've lived here all your life then who better to get us into the city?"

"He's way too old to make such a journey," said Chin angrily.

"I can agree with that!" Will rolled his eyes.

"No, wait no," sighed Odo waving his hand at Chin, "maybe I would like to see the city one last time. I'm not so old that I can't make my way slowly towards the coast. I've been sitting in this cave far too many years now."

"Is there any way to get an advantage over the Citons?" I asked hopefully.

"None that we know of," said Chin leaning back on his elbows.

"How do they communicate." Will looked at Chin.

"I read that they have partially developed vocal chords which they trained to talk to humans, but with each other, they used clicking noises and sonar, very much like dolphins. Their language is a kind of sonic beam, which forms picture bubbles in the water; similar to ultrasound."

"How are they so advanced though?" I asked curiously. "They have no satellites or communication devices in space that could connect with our quantum."

"I read that they all have what we called a galactic contact lens," replied Chin.

"A what?" said Will knitting his eyebrows together.

"A galactic contact lens," repeated Chin. "It's way advanced beyond anything that humans can understand. It's almost like magic to us."

"What does it do?" asked Tom, immediately putting down his empty soup cup.

"It's worn in their right eye, and from what we understand, somehow it connects to the galaxy. All of Citon knowledge and much more transmits via the lens directly into their brain. It was suspected that they also communicated through it, in some sort of telepathic network." Chin paused and pushed his long black hair from his face. "We know about the lens only through what was recorded in the quantum archives when Citons arrived on Earth. Only a handful of humans ever saw one."

"It would be very handy at this point to have one of those lenses," I sighed.

"The problem would be how to get one out of their eye," said Sookie glumly.

Julia threw her hands in the air. "Okay, so to summarize, we have to get to Seattle, maneuvering a granny on a stretcher over a mountain while avoiding crazy killer jellyfish aliens, to ask a computer how to find our parents, and if we can fit it in, grab a spacey contact lens out of a sleeping alien's eye." Everyone looked at one another.

"Well, I wouldn't have put it quite like that Julia," I said, and then continued quickly, "Listen everyone, why don't we all get some sleep now and talk again in the morning." I yawned, eager to avoid another argument. Julia looked mutinous.

Emily said quickly, "Yes, let's get some rest. I'm sure you all need to sleep as well." Seffie was leaning wearily against Sookie's arm.

"We are safe here aren't we?" Emily looked around hesitantly. "I mean the aliens couldn't break in while we are sleeping?"

Odo got up and put his hand on Emily's shoulder. "You are safe. We have been living here for many years."

"I'll shoot them if I see them," said Julia defiantly brandishing her pistol. "Do laser guns work on them?" she looked at Odo uncertainly.

"I'm afraid we'll have to sleep in this room and the room at the rear," Seffie said. "We don't have much space. Julia and Emily come with me, and the guys can stay in here. I'll get some blankets from the storage center." I thought that Julia would say something about having to share a room, but she was so weary that she simply nodded. Emily struggled to her feet and held out her hand to Julia. She pulled her up off the cushions. I saw Julia's other hand check her pocket for Henley's gun. I stood up and put my hands on her shoulders.

"Are you okay?" I asked.

"Yes," she sighed and nodded. "I'm hoping to wake up in the morning and find that this is all a very bad dream!" Sookie put her arm around her and they followed Seffie out of the door. Seffie returned after a few minutes bringing blankets. We stacked large heaps of cushions together and lay down. In the corner, by a pile of abandoned machine junk, Mrs. Henley lay motionless on the stretcher.

"Anyone mind if we leave the lights on?" asked Will quietly. I shook my head. We settled underneath the warm covers. I remained awake for some time, my mind in turmoil, unable to comprehend the enormity of what had happened. The last sound I heard was Odo's loud snoring.

Chapter Seven

CAPTURING THE GALAXY

"If aliens ever visit us, I think the outcome would be much as when Christopher Columbus first landed in America, which didn't turn out very well for the Native Americans." Stephen Hawking

I awoke to Seffie leaning over me stroking my face. "I've brought you some nettle tea," she whispered.

"Thanks," I whispered back gratefully. My eyes flickered wearily around the dull concrete walls. Odo was gone. Tom and Will were still asleep. The room looked the same as it had last night. If only it had a window and some sunlight! I sat up and looked in the direction of Mrs. Henley. There was a space where the stretcher had been. My heart sank.

Seffie read my thoughts. "Don't worry, Odo and Chin have taken her to the exam lab to see if there is anything more that can be done."

Tom groaned and turned over. "What time is it!" he asked sleepily.

"Early morning," replied Seffie. "I have some tea for you."

"Is there anywhere to shower here?" I asked, standing up and smoothing the creases from my smart suit.

"Unfortunately not," Seffie replied, putting down the mugs. "The water supply failed some time ago and we don't want to start digging and re-routing the pipes outside in case it's noticed. We all just wash in the stream not far from here."

"Funny, I'm not so keen to go wandering around outside on my own," I yawned. "I'll go and see Odo first."

"It's down the corridor, the room on the left," whispered Seffie handing a tea to Tom. I wrapped myself in the blanket and stumbled down the dim corridor. When I found the exam lab, Odo was bending over Mrs. Henley fixing some kind of line into her arm. He looked up.

"I can keep her going like this for about a week," he sighed. "After that, we have to find an alternative or..." his voice trailed off, we both knew what that meant. I looked down at her pale wrinkled face.

"You would have liked her," I said thoughtfully. "She was funny and extremely clever."

"Don't give up on her just yet," replied Odo patting my arm. "I should stay here and care for her. I can't see her surviving a trip through the mountains. I'd hoped to find some medical supplies in the city, but I'll give Chin a list of what we could use, if he can find anything!"

"When were you born and how long have you lived here?" I asked curiously, leaning back against an old, carbon workbench.

Odo stroked his beard thoughtfully. "I'm not sure about all of that now," he sighed. "So much time has passed. I was born after the catastrophe. My parents brought me here for safety. They died when I was an older man. They were very old themselves." He paused and shook his head. "So much time," he murmured.

"Have you ever seen a live Citon?" I asked.

"Nope, only ancient news downloads showing their spaceship landing, and a few science programs about them. I have an antiquated quantum that we manage to power up occasionally," he gestured to an unrecognizable machine fixed to the wall. "We have concocted a generator to run everything in the bunker, but we have to use it sparingly."

"What makes you so sure that the Citons are still out there then?" I continued. "Maybe they've had problems of their own in the underwater cities, perhaps they never come out now?"

Odo shook his head. "They are there," he said firmly. "I've seen strange lights in the night sky, lights that aren't made by nature. I don't know what they're up to, but I do know that they are still out there."

"Why don't you go looking for other people?" I asked scratching my head. "Surely it would make sense especially for Seffie, Sookie and Chin to join a larger group if you could find one."

Odo looked at me with a vague expression. "We are content enough at present, but yes, soon the young ones must look for something more. Perhaps you will help them find it." He smiled at me kindly. "Today you must go. It won't be long before the Citons come to see what came through the sky, and when they find your Time Train they will begin to hunt for survivors."

I shivered. "But how will you be safe then? Aren't you worried?"

"No one has ever found this bunker yet," Odo replied. "It's well hidden and I take many precautions to keep everyone safe." He paused and leaned back against the table folding his arms. "I have some questions for you now. Where did this Future Project have its base?"

I sat down wrapping the blanket tighter around my shoulders. "The project was located in Pennsylvania, about six miles from the Presidents' retreat, Camp David. It was known as Site R. Of course no one knew what went on there, including us. The Time Train that brought us here was built on Moonbase in absolute secrecy."

"I wonder," asked Odo stroking his beard. "Why didn't your quantum land you at Site R? Why bring you here and then send you to Microsoft?"

"I don't know," I said rubbing my eyes. "Our train's quantum was damaged in the crash. Perhaps it can repair itself at Microsoft, perhaps Site R no longer exists, or it could be that we will be able to access information in Seattle to find our parents. I don't know," I repeated. "But unless we have some form of transportation, we'd never make it back home anyway. Pennsylvania is on the other side of the country."

Odo looked serious. "You are better to go everywhere on foot Jake. The Citons will find you if you start using anything electrical or hydrogen powered, even if you could still find something that worked."

Seffie slid through the door and handed Odo some tea. "How is your companion?" she asked looking at myself and Odo.

"She can't make the trip," replied Odo blowing steam off his tea. "I must stay here with her."

Seffie looked immediately concerned. "Odo, the Citons will surely search this entire area once they find that train."

"I will be fine," Odo said shaking his head. "In all these years they haven't found me yet."

"But they haven't really searched the forest before." Chin appeared in the doorway. "It would be safer if we all got out of here as soon as we can."

"We can't move this woman and we can't leave her behind," replied Odo slurping his tea through his teeth. "I won't go out until you return. You must leave within the hour though, so that you can find shelter near the city before dark."

Julia strode loudly through the door. "No shower, bath, nothing," she said looking at me in disgust. "I mean how can you stay clean in a dirty old stream?"

"I'm sorry," Seffie said quietly. "The plumbing was damaged many years ago."

"Listen Julia," Emily's voice floated in from the corridor. "I packed some instant wash, let's just use that for now." Julia stomped back out of the door, muttering under her breath.

"Everyone must be well covered with the particle spray," cautioned Odo. "You should take some cans with you," he said turning to Chin, "and of course, you must take your quantum," he said looking at me.

"Can you show me where to get a wash outside," I asked Chin. He nodded and beckoned me over to a cupboard, taking out some towels that had obviously seen better days.

"Come on, let's go now," he said in a low voice. We left Odo putting more thermal blankets around Mrs. Henley and rode the elevator up through the cavern to the crawl space.

"How do you know that there's nothing outside? I asked nervously.

Chin pointed to a small screen set in the rock face. "Motion and body heat detector. We wait a couple of minutes, and if anything that has a body temperature even moves a whisker then we don't go outside." After a couple of minutes in silence he said, "Come on." The door opened and the sun shone brightly. Shafts of light were cutting through the trees. I gulped down the fresh air eagerly.

"Chin, what were you doing so far away from here when you found us?" I asked curiously, while following him closely.

"Exploring," Chin replied. "It can get boring sitting around here all the time!" I nodded, scrambling down the bank towards a shallow stream.

"What month is it?" I asked, the soil felt damp beneath my smart boots.

"August," he replied. "A good time to travel. If you had landed in winter we would have had to wait many months for a thaw."

"Have you been to the city before?" I asked, trying not to slip on the mud.

"Never," he replied curtly, sitting by the bank and pulling off his boots.

"You might not want to share that information with Julia," I said peeling off my smart suit. The inside odor protector had ensured that although I had been wearing it for twenty-four hours at least, it was still fresh. Chin threw off his body suit and waded into the shallow water nearby. He was extremely muscular and I felt all white and skinny in comparison.

"You must work out quite a bit," I commented, shivering in the cold water which came just above my knees.

"Work out?" he said looking puzzled

"Your muscles," I asked, "do you lift weights or something?"

"No," he replied splashing his head with water. Now it was my turn to look puzzled.

"Then how do you stay in such good physical shape?" I asked.

"It must be our protein powder, although too much, as in Odo's case, can add more weight than muscle," he chuckled with his back to me. I drizzled some water and cleaner through my hair.

"I think I'll try some of that powder. I'll be a big hit with the girls if I get a six pack like that!" I laughed.

Chin turned and smiled. "You, like a girl?"

"My friend Emily," I said quickly. I didn't want him to think I was hitting on one of his sisters, not with muscles like that.

"She's very quiet," he replied wringing the water out of his long black hair.

"I think she's just shocked and upset at how things have turned out. She was really popular back at school, not quiet at all, but now... " I trailed off, wading out of the water.

"In a difficult situation people often change," Chin said wisely.

"I'll say," I replied. "Who would have thought that my sister would be carrying a gun. She was more of a fluffy dress and lipstick sort of girl before."

Chin smiled. "Your sister is very fiery, like a wild horse."

"Well she does have quite the temper," I said lightly.

Chin dried himself off with one of the ragged looking towels, and then threw one over to me. "Let's go now." We made our way back to the entrance and crawled through.

"Why don't you dig a bigger opening? I asked, squeezing inside. "

"Odo says Citons are not very flexible in their exoskeleton suits so it's just a little extra, that makes it a bit harder for them to find us." The elevator was waiting, and when we emerged, I saw bags packed up against the walls.

"I'd better go and sort my stuff," I said to Chin. He nodded and disappeared through the door leading to Odo's lab.

Inside the room filled with cushions, Tom and Will were going through their gear.

"Hear you've been out in the jungle Tarzan," said Will rolling his eyes.

"I had a wash," I replied.

"Nothing's making me go out there," said Will. "Not without everyone else and Julia's gun." He lifted up his arm and sniffed. "I don't smell at all, I think I'm good for a few days in this suit."

"You're good for much longer," replied Tom in an authoritative voice, "the suits dissolve body odor and sweat with antibacterial nano-matrix finishing technique. You could, in theory, wear your underpants for twenty eight days but," and Tom smiled "I'll tell you when it gets really bad."

"Thanks bro," said Will grinning. "I'll return the favor."

I tipped the contents of my bag onto the ground. Will began to laugh. "Tom, look, he's brought his doggy!" Kiki lay motionless on the floor.

"It's not as far out as it may seem," I said calmly, although inside their teasing made me seethe. Tom folded his arms smiling.

"And that would be why Jake?"

"Because the dog can be programed for silent mode. It creeps along ahead of us and will alert everyone if anything moves."

"I think he just wants his doggy," said Will still laughing.

"That from the guy who's scared to take a shower outside!" I replied rolling my eyes now.

"Point taken," said Tom nodding and counting the energy bars. "The dog comes along."

"Who's carrying the quantum?" asked Will, trying out the weight of his backpack.

"All of us," I answered. "We can take turns."

145

"Does Chin know his way to Seattle?" asked Tom.

"Er, not exactly. We might need those old Pid Pad maps from the data banks to find our way," I replied, folding my smart blanket into my belt.

"You know, I don't have much power left in mine," said Tom. "The hydrogen fuel cells should last a couple of weeks, but we might want to use the Pid Pads sparingly. Once the power is gone, I don't know how and if we can charge them again. I'm hoping to get the quantum working at this Microsoft place but if not..." Tom looked concerned. "We could be stuck for a long time, and we need those Pid Pads for information."

"Okay I'm almost packed, shall I check on everyone else?" I set Kiki's motion detector to tracking mode.

"Yes, make sure that Julia has all her hair curling appliances and cosmetics at the ready," said Will.

"And her gun!" I added.

"Of course," he replied. "Shooting at aliens is so much more glamorous while wearing lip gloss."

Even Tom was smiling now. "I can't believe we can laugh when so much has gone wrong," he said shaking his head.

"We have to," I replied seriously. "Just as we have to believe that our parents are okay and that we'll find them."

"You don't think the aliens have them do you?" asked Tom, suddenly solemn.

"No, I don't," I replied. Will shifted uncomfortably on the floor and kept his eyes on the ground.

"Come on, nothing could get past Henley and Previn," I said, sounding more confident than I felt.

"Well, where are they then?" asked Will, sighing and unbuckling his backpack.

"I think somewhere else, hopefully Seattle, or in another time line."

"In another time is no good to us," said Tom glumly.

"We may find the answers at Microsoft," I answered. "Let's keep our hopes up until then." Sookie and Seffie arrived a few minutes later to tell us that they were ready. They loved Kiki and soon had him rolling around the floor.

"Ah, not the dog," said Julia appearing with Emily.

"Are you sure you can stop it," asked Emily looking dubious.

"The remote is in my pocket," I replied and patted my smart suit leg.

"Well," said Odo shuffling towards us. "Are you all ready?"

"I'm worried about you Odo," said Sookie tearfully, hugging him around the waist.

"Pah, I'll be fine, don't you worry about me."

Chin took Odo's hand. "If we aren't back in a few days, you should move from here, in fact you should maybe move anyway."

"Why would he do that Chin?" asked Seffie looking annoyed. "How can he go anywhere on his own?"

"If we're captured, we may be forced to give details about our hiding place." There was silence as the weight of Chin's words sank in.

"We don't have to pass the Time Train do we?" asked Emily anxiously.

"No we can go another way" replied Chin, "and remember, everyone needs to be well-sprayed for protection. The particle solution was specifically developed to prevent Citons detecting a human presence."

Odo put his hands on Chin's shoulders. "I know you can get everyone to the city. If you can't get back don't worry about me." Odo then turned to the rest of us. "I'll take good care of Mrs. Henley for you. I want you to fix the quantum, and find out where your parents and friends have gone."

"If Mrs. Henley wakes up when we are gone, tell her I said hi," Julia grinned mischievously, "I was always her favorite."

"You were so not," said Will pretending to swat Julia. Everyone was shouting now and pushing Julia who was laughing.

"Let's go," said Chin abruptly. We all gave Odo one last hug and made our way to the elevator. Once we were outside our good mood evaporated instantly. Everyone glanced around nervously and Julia held the gun in her hand. I set Kiki on the ground and he trotted ahead of us, silently snuffling through the leaves. We pushed aside hanging branches, huddling together.

"I think we should keep our voices down," said Chin quietly "Just in case."

"Has anyone ever seen a Citon?" whispered Julia.

"No," whispered Chin back at her.

"Then how will we know what they look like?" she asked.

"Let's put it this way," said Will. "They won't look like us and they won't be saying hi how you doing!" Julia punched Will lightly and we crept forward trying to avoid stepping on twigs and making noise. After a few hours we began to relax a bit. Tom consulted the Pid Pad and said he thought we were on a centuries old overgrown trail. We stopped, and everyone took a break for a drink.

"How come you guys are never thirsty and never seem to need the bathroom?" Julia asked, swigging from a water bottle.

"We take powdered nutrition now," replied Seffie. "Given the difficulty in finding food, especially in winter, we have adapted our diet in order to survive here."

"Well, I'll take that over Mrs. Henley's constant bathroom visits any day," snorted Julia.

"We need to press on," said Chin. "If we can make it to the outskirts of the city by nightfall we can hopefully find shelter in one of the buildings."

"Do you think they've found the train yet?" asked Emily who still looked fearful.

"I don't know," replied Chin gently. "I know so little about the Citons and what motivates them. It's impossible to say."

"Okay." I took one last swig of water. "Let's go." I felt for my remote and checked that Kiki was still in alert mode.

We tramped on, the sun's rays occasionally peeping through the trees.

"I hate not having GPS," said Tom brusquely.

"What's GPS?" asked Chin blinking rapidly.

"Global positioning system," replied Tom. "In our time we had satellites in Earth's orbit. We could connect to them and they would tell us our position on the planet at any given time."

"So you never got lost?" asked Chin.

"Well maybe Julia would," sniggered Will.

"It's your turn now to carry the quantum," butted in Julia rudely. I bent down and Kiki's remote fell to the ground.

"Get that for me Julia will you," I asked, fastening the quantum pack on my back. Chin helped me.

"It must have been wonderful to live in your time."

"Well that's the funny thing," said Tom sadly. "We came here because we thought it would be wonderful to live in your time."

"And now we find we're in the Stone Age," sighed Julia.

"We don't know that for sure," said Emily looking appalled. "There could be other towns with a lot more people inland. It may be, because it's so close to the ocean, that no one lives here."

Chin sighed, "We have no communication system, so we simply don't know. In all my years of living here, I've never seen anyone else."

"But you're only, what fifteen?" asked Emily looking at Chin. "Who knows what we might find in the city."

"If the quantum wasn't sending us to this Microsoft place, I would have said we should travel deeper inland," I murmured.

"How much further now?" puffed Julia.

"We should be able to see the city in a few hours," replied Tom authoritatively, looking at his Pid Pad.

"You do realize it won't look like it did in your century," said Chin. "It's been uninhabited for longer than anyone can remember and parts of it will have collapsed."

"We should still be able to find Microsoft though?" Emily's anxious question was something that all of us were wondering. To come all this way for nothing would be devastating.

"Look, I think that the trees are getting thinner now," said Will. "I can see rocks and fields ahead." We emerged from the forest. Kiki bounded forward into a clearing and began to run in circles barking like mad.

"Julia, you've done something to the remote," I shouted over my shoulder. Suddenly, a strange clear bubble appeared in the sky and hovered down over Kiki. Sookie shrieked and grabbed Emily by the shoulder pulling her backwards violently.

"No," screamed Seffie, "Citons." I felt my heart pounding and looked at Chin, terror stricken.

"Back in the trees," cried Tom in panic. We almost fell over one another as we turned and ran.

"Julia the remote," I panted as we raced out of the clearing.

"I'm trying, I'm trying," she said pressing every button while running and stumbling.

"Stop," said Chin gasping. "We're making too much noise." We crouched down and peered through the branches. The bubble floated softly onto the grass and slowly faded away. A tall thin figure began to emerge. Emily clutched at my arm in horror. My legs shook uncontrollably.

"Don't move," whispered Chin. Kiki continued to bark and jump. The Citon stood still. It was wearing some kind of dark exoskeleton suit. White pieces of tissue floated out between the cracks. The head turned around.

"Holy crap," said Julia quietly. The Citon moved slowly towards Kiki who continued to bark and jump. Julia reached for her gun. Trembling, she dropped Kiki's remote on the ground. Kiki whirled around in a circle and ran forwards. The Citon moved towards the yapping little dog, arms outstretched, gathering speed, and then suddenly tripped on something sticking out of the grass. It fell forward and hit its head on the ground. The skeleton suit crumpled, relaxed and lay still. Kiki scampered away until he disappeared into the trees. No one moved. No one spoke. All that could be heard was our breathing. Emily had her arms wrapped tightly around me, her head hidden in my shoulders. I could hear Kiki barking in the distance.

"Is it dead? asked Julia quietly.

"I don't know," replied Chin whispering. "We should back out of here quietly. It could just be stunned and others may be following." Seffie and Sookie huddled together looking terrified.

Will ran his hands through his hair. "Can anyone smell prawn stir fry," he whispered looking frightened.

"There's a definite fishy smell around here," replied Julia crouching down next to him.

"Let's go" said Chin in a low calm voice, "Let's get out of here now while we have a chance."

"Wait," Julia put her hand on Chin's arm, "just wait."

"Are you nuts Julia," I whispered, "wait for what?"

"Listen to me," Julia whispered angrily. "Listen all of you. I've walked a gazillion miles to reach Seattle and find my parents, and I'm not turning back now."

"So what, do you want to just stroll by it?" I responded furiously.

"No, I want to open that helmet thing on its head." she replied.

"Are you insane?" Will could barely contain himself. "Getting out of here alive will be a miracle, and you want to go poking around an alien?"

"Didn't you say it had some kind of magic lens in its eye?" Julia turned towards Chin.

"It's not magic Julia," replied Chin "it's just science way beyond what humans could ever understand.",

"Why don't we grab it," said Julia fiercely. "One of us should creep up on the alien and steal the lens out of its eye."

"That's presuming that we can find its eye," I whispered.

"Let's just go Julia," begged Emily shaking all over. "It might wake up."

"I agree." Seffie crouched down further. "We don't even know where the eye is."

"I'm guessing the same place as ours, since it turned its head around to look at Kiki," replied Julia.

"It's the most optimum design in nature for vision," whispered Tom.

"The most optimum design in nature for predators you mean," said Will angrily. We all sat, crouching down low behind the trees looking at one another. "We need to get out of here now," continued Will frantically.

"Okay cool it, someone needs to get the lens out, then we'll be able to find Mom and Dad," said Julia. No one moved.

"It's just a big jellyfish." Julia began to shout, and memories of childhood tantrums sprang to mind. She looked at us all fiercely. "You're supposed to be the clever kids," she hissed at Tom and Will. "Do something!"

"You've got that right, we're smart not stupid," Will replied angrily, "No one that has any sense is going to mess with that alien."

"I'll do it myself then," Julia screamed in fury and charged out of the trees. As she ran her arm was raised, firing the laser gun into the air. Branches crashed down in the undergrowth on the far side of us and the air was filled with a burning smell.

"She's lost it," whispered Will terrified. "She's cracked." There was nothing else to do but watch, shocked, as Julia ran towards the Citon. She pointed her gun at the exoskeleton's helmet and kicked it hard with her boot. It moved where she kicked it but otherwise lay motionless. Chin leapt out of the trees and ran towards Julia at full speed.

"Just great," cried Will almost hysterical.

I edged further out towards the clearing. I could hear Julia say, "Get the helmet off. I'll shoot if it moves."

Chin stood for a second looking uncertainly at Julia, and then he knelt down next to the fallen alien. He put both hands around its head. "It won't come off," grunted Chin panting and pulling at the helmet.

"Let me try," said Julia, handing her pistol to Chin.

"No," he turned away from the gun. "I can't fire it."

I don't know if I decided to go, or if my legs were on autopilot, but I gently pried off Emily's arms and ran into the clearing. I reached Julia running at full speed.

"Hold the gun, I'll try," I panted and knelt down in the grass. The smell was overpowering. I almost gagged. "It stinks," I coughed.

"Well, we can discuss its poor hygiene habits later. Let's just get the magic lens thing out of its eye and get out of here." Julia whirled around pointing her gun at the trees and then back at the body of the Citon.

"Is it dead?" asked Chin.

"No idea," I said, pulling at the side of the helmet. I sat back and looked at it. Then, I ran my hands over the covered face. The helmet visor shot open and I fell back. "Crap," I shouted.

"What?" shouted Julia jumping and shaking the gun over my shoulder.

"It's open, look its open." The Citon's face had no nose just nostrils and a smiley dolphin mouth. Its eyes were closed and a sticky gel covered the smooth white skin.

"It doesn't look too bad," said Julia, doubtfully peering over my shoulder.

"Get the lens out of its eye," whispered Chin frantically. I opened the right eye, which was bright blue, staring straight at me. I shuddered, feeling sick, and put my finger in gently. I moved it around on the surface and to my amazement something came out and stuck to my finger. It was small and clear, with fine, bright blue veins running through it.

"Julia, give me your water bottle," I said my hand shaking. She took a small bottle from a clip on her belt and handed it to me. I dropped the lens inside, and hastily threw in a salt tablet, tightly fastening the top. Then on impulse, I took the smart blanket out of my waist pack, and gently covered the fallen Citon taking care to shield its face from the sun.

"Let's go now," I said urgently. We sprinted back into the trees at full speed. "We've got it!" I held up the bottle triumphantly.

"Great," said Will glaring at Julia. "We risked our lives for a piece of plastic alien hardware that we haven't got a clue how to use."

Tom angrily motioned past the clearing. "Let's get out of here now! All of you. Over there." He pointed to some trees in the distance. "And no more heroics." He added coldly. Everyone was silent.

Tom glared at Julia, who stared back sulkily. "Who put you in charge, anyway! Come on Chin," she added moving ahead.

"Are you okay, Emily?" I asked. She nodded weakly and Seffie helped her to her feet.

"Is it alive?" Sookie asked trembling.

"It was warm," I said quietly. "So I closed its eyes just in case and draped my smart cover over it."

"They took over the planet, wiped us out, and now we're taking care of them and wrapping them in a blankie!" whispered Tom angrily.

"I don't think we know exactly what happened," I said uncomfortably. "Let's not go down to their level, we're still human."

"I think it was a very generous gesture Jake." Sookie hugged me and there were tears in her eyes.

"Talking about being human, let's get running now," Will said impatiently. "In case any more aliens suddenly fall out of the sky!" We made our way quickly around the side of the clearing and emerged in the far trees. The Citon still lay motionless in the midday sun.

"We need to get out of this area as fast as we can," Chin said urgently.

No one argued. We pushed aside branches and overhang, running as fast as we could. Chin led the way, followed by Julia, who was still holding her gun. I really wanted to find Kiki, but now was not the time to ask if I could go looking for my bot dog. I'd picked up the remote. It was still in my pocket just in case. Furtively, I clicked it every so often, but heard nothing. Hours passed and our panic began to subside as we got further away from the Citon.

"How far now?" asked Chin, pausing to catch his breath and looking at Tom.

"We should be able to see the city soon," Tom wheezed, consulting his Pid Pad. "Keep going."

The sun began to fade. I frequently checked the water bottle clipped to my belt. We had all agreed that until we reached the city, and found some kind of shelter, that no one should look at the lens. I knew that Tom was impatient to get his hands on it. Julia thought it would tell us where Mom and Dad were, and had to be talked out of trying to use it immediately. We tramped, on half running, half walking, stopping only for water and energy pills. Sookie, Seffie and Chin ate, but hardly anything. I found some food that Sookie had dropped, but she said she wasn't hungry. Finally, as dusk began to fall, we reached the top of a hill and broke through the forest.

"Look," said Tom breathlessly. The ruins of Seattle lay before us; a once great and vibrant city, crumbling to pieces. The architecture and building materials seemed different now. They must have rebuilt in the centuries after our departure. I felt the tears behind my eyes, as I suddenly realized that the destruction of civilization had really happened. Back in the forest, we could have made believe we were still in 2085, but now, faced with this nightmare truth, it finally sank in that everything we knew had vanished. I almost wished I hadn't lived to see this devastating sight. Everyone was silent before the epic, Armageddon-like picture, that stretched out for miles in front of us.

"I don't know what you can hope to find in there," said Julia despondently, turning to Tom.

"Man, that is one huge mess," sighed Will.

"It's terrible," said Emily quietly. Her hands shielded her face, as if she couldn't bear to look.

"Did it look very different in your time?" asked Sookie gently.

"Here," said Tom roughly, overcome with emotion, and held the Pid Pad in front of Sookie's face with a picture of Seattle on it.

"Oh," said Sookie quietly pursing her lips.

"That's why I wouldn't have put a blankie over it." Tom shook the Pid Pad angrily at me, and I sat down wearily on the grass.

"Everything isn't always so black and white Tom," I said, brushing my hair off my sweaty forehead with grimy fingers.

"There's no point in arguing now," Julia stood next to me. "This happened so long ago. Who knows if the Citon back in the clearing was even born then?" I smiled at Julia, grateful for her unexpected support. She smiled back at me, and held out her hand to pull me up.

"Come on," said Chin, "let's climb down the embankment before it gets dark." He motioned us forward and began to descend. We scrambled down hillsides and through overgrown thatch. By the time we reached the outskirts of the city, night was falling.

"Where should we go to find shelter?" asked Julia stumbling over some rubble on what appeared to be an old sidewalk.

"Let's find a building that has a roof and doesn't look like it will collapse on us," replied Tom gloomily. We slowly walked down the deserted street, staring in wonder at the huge crumbling structures surrounding us in the fading light.

"It's so scary here," whispered Emily looking around and shivering. "Like the ghosts of all the people who once lived here are watching us."

"Shut up Emily, you're giving me the creeps," said Julia sharply.

"Coming from the girl who charged an alien that's funny." Will carefully stepped over some rocks.

"Yeah, well it was alive. It's the spooky stuff I don't like," replied Julia fiercely.

"Over here," said Chin motioning towards a building that still had a partial roof. "Let's have a look at this place." We clambered over the collapsed rubble behind him.

"It may have been a bank once," I whispered looking at the carving that was still visible in the marble entrance.

"Why are we whispering?" asked Sookie quietly.

"I don't know, it just feels like we should," I replied in a low voice.

Chin produced a flashlight from his pocket. "I'll put in on dim just in case," he said. "I could switch it to full and light up the whole building but I'm worried that the Citons are searching for us."

"Just keep it down, and point it at the ground" whispered Tom. "Let's take a look inside."

We picked our way through the rubble and found the iron-wrought doorway. Inside greenery flourished everywhere. Ivy climbed around old quantum screens and prickly weeds grew through the cracks in the tiled floors. Deserted marble banking stations echoed with the customers of long ago. The enormity of what had happened suddenly overwhelmed Emily.

"It's gone," she said her voice cracking. "Everything that we had, everything that we worked for, human cities, all our civilization gone. Even Moonbase must be decaying, not that any human could ever reach it now." There was silence. We stood gazing at one another in crushing despair.

"Don't give up hope just yet," I said. "When we find our parents they'll know what to do."

"Jake," Julia said quietly. "I'm beginning to think that we may never find our parents or the others. Perhaps we are on our own now."

Chin, Sookie and Seffie observed us silently. It occurred to me that they had also lost their parents. I longed to know what had happened, but I knew that this wasn't the time to ask them.

"We should look for the bank vault," I said instead. "I'm assuming there must be one. We'll be well-sheltered and fairly safe from detection if we can hide in it."

"Good idea," said Tom brusquely.

Emily wiped her wet face with a corner of her smart blanket, which she tugged out of her belt. Chin led the way over the stones and fallen walls. I ran my fingers over the composite. It was some kind of super, reinforced, carbon atom structure. This stuff was built to last forever. It would be impossible to guess how long the city had been decaying.

"Normally the vault would be further back," I said, glancing at Tom. "Let's keep moving."

Chin shone his flashlight ahead of us and we huddled together, slowly inching our way down a corridor. The doors hung off their hinges and the rooms smelled musty and damp.

"Over there," I motioned with my hand. A heavy, carbon, steel door lay to our right. We picked our way carefully through the debris. A keypad hung on the side of the wall.

"Do we need some sort of code?" Sookie asked uncertainly.

"Let's just try it manually first," I replied.

Chin and I took hold of the lever and began to pull. The door swung open with a creak. Virtual safe deposit boxes lined a huge circular room. Compared to the rest of the structure it was still in pretty good shape.

"Good idea Jake," said Tom looking around. "We can close the door, leave the light on, and no one will be able to see in from outside."

Julia began to unload her gear onto the table in the middle of the room. Will heaved the quantum pack from his back and set it down with a sigh of relief.

"Let's inflate our smart bags on the floor," I said, taking in my surroundings. "It won't be that comfortable, but it will do for tonight."

"What happens if we can't reopen the door?" asked Emily biting her lip.

"Might as well give it another try now," said Will patiently, "just before we close it for the night." He gave a tired, sympathetic smile to Emily.

Sookie and Chin stayed outside until we opened and closed the door a few times. Finally, we were ready, and it slammed shut, the lever pulled down.

"I hope Odo is okay without us," Sookie muttered to Chin.

"He will be," said Chin, trying to reassure her. "Once we've found Microsoft we'll head back to him. It shouldn't take more than a few days."

"Okay," said Julia sharply. "Let's get that magic lens thing out and have a look at it."

"Should we?" breathed Emily. "What if it helps the Citons to find us? I think it's too dangerous. We should leave it until we get back to Odo."

"What do you think?" I asked Tom, deferring to his tweakie judgement.

Tom sat down in contemplation. "Chin, are we taking a huge risk if we put this lens in our eyes?"

"I don't know enough about it," replied Chin. "All I know is that the lens is a very, powerful, knowledge, device."

"We don't even know if it will work on a human," sighed Will, resting his head on the table.

"Someone has to try it," Julia looked around the room. "Someone really smart, who can figure out how it works," She looked at Tom and Will, her stare was full of meaning. I took the bottle from my belt and stood it carefully on the table. The lens, with its blue veins threaded over the surface, stared right back at us. Emily shivered.

"We need to make up some seawater solution of the same density as the North Pacific," ordered Tom, "that way we'll know the lens will be in optimum working order."

Sookie began to unpack a small bag from her belt. "What do you need?" she asked.

Tom sighed, and closed his eyes deep in thought. "We'll need one pinch of salt for every teaspoon of water."

"Are you sure?" asked Will looking at Tom intently.

"Of course," said Tom authoritatively. "Salt water has 35 grams of salt per liter; one liter of seawater is roughly one kilogram. There are approximately 200 teaspoons per liter and one pinch of salt is equal to a quarter of a gram, so if you divide 35 by 200 you end up with 0.175 grams per teaspoon, which is roughly equal to one pinch of salt." He paused and added "It takes a few minutes for the solution to reach equilibrium."

Julia stared at Tom and shook her head. "I would say you really need to get out more, but that's just so inappropriate now."

"Let's just get on with it," I said impatiently.

Sookie carefully measured the fresh water into a clean container with a spoon and added the salt. Julia picked the lens out of the water bottle, and transferred it to Sookie's mix.

Tom looked at the container apprehensively and gave it a swirl. "I'll try it, but I want you all to stand right next to me and take it out if anything happens."

We crowded around him and he laid the lens on his finger. "Okay, here goes." He gently positioned the lens in the center of his eye and stood up, blinking hard.

"Well?" asked Julia excitedly.

"Nothing," said Tom disappointed. "It feels like a piece of grit."

"See, I told you that it probably wouldn't work," sighed Will.

"You try it." Tom rinsed the lens and handed it to his brother. Will nervously fumbled around with his eye and like Tom nothing happened.

"I think it doesn't work on humans," he said, balancing the circular, blue-veined, eyepiece on his finger.

"Do you want to try it?" Will held the lens out to Sookie and Seffie. They shook their heads and looked away. Will put the lens back in the bottle and stood it on the table again. Julia sighed in disappointment.

"I might as well have a go," I said, rattled that no one had asked me. I picked the lens out of the bottle and without a moment's hesitation stuck it straight in my eye. What happened next was indescribable. It felt like the world exploded. I saw stars, planets, nebulas and whirling cosmic gas. I gasped, and my whole body went rigid. Suddenly, I was swimming gracefully through clear blue water. A beautiful, long, white fish swam next to me, except when I looked closely, it wasn't a fish at all. It had bright blue curious eyes and tendrils of wispy, white, hair floated around its face. I suddenly realized, that I couldn't breathe underwater and began to panic. I kicked wildly, feeling something was holding me down. I surfaced, gasping for air and looked up at the luminous blue sky. Three suns were on the horizon. I splashed around confused and disorientated. I could only see blue sea everywhere. Where was I? The water filled my eyes and I thrashed around frantically in the darkness. Someone was shaking me. I woke up lying on the floor. My heart was pumping so fast I could hardly breathe.

"Are you alright Jake, speak to me!" Tears ran down Julia's face as she held my arms.

"I got it out," said Tom balancing the lens on his fingertip. "He's okay, he's okay."

"He's in shock," Will said, "get him a blanket."

Chin and Sookie wrapped a smart blanket around me. My teeth were chattering.

"What happened?" I asked trying to speak.

"I don't know," said Tom. "You suddenly freaked out and started yelling and screaming."

"Man did you see something?" asked Will in amazement. Emily knelt on the floor holding my hand. Seffie sat beside her.

"Give him a warm drink," Tom commanded, and Sookie pulled out her flask. Remembering her soup I quickly said,

"No, I'm fine."

"What happened?" asked Tom. I shook my head.

"I don't know. I felt like I was spinning among the stars and then suddenly I was swimming underwater with some weird white fish creature." Everyone was quiet.

"Perhaps it was the memories of the Citon," said Chin looking concerned.

"Should we all try the lens?" asked Julia.

"Put it in," I nodded, "we'll hold you."

Julia rinsed the lens and tried it with great hesitation. She blinked. "Might have known, nothing." She took the lens out and handed it to Emily.

"Are you sure?" I asked, as Emily glanced around nervously. She nodded and put it in her eye. I held her arm tightly.

"It's like grit," she said, taking it out and wiping the streaks off her face.

"It's your turn, Chin." I held out the lens to him. He immediately inserted it, and then pulled it out again.

"No nothing for me either."

Sookie and Seffie tried it really quickly. "You're not leaving it in long enough," I suggested.

"Okay," said Tom, looking annoyed. "You're the only one who can use it Jake. For whatever reason, you have a connection to the lens."

"I'm not so keen to try it again," I admitted a bit sheepishly.

"I'm sure it's all about learning how to use it," said Chin soothingly. "Think about what you want to know and see if that works."

"Can we try in the morning?" I asked.

"No," replied everyone in unison.

"Listen," said Tom persuasively. "We need answers, perhaps you can find out more with the lens than Microsoft can tell us." He hesitated. "Please Jake; just try, just one more time." Everyone looked at me.

"Pretend you're Spock from Star Trek doing the mind meld," added Will, "and force the information out of that fish." He slammed his fist down on the table.

"Okay," I said. "On one condition. You stay near me."

"Agreed," said Julia, and everyone nodded.

I rinsed the lens in the water to soften it and held it up, breathing deeply and carefully inserting it into my eye again. The stars exploded into view once more but this time I forced myself to think. I tried "Where do Citons come from?" and instantly, a map of the galaxy appeared with a circle around a planet on the edge of the Milky Way. I zoomed in on the blue planet completely covered in water and its bright three suns. It was breathtakingly beautiful. I zoomed in further, "I want to see the surface," I thought. Huge calm oceans appeared before me with crystal like structures visible underneath clear, tranquil water. I concentrated hard. Why did the Citons come to Earth? I asked. Immediately I saw one of the bright suns begin to glow red and move nearer to the ocean. Crystal spaceships glided out of the water and rose up silently. It seemed as if millions of white, fin-like hands poked out of the waves in a silent goodbye.

The water began to bubble and boil. "What happened to the space-ships?" I asked? Stars and planets whizzed by at a fantastic speed. My head began to spin. Suddenly, I saw the planet Neptune, and the Citons cruising in orbit. I could see them waving their fin-like arms in a celestial dance with each other. Earth television signals... time passing... the Citon spaceship raced towards the asteroid. Crowds of humans knelt and prayed. "Where is everyone now? Where is everyone now?" My heart was pounding in my chest. My eyes seemed to zoom in and out at the images rolling past them. I struggled to comprehend. I tried to slow it down and concentrate. Strange planets appeared, some silent, and others teaming with incredible animals. I could see Mars now. A Mars, with a small lake of water and bright green plants. Domes like those at Moonbase nestling together on the red desert sands. Then, abruptly, the cosmos was yanked from my field of vision.

Julia face was close to mine, "You okay?" she asked tentatively. "Did you manage to find out anything?" I sat up and rubbed my eyes. She put the lens in my hand. Everyone looked at me in anticipation.

"They left a dying planet," I said slowly. "I think they gave humans the engineering technology to terraform Mars."

"You're lying," said Tom angrily. "They've put that notion in your head. They wanted our planet and were willing to kill us all for it."

"Shut up and let him finish Tom," interrupted Julia.

"I... I'm not sure, maybe some humans are still living on Mars. It looked like Moonbase with the domes. I need practice, to control my thoughts more. It's really hard."

"You've done well as it is," said Chin encouragingly, putting his hands on my shoulders, "I think we should all rest now, it's late, and we need to find Microsoft tomorrow."

"Do you think the Citons are looking for us?" asked Emily nervously, "Do you think they would do something to us if they found us here?"

"Don't worry," sneered Tom. "According to Jake, they would probably tuck us in and sing us a night, night song."

"Look," I said standing up, my voice getting louder. "I don't know what the truth is here; I only know what I saw."

"And I know what I see," shouted Tom angrily. "Once great cities falling to pieces, people hiding in caves, the population decimated and a civilization in ruins."

I turned and looked suddenly at Seffie, Sookie and Chin, "I'm sorry to ask you this, but we need to know." I paused and took a deep breath. "What happened to your parents? When did they disappear and how?" There was a silence in the room as the three of them looked at one another, Seffie's eyes were pleading with Chin.

"It was some years ago and we don't really know," he said abruptly.

"Did they leave the bunker and not come back?" asked Emily gently. Seffie nodded looking at the ground.

"So you don't know for sure that they were captured by Citons," I persisted.

"No one leaves their three children and disappears for no reason," said Tom a bit more calmly.

"Perhaps it was wild animals..." said Julia her voice trailing off.

"Maybe they went in search of another settlement and meant to return but couldn't get back," Emily replied quickly.

"What did Odo say?" I asked.

"He said we must accept those things that we cannot change," answered Sookie sadly.

"Please," Seffie held up her hand. "Enough. We have come to help you. To find answers to where the rest of the people on your train have gone, and we hope that in helping you, there may be a place for us with you. A better life that we can make together."

Tom hung his head and sighed, then he looked at me, "I'm sorry Jake, I just have no sympathy for these alien creatures when I see what's happened here and how our futures have been destroyed. They must have been the ones that attacked the Time Train. It had to have been them, and because of that, we find ourselves alone here." He looked around the room.

"You are not alone," said Sookie softly. "We are with you, and at the risk of sounding selfish, we're glad that you ended up here." She leaned against Tom and rubbed his arm.

"Group hug everyone," said Will, holding out his arms, and we all laughed. The tension was broken.

"I'll try to find out more from the lens tomorrow," I sighed looking at Tom.

"That's okay," Tom replied stiffly. "I think you may be seeing everything from a Citon perspective. After all, they wrote the firmware. We should concentrate on finding Microsoft first."

"Agreed," said Emily, "Let's sort out the smart bags and settle down for the night. I'm just going check the door one more time."

"Don't worry Emily," said Will. "Julia has hardly taken her hand off that gun all day, and she seems to have a hair trigger reflex. The only thing I'm concerned about is her waking up and firing if someone rolls over in their sleep."

Julia pushed Will and he pulled a face at her. "Jake, get into your bag," she ordered. "I'm turning the lights off." She laid the gun down beside her.

Typical bossy older sister," I smiled at Chin "You don't seem to have that with your two sisters. Who is the oldest?" I suddenly asked in confusion realizing I didn't know.

"I am," said Seffie, "now go to sleep." I laughed, secured the lens, and snuggled into my smart bag. I could hear the others shuffling around for a few minutes, then everything gradually went quiet. The only audible sound was our deep breathing within the dank and crumbling bank vault.

Chapter Eight

THE BUNKER AT MICROSOFT

"We shall require a substantially new manner of thinking if mankind is to survive."
Albert Einstein

When I opened my eyes in the morning there were shafts of sunlight streaming into the corridor behind the open door. I sat up sharply, terror surged through my body. The door was open! The lever was in an upright position! I looked around the room. Everyone was sleeping, and accounted for inside the room. Julia lay half sitting half slumped, snoring with her gun in her hand. My eyes darted wildly. Tom was the nearest. I crawled over to him.

"Tom," I croaked, "Tom, wake up." He turned over and I shook him urgently. His eyes opened and he yawned.

"What time is it?"

"Tom," I whispered, "Tom, someone has opened the door!" Tom sat up confused. He quickly looked around the room and fear sprang into his eyes. He pointed at Julia and began to crawl over to her. I followed him. When he reached her, he placed his hand over hers holding the gun to steady it, and shook her gently. "Julia," he whispered, "Julia, wake up." Julia opened her eyes groggily, glanced around, and quickly sat up.

"What happened to the door?"

One look at Tom and I told her all she needed to know. Carefully she pointed her gun in the direction of the corridor outside and we crouched down.

"Wake the others," Tom whispered and I set off crawling around the room. One by one, we gathered around Tom and Julia.

"Listen," I said in a low voice. "If someone wanted to harm us they would have done it already, or at the very least taken the gun."

"What if they're waiting for us outside?" shivered Emily almost in tears.

"What would be the point of that," I replied trying to comfort her.

"They could have rounded us up already."

"Okay" said Julia firmly. "We have to at least check outside before we do anything else, come on follow me."

"That's our plan?" whispered Will fiercely. "That is our plan?"

"Can you think of anything better?" Julia almost shouted. Will shook his head. Julia held the gun firmly and took some deep breaths before stepping sharply outside the door. It struck me that if it weren't so terrifying it would be almost comical; Julia copying the moves of all my favorite TV police dramas.

"No one is outside," she called back in a relieved voice.

"That's because there's probably a fish army out front," said Will still panicking.

"Don't be ridiculous," I whispered. "For a bunch of kids with one gun, hardly!"

"All the same," said Tom quietly. "Let's check it out first." We picked our way through the rubble towards the front entrance. Julia advanced in the direction of the bank's main gate with Chin closely behind her. She tentatively stuck her head through the wrought iron gate. Then she stepped into the street, and for a few seconds we couldn't hear anything.

"I'll say one thing about your sister," whispered Will. "She's got some nerve." Seffie, Sookie and Emily huddled behind a teller station.

"Outside is deserted," said Julia stomping back through the entrance. "Chin, check out further down the street and I'll cover you." Tom and I moved quietly towards the gate.

Chin crept outside while Julia tiptoed behind, pointing the gun in his direction, and turning every couple of seconds to look up at the derelict buildings. Then they disappeared from sight. After a few heart stopping minutes Julia stepped back in again.

"Nothing to see," Chin said, sighing in relief behind her.

"Could the door have just swung open?" asked Seffie confused.

"Unlikely," replied Tom. "It's way too heavy."

"Perhaps it opens when the bank does," said Will excitedly. "You know like one of those time delay locks."

"What's that?" asked Chin looking puzzled.

"When the bank opens, the vault automatically opens," replied Tom looking thoughtful.

"It could have happened that way," said Julia, looking doubtful. "I mean there's no other explanation really. Why would anyone just open the door and leave?"

"Perhaps we are an experiment," said Emily slowly. "Perhaps the Citons found the Time Train and they are watching what we will do next," she shivered.

"It's possible," Tom replied, scratching his head.

"I think it was a timer on the vault," insisted Will. Everyone wanted to agree with this explanation. The doubts I had about the human genome project came into my head again. If Tom and Will were so smart then why didn't they realize that would mean the door should have been open when we entered the bank? Or did they? I thought about saying something but decided against it. The unlikely explanation that Will offered was much more comforting to believe.

"I don't want to stay here," whispered Emily.

"Let's just get our stuff and go," agreed Tom.

"I'll wait here and keep a look out with Chin," said Julia "You all go and pack up".

Back in the vault we began to load our bags in a hurry and fold up our belt supplies. I helped Will with the quantum and then bent down to roll up my smart bag. Next to it, where I'd been asleep, was my blanket! It was the same one that I had laid on top of the fallen Citon! It was smeared with some kind of gel. Blood rushed to my head and my hands began to shake. I looked around. Everyone was busy, dashing about collecting and stowing gear. I stuffed the blanket inside my bag. I looked around again, double-checking to see if everyone had a smart blanket on their belt. My heart sank.

"Are you daydreaming Jake?" asked Will, glancing up from his bag at where I sat with my mouth open.

"I was just thinking," I said quietly.

"Anything you want to share with us?" queried Tom, looking at me suspiciously.

"Nothing, I'm just hungry," I replied.

"Grab a bar," he said, and threw me a nutrition meal from one of the packs. I caught it with one hand. Inside my pant leg pocket was the precious lens. I'd hidden it there before going to sleep. Feeling around carefully, I transferred the bottle to my belt. I felt like I was a computer hacker, and possibly like all hackers, I had been traced to my source. I considered telling everyone about the blanket, but it would scare them even more. Perhaps it's a good Citon. It must be, or why would it leave it without disturbing us. Suddenly, I thought, another shiver running down my spine, how did it know the blanket belonged to me? It was out cold after smashing its head against the ground. Well at least I knew it wasn't dead, but why didn't it take the lens back? Visions of an alien, slimy, fishy hand groping down my pants was not appealing. I shuddered. Surely it must realize that by leaving the blanket, I would know that it had been in the room. Did it mean to help us? What was the explanation for it all? My head spun round, and I longed to speak to Dad.

"Ready?" asked Tom.

"I'm good to go," I replied in a weak voice.

"We're ready as well," said Seffie.

"Who's got the lens?" Will asked tightening his backpack straps.

"It's here," I replied patting the bottle clipped to my belt.

"Okay, let's go then," said Tom swinging a backpack over his shoulder. Julia and Chin were chatting at the entrance. It struck me from the way she looked at him while twirling the ends of her hair, that she really liked him. It also struck me that Tom frowned when he saw them. I had enough problems I thought. They would have to work that one out themselves.

"Okay Tom, have a look at the Pid Pad and let's get an idea in which direction we need to travel," said Will.

Tom held it up and studied the screen. "Microsoft is miles to the east of Seattle. It's in a place that was once called Redmond. I have Microsoft's address in here so if there are any street signs still hanging I can use the old street maps to guide us." He looked around at everyone. "We'd better start walking. It may take us the better part of the day to find Microsoft, if it's still standing."

"Great," said Julia sarcastically. "More walking! All I've done is walked, and all I can see myself doing in the future is walking. I could be a gold medalist hiker at this rate."

We set off cautiously down the street. In the morning light it looked even more decayed than when we had first seen it last night. Julia's voice droned on as we trudged out of the edges of the city into more trees and bushes. Everything was overgrown. The pictures of neatly, well-manicured parks and flower beds on the Pid Pad only seemed to enrage Tom further. I decided against saying anything about the blanket. A few birds flew overhead, and the sun shone pleasantly. I almost felt happy despite my misery. We passed derelict churches and restaurants with their twisted metal chairs. Battered tables were exposed to the elements. Piles of rubble that had once been apartments, houses and offices lay in heaps. Thorny brambles wound themselves around the concrete. Nature was reclaiming the land as its own. The perfect silence was the hardest thing to bear. I'd been to cities like New York, and remembered the noise, lights, and twenty-four hour vibrant hum of the population at work and play. This desolation was overwhelming. I looked around and sighed deeply. I doubted humans would ever rise up again. Our time had passed. Perhaps the asteroid would have been a better end. The sun rose higher in the sky and we stopped to eat and drink from our water flasks.

"I don't know how you stay alive," Julia was saying in a loud voice to Seffie. "You eat almost nothing. You'd make a great model though."

"I think you should consider a career change Julia," said Will drily. "Not too many people around to buy dresses now."

"Duh, do you think so?" said Julia and threw a crumb at Will. He ducked and laughed.

"You're so quiet Jake." Emily sat down beside me. "Is it because of the lens?"

I shook my head. "Look around," I said despondently. "How do you think we can survive here, there's nothing left."

Emily put her hand on my arm. "When we find the others they'll know what to do." I wanted to say, if we find the others, and I was not convinced now that we would.

"I'm so afraid Jake," she continued. "I'm more afraid than I ever thought possible, but I'm trying to be brave. I'm not like Julia. I don't have a lot of courage."

"You have more than you think," I replied firmly. "And many other great qualities."

"Well I've always been a fast runner," she laughed. "That could come in really useful now!"

I put my arm around her and said encouragingly, "We'll find them. It's a shock to see Seattle looking like this, but don't worry, we'll be okay." She nodded and smiled.

"Let's keep moving," Tom commanded, standing up and swinging his backpack across his shoulders.

"Do you think the Citons have found the train yet?" asked Emily again, looking at him for answers.

"If they haven't they can't have put much effort into looking for us," replied Will.

"Apart from the guy in the forest," said Julia, "and when they find him, they are going to be majorly fed up with us."

"It was a girl," I interrupted. Everyone stopped and looked at me in astonishment.

"There's no way you can know that," said Tom.

"What are you, suddenly an expert on Citon anatomy," laughed Will uncertainly.

"No," I replied. "I just felt it from the lens that it was a young girl."

"You never told us that last night," said Tom suspiciously.

"I didn't realize it until now," I replied keeping my eyes on the ground.

"Weird," Will said, staring at me closely.

"Maybe, she wasn't really looking for us," Sookie added looking hopeful.

"Then why was she not in the ocean?" asked Tom brusquely.

"Perhaps she was just curious about our planet and now we've killed her," said Emily sadly.

"We didn't kill her, she tripped on a rock... totally her own fault," said Julia still chewing on an energy bar, "and we don't even know if she was dead, she may have just knocked herself out." She threw her wrapper on the ground. "And really Emily, we're going to feel sorry for a Citon now?"

Tom waved his hands. "Enough, this isn't helping us find Microsoft."

Everyone packed up. Tom was glaring at me. As we walked towards the trees he beckoned me to join him. "You're not holding anything else back are you?" he asked, trying to sound casual.

"No," I lied. "It was just something that came into my head."

"It's a shame that only you can use the lens... it would be better for all of us if someone else had been able to wear it."

"I agree," I said. "Maybe everyone could try it again?"

Tom shrugged his shoulders. "I doubt it will work a second time when it didn't work the first. I'd love to know, though from a scientific viewpoint, how it only hooks up for you."

I sighed. "I can't answer that Tom." He cast a sullen look at me and quickened his stride catching up to Will ahead of me.

We walked on in silence. Chin was setting a fairly fast pace, and apart from the occasional complaints and groans from Julia, everyone conserved energy for moving, not talking. The hours wore on.

"How much further?" groaned Julia. Tom consulted the Pid Pad.

"I think we are almost in Redmond."

"How will we know this Microsoft building?" asked Chin.

"It's very distinctive," replied Tom. "Big and silver."

"Might not be now, Tom," said Will looking around at the derelict ruins. "It's hard to recognize anything here."

"Let's just keep moving," I added. "We need to find shelter again by nightfall."

"I agree with that," said Julia. "But no more bank vaults, please?"

"Show me the picture of Microsoft," I asked Tom, and Sookie took the Pid Pad out of Tom's hands, passing it to me.

"Can't see what good it will do looking at that now," grumbled Will.

We walked on with everyone scrutinizing the picture. Soon we came to the outskirts of a dilapidated suburb. Ruin after ruin appeared before us. It was hard to make out where the streets had been. We searched for more than an hour among the buildings where we decided Microsoft might be. By now the light was fading.

"That's it over there," cried Chin suddenly pointing at an enormous, dull silver structure. "I'm sure of it."

"You think?" said Will looking doubtfully at the Pid Pad. Chin was already clambering up the rubble with Sookie and Seffie behind him. Their agility and fitness never ceased to amaze me. You never heard them complaining about the walking, climbing or needing to go to the bathroom.

Tom quickly followed behind them and shouted. "Hey come on, I think Chin might be right."

The steps to the entrance had long since crumbled. Chin held out his hand, and guided us through the gap where the door had once stood into a darkened interior.

"Wish we'd found this earlier," said Emily, glancing around nervously.

"Which way?" asked Julia looking at Tom for directions.

"There has to be an underground bunker, so anywhere that leads us down."

"That's just as well Tom," said Will pointing at the holes in the roof high above us. "Because I don't think that going up is an option."

We picked our way through the dust, leaves and fallen stones. I gulped back a lump in my throat when I saw the famous Microsoft logo on the wall, it's four, colored, squares chipped and smeared with dirt. Chin switched on his flashlight.

"I really don't like this," whispered Emily.

"I'm with you on that one!" replied Will. We tried door after door. There were large rooms filled with rusted, rotted, overturned furniture, some of it made from materials that I didn't recognize. Finally we wandered down a corridor with a small elevator at the end. I could still make out the words carved in carbon steel above it, Secure Personnel Only. An old scanner hung loosely to the side.

"What do you think," I said, looking at Tom.

"If that's our only option we'd better unpack the quantum," replied Tom. "See if it can crack whatever code they used."

I lifted up the cover and ran my finger over the surface of the scanner to remove any dust. "Jake Ellis Future Project, subject number twelve please identify." I froze and looked behind me. The female voice was soft and low. Julia whirled around with the gun. Chin almost dropped the flashlight.

Tom's face was white. "Was that a computer voice?" he whispered.

"Yes," said Chin focusing his light on the scanner. "Jake, put your palm flat on the screen." I tentatively held out my hand and pressed it down.

"Jake Ellis identified," the voice said.

"Julia, you do it," I said excitedly. Julia pressed her hand down.

"Julia Ellis identified. You may proceed." The elevator doors slid open.

"Do you think this is really safe after all this time," asked Will sticking his head inside.

"Just get in," said Julia impatiently. "The scanner is still working so why shouldn't the elevator?" As Emily tried to step inside the elevator a computer voice said softly,

"Identify."

Emily pressed her hand down on the scanner. "Emily Watson identified."

Tom stepped forward with his hand out. "Thomas Howard identified." Then it was Wills turn. "William Howard identified."

Chin still stood outside looking nervously at Sookie and Seffie. "I think we should just wait here," he said.

"No way," insisted Tom. "Just put your hand out and see what happens."

Chin held out his hand, "Negative entity may proceed."

"Man that's a bit harsh," said Will laughing.

Chin stepped inside and the same thing happened to Sookie and Seffie. They looked at one another with a somewhat secretive glance and Sookie shrugged her shoulders.

"Okay here goes," Tom pressed the button and the doors closed. We slid smoothly and silently down the chute. Julia had her gun ready. The doors opened onto a brilliantly lit white room filled with high tech quantums and workstations. Camera monitors in the wall flickered with views of the darkened space above us and the outside of the building.

"Well, at least there's no chance of anyone leaving this door open tonight!" said Will, as the elevator closed behind us.

"Tom where's the power coming from," I asked taking a step forward. He shook his head.

"I'm not sure. Perhaps the elevator activates an emergency supply. They must have a back-up generator in here somewhere."

"Oh my gosh," I said breathlessly. "Julia look!" I ran towards the table in the middle of the room and picked up the object from the center. "It's Mom's necklace, it's Mom's necklace! The one I bought her for Christmas last year." I could feel a lump in the back of my throat. Julia ran towards me and tore the necklace from my hands. Everyone gathered around.

"It is," she gasped, "it really is. I remember when Jake gave this to Mom, and I insisted that she kept it in her closet because it was so un-fashionable."

"Thanks Julia," I said taking back the necklace and fastening it around my neck defiantly.

"So your parents were here," said Sookie excitedly. "Maybe they've left a message somewhere?"

"Of course they have," said Tom firmly. "They'll have made sure that we can access it somehow."

I looked around the room. "Let's set up the quantum and see if we can't get some of this other equipment working."

"Do you think they were all here?" asked Emily breathlessly.

"I'm sure of it," I replied. "Will, help get the crystals in line," I continued, unpacking the quantum.

Chin walked around the room with Tom pressing pins, checking crystal configurations and waving in front of the virtual screens. Suddenly, one of the virtual wall panels began to flicker with static.

"Over here," shouted Tom. We stopped assembling the quantum and raced across to the screen. To our amazement the static cleared and Previn's face appeared.

"I've got it Jerry," I could hear him saying. "It will start to record now."

We could hear people talking in the background as Previn turned the back of his head to the screen. "Alright," I heard him say as he moved out of the way. Dad's face appeared. I looked at Julia. Her eyes had already welled up, and Sookie had her arm around her.

Dad looked strained and unhappy. "Listen up kids," he began softly. "If you're watching this transmission then you've made it this far. The train, as you now realize, separated when it appeared that we were attacked." He paused and turned around. I could hear Previn talking in the background. Dad faced the screen again. "We've read in the Microsoft history files about a species that came to earth after we left. This new alien species seems to have caused the destruction of human civilization, and apparently they live in our oceans now. According to the records here, they are patrolling the Earth from space with attack droids designed to keep anyone from attempting to land." Dad paused again, and then covered his face with his hands.

Henley appeared in front of the screen, and said in a strong firm voice. "You have to avoid these aliens at all costs. There are guns in the cabinets behind you. Take them and use them if you see any of these creatures. Now listen carefully, especially you Julia, my little spy!" He winked at the screen. "We have read that a human colony has been established on Mars and we've discovered the entry codes, which will appear at the end of this message. Our plan is to employ our quantum to launch the rear time train using our remaining antimatter, and try to fly past the alien defenses. We hope to make it to Mars and join any settlers that may still be there."

"Why can't we wait for them?" I could hear Mom's voice pleading in the background.

As if in answer to this Henley paused and looked firmly into the screen. "We've scoured the planet surface using the quantum and it's picked up no sign of the other train, no signs of any kind of human activity. This is why we need to leave immediately." I could hear voices in the background arguing and Henley moved to the side.

Previn appeared again, looking exhausted. "I want you to listen carefully to my instructions," he said gravely. "To the rear of this chamber is a concealed door. The program will give you the exact location and entrance key. Behind it lie two things that will help you. Microsoft has left quantum robotic horses designed to ride over any terrain. They have hydrogen fuel cells inside which should last well over a month. These horses will return you quickly to your train, so that you can reprogram your quantum and hopefully join us on Mars. More on that in a moment. The horses have satchels that contain smart dust in green canisters. Throw the smart dust in the direction that you are headed, and the nanotechnology that it contains will scan an area of fifty miles in order to secure it for you. If any smart dust returns, it's a warning of danger ahead and you should immediately change your route. We don't know if your quantum was damaged during the landing. If this was the case and you can't take off, we have a second plan for you, which is a long shot, but if you are stuck here you can try for it."

Previn paused and rubbed his eyes. He leaned in towards the screen and appeared to take a deep breath. "There are codes contained within this system to release the secure, emergency signaling system for Starship One. The codes have to be entered into a strong enough telescope to transmit and reach out in the direction that the ship took. I can't help you with the codes. Our quantum doesn't have enough power left to both look for them and take off for Mars. We are also running out of time if we want to make it back to our train and not be detected by the aliens. Tom and Will, you kids are smart. I think you'll be able to find the codes embedded in the software. If you can, you'll need to make your way along the coastline to the Allen Array telescopes at the old SETI facility in California, and transmit the message from there. I know that will be difficult but it's all I can suggest to help you." Previn moved away from the screen. "Good luck kids," he said sadly.

Dad appeared again. "We'll continue to search for you," he said. "Don't give up, we'll find a way on Mars to get help to you." He turned around again, and Mom squashed in next to him. She looked terrible, as if she'd been crying for days.

"We love you very much," she said, her voice cracking. Dad held her as she wept and looked the screen. "I'm sorry," he whispered. His face was white and gaunt. "So very sorry." They got up and Emily's parents sat down. Their faces were haggard, and they had aged since I last saw them. Emily sobbed as Seffie put her arm around her sympathetically.

"Emily, try to make it to Mars with the others," said her Dad.

"We love you," her Mom wept.

Henley came back into view. His face was tight and grim. "I hope you're bearing up Mam, I'm relying on you to help everyone with that magnificent mind of yours. Don't give up on seeing me again as I'm going to leave no stone unturned in trying to find you." Henley paused and moved closer to the camera. "Take care of my old Mam, Jake," he said. "She'll help you all she can, and remember, shoot those damn alien creatures if you see them." He suddenly looked unbearably sad. "Sorry about Paris, Julia."

No, I thought to myself, as I looked at his open and genial face, he couldn't be the traitor. No man who was about to betray anything or anyone could be so genuine. I was convinced that somehow there was another explanation for the gun.

He stood up and Tom and Will's parents appeared on the screen. "Tom," said his Dad sternly. "You can decipher the codes if your quantum is working. Don't get too near the coastline."

"Will, you work with Tom and stick together," their mother whispered calmly. "Boys we love you both. I know we will see you again." The screen went blank, and then began to reel off a string of data.

"It's how to reprogram the quantum for Mars," said Tom quietly. We all continued to watch the screen in silence until the numbers stopped. At the bottom left hand corner the time and date of the message were recorded. My heart stopped.

"Tom," I took hold of his arm, shaking it hard. "Tom, look, the message was recorded in 2585 that's fifty years ago, they were here fifty years ago!"

"Oh no," groaned Julia jumping around in agitation. "What's happened? How can it be fifty years ago?" She sat down. Shock and horror written all over her face.

"We must have moved further forward in time to avoid the attack," said Tom, his voice sounded hoarse. "Which is why they couldn't find us." He held his head in his hands. "I'm not even sure that the quantum got the date right. Judging from Seattle's decay I think we are even further down the time line."

"This is bad," whispered Will, his face white. "This is really bad, suppose even if we could get to Mars, what if they are gone or didn't make it?"

"Of course they made it," shouted Julia tearfully.

"The bigger problem is getting to Mars," said Tom, walking around and stretching out his arms in agitation. I could see he was struggling to maintain his composure. "Our train has been out in the open for days now. I'd be surprised if the Citons haven't found it, especially, given the fact that they will be searching for the missing Citon as well." Tom looked at me and to my surprise asked. "What do you think Jake?"

"I think it might be better to send a signal if we can," I replied feeling sick. "At least that way we have a chance of being rescued."

"Ah crap," yelled Julia. "You don't know if we can do that. Previn said it was a long shot. We could be waiting for years and who knows if someone will ever turn up." Seffie, Sookie and Chin stood in silence watching us.

"What do you guys think?" I asked.

"Are you sure the SETI telescopes are still working after all this time?" asked Chin, practically.

"Good question," replied Tom, still pacing up and down. "One which we have absolutely no way of knowing until we get to where they were last standing."

"How long will that take?" asked Emily in an anguished whisper.

"Probably a few days on one of those robot horses," said Tom. "If they are still working."

"Maybe we should go back and ask Odo," Sookie looked at us evenly.

"Makes no sense," interrupted Tom. "We'd be going back on ourselves and it would be further to travel, we might as well go on from here."

"Why don't we just go back to the train," Julia pleaded. "We'll have plenty of weapons."

"We can't do that Julia," I replied. "Firstly, we have to go back for Mrs. Henley, and secondly, we don't know how many Citons could be at the train, that is, if they haven't removed it by now."

"We don't even know if the colony on Mars is still there Julia," said Will. "That message was recorded at least fifty years ago. Who knows what's happening on Mars now." Julia sat down with her head in her hands.

"This is the mother of all bad situations," continued Will, looking at Tom, his hands on his hips.

"Look, we're all tired," sighed Tom. "Why don't we sleep in shifts. Will and I can try to break into the system for the codes. If we can't retrieve them then we can't send any signal. In the meantime we can attempt to reprogram the quantum for Mars. Let's wait and inspect the horses in the morning, and then we can decide." He looked around for our consent, and we all nodded. Julia seemed sulky but she nodded as well. Seffie began to unpack the smart bags and inflate the beds.

Sookie smiled at Julia consolingly. "You'll see your parents again,

I'm sure of it." Julia didn't look convinced and flung herself down on a smart bed.

"Seffie," I asked slowly, "the message said that the planet scans didn't see any human activity. Odo seemed fairly sure that there were other people living in small settlements inland."

Seffie and Sookie exchanged glances. "Perhaps they are in hiding like us," replied Seffie somewhat evasively.

"Or perhaps Odo is wrong," Chin shrugged his shoulders, "He's very old, his memory isn't good, and it may be that he remembers this incorrectly from a long time ago." I looked hard at the three of them. Why did they all seem uneasy? Was it just my imagination?

"Julia," I sat down on the bed, "it's possible that Starship One has established another human civilization out there somewhere in the stars. Wouldn't you rather make a try for that?" I was trying to sound positive. If we all gave in to despair what would happen to us then?

"I wish we could just go back to Odo," said Emily tearfully.

"And live out your life in a cave, stuck in a forest hiding from aliens Emily?" said Tom angrily. "Suppose you get sick, or injured. Who can help you then? Not to mention, our parents could be waiting for us on Mars."

"Emily, I'd rather go back as well," said Will sympathetically, "but what's there to do except sit around all day and wait for Julia to come back in from hunting, shooting, and fishing?" Emily smiled through her tears. "At least we all have guns now," grinned Will opening a cabinet. He took out a massive machine gun and examined it carefully. "Take a look at this huge sucker Julia!" She couldn't help but glance in Will's direction. Her face brightened when she saw the amazing high tech weapon that he was holding.

"Can you help me over here Will," asked Tom in a grumpy voice. "I'm going to need more than one brain to crack this system."

Will handed the gun to Julia. "Careful." She began to examine it, smiling.

"Wake me in a couple of hours then." I yawned and lowered myself onto the smart bag. Chin, Sookie and Seffie also lay down. I looked over at them. "We owe you big time," I said gratefully. "You were safe in the forest. Now you've put yourselves in all sorts of danger to help us." I observed them closely.

Seffie smiled. "We wanted to help you. We've been on our own for so long, with nothing else to do."

I laughed, watching Julia still examining the new guns. "Yeah right, just keep an eye on gunslinger over there will you?"

Seffie began to chuckle and snuggled down into her bag. I turned over and tried not to think about Mom and Dad. Would they have given up by now on ever seeing us again? Were they on Mars, alive and waiting for us? I felt my eyes grow heavy and gave in to my need for sleep. When I woke up hours later, Tom and Will were still sitting at the console. Seffie had joined them.

"How long did I sleep?" I asked shuffling over to them yawning.

"Four hours," replied Seffie, "and you were snoring."

"Not as bad as your sister though," said Will pointing over at Julia who was lying with her mouth open breathing heavily.

"How's it going?" I yawned again.

"Terrible," replied Tom in disbelief. "This thing has been securely sealed with a watertight encryption in case the Citons tried to access it."

"Can't the quantum get in?" I asked surprised.

"The quantum has been working through it for hours," Tom said tiredly. His eyes were puffy and ringed by dark circles.

"Why don't you and Will get some sleep," I suggested. "I'll sit with Seffie for a few hours and if we need help I can wake you."

"Come on Tom," sighed Will. "We need to rest. We're no good to anyone like this."

Tom nodded trying to keep his eyes open and stood up wearily. Will inflated their smart bags and as they lay down I slid into Tom's seat. Seffie and I stared at the screen as the hours ticked by.

"I don't think that the quantum is going to be able to break this down tonight," Seffie finally whispered, "I think it's going to take days."

"Nonsense," I said. "Do you know how powerful these things are?"

"Actually, this one is quite dated compared to others I've seen," she said quietly.

I looked at her puzzled. "How can you have seen quantums before if you've been living in the forest with Odo for years?" I asked curiously.

"I viewed some different models on his old quantum once," she replied. "It's stashed away in the exam room. We rarely use it. I have to tell you it was more advanced than this one, despite being ancient and in poor working condition." There was something about the way she didn't look at me directly that I found disturbing. I was silent, wondering if and why she would lie to me. When I looked at her again she was smiling, all silky blue hair and dimples.

"So we might sit here for hours?" I said tiredly.

"Days," she repeated leaning forward, a real sense of urgency in her voice.

"That's your opinion," I answered irritably. She shrugged her shoulders and looked annoyed. I suddenly realized how little we knew about Seffie, Sookie and Chin. Our situation was one of an ongoing crisis. Who were they really, I wondered, and stared at her profile intensely.

"What do you suggest?" I asked, feeling there was so much more going on behind those bright blue eyes than I could even guess at.

"You won't like it," she replied her eyes fixed on the quantum.

"Okay, hit me with it then," I said.

She moved closer to me. "You're going to have to use the Citon lens," she whispered.

"Are you kidding me?" I whispered back angrily. "I can't control that thing. I could end up bringing the whole Citon army down on us."

She put her hand on my arm. "You won't, if you listen to me, and do exactly as I say. We don't know for sure, that the Citons can track anyone who uses the lens, and I can make sure that the quantum gates are closed before the codes come into sight. We just need to find the path to them."

I looked around at the sleeping figures curled up on the floor. "You want me to do something like that without waking anyone?" I said. "Are you mad? I can't just do that."

"Listen," she said in a serious voice. "We can do this together. The others need to rest and we know how uncomfortable Tom is with the lens."

"What exactly do you want me to do?" I asked nervously.

"You need to insert the lens and ask it to guide you through the system to find the codes. Once you are within sight of them I will take out the lens, secure the quantum gates and retrieve the codes myself."

"How?" I looked at her incredulously.

"Trust me," she said, placing her hand on my arm. I crept over to my smart bag and with a shaking hand took out the bottle containing the lens. When I returned to the Microsoft console Seffie was already at work, her fingers flying over the pins. The quantum crystals were glowing.

"Sit here," she said, without looking up. I sat down apprehensively and positioned the lens on my fingertip.

"I hope you're right about this."

She swung round on the chair. "Okay hold the pins and stare at the quantum crystals once the lens is in your eye; focus Jake."

I took a deep breath and let the lens meld to my eyeball. The cosmos exploded into view. I struggled to think and reached out my hands. Like a blind man I groped around for the quantum pins. In the background I was dimly aware of Seffie's hands on mine guiding them to the crystals. I concentrated and imagined myself walking through the many particles of light reflecting in the machine. Different subatomic routes opened up in front of me. Dizzying possibilities, so many of them. Atoms danced around me. I thought of Starship One and our need for the codes, repeating my mission like a mantra. Suddenly, I was racing down a brilliantly lit circuit pathway. Beams of light criss-crossed in front of me. I was twisting and turning as though trapped in a corn maze. I came to dead ends and turned around time and time again. Electron clouds floated above my head and pixels wrapped themselves around me. I quickly untangled myself and slipped inside the data stream. One's and Zero's, billions of computations passed before my eyes. My mind was going so fast my breath hurt. I could see the codes now or rather I could sense them getting nearer. I stretched out my mind still further and ran faster than ever towards them. My hands grasped at the air and I felt power surge through me. Dimly in the background I was aware of Seffie. My head was wrenched backwards.

"Jake, are you alright?" Seffie's blue hair hung over my eyes and tickled my nose. I nodded, hyperventilating. She held the lens on her fingertip. I took it from her and let it sink down into the bottle. My hands were still shaking. She leapt back up at the console and began a series of hand movements so fantastically fast that I couldn't make out what she was doing.

She blinked quickly and then with a quiet cry of joy punched the air.

"Got them," she said grinning at me. Her smile faded as she saw the confusion on my face.

"How do you know how to do that?" I whispered. "You're ten times faster than Henley and he was a quantum expert."

She lowered herself slowly into the chair. "Jake, I feel that you are more open minded than the others, and I suspect that's why you can use the lens. Would you take me on trust, when I tell you, that I only have your best interests at heart and would never do anything to harm you or the others."

I nodded dumbly staring into her bright blue eyes.

"We all have secrets don't we?" she looked at me slyly. "I noticed that you have your smart blanket back."

I blushed deep red and stared at the ground. How could she know? It was still tucked at the bottom of my bag. "I don't know..." I began.

She held up her fingers and put them to my lips. "I know," she said softly. "Sometimes we keep things to ourselves so as not to worry the others, and that's what I'm asking you to do now." She was so close to me now that I could see the tiny pores on her skin. Her eyes seemed so weirdly unfocussed that I hesitated. Our lips brushed lightly against one another. In the background I heard someone clearing a throat.

"Er, hate to break up the party but are we any nearer to finding the codes?" asked Julia looking at me in astonishment. I moved away from Seffie in confusion.

"We've got them," I replied pushing my chair back and patting the quantum.

"Great," said Julia glancing at Seffie, then back at me in amazement. "Can we open the door that leads to the horses now?" Seffie waved her hand at the quantum and a panel set in the side of the wall slid open.

Julia put her hand on her gun and walked forward slowly. "Look Jake!" She gasped. The large cavern lit up in front of her. It was filled with the most lifelike bot horses I had ever seen. They might have been real except for the fact that they were standing perfectly still.

"Why horses?" asked Julia in awe, to no one in particular.

"They are the best design that nature can offer when you have a surface with no roads, and unpredictable terrain," replied Seffie.

Julia walked slowly into the cavern and stroked one of the large white creatures. "They are amazing," she said in wonder "and you know the best thing about them?" she laughed, turning to me, "they don't smell!"

I smiled. "Add that to the list of things you thought you'd never do, ride a mechanical horse!"

"I want this white one," said Julia excitedly. "It's so pretty."

I joined her and we wandered around the horses. I couldn't resist stroking their manes and patting them. Chin and Seffie stepped into the cavern whooping with delight, and we started to pick out which ones we wanted.

"Shouldn't we wait for the others to wake up before we decide?" Seffie asked hesitantly, her arms around a beautiful American albino.

"There are plenty to choose from," Chin replied, his face glowing.

"Please don't try to start one up yet, Julia," I said cautiously "You could begin a stampede in here!"

She looked at me slyly. "So which one are you going to pick Jake?" she winked at me.

I leaned against her horse. "Look, don't say anything," I whispered.

"I would never have believed you were such a ladies man Jake," she said, smiling and batting her eyelids comically at me.

"And I would never have believed you were such a natural with a gun Julia," I said, smiling back at her and pointing my fingers in a shoot position.

She laughed. "Point taken," she replied. "But Jake," she was suddenly serious, "don't upset Emily." I was serious as well.

"I won't... I promise."

"I think we should pack up and leave now," Julia announced loudly. "I'm so thrilled not to have to walk anymore."

"I'll think you'll find that riding is just as tiring after a while," said Chin, inspecting a huge grey roan in front of us.

"How do you know?" asked Julia inquisitively.

"I used to ride horses when I was younger," said Chin, burying his face in the horse's mane. "Appaloosas on my Dad's ranch."

"Really!" Julia looked at him in amazement. "When was that?"

Chin appeared momentarily confused. "It was a long time ago," he said quietly looking away. Julia opened her mouth as if she was going to ask Chin something else, but he was saved from her questions by the appearance of Emily.

"Cool," she gasped. "Which one is mine?"

"Anyone you want," I said, avoiding Seffie's eyes. "We're just beginning to choose. I think Julia wants the white one though."

"It's an Andalusian," remarked Chin knowledgeably.

"How lifelike these things are!" Emily ran her hands over the fur and buried her face in it. "They are amazing."

"Let's start to pack," I yawned. "Then once Tom and Will wake up we'll be ready to go." I turned back, stepping through the panel into the quantum room.

"Should we record the Starship codes?" I asked Seffie, who followed me. "Just as a precaution."

She nodded. "I'll jot them down and give them to you. If anything happens to the quantum at least we can enter them manually. That's supposing some kind of array is still standing in California," she sighed and tightened the band around her blue ponytail.

"Thank you," I said my eyes meeting hers. We stood staring at one another awkwardly.

I didn't understand why I had kissed her. She seemed so sympathetic, it just happened. Her strange exotic beauty was haunting but somewhat cold. I shivered and looked away. Seffie continued to regard me calmly.

"I removed the lens from your eye before the codes appeared, just in case the Citons could trace you."

"Thanks," I whispered. "I feel like a hunted man."

"The lens has powers beyond our comprehension," Seffie said softly. "You just need to learn how to use it Jake."

Emily and Julia continued to giggle and run between the horses with Chin close behind. My thoughts wandered. I was reminded of Julia on Christmas Day with her new toys.

Seffie touched my arm. "Are you okay Jake?"

"Yes," I sighed. "Just thinking of past times with my family."

"Maybe you'll see them again someday," said Seffie with a hopeful look on her face.

"Perhaps," I replied glumly.

"Seffie," I whispered and I looked across at Sookie, Tom and Will, who were still fast asleep. "I don't know how my blanket got back into the bank vault that night."

Seffie sat down and looked at me strangely, "Perhaps for now, it's best that you don't think too much about that."

"You're not involved with the Citons are you?" I looked Seffie straight in the eye.

"No," she replied looking straight back at me. "I've always told you that I will do anything and everything to help you."

I continued to stare at her. "There's something else. I don't know what it is, but the more I get to know you and Chin and Sookie, the more I feel that you are hiding something from us." Seffie continued to meet my steady gaze. She put out her hand and rubbed my arm.

"Why don't we concentrate on finding the SETI facility Jake? Everything will be alright, I promise you."

She turned to the quantum and started to pack up. I noticed that she hadn't denied my accusation. Perhaps things were worse than we'd been led to believe, and she wanted to let us down gradually. Tom snored loudly and Sookie woke up and yawned. I started to gather my bags while Seffie explained to Sookie about the horses. Tom and Will stretched and sat up, still dozy and warm.

"We have the codes for Starship One," I said, in a low and weary voice.

"I knew the quantum would crack it," grinned Tom. Yet another lie I thought uncomfortably.

"Where's everyone else?" yawned Will, rolling up his smart bag.

"Choosing their quantum horses," I replied.

Will leapt up. "I'm off to find my ride, yee ha!"

"You seem unusually serious," Tom said to me, as Will ran towards the horses. "Is anything the matter?"

I sighed. "No, I just hope our plan will work. It seems such a long shot to me."

"Jake, the only other option is to fly to Mars, and can you imagine even if we did manage to get there. Suppose it's deserted. Suppose we can't get back?"

"I know," I sighed again. "I've already thought that one over, and at least we can survive here on Earth, as long as the Citons don't find us. Hopefully those horses can get us to the Allen Array in California. Everything depends on the telescopes still standing."

"They will be," said Tom optimistically. "The Citons don't seem to have deliberately destroyed anything, they seem to just let it decay and fall down."

"Because they are so infinitely superior to us, what would be the point?" I asked gloomily.

"Ah, but you're wrong," Tom said decidedly. "They haven't reckoned with human ingenuity and determination."

"No," I replied. "What they hadn't reckoned with was a bunch of kids traveling through time and crash landing on Earth."

Tom frowned. "It's the same thing. We were clever enough to send that train without them knowing."

"But they attacked us," I persisted. "It was only luck that we survived."

"No," said Tom firmly. "Our quantum technology evaded them and landed us safely and," he added looking at me fiercely, "our own resourcefulness has kept us alive."

"Whatever," I said tiredly shrugging my shoulders. "You're determined to have the last word on this and I hope you're right."

"Tom," Will shouted from the open cavern that now resembled a riding stable. "Come and see these things, they're fantastic!" Tom thumped me firmly on the shoulder.

"Let's go and find SETI."

Chapter Nine

SEARCHING FOR SETI

"The dishes remind me of big flowers pointing their petals to the skies waiting to receive what's out there. There's nothing between my dish and the end of the universe."
Rachel Tortolini

Within the hour everyone had packed up, chosen a horse and given it a name. Seffie and Sookie picked Sunshine and Bluebell. Julia stuck to her fashion background and called hers Calvin Klein. This was apparently some kind of vintage, American designer who, she informed us, was a minimalist. Will laughed at this, saying it was a good name, as you couldn't get more minimalist than our present situation! Emily named her horse Hope. Chin decided on Fireball, which was the name of a horse he had once owned. I saw Seffie frowning at him as he told us. Will said he wanted to call his horse Mr. Benkie after his physics teacher, who was an inspiration to him and hated animals. Tom decided on Lightfoot, and I called my horse Hawking, after the professor, whose science had led to the creation of the Time Train. Chin helped us to fasten the saddles onto the horses' backs. They were beautiful, soft, brown leather, padded seats of the highest quality.

"Western saddles," remarked Chin stroking one wistfully, "they spread out the weight more evenly, so that we can maintain good balance even with our equipment strapped to the sides." Will swaggered around the horses pretending to be bowlegged.

"Get off yer horse and drink yer milk."

Chin blinked hard and began to laugh. "John Wayne, right?" he said.

Will's face was a picture of astonishment.

"That's right, how could you possibly know about John Wayne."

Julia butted in, "I haven't the faintest idea what you are talking about!"

"He was a twentieth century movie star, no chicks or aliens allowed in his films. It was straight up cowboys and Indians." Will said, patting his horse.

Seffie interrupted him, "Are we ready yet?"

Once everyone had saddled up, we checked our smart dust canisters in the satchels and doused ourselves with particle spray. Will handed out the guns to everyone, and we strapped them to our saddles.

"This isn't difficult," said Tom confidently. "The horses are voice activated, and once we start to ride, if you shout fast, slow, jump or stay they will do as requested."

"How do we actually get out of here though?" asked Emily, looking around the circular chamber.

"According to the quantum, the horses know how," replied Tom. "Is everyone ready to activate?" We all shouted yes and lifted the horse's reins. One by one we began to whisper the codes into the area behind their ears. I felt movement beneath me as the old mechanical beast built so long ago began to come alive.

"Welcome rider," said a deep voice.

"Holy crap they talk!" shouted Will.

"Do you know your way out?" I whispered in Hawking's ear.

Hawking stamped his feet and replied simply, "Yes."

"Talking horses!" screamed Julia "Fabulous!"

"Let's go," shouted Tom and Lightfoot began to move forward. The wall in front of the horses that had seemed so impenetrable suddenly slid open. Tom's horse stepped forward. Lights shone from the horses' eyes, and we followed each other in single file down a long pitch-black corridor, mile after mile through twists and turns. After an hour or so, the horses picked up the pace to a rocking canter.

"Where are they taking us?" shouted Julia.

"I'm guessing this tunnel leads out of the city," Tom shouted back over his shoulder. "It's going to take a few hours so try to be patient."

We rode for six hours, the darkness illuminated only by our horses' eyes. I began to feel slightly motion sick, and chatted to Hawking to pass the time. I could hear the others doing the same. He told me, that he had been assembled long after the arrival of the Citons and was placed in the cavern following the Great Alien War. This was at the beginning of the time when the Micro Virus began to decimate the human population. I was relieved to have Odo's story verified, and know that everything Seffie had told me was true. Hawking knew nothing about the Time Train. His knowledge base contained an extensive repertoire of geography, but only a brief history of his origins. Given that he had been set up to connect with a now defunct global positioning system, it was clearly going to be a journey using the old stored maps for reference. He seemed unable to comprehend a world without satellites and a human population, so I let it drop. As he had been stored during the decline, there was little he could tell me about what had happened since.

"Hawking, were all of the horses that were placed in storage still in that room?" I asked, grasping my reins as I leaned forward.

"No," he replied. "Fourteen are missing."

"What do you know about that?" I asked hopefully, thinking Previn and the others must have taken them.

"Nothing," he answered. "Only that they were accessed for service."

"Is there any way of knowing what happened to them?" I asked.

"No," he repeated. "We are not in communication with one another."

"Thanks," I sighed and patted him. I pulled up my hand and smiled remembering what Dad used to say to me about talking to coffee machines. How easy it was when something looked so real to treat it that way. We rode on, occasionally calling out to one another in the darkness. Tom's horse slowed down and we all nervously halted behind him.

"What's wrong, why are we stopping?" shouted Julia immediately.

Tom turned around in the saddle. "We've come to the end of the tunnel. Lightfoot is asking if we want to exit outside."

"Of course," shouted Julia impatiently.

I watched Tom lean forward and whisper into Lightfoot's ear. A whirring and creaking noise filled the tunnel, and suddenly light was visible in the distance. Lightfoot started towards it and everyone followed. I felt for my gun and my heart began to beat loudly. The light got brighter, and I could see Tom reaching into his saddle throwing smart dust ahead of himself. It looked like gold glitter. Then suddenly it disappeared. We continued to canter forward, and after a few minutes Tom turned and stuck his thumb in the air.

"Okay," he shouted, and we galloped faster towards the light. There was a slight breeze as we exited the tunnel, emerging onto a grassy open field. I looked up at the sky and closed my eyes breathing in the fresh air, ridding my lungs of the damp, stale, atmosphere we had endured. Emily happily rode next to me on Hope, her curls blowing in the wind.

"Hope has told me that the area around us has been secured for a fifty mile radius."

"Let's not rely on that though," said Tom riding around us. "We don't know if the Citons have developed any technology that can counteract or destroy the smart dust." Emily's face fell.

"There's no reason to think that at present," I replied reassuringly, shooting a warning glance at Tom.

"Okay," said Tom ignoring me. "Listen up. We'll ride now as fast as we can towards California. I'll lead. Lightfoot has the maps and he'll take us by the quickest route. Given that his maps are years out of date, we may have to make a few detours. We can stop for food and water. At night we'll look for shelter and grab a maximum of six hours sleep. The quicker we find SETI and the Allen Array telescopes, the quicker we can send our message and get back to Odo.

"That's going to take a couple of weeks now," Sookie glanced at Chin with an expression that was hard to read.

"Maybe, one or two of us should ride back to Odo," said Chin, looking concerned.

"No," replied Tom firmly. "We all stick together, and besides, you can't go back alone."

"I agree," Sookie looked around. "Perhaps Chin, Seffie and I should return to the forest together."

"You're joking," said Tom angrily. "I thought you were going to stay with us and help?"

"You asked us to take you to Seattle and find your Microsoft for answers. We have done that," replied Sookie evenly.

"We don't have any answers yet," said Will looking surprised.

"You do," replied Chin calmly. "You can attempt a Mars flight past the Citons, which may or may not succeed, assuming that you can still gain access to your train. You can also attempt to contact a spaceship that left Earth over 500 years ago," he paused. "The latter is your decision."

"Let them go," said Julia, pulling a face in disgust at Chin. "If they're frightened and want to go back to their hidey place in the woods then just let them go. We don't need them."

"Oh, but you do," said Seffie emphatically. "You will need help, to align the telescopes and work the quantum." Seffie and Chin faced one another.

"We need to talk," she continued. Chin gave his horse a kick, and the three of them rode out, stopping a hundred meters from where we sat. They formed a small, tightly-knit circle in the shade of a large cedar tree. I watched them talking among themselves.

"We don't need them," said Julia fiercely.

"Shut up, we do," shouted Tom angrily.

"Don't tell me to shut up," roared Julia, riding her horse right up to Tom, as if in a stand off.

"Listen Julia, it's safer if we all stick together."

"Oh suck it up Tom," she continued still shouting, "just like I've had to suck up the fact I'm riding a bot horse on the run from aliens instead of sitting front row at a Paris fashion show. Do you hear me complaining?"

"Er, you may have mentioned it a couple of times!" said Will. Julia glared at him. "Just a few though and hardly at all recently!" he hurriedly added.

"What's changed their minds?" interrupted Emily. "Have we offended them in some way do you think?" Julia looked at me and I stared at the ground.

Will groaned and ran his hands through his hair. "They've done what they said they would do, and who can blame them for being worried about the old man. They've lost their parents; he's all they have left."

"It's safer for all of us if we stick together," insisted Tom again. "Plus they are way quicker and fitter than us."

"If only I'd known I'd have to run, ride, shoot, and hunt when I was at school," said Julia sarcastically, "I would have thrown down my fabric scissors and joined the cross country club."

Will didn't look convinced. "I doubt that Julia."

"I think they will come with us," I said cautiously. "But you have to understand we've decided what we want to do, without so much as asking them. We just keep assuming what we want, is automatically what they want."

"How come Chin had a horse anyway?" asked Julia unexpectedly. There was a silence.

"Wasn't he a child?" ventured Emily.

"I thought they grew up in the forest," said Will in a puzzled voice.

"They aren't very clear about that," Tom replied, looking thoughtful.

"So are you saying we can't trust them?" asked Emily, looking shocked.

"No," I said firmly. "We can totally trust them, I'm sure of it."

"It's not as if we have much choice now anyway," said Will gloomily.

"I hope they decide soon," Tom sighed. "It's late afternoon and we need to find shelter again before nightfall." We dismounted and stretched our legs.

"I have pain in places I didn't know existed," said Julia squatting and bending over.

"Better get used to it," replied Tom. "It's going to take us a few days even galloping at full speed to reach SETI."

"I wonder if Mrs. Henley has recovered," Emily suddenly said. Everyone shifted around looking uncomfortable.

"She was badly injured Emily," said Tom gently, "swelling on the brain is very serious, and even doctors in our time couldn't have repaired it."

"She's as tough as old boots though," Julia piped up unexpectedly. "I think she'll be okay, and we'll probably get a tongue lashing for leaving her with Odo."

Will laughed. "She's probably driven him crazy by now, using his bathroom constantly and talking nonstop."

Julia nodded. She began to pick at blades of grass, and as Emily sat down next to her, she said "They have a weird diet don't you think?"

Emily shrugged her shoulders.

"I don't think I've seen them swallow a whole piece of food," Julia continued.

"Whatever those powders are that they take seem to work though," said Will. "Have you seen Chin's muscles?"

Julia smiled. "I have." Tom frowned.

"That's more than likely because he does hard manual labor," I said. "He hasn't had a luxurious life of ease and leisure like the one we had back in 2085."

"Shh, they've decided," whispered Emily getting up off the grass. Sookie, Seffie and Chin rode back slowly towards us. Chin leapt off Fireball in an experienced casual manner. No one spoke.

Seffie dismounted slowly. "We'll come with you," she began and then held up her hand, as Emily and Tom tried to speak.

"We are going to help you align the dishes, but after that, no matter what happens, we must return to the forest to ensure that Odo is safe and well. So don't ask us to accompany you further if you change your plans."

"Thank you," said Tom "We appreciate your help."

"The day will come when I will remind you of that Tom," said Chin strangely. There was an awkward silence.

"Well if that's sorted, then let's get going," said Julia jumping up. The horses stood patiently, waiting for their commands. Sookie looked unhappy and pulled at her reins.

"Thank you Sookie," I said walking over to her horse, "I know that Odo means a lot to you and you want to get back to him."

She nodded. "I know YOU understand Jake." I mounted my horse somewhat puzzled by her tone.

"Are we finally ready?" shouted Tom.

"Yes!" came Julia's reply loud and clear.

With that, Tom activated Lightfoot into a gallop and everyone followed. We rode over fields and through trees for the rest of the day until dusk. A small wooded area was deemed suitable to set up camp. The horses stood silently around us. It was a full moon, and as I gazed at its soft, yellow, glowing surface, I wondered if Moonbase still existed. We lounged on smart covers facing one another. A thermal smart heater stood in the center of our bedding arrangement. The stars winked down on our little, peaceful camp. It could have been a school Outward Bound trip, so unbelievable was the idea that we were possibly the only humans left on Earth. Looking around, nothing had changed, yet everything we knew was gone.

Will sat cross legged gazing into the thermal glow. "Hey Julia, what did the alien say to the gardener?"

"Very inappropriate given our present circumstances," Julia replied sharply.

"Take me to your weeder," said Will in a deep voice.

I laughed in spite of myself. "What do you get if you cross an alien with a hot drink?"

Will smiled and shook his head.

"Gravi-tea!" I chuckled.

"Oh it's all so funny now," said Julia crossly. "No one will be laughing if those fish in spacesuits suddenly turn up."

"Would they really harm us?" asked Emily quietly. "I mean we're just kids, we haven't done anything."

Chin's next words sent a chilling reminder to our cozy gathering. "They would kill us for sure, no question about it. Why do you think Odo goes to such extraordinary lengths to hide everyone?" There was silence as we all digested this terrifying prospect. I could see Julia checking her gun under the covers.

"It's amazing how houses, roads, cars, space shuttles, all signs of civilization have disappeared," said Tom abruptly, changing our topic of conversation.

"I wish you had known the Earth in our time," Emily said to Sookie, pulling her smart covers up to her face. "It was fun."

"No it wasn't," sighed Will. "You're forgetting we left in the middle of an energy crisis, with a war over resources on the horizon. Things were beginning to fall apart even then."

"We achieved great things though," persisted Emily.

"That's true," I agreed. "You only have to look at medicine, space travel and the quantum revolution."

"I wonder if Moonbase is still standing?" said Julia, looking up at the sky. I smiled at how she had read my mind.

"Doubt it," replied Tom gloomily, clutching his thermos flask.

Seffie asked, "Could there have been other time travelers after you?"

Tom shook his head. "The Future Project had already run out of money. There's no way they could have built another train. It cost trillions of dollars."

"Do you really think that Starship One has settled other worlds and can rescue us?" Emily asked Tom sleepily.

Tom looked up into the night sky. "They must have made amazing technological advances by now and who knows, perhaps they've been trying to contact Earth, wondering why there's no reply."

"Maybe even if we could get a message to whoever is out there, they might not be able to help us," sighed Will. "The Citons may just be too powerful and too advanced for them to get past their defenses."

"Why don't you try the lens again Jake?" suggested Seffie suddenly.

Tom and Will both said NO at the same time.

"Why?" asked Seffie.

"Because, it seemed like a good idea at the time," replied Tom. "But now I'm not so sure. It may lead them to us. We still just don't know enough about how it works."

"Could it show you if the Allen Array is still standing, or if this is a wild goose chase?" asked Julia, wriggling around in her smart bag. I shrugged my shoulders.

"I don't know." I took the bottle from my belt and looked at the lens floating around in it. "If this contains a map of the galaxy shouldn't we be able to see if other planets are settled, or at least suitable for humans to live on?" I pondered.

"Exactly," said Seffie.

"It is tempting," Will looked at Tom. "It could save us a lot of time and wasted effort, perhaps even show us what's happening on Mars."

Tom pushed his hair back from his face and sighed. We all watched him carefully. He had become our leader partly because of his bossy personality, and partly because we all believed him to be the cleverest. It dawned on me, that he might have conflicting feelings of jealousy and disappointment at his inability to use the lens.

Seffie challenged him again. "Tom we have this amazing device in our hands, why not use it, or at the very least try it?"

"I agree," said Julia turning over and stretching. "Put the lens in Jake."

"Okay, Okay," Tom grunted. "I'm sick of being the bad guy."

Seffie slid out of her covers and took my hand. "Put the lens in and squeeze my fingers if you get into trouble and need some help." I looked around.

"Just do it," said Will impatiently.

Tom stared ahead, resigned to the situation. I dabbed some fluid on my finger and tentatively placed the lens into my eye, bracing myself for the flash and the spinning. I focused in as hard as I could, emptying my mind of all thoughts except one, Mars. I felt as if I was standing on a moving conveyer belt hurtling towards the Red Planet at an unimaginable speed. The surface came into view. I could see domes similar to those on Moonbase. Some green areas were scattered around. The whole place had a look of neglect to it. No humans were visible. Perhaps inside the domes? No I couldn't go inside. Lines of code appeared in front of me. I focused again and sped back out into space. I saw millions of rocky planets, gas giants, frozen worlds, and multiple sun systems. Billions of stars, worlds of stripes, colors, rocks, fire, and ice hurtled past me at an incredible speed. Then silence, as I made my way carefully around the middle of the Milky Way, avoiding the super massive black hole in the center. Then, more stars and planets, some with plants, some with animals. I registered this in my brain without pausing, then, I stopped. The edge of the galaxy was near. In front of me appeared some kind of extraordinary, indescribable structure. Who built it? I circled it with my mind and zoomed in on it closely. Its vastness overwhelmed me. Could it be a monument? A gate? A building? A ship? What was it? I strained further towards it and looked more closely. It came to me. There on the side, like a pebble on a beach, was a plaque. I recognized it from my history lessons. The shock ran right through me. How was it possible?

"Pioneer," I whispered. The etching was on gold, of a naked man and woman waving. That was the last thing I saw. When I regained consciousness Seffie and Emily were bending over me.

My head lay in Julia's lap. "Jake," she cried. "Are you alright? Say something."

"Pioneer," I croaked. "Pioneer."

"He's delirious," I could hear Julia saying, "he's dreaming he's a pioneer in the Wild West or something!"

"Give him some time," said Emily softly, kneeling next to me. "He hasn't come round yet."

"What's he saying?" I heard Seffie's voice from a distance.

"Pioneer," I croaked again.

"What's Pioneer?" asked Seffie, helping to lift me into a sitting position.

"I don't believe it," said Tom in amazement. "Pioneer was the first human made object that was sent out into the solar system. It was used to transmit the first images of the planets. I think it was 1977?"

He looked at Will, who nodded. "It was. I remember reading about it in space history. But why is Jake saying Pioneer? Do you think he means the same one?"

"Wasn't that the one with the golden plaque depicting the man and woman on it?" Tom looked at Will.

"Yes," I said my voice coming back, "the man and the woman etched in gold. I saw it."

"That's impossible," Tom replied sitting back on his knees. "It was sent over 600 years ago."

"Just tell us exactly what you saw," Seffie said calmly. I stumbled over my words, breathing hard. Julia rubbed my back.

"A huge, weird, beautiful structure at the end of the galaxy. It was kind of like a geometric pattern," I paused "perhaps a snowflake, but not quite."

"A fractal?" queried Tom.

"What's that?" asked Julia staring at Tom.

"A shape that's been found to be common in nature on Earth. Fractals are everywhere. Snowflakes, leaves, mountain ranges, even the human heart has a fractal design running through it."

"Okay, okay, information overload," Julia waved her hand. "Save the science lesson for another day."

"So what was it?" continued Seffie.

"I don't know," I replied. "All I can tell you, is that the golden plaque from Pioneer was pinned to its side. I mean it was like a speck of dust, this fractal thing was so huge."

"What does it mean?" asked Will looking at Tom.

"It means that it's the last outpost of humanity," said Seffie solemnly.

We all stared at her. "The fact that the design of the structure is fractal like on Earth and the Pioneer sign is attached to it, is like a message, you know, like, hey here are the humans, or humans follow this sign."

"Did you see anything else?" asked Emily hopefully.

"Lots of planets and stars," I replied. "But," and here I struggled to put my thoughts in order. "There's no one else, I mean planets with simple plants and animals, but nothing like us, nothing that's intelligent."

"What in the whole galaxy?" cried Seffie, in astonishment?

"It seems like only us, in all of space," I said sadly. "I don't know what happened to the crew of Starship One, but they definitely haven't settled any planets that I could see. "And," I added, "it's strange, but I was only aware of two other planets with a significant amount of liquid water. I think planets with oceans are definitely in short supply."

"So what now?" asked Will gloomily, slumping to the ground.

"We send our message to the fractal structure," said Seffie simply.

"Are you nuts?" replied Tom. "Have you any idea how long a message will take to cross the galaxy?" Tom then looked at Will intensely, "I can't believe it, but Frank Drake was wrong!"

Will nodded, staring up at the night sky. "Man who'd have thought it," he sighed.

"Okay I know I'm going to regret this, but who was Frank Drake, and why was he wrong?" asked Julia.

Tom cleared his throat and said quietly, "Frank Drake was a SETI astronomer who devised an equation to express the likelihood of extraterrestrial intelligence in the Milky Way. $N = R^* \times Fp \times Ne \times Fe \times Fi \times Fc \times L$, which is considerably less than what Jake saw!"

Julia blinked. "Can I have a translation from tweakie to English please."

"It means there should be a lot more dudes out there," said Will sadly.

Emily stood up and stretched, wrapping her blanket tightly around her shoulders. Stars twinkled above her head. "Have you any idea how precious we all are now," she whispered.

It might have been hours in the heavy silence that followed Emily's words. Finally Will spoke.

"So now what?"

Seffie looked up at him unperturbed. "I believe that we will think of something."

Will raised his eyebrows. "Please, someone think of something, any ideas Julia?"

Julia shook her head. "Ha ha, not my department, you're the one with the super intelligent brain gene."

"I want to say something," I said slowly. "We have all been under the impression that the Citons are so much more advanced than us. But the question is, how much more advanced?"

"What do you mean?" asked Tom in bewilderment.

"Well, suppose that Starship One has developed new technological advances in its hundreds of years of interstellar travel. We know some crew were frozen, and I suspect some were not, or at least not all of the time. We also know that the human genome project was at Moonbase although we never found out why," I looked around at everyone. "Don't forget even before the Citons got here, we had discovered faster than speed of light travel via antimatter, time travel and quantum. That has to make us at least approaching their equal. A few more centuries would probably have evened us out."

Tom stroked the back of his head deep in thought.

"Well, if we are so smart Jake, how come no one is left"? asked Julia, drily. I thought hard and screwed up my face in concentration.

"I think some kind of genetic experiment went wrong," I replied. "I mean wrong for everyone. I think the fact that the Citons are a mainly a water based species means they had to seek a similar environment to survive after their planet was destroyed. Perhaps, Earth was the best they could find at such short notice. But it could be that it wasn't such a piece of prime real estate after all. Maybe something has happened, and now they are stuck here. Does that make sense?"

"Absolutely none whatsoever," said Will cheerfully.

"What about Mars?" asked Seffie gazing at me.

"Couldn't see anyone," I replied. "Although, there were signs of a settlement, similar to Moonbase."

"Could you see SETI?" Julia asked blinking tiredly. "Are the telescopes still standing?"

I sighed and rubbed my eyes. "I can't seem to focus in on specific areas or buildings. I don't know if the lens contains that much detail or," I paused, "perhaps I just haven't learned how to access that information."

"So what now?" asked Will, scanning our disappointed faces.

"We carry on to SETI as planned," said Seffie firmly. "We look for the telescopes, we think about how we can send a transmission to the fractal structure, and when Jake is recovered, he can put the lens in again and try to find out more, agreed?" Seffie pulled her blanket tightly around her shoulders.

Tom nodded glumly. "Can't think of a better plan, how about you Will?"

Will shook his head, "Magic lenses, talking horses, fractals in space. I'm right out of ideas on this one Tom!"

"Let Jake get some sleep." Julia got up and gently tucked the blanket around me.

"Have you secured the area with smart dust?" Will yawned.

"It's been done," said Seffie quietly. "We'll stay awake first," she looked at Chin.

"No," said Tom firmly. "I'll take the first shift with you." There was silence.

"Very well," said Seffie evenly. I had to admire her calmness, but I felt angry at the lack of trust that Tom was now openly showing. Even though Seffie, Sookie, and Chin had wanted to go back to the forest, they had always been honest with us. I didn't think for one moment that they would leave us here.

My sleep that night was full of dreams. The weird and wonderful fractal structure with the golden plaque played over and over in my head. Mom and Dad looked out of a window and I shouted until my lungs almost burst, but they didn't hear me. There's no sound in space.

I awoke to Seffie shaking me, "Jake you're talking in your sleep, in fact, no, shouting would be a better description."

"Sorry," I mumbled.

"Are you okay?" she asked quietly.

"I was dreaming," I replied sleepily.

"About your parents?"

"Yes," I sighed.

"I think we all dream about our parents," Tom whispered, looking into the thermal heater.

"What about you Seffie?"

The two of us looked at her. She was silent, gazing at the ground, deep in contemplation. "It was another lifetime," she finally replied. "It all seems like a dream now." We were quiet. "Go back to sleep Jake," she said softly, and I lay back down pulling up my covers. When I woke again, Sookie and Will were already preparing breakfast. The horses stood motionless nearby.

"It's not quite a bacon, breakfast sandwich," grinned Will handing me a tin of mixed nutrients. I yawned and looked up at the rising sun.

"Cheers Will," I said, my stomach already protesting at the mush inside.

Julia was up next. "Crikey, what I wouldn't give for some proper real food," she said, when she saw my can of nutrients. "Even Sookie's soup is beginning to seem appealing now," she whispered in my ear. Gradually everyone awoke, grumbled, ate and packed. Sookie seemed unusually quiet. I wondered if she was still upset at the decision not to go straight back to Odo. I waited for a moment until Seffie was alone, and I approached her rather sheepishly.

"Hey Seffie, I just wanted to ask if Sookie is okay?"

"Why, what's wrong," she quickly replied.

"Nothing, just she seems so quiet, I mean she's hardly said a word."

Seffie sighed. "Sometimes Sookie gets that way. We call it her blues. There's nothing we can do except wait for it to pass," she paused. "It's not this trip, although she does want to be back with Odo. It's more." Seffie struggled to continue, and then she put her hand on my arm. "There's so much I want to say to say to you Jake, but it will have to wait for now." I nodded.

Tom shouted over, "I think we're packed Jake, are you ready?"

"Coming," I shouted back at him.

I wandered over to Hawking. I wondered if it was just to me that Seffie, Sookie and Chin seemed sometimes so different. No one else asked any questions about their appearance. There was definitely something though, and I couldn't put my finger on it. If I had to say what it was... on occasion their eye movements seemed rather odd. Nothing that I could say for sure.... Seffie's skill as a quantum expert, that she wanted to conceal from the others. Chin's ability to ride a horse like a rodeo champion. Sookie's moods, and uncomfortable expressions. I shook my head, mounted Hawking, and whispered the start-up codes in his ear.

"Morning Jake," he said in his deep voice.

"Lightfoot is going to lead the way using the old maps of the area," shouted Tom.

"Have you thrown the smart dust?" asked Emily immediately.

"Yes," everyone shouted together and Julia and Will started laughing. I knew that Emily was always worried. We hadn't seen any signs of the Citons since that morning in the forest on our journey to Seattle. I still wondered though about the smart blanket and what that was meant to signify. Was it a sign of a Citon truce? That they were going to leave us alone? Or were they watching us, waiting to see what we would do next? Lightfoot galloped forward and we followed racing through the fields.

Signs of long abandoned freeways appeared through the grass and weeds. Our smart suits kept us cool and comfortable. Surprisingly, Julia seemed to have taken to riding, and laughed, tossing her hair back as she cantered alongside Chin. Who would have believed it! I wished with all my heart that Mom and Dad could have seen her. Seffie and Sookie rode together, their long blue and blonde hair streaming behind them in the wind. Emily rode next to me. From time to time she glanced around nervously especially when we entered a very exposed area, but she seemed calmer and less jumpy than the last few days. We stopped briefly and took quick snacks, but Tom was anxious to press on as fast as possible. I questioned Hawking as to our location and distance to go, but without a GPS to refer to, he was often uncertain.

We galloped by deserted towns, once thriving areas now crumbling and dilapidated. It was still astonishing to see the extent of destruction, and the eerie silence of roads and towns with no people. In a few hundred years or less, perhaps most signs of humans would have begun to disappear altogether, and after that nature would paper over the last remains of our civilization. What had happened, I wondered once more? I questioned Hawking but again drew a blank. All he knew was that he had been put into storage pre-catastrophe to be used in case of an emergency. It seemed the answers that I longed to find would be impossible to uncover at present.

Evening came and Tom divided up the watch. Things seemed calmer now between him and Seffie, or maybe, he had calculated that because we were past the half-way point, it would make more sense for her, Chin, and Sookie to carry on with us than to take off on their own. I slept badly. No one mentioned the lens. After only a few hour's sleep, we set off again, riding furiously towards what was once the Hat Creek Radio Observatory. I couldn't even bear to think about what would happen if it was no longer there. The Citons seemed happy to just let everything fall down, so I hoped that the Allen Array would be no exception.

We crossed the State line at some point. No sign or building marked the border. Seffie handed out pills to keep us awake and we rode quickly through California. The horses avoided all built up areas, and took us to higher land. On our fourth day of travelling we finally began our approach to what was once the home of SETI.

"Ironic isn't it," said Will, slowing down to ride next to me. "We have to go to where humans once searched for aliens, to now search for humans!"

I laughed. "Yes there is a certain kind of black humor to that, which I think the early SETI astronomers would have appreciated."

"Well they certainly found their aliens," shouted Tom from the front.

"With a vengeance," agreed Will.

"How much further now?" asked Julia, pulling her horse over to ours. "We surely must be near?"

"If the telescopes are still standing, we should see them soon" panted Tom, speeding up his horse.

We all rode faster now, the thrill of anticipation driving us forward. I saw them first; hundreds, and hundreds of white dishes pointing to the sky. The elements had not yet broken through their protective coating. They stood silent, looking up towards the cosmos probably very much as the last SETI astronomer had left them. Their mission had been accomplished. Alien life had been found. Now they had a new mission, to find human life!

"Do you think they still work?" shouted Will.

"They'd better," shouted back Julia. "Or you have a lot of those dish things to fix!"

"They are beautiful," beamed Sookie and for the first time in days she seemed more like herself again. I looked over at Seffie and she smiled happily back at me.

"We need to find the control room first," puffed Tom over his shoulder at us.

"This way I think," Will shouted waving us forward, and we followed galloping through the white dishes which surrounded us on every side. Finally, we came to what looked like the main SETI operations building. It hadn't fared as well as the telescopes, and looked more run down. Everyone dismounted in front of the entrance.

"Who's going in first?" asked Julia pulling out her gun.

"You," said Will laughing.

"I'll go," replied Tom pointing his gun at the building. He tentatively tried the door and it slid open silently. A huge reception area stood littered with pieces of rusted metal and broken glass. Bits of grass grew through some of the floor tiles, and a few pieces of an old quantum lay smashed on the floor. The sun's rays shone through the heavy duty glass material that was still intact. We advanced nervously into the main hall.

"There's no one here," said Tom, more to himself for reassurance as we slowly looked around.

"This place has been abandoned for a very long time," whispered Seffie gazing up at the mosaic ceiling.

"Now there's a surprise," sighed Will, tossing his backpack on the floor.

"It's still in good condition though," said Emily running her fingers across the wall. "I mean compared to some of the buildings in Seattle."

"It was made from more expensive and durable materials," commented Chin touching a marble work surface.

"Let's split into two groups and take a look around," ordered Tom. He motioned for Julia and Chin to join him.

We wandered around the labs looking at all the machines and computers; microscopically thin slivers of graphene. They were way more advanced than those we had used in 2085. I doubted if we could figure out how to operate them. A huge room contained all of the telescope connections. Millions of wiring lines, and complex, strange looking black boxes with unreadable markings on them.

"You need to see this," Tom reappeared, gesturing towards the door behind him. "They have what I think is a mini particle accelerator in here."

We followed Tom into a massive hall. At the end of the room, a huge carbon circle stood silent and dusty. Everything looked grey, gloomy and desolate. I studied the small machines fixed to the walls.

"Tom, I'm not an astronomer, but I'd say those dishes outside aren't sending radio signals anymore."

"What are they doing then?" asked Will, pressing some pins at random.

"I haven't got a clue," I replied, shaking my head baffled.

"Neutrino beams," said Seffie hauling herself up on one of the metal workbenches and running her fingers over a dirty screen.

"What?" asked Julia, "and keep it simple please."

"The neutrino beams are made at the particle accelerator, and encoded messages are then flashed across the galaxy in them." We all looked at Seffie in astonishment.

"Er, how do you know that?" asked Will looking puzzled, "and why does everyone seem to know more than me these days!"

"Read about it on Odo's old quantum," she said, looking at the ground.

"So, we can use these beams to send a message to the fractal structure?" I asked hopefully.

"Probably not," she replied, Even though they can travel faster than the speed of light, it would still take too long."

"How long?" asked Julia, her hands on her hips.

"Centuries," said Seffie regretfully.

"So, can we make the beam go faster?" asked Tom.

"Perhaps, if we can figure out how to send the neutrino message via different dimensions," replied Seffie thoughtfully, "but we need Jake to look in the lens and see if that's possible."

"This is the perfect time to tell one of my best jokes," chuckled Will, propping himself up next to Seffie. "The barman said, sorry we don't serve neutrinos. A neutrino enters a bar!"

Julia looked at Will with a stony face, "You really need to get some better jokes, because I haven't understood a single one," and then she shouted, "in five hundred years!"

Chin roared with laughter.

"I still find it hard to believe," said Emily, ignoring Will and Julia "that apart from the one Citon in the woods, no one has come after us. I mean they must have either found the train or the Citon by now, and discovered that we took the lens." Everyone was silent.

"What if something else is going on with them?" suggested Chin. "They could be caught up in their own struggles, perhaps with their government or sickness..." he trailed off.

"Maybe they just don't think a few kids running around the planet are enough to justify the trouble of chasing us," said Sookie quietly. "They may think we will be gone soon enough."

"Don't say such a thing," said Julia looking shocked.

"Er, well, reality check Julia, Sookie may have a point. We've survived so far on luck and our small supplies," said Will.

"No," Tom corrected him. "We've survived so far because we have a plan and a purpose."

Seffie nodded. "Tom is right. We need to start up the accelerator and check out the dishes. Once we have everything up and running, Jake will play his part. He needs to use the lens to find the coordinates of the fractal structure, and a quick route for our neutrino beam to reach it."

"Then what?" asked Julia. "How will we know if the message has been received or if a rescue attempt is going to happen?"

"We won't," said Seffie. "We'll transmit our coordinates here in what was once known as North America, and go back to the forest to wait."

"That's our plan?" asked Julia incredulously.

"Got a better one?" replied Will rolling his eyes.

"Blast our way back onto the Time Train and take off for Mars," shouted Julia shaking her gun fiercely.

"Okay," said Will. "So thinking about how exactly we're going to do that might just take you the rest of the evening, Julia, but please feel free to give me the details when you've planned them out. Oh, and by the way, just in case you didn't know, leading a machine gun assault on an alien fish army isn't something I learned at the academy!"

"I'll go back to the forest," Julia replied looking mad. "But I'm not sitting around for the next few years, just waiting while hiding in a hole."

"Once we've sent the message and returned to Odo, we can think about our next course of action," said Tom diplomatically. "Let's just send the message first of all and then see what happens afterwards."

Emily began to unload her backpack. "I think we should sleep in the control tower."

"Chin you ride around the dishes with Sookie and check as many as you can," Tom ordered. "Julia and Emily, set up camp, Will and I will look at starting up the accelerator, and you, Jake, can put in the lens with Seffie and see if you can find anything to help us."

I groaned, although I should have felt privileged to be the one that the lens responded too, it was also a bit like a visit to the dentist. You dreaded it, you didn't know what would happen, and you were extremely relieved when it was over.

Tom and Will stayed in the accelerator room while we made our way to the control tower. Chin smiled at Seffie and Sookie picked up her gun.

"How come we get to play house?" Julia grumbled looking at Emily.

"Come if you want," said Chin.

Emily smiled at Julia. "Just go. It's okay. I can manage here."

Julia didn't need to be told twice, she was out the door after Chin and Sookie before the last words left Emily's mouth.

"Let's go and sit in the corner by the window," I said to Seffie.

"We'll be over there," Seffie pointed. Emily nodded and continued to unpack.

Seffie and I sat cross-legged on the old tiled floor. "Concentrate on finding a way to transmit the neutrino beam to the fractal structure and nothing else," said Seffie settling herself comfortably in front of me.

I nodded, took out the lens, breathed deeply and placed it in my eye. My mind was an explosion for the first few seconds and I focused hard.

Show me the way to the fractal I repeated over and over again. I opened my mind up and I was sitting just outside Earth's orbit floating in space. Equations flashed in front of me. I began to repeat them as I raced further and further away. Huge tunnels filled with bright lights blazed, hurting my eyes. I was aware that I was shouting the coordinates, and yet, I was looking around me in fascination at the beauty of the cosmos. The fractal loomed. I had arrived at the gateway to humanity. Seffie was right. I was sure of it now. My mind zoomed in on the Pioneer plaque and I looked at the golden woman and the man waving at me. Then suddenly I was rushing backwards, a huge whooshing sound in my ears. I was in Earth's orbit again, but it felt like I was floating in the sea. I saw her drift towards me, her friendly dolphin smile, her arms outstretched, but I was afraid. She stopped in front of me and lowered her arms. Did her mouth move or did I just hear her words in my mind. I wasn't sure.

"I am the Citon whose life you saved," she whispered.

"You tripped," I replied uneasily, backing away. She shook her head.

"If you had not covered me I would not have survived. That you let me live, after what my people have done to your kind, was astonishing. Such compassion for a mortal enemy marks you out as truly unique. We have taken everything from you and still you would protect us."

"We stole your lens," I stammered. "But of course you already know that."

"Understandable," she replied softly. "But what is truly incredible is that you were able to use it. Even when humans inhabited the Earth in enormous numbers, only a handful could access the lens."

"Why didn't you take the lens back from us in the bank vault when you had the chance?"

The dolphin mouth began to smile wider. "I couldn't find it, and I knew I would be able to obtain a replacement."

"Are you going to try and capture us?" I asked nervously.

She shook her head. "There are some like me who wanted only to live in peace with mankind, but we are unfortunately very few in numbers. Most of my people wish to isolate themselves from man and are glad that he has gone."

"Why and how did you return my blanket to me?" I asked curiously.

"I rendered you and your companion's unconscious in order to examine you and to return your cover." She floated cautiously towards me. "I wished to do this, as a sign of my goodwill and gratitude. I am a mother myself, and I was surprised to find that you are only children, perhaps the same age as my own."

"How did you find us?"

"My craft recorded what happened in the forest." She tilted her head and looked at me searchingly.

"Do the other Citons know about us?" I asked fearfully.

"Not yet," she said. "I was a lone explorer when you came upon me. My job is to collect and analyze different kinds of plants."

I stared at her smiley white dolphin face with its soft floating tendrils of hair. A pale blue outfit billowed and spun out around her, accentuating her kind blue eyes. "I have been given another lens by friends who wish to protect me," she whispered, then paused and looked at me sadly.

"An expedition has been organized to investigate the entrance of an unknown entity through the Earth's atmosphere. At present, no other Citon is aware of your existence, or your possession of the lens. I know about the Time Train, for the lens can work both ways and has revealed your history to me. We are linked, but be assured, I will not betray you. Take the other children and the quantums. Go deeper inland and hide there."

"But our people will rescue us."

She interrupted me. "Jake," she said sadly. "Your people are long gone."

"No," I cried out. "Humans still exist and they will come for us."

"Save yourselves," she whispered, her white tendrils floating dreamily around her face. "Save yourselves."

"Jake, Jake," Seffie was shaking me excitedly. "Jake, I've got everything written down; you've given me the exact coordinates for the beam to pass through a series of wormholes. It can reach the fractal in a matter of hours."

"We may not have much time," I said, looking at the lens in my hand. "The Citons are about to launch a search expedition where our train landed."

"What?" said Emily walking towards me her face white and panic-stricken.

"We need to send the message and get out of here."

"Did the lens tell you that?" asked Seffie, putting her hand on my arm.

"Yes, I need to speak to Tom." I jumped up and ran quickly towards the accelerator room. Tom and Will were standing with wires between their teeth re-routing code, and moving quantums around. Graphene screens glowed with lines of green data.

"I've used the lens," I panted quickly. They put down all the equipment.

"And," asked Will, raising his eyebrows. "What does the oracle say?"

"We need to send the message quickly. I have coordinates that can get the beam through a series of wormholes. It will reach the fractal in a matter of hours, but the Citons are preparing to search the area where we landed. They don't know about us yet, but it's only a matter of time." Tom and Will glanced at one another worriedly.

"Are you sure?" asked Tom, running his hands tiredly through his hair.

"I'm positive," I replied.

"We'll have this figured out hopefully within an hour," Tom sighed. "I'm just hoping that a sufficient number of telescopes are in good enough condition to transmit. We won't know until Chin gets back."

"I have something else to tell you," I swallowed and looked at Tom.

"The Citon from whom we stole the lens, well she's part of some kind of pro-human group. I mean she sympathizes with us. She wants us to run and hide inland as far as possible."

"You've talked to a Citon," asked Will incredulously his mouth open in disbelief.

"Yes!"

"Are you crazy?" shouted Tom dropping all the wires as if they were live. "I knew that lens was dangerous."

"No," I insisted. "Why would she warn me if she meant to harm us?"

"It's a ruse until they can get to us," roared Tom, his face red with fury.

"They already did." I replied quietly.

"What do you mean?" whispered Will, looking terrified.

"The night we spent in the vault," I said. "The Citon followed us, somehow knocked us all out, and left my smart blanket beside me as a goodwill gesture. To show she meant us no harm."

"You knew that and kept it from us?" said Tom in amazement, putting his hand on a machine to steady himself.

"I only knew that my blanket was back, I didn't know how," I replied unruffled.

"I don't know if we can trust you," said Tom glaring at me now, in cold fury.

"We'll you'd better," I shot back angrily. "Seeing as I've given you the beam coordinates and seeing as I'm the only one that can use the lens." I stopped, "And another thing, why would I tell you that we should get out of here if I was going to turn you over to the Citons?"

"He has a point," replied Will, recovering slightly. "Man, Jake, I don't know whether to think you're one awesome dude or a dangerous idiot!"

"Okay no more secrets," Tom ordered, pointing angrily at me, "and no more using the lens without me being around."

"Tom, you're not in charge of me," I said calmly but firmly. "I know you want to try and advise us how to get out of this mess. We all have something to contribute to our survival. Don't go thinking that you can order everyone around."

Tom stood up straight, his fists clenched, his face bright red and I thought for a second that he was going to hit me, but Will put his hand on Tom's arm.

"Look, if Jake is right, then let's concentrate on fixing up the beam and sending the signal." Will stared at me intensely, "How much time do you think we have?"

"I'm not sure," I hesitated. "The Citons don't yet suspect it's a space-ship that crashed through the atmosphere, so they aren't in a rush to nose around our landing site. However, an expedition is getting ready to investigate. If we want to make it back to the forest and get to Odo and Mrs. Henley before they do, then we should hurry."

Tom picked up the wires from where they had fallen. "Once Chin has finished inspecting the dishes, we'll get started." His expression was still thunderous as he turned his back on me. I nodded at Will who looked worried, and made my way back to the workroom. Chin, Sookie, and Julia had finished evaluating the dishes and Seffie was telling them about my experience with the lens. They all stopped talking and stared at me.

"Are the dishes in good shape?" I asked Chin apprehensively.

"They seem to be," replied Chin. "There are a few that are slightly weather damaged, but on the whole they've been so well insulated with some kind of carbon material, that they're still in fairly good condition."

"The more we have, the stronger the signal," I pondered. "So if only a few are out, then we should be able to send a message."

"I can only see one problem," added Seffie. "The signal might be picked up by the Citons. We should either send our transmission now and leave, or send it in the morning and set off straight away."

"Let's get some sleep then send it," I answered.

"Agreed," replied Julia sharply. "I don't think anyone can ride any further now, especially in the dark."

"I'll go and talk to Tom," said Chin, walking out of the room and casting a strange backward glance in my direction as he left. Everyone flopped on their Smart beds totally exhausted. I was too tired even to eat. My eyes wandered to the open window. Where was Starship One? My last thoughts before darkness surrounded me were, please let there be a rescue from this nightmare.

I woke to find Seffie shaking me. "It's almost morning. Tom and Will finished setting up hours ago. We've got the last watch. Let's get everything ready."

I yawned and crept out of my smart bag. She handed me a can of nutrients.

"Be with you soon," I mumbled, and Seffie left the room silently. I looked around at everyone sleeping. Julia was snoring lightly and Emily was curled up in a ball. I finished spooning the mush in my mouth and stood up. I straightened my Smart suit and combed my hair. It had grown and needed to be cut. We were all starting to look rough now. Seffie, Sookie, and Chin still looked the same. They were used to living this way. Perhaps in time we would be too. When I arrived at the accelerator room Seffie was inspecting all of the connections.

"What message are we going to send?" she asked, her back to me as she pressed some pins and blew some dust off the screen.

"I think SOS," I replied "It's short, simple and to the point."

"I like it," smiled Seffie, turning and facing me.

"It's not exactly original."

"What's not original?" Julia appeared, scratching her head. If I didn't know better I'd have thought that she was trying to minimize any time that Seffie and I might be spending alone together.

"The message SOS," I replied. "Save Our Souls."

"Hmmm," Julia looked around. "I'll wake the others."

She flounced out the door and as I looked at all of the wires and strange pins, I could hear Tom and Will discussing what message we should send with Chin and Sookie. Everyone made their way down the hallway and gathered in front of the accelerator. Three large rings spun and whirred simultaneously.

Tom spoke confidently. "The first message we'll send will be SOS. We'll send it three times, and after that, we can send a slightly more detailed transmission. Let's see if this works."

Will began programing, and as we looked out of the window, the white dishes began to turn in unison. When they were all pointing up at the sky, Will's fingers began to move across the pins. He tapped out the SOS signal onto the clear graphene screen. The bright green letters glowed. "Here goes," he said. The carbon circles spun and the neutrino beam fired.

"Has it worked?" asked Emily anxiously.

"I think so," replied Will scrutinizing the quantum.

"Okay, I'm sending again," Will pressed the pins. "What other message should we send?" He looked around, "Any ideas?" Everyone looked at one another, waiting for someone to speak.

"I know what to send," I said, and bent over Will who got ready to transmit in rudimentary Morse Code, an ancient system still taught in the academy.

"We are a group of time travelers trapped alone on earth - the planet has been taken over by hostile aliens - we failed to detect them in a nearby star system - despite a leaked transmission from their ship in 1977 - the Wow! signal as it came to be known - could have saved mankind if we had carried out further investigations - we are uncertain of events since our departure in 2085 - we ask you to send a rescue mission - no other humans seem to have survived - be warned that the aliens have attack droids in orbit - here are the coordinates - hurry -"

"That's good enough," said Will his fingers stabbing at the pins. "It's sent."

Suddenly, Julia let out a wail "No, No!" Everyone looked alarmed; my heart beat faster.

"Julia, what's wrong?"

"Can't you see what you've just said?" she groaned in despair.

"What?" I asked in confusion. Julia took me by the shoulders, shaking me hard.

"Don't you remember on the Time Train, Dad said the reason scientists were so confident that our mission would succeed was that they had received a message twenty or thirty years earlier saying Wow! The message came from the future. Oh my gosh, Jake I think it was you. I don't understand, but what you've said in the message it, it..." she trailed off. "Don't you remember I said at the bunker that we should send the word crap?" She looked horror stricken.

"You think that was Jake?" asked Emily astonished, "how?"

"I don't believe it," groaned Will his head in his hands. "But I think Julia's right. We've sent the message through a wormhole, through time, through a particle accelerator, which can be picked up by another particle accelerator in another time."

"The Hadron Collider in Switzerland 2065," finished Tom grimly. "Remember what I said, when Odo first told us about the Citons. My theory was, that we sent the message." He shook his head, a look of intense concentration on his face. "It's an information paradox that we'll never understand, and I'm not even going to try. It's like the old what came first the chicken or the egg saying?"

"No," I whispered, "it can't be, I haven't been here before. It would have had to have happened before."

Tom stared ahead deep in thought. "Remember Previn's all time is entangled theory?"

Will nodded, "Chop! One of King Henry's wives just lost her head!"

Julia slumped against the wires, her hands over her eyes. "I don't understand this, but it's too late, the message has been sent. Remember those Higgy thingy's that Dad talked about when we were on the train? The stuff that can time travel through a particle accelerator!" she sighed. "You must have.... I just don't know though, why you would mention the Wow! signal."

"I don't know either," I paused confused. "It just came into my head, and well, no one stopped me." I said defensively. "You all sat there and let Will send my message."

"It doesn't matter," sighed Tom. "It's done now and there's no way that we can un-send the transmission. It was meant to happen this way Jake. The message, for whatever reason, had to be sent. He stood up. "All we can do is hope that the fractal received our plea for help, and that someone out there is still around to send a rescue mission to save us. In the meantime, I say we get out of here right now in case the Citons have seen the neutrino flashes and mobilize that investigation team out of the ocean even faster."

"Let's leave right now!" said Emily, jumping down from the work-bench. Her sense of urgency affected everyone. We threw our stuff together quickly, falling over backpacks and bags in a panic.

"Do you think we should try and disguise the fact we were here?" I asked Tom tying up my belt at the double.

"No point," replied Tom. "There's nowhere else you could send a neutrino beam from in this area, possibly even in the whole of North America. It had to have come from here."

"Come on, let's move it," said Will, hurriedly slinging his machine gun over his shoulder.

Chin already had the horses ready out front. We jumped on our mounts. Tom threw out smart dust. Sookie ran round and sprayed everyone quickly with the particle spray.

"We should ride immediately," Tom shouted. "Is everyone ready?"

He looked at us reassuringly, sensing our panic. We had laid ourselves wide open to detection now. I could see that Emily's hands were shaking as she held on tightly to her reins. She took a deep breath and winked at me. "I'm okay."

Tom cantered in a circle around our horses. "I've asked Lightfoot to get us back to the forest directly, avoiding Seattle, and keeping us in covered areas as much as possible."

"Hurry," shouted Julia, her growing collection of guns slung around her saddle. We began to gallop back through the dishes, at break neck speed, leaving SETI behind.

Chapter Ten

QUANTUM MINDS

"Extraordinary claims require extraordinary evidence."
Carl Sagan.

We rode hard day after day, stopping under cover for only a few hours of sleep at a time. Seffie gave us pills that kept us awake and alert. Emily worried constantly that the horses would breakdown, but they showed no signs of slowing. We had given ourselves away twice now; firstly, with our crash landing, and secondly, with the neutrino beam message. Would our luck hold out long enough to get us back to Odo? I resisted trying to use the lens, as I was concerned it could reveal our location if a non-friendly Citon managed to connect up with me. At last, we reached the forest.

Everyone became more nervous, as we skirted the area where the Time Train had landed. The smart dust was thrown out twice as often and we were silent as we galloped behind Tom. Every twig that cracked underfoot, every rustle of the wind unhinged me. Julia rode in front of me, putting her hand on her gun every few minutes. Emily looked worn out with terror and Seffie, Sookie, and Chin looked grim. Tom alone seemed confident, and Will, although nervous, relaxed whenever Tom encouraged him. I couldn't decide whether Tom was truly brave, or just so arrogant that he thought he could never get caught.

The horses took the mountain terrain in their stride. Microsoft had been wise in going with nature's design. Although not the fastest, it would have been impossible to get any other sort of transport vehicle through trees and over the steep hills and rocks. The forest had never seemed so dark and scary, the silence never so frightening. As we approached the bunker, my heart was pounding. We all dismounted. Tom and I had talked about the problem of the horses. Obviously they couldn't get through the crawl space, and to keep them near by would mean they could inadvertently reveal our hiding place. We agreed that they should be freed to ride out and away as far as possible.

"Hawking, we are going to walk from here," I whispered stroking him gently. "We can't take you any further and you can't know where we are going in case you should be captured and questioned by a Citon."

"I have fulfilled my purpose," said Hawking directly. "I will return with the others to Microsoft."

"Is that wise?" I asked. "Wouldn't you rather roam further inland?"

"That is not my purpose," replied Hawking, standing perfectly still.

"Thanks for all that you've done for me," I said rubbing his nose.

"You are most welcome," Hawking continued, lowering his head and nuzzling my hand.

Everyone stood awkwardly, not wanting to lose the horses, but knowing that they had to go. Tom spoke first, "Go Lightfoot go."

He galloped away and the other horses followed him. Soon, we could hear the sound of their heavy hooves fading away into the distance. Tom threw smart dust around us as we crept quietly through the trees towards the bunker. Chin edged his way carefully over to the crawlspace first. He seemed to check a few things out and then beckoned us over. We crept inside one by one. Seffie waited until last. Once inside the cavern we squashed into the elevator. Chin had already gone ahead and sent it back up. I was still nervous. We had been away almost three weeks.

The elevator door opened and the passage was empty. Now it was Seffie's turn to look uneasy. She and Sookie exchanged a glance that I couldn't quite place. We could hear loud voices arguing. Chin came out of the cushion room and shut the door. He seemed to be breathing hard and looked uncertainly at us.

"What's wrong?" Tom asked immediately. Julia reached for her machine gun!

"I don't know how, I don't..." Chin looked at Seffie and Sookie. "It's going to be a shock."

"Odo?" asked Sookie, fearfully.

"Serena," Chin replied his voice shaking.

A young woman appeared in the dim light of the passage. She was incredibly beautiful with thick, bright red hair, and an impish grin. Her silver, tight, body suit showed off her tall lean frame. "Ah, just tell them will you and get on with it."

Odo appeared shuffling behind her.

219

"Who are you?" asked Tom, the amazement in his voice mirroring how everyone felt.

"Why don't you know me?" she smiled kindly and tilted her head examining us closely. "Julia, dearie what's happened to your lovely hair? You look decidedly bedraggled."

She tapped her boot and peered at us mischievously. I looked around. Our appearance was rough to say the least. Tom and Will's dark hair was messy and tangled. Their smooth, short, sleek, parted styles had long since disappeared. Emily's curls were wilder than ever. I hadn't been near a mirror in days, but I could feel soft hairs growing on my chin.

"You don't know me," said Julia in confusion, turning from the girl to look at me for help.

"Cat got your tongue Jake?"

Now it was my turn to stare. I don't know why or how but the words, "Mrs. Henley?" escaped from my lips.

"Told you he was the clever one," said the girl smiling at Odo and folding her arms. "Doesn't look it mind you."

"What's going on?" asked Tom bewildered.

"Where's Mrs. Henley?" Emily stammered looking around.

"Now don't you go upsetting yourself my dear," said the girl, walking towards Emily and hugging her. "Odo told me how concerned you were about me." Emily stood rigid staring at the girl's face.

"Er, can someone tell me what is going on, and why you are impersonating Mrs. Henley?" asked Will his eyes fixed on the beautiful redhead.

"We'd better all go inside and sit down," said Odo looking sheepish. "Chin tells me that you have traveled this last week nonstop. I've got some drinks ready, now come on all of you." He beckoned us in and we followed him as if in a dream.

I flopped down on one of the big old cushions, confused and exhausted.

Julia stood, her hands on her hips defiantly. "Someone better tell me what's going on and where's Mrs. Henley?"

"I'm touched," said the girl, perching on the arm of Odo's chair. "Never knew you liked me so much."

"Oh shut up," replied Julia rudely, looking at her aggressively.

Odo sat down in his rag tag chair and regarded us solemnly. He took a deep breath. "Here's the thing."

"Don't," interrupted Seffie, putting out her hand to silence him. "We agreed."

"I have no choice now," Odo sighed, patting Seffie's arm reassuringly.

Chin threw himself down, his head in his hands and Sookie leaned in next to him.

"Go on," she encouraged Odo.

"Apart from me," and he waved his hands around the room, "the others here are quantums."

There was a stunned silence and Julia whirled around in a temper, "You've got to be kidding us, it's a joke right?"

Odo sat still facing down her fury, while everyone else stared at each other in stunned silence. It seemed as if the very air had been sucked out of the room, so complete was our shock and bewilderment.

Seffie broke the silence and spoke first. "I was once a young girl called Stephanie," she cleared her throat and seemed to struggle to continue. Her eyes filled with tears, but she carried on. "I was born in New York. It was centuries ago. My quantum clock is damaged so I can't give you an exact date. When I was sixteen, I was waiting for a transit vehicle with my parents. I lost my footing and fell in front of it. My body was so badly damaged that transfer to a quantum was my only option."

She rested her head in her hands and looked miserably at the floor. There was an amazed stillness in the room. I stared silently at her. I felt sick. She was a machine!

"I grew up on a ranch in Wyoming," Chin sighed, looking around at everyone, but avoiding Julia. "I was out riding. My horse got spooked and threw me over a cliff. I was fifteen at the time. It took the authorities two days to locate me. When I woke up, I was a quantum. My name was Stephen Chinley."

Sookie rubbed Chin's arm and rested her head against him. "I was called Susan," she smiled. "Sookie was my nickname after a cartoon character. My family lived by the sea and I loved to sail yachts. One day, just after my thirteenth birthday, I took my new boat out too far from the coastline and got caught up in a hurricane. I was picked up after three days in the water. The medics took me to a leading quantum center. That was where I met Chin, Seffie, and Serena, or should I say, the girl that used to be Serena," she paused. "I've gotten used to being a quantum but I would still love to be human again and eat pizza," she sighed.

Seffie looked up wistfully, "I miss ice cream the most."

"How did you end up here with Odo?" I asked slowly, dumbfounded at their revelations.

"We were in the quantum suspension lab, in suspended animation after our port," Seffie answered quietly. "This must have protected us from the virus," she paused and twisted her blue hair in her hands. "When the four of us awoke everyone was gone. We haven't got a clue if we were in suspension for months, years, decades or even longer. We don't know what happened while we slept. All we do know is that at some point the power to our hospital was cut. Our new quantum bodies were fully operational but had sustained some damage after our extended hibernation. Later, we made our way out of Seattle to the forest here and found Odo."

"Seattle?" I repeated staring at her.

"I'm sorry Jake," she said, returning my gaze. "The laws of robotics permit me to lie when I feel it's in a human's best interest. I thought it advisable given your distress, that we shouldn't add to it by revealing our true nature and our stay in Seattle's quantum facility."

"Which is why," added Chin, "I couldn't take the gun from Julia when she stood over the fallen Citon. I have an inbuilt inability to harm any living creature."

"We have to protect all human life," added Sookie passionately. "Which is why I was so concerned about Odo. The great power of being quantum also has limitations, so that our amazing advantages over biological humans can't harm them in any way."

"They can't be bots, they just can't," said Tom his eyes still wide in amazement. "I've felt their skin, they cry and think, and reason."

"See, we are already 'they,'" said Seffie bitterly looking up at Odo.

"It's impossible," shouted Julia stamping her foot and looking at Chin in a fury. "You cannot have been fooling us all this time." Her eyes glittered dangerously as she clutched her machine gun. A vein on her forehead bulged in anger and distress, as her face turned redder and redder. It was obvious to me that she was suffering from a bad case of uncanny valley. I looked at Seffie, but she avoided my gaze. Henley's words floated into my mind that one day, man would join with a machine to form a singularity. How right he had been. Julia stood in front of Chin, her hands on her hips, examining him in silence like a specimen at a science fair. He looked sadly at the ground unable to meet her ferocious gaze.

"Hang on a minute." Will scratched his head struggling to comprehend this new unforeseen situation. "You're telling us that you were all humans and that somehow you downloaded yourselves into bots? Man, that's even freakier than the fish aliens!"

"Quantums," replied Odo. "We don't use the term bots anymore. It's considered rather insulting. The human factor is an interesting one because when the human brain joins with the quantum, it becomes so much more in every possible way. I don't know if you kids learned about a scientist called Alan Turing in your history lessons?" He looked at us, but we were all silent, our minds still reeling from the impact of the astounding revelations. Odo continued. "Well, this scientist devised a test, the so called Turing test. You put a machine and a human in two separate sealed boxes, then you ask them both a series of questions. If you can't tell the difference between the answers of the human and answers of the machine, then the machine has passed the test." He paused and stared hard at Julia. "Therefore, you should regard the machine as being the equal of a human."

"What has this to do with her and Mrs. Henley," Julia said, slowly pointing and looking at the impish red head, who had been quietly listening to all that was being explained.

Odo sighed. He looked so old and frail. "Your companion was dying. I made the choice to download her into quantum in order to preserve her. It's not a decision I took lightly believe me. According to my history program, no one that old had ever been transferred. It's normally too much of a shock for the mind to cope with at such an age."

"You expect us to believe that this is Mrs. Henley?" said Will, pointing at the girl with his mouth open. "Mrs. Henley did not look like that the last time I saw her!"

"I can tell you," said the girl folding her arms, "it feels a heck of a lot better than being old, although I do miss a nice cup of tea." She smiled at Sookie.

"How?" said Tom sitting down slowly. "How is it possible?"

"I have the equipment in a concealed lab outside my room. It was left in the bunker post catastrophe by whatever science team was here before my parents arrived," replied Odo. "The brain is scanned. Its entire synapses and every single one of its millions of neural components is reorganized and recreated on the quantum brain, including memories and feelings. The consciousness field on the human is transferred down a consciousness channel into the quantum with all that made that person unique and who they were, including Mrs. Henley."

"What about the old Mrs. Henley?" I asked, slowly trying to reason it all out.

"I buried her," said the girl cheerfully. "I thought about saying a few words over myself but it seemed so ridiculous, that I decided against it. Not many people get to be at their own funeral!"

"I have no words for how creepy that sounds," said Will, shaking his head in disbelief.

"So what, you have a stash of bot bodies in a secret room somewhere?" Julia's face was incredulous.

"No replied Odo." Mrs. Henley's body belonged to a quantum called Serena. After civilization crashed, she came here with Seffie, Sookie and Chin. Years passed and she could no longer cope. We woke up one morning to find she had deleted herself.

"Deleted herself?" repeated Will his mouth still hanging open.

"She left no back up, nothing" said Odo, very matter of factly. So we stored her in case the time should come when I needed to be transferred."

"And now we don't have a quantum for you," said Sookie, looking at him sadly.

Will stared at Odo as if he had gone mad, "You planned to become a female computer?"

Odo ignored him. "We'll think of something else." He smiled, not looking in the least bit worried.

"I'm very grateful for your sacrifice," the girl said, and patted his hand. "You've given me a second chance at life and I won't let you down."

"So you want us to believe that you are really Mrs. Henley?" asked Julia.

"Well, I can tell you all about our time on Moonbase." The girl smiled at Julia. "The first time I met you, you were wearing a beautiful white dress. And of course," she continued, "our trip on the Time Train. Remember when we woke up and poor little Alex had aged ten years."

"We didn't tell that to anyone," said Emily quietly, biting her lip. "There's no way anyone could know about that."

"How do you feel?" I asked the girl.

"Amazing," she replied. "I'm still me, but better. I can think and work things out in math that I would have needed a computer and weeks of research in the past to accomplish. Now, it's like I have a Pid Pad in my head. All the information I need is right here in seconds."

She tapped her bright red hair. I looked at Seffie. It made sense to me now, all her abilities with the quantum at Microsoft and her peculiar eye movements. The eyes truly are the windows to life, I thought to myself. The girl's eyes had a similar blank expression like Seffie's. I shook my head in wonder.

"How are you all so real?" I asked. "When we left Earth, quantum technology in bots was still in its infancy." I was thinking of Tale and Sugar, although the days of World Sing Song seemed so far away now that I could hardly believe they had ever happened.

"Humans learned to port, or transfer themselves, not long after the Citons arrived," Odo said. "They were aided by Citon technology and for those few people for whom medicine had no answers, it was the perfect solution. The science of growing a much-toughened version of our skin evolved, along with a realistic machine-based body. This meant that the person could be ported as hardware into a new being... into a brain, based on quantum principles, which would then enable the person to be the person they were before, just in a different body. A better and stronger body."

"What if there were two?" I asked.

Odo shook his head. "The transfer of the old to the new, automatically destroyed the old. Like emptying water from one glass, to another glass. I emptied Mrs. Henley out of her old body into the quantum."

"I don't get all of this," said Julia, pacing around in agitation. "All I know is that you're trying to tell me that this is Mrs. Henley and these are bots." She waved her hand around the room.

"Perhaps you should call me Violet now," said the girl. "Mrs. Henley

225

seems a bit old don't you think?" She tossed her red hair, got up off the chair arm and twirled around in front of me. "What do you think Jake? Am I a looker or what?"

I had to laugh. The sheer absurdity of it all was so comical. Violet began to laugh as well and soon we were shaking, clutching our sides.

"I don't know what's so funny," said Julia crossly. "Here we are stuck in a cave with a load of bots and a sea full of smelly, fishy aliens to hide from."

"Mrs. Henley, I mean Violet, you're a bot!" I said laughing.

"All the way to the future to become a bot! It's one heck of a way to solve a leaky bladder," she said, and we laughed even harder.

"You were nuts when you were Mrs. Henley, you're completely insane now," shouted Julia, as mad as could be!

Violet and I clutched at the cushions still chuckling, and she threw one at me playfully.

Will leaned back staring at Violet, "They're both crazy." Tom shook his head and ignored us.

"I'd like to see this lab of yours Odo."

He nodded tiredly.

"Is that why the Citons haven't captured you?" asked Emily perceptively, looking at Sookie and Seffie. There was silence in the room.

After a pause Seffie replied. "It's likely that after scanning the Earth, and finding perhaps only a few people and quantums, the Citons decided that it wasn't worth their while to hunt us down. We can't have children and therefore increase in numbers, so what's the point. Quantums are no threat to the Citons."

"Are there really other settlements then Odo?" I asked.

He relaxed back into his recliner and folded his hands. "Truthfully, I don't know," he replied. "I didn't want you kids to lose hope after the shock of your landing. I don't know what has happened in other countries, I just don't know." He shook his head.

"The demise of humans was certainly the fault of the Citons," said Violet perching back on the arm of the ancient recliner. "I've accessed a lot of files on Odo's old quantum and piecing together what happened it seems likely that humans were infected by a manufactured Citon robotic virus, which unfortunately for the Citons, then backfired on them."

"What?" asked Julia finally sitting down.

The atmosphere in the room was calmer. I sipped at the warm drink that Odo handed to me.

"How did the virus backfire?" I asked.

"It appears humans were using nanobots in medicine to stop aging and greatly prolong human life," replied Violet. "These nanobots mutated with the Citon virus. The virus appears to have been originally targeted with particles to destroy the human respiratory system."

"So you couldn't breathe?" asked Julia.

"Precisely," replied Violet. Then it spread through the entire population eventually killing everyone. The Citons were also infected with the virus when it merged with the human medical nanobots. They retreated to the ocean to look for an answer. It seems they found some kind of solution for themselves, but of course not for us." Everyone was thoughtful.

"Still can't believe you're a bot," said Julia, suddenly looking at Seffie. Sookie looked upset.

"It doesn't matter what anyone is," said Emily, glaring at Julia. "All that matters is that we are among friends." Emily rose and sat next to Sookie, holding her hand. Sookie smiled at her gratefully.

"Why didn't you tell us this to start with?" I asked.

"We didn't want to frighten you," Sookie answered. "It was a big enough shock that your entire world had disappeared. We thought it best not to say anything about our quantum state until you had accustomed yourself to us."

"Good call," said Will. "It would definitely have been a case of too much information on our first night down here!"

"We need to accept everyone for who they are," said Violet sternly. "If we do that and help one another we have a chance, a small chance of staying alive."

"Why do you say that?" I asked.

"Because sooner or later, the Citons are going to come looking for us." replied Violet. "They are going to locate the object that entered the atmosphere and discover the Time Train. Then they will want to find out who was onboard. It seems unlikely that the train would fly here all by itself, and because there were no bodies, they will put two and two together and the search will begin."

"Don't," said Emily covering her face, "perhaps they won't bother."

"Oh, but they will," said Violet grimly. "And then we have to decide what to do."

"Isn't this place safe from detection?" I asked Odo.

"I have always thought so," replied Odo. "But if the Citons come looking and turning over every last blade of grass, then I'm not so sure."

"Oh great," groaned Will. "Now you tell us. We might have been better off staying in the Microsoft bunker."

"So you made it then," said Violet, leaning forward.

"Yes," I sighed. "It's a long story."

"We saw a Citon and stole its magic eye lens," interrupted Julia, blowing on some tea that Seffie handed to her.

"What?" exclaimed Odo. Now it was his turn to look surprised.

"It will only work for Jake." Then she added, "No one can explain that one!"

"I can tell you now that the lens will never work for a quantum," Seffie said, "it was always designed for a biological organism, although I was shocked given the statistics of humans who had tried them, that it worked for you at all."

Julia looked at Seffie strangely. "I'm sorry, it's going to take me a while to adjust to the fact that you're a ..." Violet stared hard at Julia.

"Quantum," Julia finished meekly.

"I want to hear everything that's happened," Violet said stretching out. "Once I know what's going on, then I can better advise everyone what our next step should be."

"I see that becoming a quantum hasn't affected your confidence at all!" Will said.

Tom just frowned. I could see trouble ahead. He wasn't going to give up his leadership of us all without a fight.

Violet laughed mischievously. "Nope, I'm cleverer than ever."

"Well, I'm glad to hear it," said Julia sarcastically, "because we are going to need some brains to get us out of this mess, and the two geniuses here haven't managed it so far." Will playfully threw a cushion at Julia and she ducked.

Everyone was slumped on the floor. I could see Emily struggling to keep her eyes open, and Chin's head was tipped back. I related the tale of how we had come upon the Citon in the woods. Violet enjoyed the part where Julia charged it, and I could see that despite rolling her eyes, Julia liked the admiration. Our visit to the Microsoft bunker had Violet in tears, especially when I related the part of Henley's message to her. By now nearly everyone was asleep. I told Violet all that I knew about the lens, the return of my blanket, and our message to the fractal in space. At the end of it all Violet sighed.

"You did so well Jake, your Dad would have been proud of you."

"Do you think I'll ever see him again and tell him myself?" I asked, sadly.

Violet looked thoughtful. "He'll be an old man now, not as old as Odo but ..." She paused, "my Henley will be old as well."

"What do you think he would say if he saw you now?"

"He'd be surprised but happy for me."

"It must have been a huge shock when you woke up." I looked at Violet curiously.

"What happened?"

Violet smiled. "I understood instantly as the first program revealed my altered state." She laughed. "And then of course Odo talked to me for hours and well," she laughed again, "when he handed me a mirror, any regrets I might have had just faded away."

"I still can't believe it, are you sure that you are you? I mean do you have anything of the other girl still in there," I tapped my head.

"No," Violet smiled. "I am really me. Serena wiped this system completely. There's no one in here," she tapped her head, "but me, Violet Henley."

"What should we do now?" I asked.

"Only you can tell us that, " she replied.

"Me! How?"

"You're sitting on the most powerful device in existence. The lens! It's the sum of all knowledge as gathered by the Citons. They had the technology to map and travel the galaxy... to tap into all its energy sources, and build huge spaceships travelling faster than light, before we had even thought of cell phones."

"And yet, here they are under our oceans, doing who knows what and why," I said.

"They may have undergone some sort of collapse of their civilization," pondered Violet. Then she hesitated. "Something has happened, perhaps to do with the virus or why would they stay here?"

"Why help us so much then turn against us?" I wondered aloud.

"The planets that you saw in the galaxy, were they habitable?" Violet questioned me.

"There were many that could potentially support intelligent life," I replied. "I saw some beautiful worlds, but no civilizations on them. I will say though, that planets like ours with a huge water supply seem very rare."

"Something is wrong, very wrong, in our galaxy," said Violet thoughtfully. "All those billions of stars, and planets, and no one out there! No trace of humanity or any other intelligent species."

"Humans must be through the fractal," I pondered. "If they aren't, if this is really it, I don't know how they will cope." I glanced around at everyone sleeping peacefully in front of us.

Violet leaned forward. "You are going to have to use the lens, I mean really use the lens. We need answers and we need them quickly."

"Violet, I'm afraid, what if I lead them right to us?" I muttered.

"You won't if you keep the lens in and master it properly."

"I can't do that. I can't see anything else once I'm wearing it, and what would be the point anyway?" I protested.

"Listen," Violet said, leaning forward. "If you leave the lens in then we can stay one step ahead of the Citons permanently. We'll know what they're up to. As for seeing with the lens, you're going to have to train your brain to flip back and forwards so that you can function with the lens still in your eye."

I shook my head. "It's not that simple," I argued. "You've no idea how it feels, Violet."

"And I wish I did," she said. "For some reason your brain is peculiarly adapted to using it. Do you know how rare it is for that to happen? I read in my data banks that only a few humans prior to the catastrophe were ever able to do that."

"I know, I know," I sighed. And then I took her machine hand and held it in my own.

"Remarkable isn't it?" she smiled, looking down at our entwined fingers.

I observed her and wondered, remembering the warning from Moonbase. Classified meant tell no one.

"Violet, why would Henley have a gun on board the Time Train?"

"Henley," she repeated in surprise, "My Henley had a gun?"

"Yes, he kept it under the quantum console. Julia saw him check it once and she brought it with her when we left the train."

"I don't understand." Violet said, blinking quickly, obviously trying to process the information. I watched her closely. If the laws of robotics were true, then she would be unable to lie to me about what she knew. "There's no logical explanation," she eventually replied in a puzzled tone.

"I received a warning at Moonbase," I said, taking a huge gamble. "There was an anonymous message on my Pid Pad, which stated that someone on board the train was a traitor."

"You think it was my Henley?" she asked, looking shocked.

"Well he did have a gun." I replied sheepishly. She blinked quickly for a few seconds.

"Yes, but you only have Julia's word for that."

"Are you crazy?" I whispered angrily "Are you seriously suggesting that the traitor could be Julia? Her head was only ever full of dresses. She made the trip partly because Dad forced her, and partly because she wanted to start her own design business with the millions that the Future Project promised all of us!"

"What millions? " asked Violet in surprise. I stared at her in horror.

"Why, the millions that the Future Project was paying everyone to make the trip... so that they could start a new life." Violet looked away from me in confusion, and tightened her grip on my hand.

"There was no such deal that I was aware of." She said softly.

"Dad..." I whispered, my voice cracking.

"Jake, listen to me." Her tone was low and firm. "We know nothing about any of this, and given our situation, it's completely irrelevant.

231

Forget it, don't think about it anymore. Don't mention it to anyone else. Whoever was, is, or could be a traitor doesn't matter now." I opened my mouth and she put her fingers to my lips.

"Sleep." She whispered. I lay down slowly, my thoughts in turmoil. I tossed and turned for hours before I eventually dropped off.

When I awoke later that morning, I found Emily in the kitchen. She immediately told me that Julia had gone into the forest with Seffie and Chin to hunt for rabbits! Julia had confessed that she absolutely couldn't live on any more nutritious shakes and broth; she wanted some real meat, something to chew on.

"So she's going to shoot something?" I said incredulously.

Emily stirred the soup that she was making, "I think it's more likely Chin will be doing that, he'll do anything for her," she replied softly.

Will burst through the door chuckling to himself.

"No rabbits yet I'm afraid."

"What happened?" asked Emily smiling.

Will was almost bent double now, holding his sides, roaring with laughter. "I told Julia that in order to catch a rabbit, she should stand behind a tree and make a noise like a carrot." Emily started to giggle as Will slapped his thigh. "She asked," he gasped, "what kind of a noise is that?" Emily's laughter was contagious. Will continued, still whooping it up. "I was sent back here with Tom after I gave her my second great tip of the day!"

"Which was?" Violet asked, appearing behind Will, carrying the train's quantum.

"In order to entice those bunnies out, she should do the hip hop!" Will exploded into laughter again, tears streaming down his face.

"Where are they all now?" chuckled Violet.

"On their way back," said Will, "I'm going to hide out in Odo's lab. Don't tell Julia where I am," he shouted as he left, still wheezing, "What noise does a carrot make?"

Violet was suddenly serious as she set the quantum down on the table.

"Seffie helped me repair the train's quantum this morning. We now have full access to the damaged data banks and it's not good." She looked grim.

232

"Why, what does it say?" I asked, sipping my broth.

"We were attacked as we left the time track. The Citons have machine droids in orbit ready to shoot down anything that approaches Earth. It appears we re-entered the time track to slip through their defenses, as did the rear of the train. But we both emerged at different times, and get this. The quantum went down as the time line opened. I don't think we can be certain of what year this is. In fact I don't even think we can be sure of how long it has been since civilization collapsed," she paused thoughtfully. "It may have something to do with the malfunctioning quantum clocks. We experienced a massive onboard time shift when Alex aged. The quantum is unable to explain it."

"How did we get past the Citon defenses though?" I asked.

"It's likely that the train re-entered time at a much lower point in the Earth's atmosphere in order to avoid sounding the droid alarm." Violet sighed. "The technology involved is way beyond anything I could ever have anticipated back in 2085."

"So is that fractal structure at the other end of the galaxy?" I replied. "Whoever built that must be advanced enough to take on the Citons."

Violet shrugged her shoulders. "There's something going on that we don't understand yet." She took the cup out of my hand and set it down. "Okay, Jake, time to put in the lens. Emily, I hope you don't mind if I ask you to leave my dear."

"No, not at all," said Emily softly, and promptly picked up a cup of broth and left.

"That was rather rude," I said irritated. "There was no reason why Emily couldn't stay."

"I worry that you'll try and impress her," Violet said smiling.

I shook my head. "You don't understand, when I put in the lens I see nothing else, hear nothing else. Only what it shows me."

"Let me see it," Violet asked, and I took the bottle out of my bag and handed it to her. She held the lens up and turned it round curiously. "Amazing how they can fit the entire Galaxy into this tiny eyepiece. You have to admire them."

"I wouldn't let Tom hear you say that, he's very touchy when it comes to the Citons."

"Rightly so," Violet answered. "However, we have to find out about them in order to understand what's going on. When you put the lens in I want you to concentrate on their recent history."

"I'll try my best." I sat down and shuffled around on the floor to get comfortable. I put the lens on my finger looking at its tiny veins. Placing it in my eye, I took a deep breath and tried to focus. The face of the female Citon appeared instantly before me.

"I've been waiting for you," she said, or did she speak at all? I wasn't sure. All I knew was that I could see her thoughts in my head. Her pretty smiley dolphin face looked sadder and weary. "My people have found your train. A small expedition brought it in three days ago. A full search of the area, involving thousands will begin sometime later today."

I suddenly felt sick. "Is there anywhere we can hide?" I asked, trying to keep the panic out of my voice.

"I know of no such place," she said quietly.

"Can't you help us?"

"We are scientists, human sympathizers that are small in numbers," she answered softly. "If we were discovered we would be dealt with severely."

"Do the other Citons know I have a lens?" I asked.

She shook her head, the white tendrils floating slowly around her shoulders. "No, because they are unaware of this they can form no connection to you."

"Then don't betray us," I said in a hard voice I scarcely recognized as my own.

She covered her face with her fin-like hands. "Never," she whispered and shook her head. "You are just children."

We stared at one another. We were separated by everything in our existence, yet we were joined by the lens. I felt her compassion and her fear. I knew she was powerless.

"I will look for my own answers," I said more kindly.

"And I will hope that you find them," she replied softly. Then she was gone.

I lay among the stars letting my mind relax. I thought back to the beginning of this journey, way back to the Future Project that started it all, and then I knew. I don't know how I knew what to do. It came to me slowly, and I let it seep into my brain bit by bit. I looked out of my other eye at Violet watching me, and I realized I could wear the lens now, it wasn't wearing me.

"Can you hear me?" asked Violet, looking worried. I stood up straight, and spoke confidently.

"Site R, in Pennsylvania, where the Future Project was based, has quantum aircraft in storage. I'm going to activate them remotely with my mind and they will reach us by nightfall. Tell the others to get ready. We'll leave as soon as they arrive, and fly straight back there."

Violet looked at me strangely. "Remotely activate them? With your mind?"

"I can start the helicopters by rearranging subatomic particles in another dimension. It's called quantum teleportation." I paused, still staring in the lens. "There's a force field at Site R which is still operational. It will protect us from the Citons."

Violet opened her mouth as if to say something, but changed her mind. She put her hand on my arm and then left the room. Something in the Cosmos was helping me. The sum of all matter and force. I felt it but it had no name, no shape, it just was. My mind expanded still further stretching out into the depths of space. I listened to the cosmic music of stars being born, to the ancient radio signals of long forgotten television shows. I smiled to myself at the sight of 'The Flintstones, Tom and Jerry,' and 'Hannah Montana' episodes beaming out to distant planets. I heard the sounds of a traveling wave falling out of a black hole, and the sizzle of a supernova. Then I realized suddenly that the universe itself was communicating with me, not in words or thoughts but in its very being. I strained my mind to its breaking point. Billions of neurons fired in my skull. My breath was taken away at the devastation.

Millions of worlds laid to waste so that the Citons could be sure of their number one place in the Milky Way. No greater intelligence would ever be allowed. I felt the hordes of replicating, locust-like, machines of destruction and then I saw them. Billions, swarming over planets that showed any form of developing intelligent life. They swam through space, their mass bigger than Jupiter, patrolling, watching, always watching. Joined with them were the human nanobots used in medicine on Earth. These two types of machine life twisted together in a deadly mutation that the Citons had never anticipated. The Citons were now as trapped as the infant life forms they had sought to destroy. Unable to return to Space, until an answer was found to the mutant killer micro machines they had originally unleashed to cleanse the galaxy. I shivered. Our alien enemies wanted any form of human life for experimental science. Research that they hoped would give them the answers as to how to destroy the swarm in Space above our heads. Their droids protected the Earth now, but the Citons could move no further, checkmate!

I turned my attention back to the aircraft at Site R. I could see them, dusty and surrounded by debris. I looked around and zoomed in on the control panel, amazed at my strength and my new-found confidence. I flicked through the start-up sequence on both machines, reaching out using another dimension. The roof of the enormous cavern began to slowly slide open. I saw it all clearly in my mind. Two helicopter type machines rose up through the cavern ceiling. I moved the virtual controls onto autopilot and set the course for a clearing in the forest nearby, then breathed in deeply. There was one more thing that I wanted to do. I cast my mind out, searching through the nearby trees. I saw him curled up and deactivated in a pile of leaves.

"Kiki!" I smiled and charged his cell instantly. He jumped up tail wagging, and I guided him on the path to our bunker.

I felt Julia tugging at my sleeve. "Jake" she said quietly, "Jake are you okay, why are you smiling?"

"Kiki is on his way here."

"I think Jake should lie down, like right now," I heard Will whisper.

"What's Kiki?" asked Violet, with a puzzled expression on her face.

"The metal mutt of a dog," replied Julia rolling her eyes.

"Let's take the lens out of his eye," said Seffie moving slowly towards me.

"No," I held up my hand. "The lens stays in."

"The lens stays in, the lens stays out, I wish he'd make up his mind" said Will irritably.

"Jake what's going on?" asked Tom, looking concerned. "You're behaving strangely and Violet says that you are remotely activating some kind of aircraft with the lens."

"Two quantum helicopters will arrive this evening. I want everyone ready. I think we'll just get out before the Citons arrive. I'll guide you to the clearing where they will land."

"He's lost it," whispered Will again. "Get that lens out now or we're going to have to tie him up soon."

"Shut up Will," said Julia angrily. "That's my brother. Jake, there are no helicopters, there is no one to fly them, and how would they know to come here anyway?"

I looked at everyone gathered around staring at me uncertainly. "Believe me the helicopters are coming. I've remotely activated them."

"Well explain how," said Tom, starting to look annoyed.

"I can't," I replied. "I can't because I'm not sure how too."

"Try us," said Tom, folding his arms defiantly and glaring at me.

"A writer many centuries ago once wrote that any sufficiently advanced technology would be indistinguishable from magic," I paused. "And so it is. I can no more explain to you what I'm doing than you could explain a cell phone to a cave man. All I can say to you is that you must do as I ask, and you will be safe."

Violet blinked a couple of times, quantum logic overcoming her human emotions. She asked quietly, "I'll get packed up. Are we coming back here?"

"No, we won't ever come back here."

Tom and Will looked at one another apprehensively.

Emily took my hand. "Jake, are you sure that the Citons are coming?"

I looked into the ocean and could see the Citons slowly gathering force along the western seaboard. "I'm positive." I squeezed Emily's hand. "I'm also equally positive that you will be safe." There was silence in the room.

"Leave me," I ordered. "I need to be alone for a while."

When the door had shut behind me, I gave myself up completely to the lens and let my mind roam around the galaxy. I wandered down winding stardust lanes, among blue cosmic dust clouds and interstellar gas. I passed stellar nurseries in the Orion Cradle full of newborn stars. Nebulas shaped like hearts, butterflies, eagles, jellyfish, and bubbles drifted by. I stood in a celestial jewel box of emerging planets, marveling at all the colors it contained. Cosmic tornados and whirlpools rushed past me. Time was irrelevant as I absorbed more and more of the wonders of the constellations. I understood that our future behavior would determine the future behavior of the stars and galaxies to the edge of all that was known to mankind. The cosmic dust that had created them had formed us too. Previn was right. Everything was entangled; everything was one, connected to all space and time. The universe was beyond human comprehension! But I was certain of one thing. It wanted to express itself through every living creature. Only then could it look out, like Julia catching sight of herself in a mirror, and see that it actually existed.

I felt the helicopters nearing. Outside in the passageway it was quiet. I walked to the kitchen where everyone was gathered around the table. They all looked up with apprehension.

"It's time," I said calmly.

"But Jake," protested Emily. "Should we really be wandering around in the dark, can't we go in the morning?"

"We have to go now," I repeated. In my mind's eye I saw the Citons rising silently out of the sea. Their gel-filled bubble vehicles idled on the sand getting ready for takeoff.

"Now," I said a sense of urgency in my voice. "The Citons are com ing for us."

"Okay let's go," said Julia, slinging her gun over her shoulder.

"He's crazy," shouted Will standing his ground.

"Look, we've argued about this all afternoon," Julia said in annoyance, sticking her face right up to Will's. "It can't harm us to go and see if these helicopters are outside, and then if not, we can come back."

"Why don't just a couple of us go," said Tom.

"No! Everyone right now," I commanded. I took Emily's arm quickly and dragged her into the passageway behind me. The elevator was open and I pushed her into it. Odo and Julia followed and soon everyone was squashed inside.

"This is insane," whispered Will furiously.

Tom looked at me angrily. "You'd better be right about this Jake." One by one we wriggled through the crawl space.

"Quickly," I ordered and began to run. Kiki was waiting, wagging his tail. He bounced along beside me. We wove in and out of the trees. I was running at full speed now. I could sense the silent whirr above my head. I reached the clearing first just as they landed. I could hear the others crashing through the trees after me. Chin had Odo, running with him piggyback style on his back.

"I don't believe it," panted Will behind me. "There really are some weird looking helicopter things here."

Everyone paused in disbelief, trying to catch their breath. The two machines made from graphene looked like huge round balls of glass with glass seats. White glowing panels lit the virtual reality controls. I waved my hands in a sweeping motion.

"Get in quickly," I said, shoving Seffie, Chin, Julia, Violet, and Odo in one of the machines and pushing Emily, Sookie, Tom and Will in the other. I jumped in the seat next to Tom and closed my eyes. Kiki squashed in next to me. Both helicopters lifted off. I led the way as we climbed higher and higher. Soon we were above the trees. Our glass enclosure turned black and we blended into the night sky. Glowing bubbles were visible now, hovering below us. We saw the forest suddenly illuminated as the Citons turned on their massive floodlights. Emily covered her eyes and buried her face in Sookie's sleeve. We flew quickly, and silently, further and further inland. The bubbles became pinpricks of light then faded out of view. Tom heaved a sigh of relief and gave me a look almost of reverence.

"I don't know how you've pulled this off Jake, but all of us are forever in your debt."

"No Tom," I replied quietly. "We're all in this together, no one owes anyone anything."

"Er, Jake, I hate to sound ungrateful, but who is actually flying these things?" asked Will looking around.

"I am," I replied.

"Okay," said Will. "That's not exactly reassuring, considering there is a Citon army beneath us, but I'm just going to accept that and move on."

"Are they okay in the other helicopter?" asked Sookie.

"They're fine," I said. "All of you should just try to get some rest. It will take all night before we arrive at Site R."

"Don't you think that at least one of us should keep an eye on you Jake," asked Will nervously. "Just don't want you falling asleep at the wheel you know."

"I won't fall asleep," I smiled.

"Just in case, I think I'll stay awake," said Will. "I know it's really cowardly of me, but there's something about being thousands of feet in the air while a kid flies two helicopters with mind control, which makes me rather nervous."

"I'm with you on that one," said Tom, raising his eyebrows. "Can I talk to you Jake or do you need to concentrate."

"I can talk," I replied.

"Are we likely to be detected by the Citons now?"

"No," I answered. "These vehicles are equipped with a cloaking device which Citon Radar can't decode. Decades of secret research and development were spent perfecting these transporters."

"What about the train," Tom continued, "how come they didn't catch us sooner?"

"The Citons were unsure how long it had been in the clearing. That, and the fact they knew nothing about the Future Project, bought us valuable time."

"Are we far away from the Citons yet?" asked Seffie, peering through the glass beneath her feet.

"At the moment they're combing the forest. Soon they will find the bunker. At first they'll concentrate on the surrounding area not thinking that we could have got further. Afterwards they'll expand the search over continents, and then globally to find us."

"So they really want to make our acquaintance," sighed Will, leaning back and running his hands tiredly through his hair.

"But they won't, don't worry."

"I'm not, Jake, or should I call you superman," Will shook his head. "You know when Tom and I first saw you and Julia, you seemed the most normal average kids anyone could meet. Now she's a fearless fighter, always with a gun in her hand, and you're flying helicopters with your brain. It's funny how things turn out."

"Where exactly are we headed?" asked Tom, still looking amazed.

"Strangely enough we're going home," I replied.

"What?" whispered Emily, putting her hand on my shoulder.

"Site R, home of the Future Project where our parents worked. We are going back to Pennsylvania, back to where it all began for us."

"Why?" asked Will, shifting in his seat.

"The Future Project built a force field around Site R that can be activated. It's unlikely that the Citons will find us there and it will buy us valuable time."

"What kind of a force field?" asked Tom, in wonder.

"It's a plasma window, reinforced with carbon atoms."

"Oh well, we'll be okay then," said Will cheerfully.

"Once we are behind the window, we are camouflaged, and more importantly, the Citons can't break through it."

"What about our message to the fractal though?" asked Emily. "Will a rescue team still be able to find us?"

"Yes, because I'll know that they're coming."

Everyone was lost in thought after this. Soon Emily and Sookie fell asleep, lulled by the vibrations of the rotors. Tom and Will still watched me in awe, unable to grasp the extent of my new abilities. Dawn began to break as we flew towards Site R. I could sense the second helicopter behind me without looking. I felt sadness as we flew over where we used to live. The streets where I dragged my Pid Pad behind me were long gone. I thought about waking Emily, but when I looked at her peaceful face resting on Sookie's shoulder, I decided to let the past go.

Echoes of our last night in Pennsylvania drifted through my mind. I thought of all the billions and billions of people celebrating World Sing Song, and looked at the empty fields and deserted crumbling villages below. I bowed my head in sorrow and wondered if mankind was lost forever. Our helicopters approached the mountains in silence. I opened the roof on the cavern in readiness for our descent.

"Are we there?" Emily yawned.

"Almost," I replied gently and smiled at her. Tom and Will took turns stretching.

"Have they found the bunker yet?" asked Tom quietly.

I nodded, not wanting to spoil the moment for Emily. I could see Citons in their gel suits scanning the cushions to count how many different recent DNA samples they could detect. They held up our soup cups and lasered their way into Odo's laboratory, smashing his equipment in anger and frustration. Bubble machines spread out everywhere. I sighed with relief. We had made it. Our helicopter descended first, slowly lowering itself into the vast cavern. Other empty vehicles stood nearby. The second helicopter followed a few seconds later and set down next to us. Julia got out first and looked around. I began to close the ceiling and turn on the lights.

"I don't know how you pulled this off Jake, but I'm proud to have you as a brother."

She put her hand on my arm and squeezed it. I smiled at her as the others appeared, yawning and rubbing their eyes. Through the lens, I saw the cavern ceiling meld into the sides of the rock and I activated the force field. We all stood still, taking in our new surroundings.

"This place is vast," I said, my voice echoing off the walls. "It was originally built as an underground city and has all sorts of facilities. First, I'm going to take you to an area which I think we can use as living quarters. Then we can decide how to organize our days until we are rescued."

Odo scratched his beard in amazement. "You sure about that rescue Jake?"

I nodded and reached for my backpack, "Let's unload and check out what's down here."

Chapter Eleven

ESCAPE TO MARS

"Mars is there, waiting to be reached."
Buzz Aldrin

I surveyed the huge expanse of cavern with Kiki by my side. It had been blasted out of the rock face many centuries ago. Jagged rough-edged walls gave way to a poured and dusty concrete floor. The landing bays, once clearly marked, were impossible to distinguish now. Heaps of abandoned machinery lay in untidy piles scattered everywhere. I closed my eyes and could almost see the last of the inhabitants in frantic consultations, looking for ways to seal the facility and preserve something of the human race.

"Where do we go now?" I heard Emily ask, her voice echoing off the walls.

"Best ask Obi dog Kenobi, the galaxy guru," chuckled Will.

Violet blinked a few times then laughed, "I like that Will."

"What are you talking about?" asked Julia irritably. "I'm cold here and I thought we were going to find somewhere to stay."

"Yes," I turned around. "I'm just waiting for our transport to arrive." Everyone looked at me open mouthed.

"Transport?" repeated Julia.

"Well I know how you love to walk everywhere Julia, but I thought you might prefer a vehicle since they are available." Just as I finished speaking two graphene transporters arrived. They slowly maneuvered their way through the debris and around our helicopters.

"This is amazing," said Tom quietly. "Are you going to operate them or do we?"

"These are really simple," I replied. "All you do is, wave your hand in whatever direction you want to go. The transporter will sense what speed it can achieve by evaluating its surroundings. I suggest I drive ahead, as I have a better idea of the facility layout."

"Jake, how are you doing this?" asked Julia, looking puzzled.

"It's a science that humans have not yet uncovered," I replied. "Unlike any we could have ever imagined."

"But how?" asked Tom, frowning in concentration. I could see that he was struggling to understand what was happening, and unlike everyone else, needed some kind of scientific explanation.

"Tom, in our century we were only aware of three dimensions in space and one in time, but there are actually eleven dimensions that I can sense now and maybe more that I have yet to discover." I paused. "Do you remember the information paradox at SETI?" Tom stared at me and nodded. "When we were on the train, in our rooms asleep, the quantum opened up an interconnected universe as we ripped through time. Do you also remember the Higgs singlet that my Dad discussed, and the particle that was found at The Hadron Collider?" Tom nodded again, looking perplexed. "Those singlets are from another dimension, transmitting information everywhere. We caused the information to come into existence even before we had sent it. I suspect, although I'm not sure, that our universe is contained in a bubble. This bubble is floating among many similar universes, in some kind of vast cosmic structure."

Will shook his head, "Trippy."

Tom whispered, "At the academy the Higgs boson, or the part your Dad called the singlet, was dubbed 'the God particle.' It was crucial in forming the universe after the big bang. What does all of this mean?"

"It means we need some Julia input into this conversation," laughed Will.

Julia leaned forward, "Okay, all I need to know is, in any of these universes, particularly the one I'm standing in right now, does everything turn out okay?"

Before I could answer Violet asked, "Where does this knowledge come from?"

"The lens," I replied. "But not just the lens itself, it seems to have opened up another voice in me that comes from somewhere else."

"I get really nervous when people start to talk about hearing voices," said Will. "In movies it never turns out well."

"This isn't a movie," I said smiling.

"Unfortunately not!" agreed Will, "because in my movie, we'd have a super stun ray gun that wipes all aliens off the planet instantly."

"And I'd be firing it!" smiled Julia, playfully nudging him.

"Let's get moving," I laughed. "We need to drive to the command center first." Chin and Will threw our packs into the transporters. Odo slowly eased himself into a seat with Seffie, Sookie, and Violet. I started up the second transporter, Tom, Will, Emily and Julia piled in. The vehicle lit up and I pointed in front of me.

"Michael Jackson isn't going to come out of one of those doors is he?" asked Will, as we inched our way down the corridor, "because if he does, I'm going to tell him to beat it!"

Julia began to laugh, "I finally got one of Will's jokes."

I glanced at them both, a vague suspicion was beginning to form in my mind. The transporter gathered speed.

"Jake, did Dad ever travel down here?" whispered Julia in my ear.

"It's likely," I replied. She was quiet.

"Even with your new understanding of everything, dimensions and all that stuff, can't you find him?"

"I'm getting closer," I replied. "And when I do, you'll be the first to know." I could hear Violet whooping in the vehicle behind me.

Julia turned around and laughed. "Can you believe it, they let her in the driver's seat?"

"Time to exercise a bit of mind control there Jake," said Will, "before this place sees its first car crash."

"She'll be fine," I smiled, waving at the virtual controls.

"Where are we now?" asked Tom, as we sped along the wide corridors.

"Driving towards central command. All the doors coming up on the sides lead to various labs and test centers. Some were also the living quarters of the people who worked here."

"You're sure this place is empty?" Emily asked anxiously.

"Positive," I nodded. "It's been abandoned for hundreds of years. When Site R was finally evacuated, it was left operational in case circumstances changed. The World Council hoped that humans would conquer the micro virus and use this facility to kick start civilization again."

"What did they do here?" Julia asked, as the vehicle slowed to move past some abandoned graphene files on the floor.

"They designed and built the Time Train components," I replied, "before they were flown to Moonbase to be assembled. Covert experiments were carried out on matter and anti-matter that were even concealed from the World Council. This place was designated to be used as a doomsday facility, where humans could survive if an asteroid hit Earth."

"Then what happened?" asked Julia

"Doomsday came suddenly with the Micro Virus, instead of the one momentous event that the World Council had anticipated. People left to be with their families, and as panic took hold, this place emptied out." Everyone was quiet. The transporter continued its journey along the bright white corridors.

"Reminds me of Moonbase," said Tom, looking around.

"I think white was the in color of the time," replied Julia.

"At last," said Will. "A return of the Julia we all know, advising us on color fashions."

Julia laughed, "I wanted to be a dress designer not an interior designer."

"I know," replied Will, "like anyone could forget!" Julia pulled a face, but Will just chuckled and shook his head.

"This is it," I said, and stopped the transporter outside two huge double doors.

We got out and Violet pulled up behind us. "You kids won't know what fairground bumper cars were, but that was even better," she said, her face all flushed.

Seffie looked at her and blinked quickly. "I'm accessing my data banks, and yes, that does look like fun."

"How do we open the doors Jake?" asked Tom, examining them closely.

"There's an access code and a retinal scan."

"So how do we get past that?" asked Violet, pushing up to my shoulder. I pulled back the panel.

"Here we go," whispered Will behind me. "Time for a bit of abracadabra!"

The code came to me easily. The override for the retinal scan was harder. After five minutes of full concentration, I had it and the doors slid open. We walked out onto a balcony. Steps led down into a huge circular white room filled with quantums. Virtual screens covered the walls and some displayed real time scenes from the interior of the building.

"The blank screens would have been connected to satellites displaying images of Space, Moonbase and later Mars," I commented, as we began our descent.

"Can we reconnect them?" asked Violet.

"No satellites," said Tom regretfully.

"Actually, among the space junk circling Earth, there are some old satellites that fell into orbit through lack of maintenance," I said. "It might be possible to hook them up again."

Emily sneezed, "Lots of dust down here."

Julia walked among the silent quantums. "These look a lot better than ours," she ran her fingers over them. A screen in front of us began to flicker.

"Julia, stop touching everything," said Emily looking worried. "You don't know what you could set off."

Out of the static an image began to form. Three women appeared on the quantum set and stepped out of it. They stood in line, a solemn holographic trio. All of them were wearing some kind of white lightweight spacesuit, with white skull caps tight around the head. The American flag entwined with the NASA logo was woven onto the front of their outfits. The astronaut in the middle looked at her colleague on the left and then at whatever was recording in front of her.

"This is possibly the last transmission of the Future Project year 3520."

"What!" shouted Tom "No, it can't be!"

"Jake!" gasped Julia her eyes open wide.

"Oh man, can it get any worse!" Will sat down suddenly.

"Quiet," said Violet breathing deeply.

"If you are receiving this transmission, you have travelled here from the Time Train and have arrived post catastrophe. Your time flow has been interrupted due to a massive rip in space time. This was caused by an abortive attempt of the Time Train to re-enter the time line. All quantums were affected. An aggressive alien race has taken control of Earth. Their technological advances have been too great for humans to overcome. Our society has collapsed due to the merger and mutation of our medical nanobots with micro cleansing chips sent out into the galaxy by these aliens. This we believe was done in order to destroy any emerging intelligent life, anywhere in the Milky Way."

The woman took a deep breath. "We are abandoning this facility in order to join a settlement on Mars. Those aliens that we have called Citons are hunting down any remaining humans. Due to the mutant chips outside Earth's atmosphere, the Citons are unwilling to leave the planet at present. We have worked out a way to temporarily disable our nanobot part of the chip, and we hope to make it to Mars."

The woman on the left began to speak. "For security reasons, although we are the last to leave, the nano codes are stored safely where we hope no Citons can access them. The force field can be activated around the facility and should provide protection against any Citon attacks. Escape ships are located in the rear of the facility; one will remain after we have left. Once on Mars, a similar force field has been erected to protect the settlement. Travellers from the past, we urge you to join us on Mars." The transmission flickered again, and although the woman continued to talk, her voice began to fade and then they all disappeared.

"Whoa," said Will holding his hands in the air. "Can someone explain to me what that was all about?"

"How can it be that she said it was 3520?" asked Tom astounded. "Our quantum registered 2635."

"And our parent's transmission at Microsoft was 2585," said Julia in confusion. "Jake what year is it?"

I sat down and searched in my mind and in the lens for the answers. "The quantum clock malfunctioned when we re-entered the time track," I said slowly. "We came out much later than anticipated. The velocity was so violent that we must have blacked out as we ripped through space time. The same thing must have happened to the quantum, which then reverted to the last known time on its clock."

"So that makes Mom and Dad..." Julia sobbed.

"Dead!" whispered Emily her face white, "over a thousand years." Sookie and Seffie looked at one another in confusion.

Chin sat in silence then spoke, "But my quantum clock says 2635, I think," he eventually added uncertainly.

"You heard what the astronauts said," Tom replied, pacing back and forwards. "When we tried to land we disturbed the fabric of time itself."

"How?" asked Odo, scratching his head.

"For goodness sake, can't you remember what year you were born?" asked Julia, shouting in frustration.

"My parents told me 2496, I think." Odo replied, still scratching his head in confusion.

"Maybe that was after the time change," Sookie said.

"No that's about right," I replied. "Odo," I spoke gently, "the nano-bots inside you have kept you free from disease and alive for over a thousand years."

He looked at me in shock, tears forming in his eyes. "So long?" he whispered. Everyone stared at one another totally dumbfounded.

"How come the buildings and telescopes aren't in a worse way?" asked Will in surprise.

"Because everything was micro coated using nanotechnology after we left. That made buildings and certain materials virtually indestructible."

"Jake, what about everyone else on the train?" asked Emily, in a voice filled with despair.

"Does it mean that Mom and Dad were mistaken about the year when they left the message at Microsoft?" Julia asked hopefully.

"I need to think," I said walking away from everyone. I hunched down on the floor and put my hands on the control quantum. I spent over an hour searching the files. From time to time Seffie would come over and look at what I was doing. Emily and Julia lay on some easy chairs while Sookie tried to comfort them. Tom, Will, and Chin wandered around with Odo looking at the quantums. Eventually I accessed the coded data stream and slipped inside, reading intently. Bit by bit I pieced everything together and retrieved the hidden nano codes. The whole shebang became clearer.

"It's okay," I said, shouting over my shoulder. "Our parents did land fifty years ago so we still have a chance of finding them."

"What's happened then?" asked Julia, flopping down beside me.

"We are in Earth year 3635 as measured by our calendar," Tom stared at me and Will asked, "Are you sure? Are you absolutely sure?"

"I am. When we came off the time tracks, droids were already patrolling in orbit. The Future Project, knowing that we were coming, wanted to push us forward in time. At that point there were serious concerns about the Citons. Having a stash of secret humans in Space was considered to be a major advantage. You have to remember that the Citons knew nothing about the Future Project. The Americans had financed it and kept it secret for centuries, an amazing feat in itself. Personnel probably lived on site with their families. That's why this place is so vast. Luckily for humans, the Citons had some kind of belief system that absolutely forbade time travel, and so they never investigated that particular field of science.

The Future Project was terrified that the Citons would discover Site R and find out about the time travelers. A NASA ship was launched as the Time Train approached. Diversions were created to hide the mission's true purpose from the Citons, and hundreds gave their lives to ensure our safety. I imagine this was the event, that caused Alex to age so rapidly. The Future Project ripped a huge antimatter hole in space time that we plunged into, which also altered the quantum clocks. Seconds passed for us, a millennium on Earth. Everyone here was born one thousand years later than on our quantum calendar. When we attempted to land, the rear of the train separated and dropped through first, as the droids attacked. It came out fifty years earlier than we did."

I paused and stroked my chin. "Starship One has been gone over 1500 Earth years. It never reported back, and the fractal that I saw is not mentioned anywhere in the quantum records."

"So what do we do now?" asked Tom. "Is there a chance that humans went beyond the fractal, or is that it? Are we the last humans?"

"What about Mars," Emily cried. "What about our parents? Are they still alive?"

I shook my head despondently. "I've been awake at least thirty hours now. I have to grab some sleep."

"If no one is coming for us, I can't stay shut up in here for the rest of my life." Julia's voice rose higher and more shrill.

"That's not going to happen Julia, just let me get some sleep before I collapse."

"Are you going to take the lens out?" Violet asked.

"No, if anything happens it will let me know immediately and," I paused "the longer I leave it in, the deeper the connection."

Violet looked worried. "Listen Jake," she put her hand on my arm. "I'm worried that the longer you leave it, in the more you are changing. You shouldn't have to feel so responsible for the rest of us."

"Yes he should," said Will cheerfully. "We wouldn't be here without him. We'd probably be fish food by now."

"I'm fine," I said, looking at Violet and smiling at Will. "I haven't changed, I'm still the same Jake, just an older, wiser version, that's all."

"Don't talk to me about ageing," said Violet. "I'm right up there with the dinosaurs now! In fact, I may soon be able to claim the honor of being the oldest human in history!"

"You're still gorgeous though," I grinned.

She laughed. "Phew, that sounds more like you."

I found a chair at the back of the room, sinking into the old creases. A warm heat spread throughout the material and the chair reclined. I felt every bone in my body relax as the soft cushion vibrated and molded itself to my shape. My eyes flickered. I wasn't sure if I was awake or sleeping when I heard her.

"Jake, Jake," I looked up at her smiley face and downcast eyes.

"Are you alright?" she whispered.

"I'm safe," I replied cautiously.

She gazed at me searchingly. "You've grown. You are no longer divided. I sense a different part of you now. A wholeness, in which everything is one. You have connected with the universe itself."

I was silent for a while. "What does that mean?" I asked. "What is the universe?"

"That, which is cut off from us at the present time," she replied sadly, and then quickly continued, "Jake, I'm to be questioned in front of our government tomorrow. They know that I was in the area on a scientific exploration near where the Time Train was found. I have only a handful of supporters, so I may not see you again. I wanted to warn you one last time, my people are determined to hunt you down. Wherever you are, they will find you."

"What do they know about us?" I asked gently.

"They know you are children, defenceless, and alone."

"Do they know I have your lens?" She shook her head, and the white tendrils floated around it softly.

"You could have killed us in the bank vault, so I know there must be good souls among you. But I also know that you have unleashed a terrible force in this galaxy, and for that your species will be held accountable." She nodded, her head hung low. I felt suddenly as if I was a judge passing sentence. Her sadness and shame at the actions of her species filtered through the lens, and I knew she was truly penitent. I looked her straight in the eye.

"I sense nothing on Mars, yet I know that humans built a colony there. What's happened to it?" I could hardly bear to see her face, a feeling of dread at the answer burning, inside of me.

"We do not know," she said, gazing back at me directly. "We cannot get past the Micro Virus."

I felt that she was telling the truth. Perhaps there was still a chance... "What about the fractal at the edge of the galaxy?"

"Citons have seen this. Many believe humans built it as a monument to their achievements after they passed out of the Milky Way, or maybe it's a gateway to another time or galaxy... even another universe. We were never able to find out because we couldn't return to space."

"Interstellar travel," I said with certainty, "will continue to elude you." She nodded sadly.

"I wish you well Jake, you and all of your companions. You are being helped now by all of the forces of the Cosmos, not just the lens. Don't underestimate my people though. You hold the key to defeating the Micro Virus, and they will bring down the whole might of everything Citon in order to capture you."

"Thank you for shielding us," I whispered. She bowed her head and floated out of view perhaps forever.

I felt Emily shaking me, "Jake, Jake wake up." My chair began to slowly right itself. "Jake, they really do appear to have a spaceship in the facility. The quantum says it's in the fourth sector. We have to go and look for it. Just imagine, a real spaceship that could fly us to Mars."

Will followed Emily over to me, his arms folded over his chest.

"Dream on Emily, you really think a few kids, an old man and a couple of... " and he lowered his voice, "walking computers can launch a space-ship? It takes hundreds of technicians, scientists and engineers to even understand the start-up sequence."

"What do you think Jake?" she asked me, her face full of hope.

"It's possible, it might take some work, but I can't see why not."

Emily jumped up. "Told you so," she said to Will.

"But," I held up my hand, "it could take weeks. First of all we need to get some old satellites working. Don't forget the Citon droids will be waiting for us."

"But we could do it," persisted Emily. "We could fly to Mars."

"Why would we risk our lives to get to Mars when we are safe here?" asked Will angrily. "We don't know if anyone is alive on Mars, or if there is a breathable atmosphere, food, heat, supplies. Think it through Emily. We all want to see our parents again, but you have to be realistic." Will paused, as Tom put his hand on his shoulder.

"Jake, what do you see through the lens? Is Mars habitable?" Tom asked.

"I've seen signs of a settlement, but no one around. I can't look any deeper, so I can't be sure."

"Then why would we go there?" asked Will again, shaking his head in exasperation.

"Describe what you see," said Violet who joined us and perched herself on the arm of the chair.

I sighed. "It looks like an old derelict kind of Moonbase. There is some form of algae covering the red sand. The atmosphere is thin, but there is enough oxygen to breathe for a short time. I can also see huge mirrors in orbit, strategically placed to increase sunlight and warm up the surface."

"So Mars has been terraformed." Violet stroked her chin, "Are there any oceans, lakes, or rivers?"

"I saw some kind of reservoir near the South Pole, but apart from that, no large areas of water."

Will threw his hands in the air. "Come on; even if we could get that ship in the air, even if we could get past Citon defenses, do you seriously think it's a good idea to fly into a desert."

"That depends," said Violet.

"On what?" shouted Will.

"On if the force field here really can hold back the Citons should they find us," Violet said, completely undisturbed by Will's temper.

"Why don't we go and inspect the ship. We could prepare it for take-off just in case it's needed," Tom suggested. Will walked away, shaking his head.

"Can the Citons get past the force field Jake?" asked Emily.

"I don't think so," I replied. "But there is an outside chance that they will come up with something. It's best to prepare for anything that might happen. The bad as well as the good."

"Can't think of much good," said Tom glumly.

"We're here aren't we?" said Violet sharply. "Against all the odds. Why don't we drive down to sector four and check it out."

"Okay, let's go and take a look," replied Tom in a heavy voice.

"I'll drive," grinned Violet. Tom looked at me and raised his eyebrows. Emily tried to cover her smile with her hand.

"Come on," I said. "Tom, ask everyone if they want to join us, or stay here."

Violet and I strolled over to the transporter. "They need something to do," she said. "They are fed up with running and waiting. All of us are holding onto the hope that we might be reunited with the others, and work out a way to survive."

"I know," I sighed. "I just wish I knew what the best course of action was. I really think we should stay here to wait and see if a rescue ship arrives."

"But Jake, we don't know if and when that might ever happen. If we can make it to Mars..."

"If... "

"Okay if, and I know it's a big if. If we can get past the Citon defenses and get to Mars, then at least we don't have to constantly dread being captured and killed."

"Violet," I said quietly. "They don't want to kill us, they want us alive to experiment on our bodies. They need to find a way to control the Micro Virus and restart their space program."

Violet looked at me and put her hand on my arm. "Don't tell the others this, especially Emily." She looked thoughtful. "That might actually work to our advantage, as they won't want those Earth orbit droids to blow us up, if there's any chance that they can take the ship and bring us back alive."

Tom returned. "It's just us three. Emily has joined Seffie, Sookie and Julia in looking at rooms and unpacking. Chin and Will are examining a quantum, and Odo is snoring in the corner."

"Let's go for a ride boys," said Violet, getting into the transporter lead seat, with a wicked grin on her face!

"Violet, take your time," I shouted, as we shot off down the corridors. She laughed and slowed down slightly, waving at the controls and looking around happily. As we descended the lights began to dim and the temperature dropped. Our smart suits heated up automatically and glowed to give off more light. Soon we were driving down a steep hill, and the transporter slowed down. We came to a halt in front of some huge, double gated doors. The words Restricted Area were still visible above them. I got out and put my hands on the security panel. I could sense that all the system needed to know was my handprint as proof of being human. The doors slid open and Tom gasped. Violet stood up and whistled. A room the size of five football stadiums opened up in front of us, exposing three central launch pads. Two were empty but the third held a massive upward thrusting rocket with small, wing-like structures attached to the sides. Slim and black, it resembled a pencil. It was at least 500 feet high and portable steps leading to the entrance lay against it. Other steps had been pushed to the sides. Violet took a few steps forward and whistled again.

"Fully antimatter integrated systems I'd guess. The age of nuclear fission is over."

"There's no way we can operate a thing this size," said Tom shaking his head.

"You'd be surprised," replied Violet. "I'd guess that it has fully automated systems and once the start-up sequence gets going, it will pretty much fly itself."

"Where does the rocket exit?" asked Tom, striding forward. His voice echoed slightly.

"Same as the helicopter cavern," I replied. "The roof will open up."

"Let's see if we can get inside." Violet's footsteps pinged off the metal floor as she made her way towards the rocket.

It took us fifteen minutes to cross the vast room. The air was damp and stale. We constantly turned our heads and twirled around, marveling at the size of everything.

"Is this where Dad worked?" Tom wondered aloud, breaking the silence.

"No, this must have come way after the original Future Project," I replied.

"Who could have believed that Site R was so immense? They must have excavated hundreds of miles of rock face," said Tom, still turning around as we walked.

Massive quantum consoles surrounded the rockets. Metal carbon compressed walls and floors in dull grey gave off a somewhat gloomy atmosphere. Finally, we reached the steps. Violet bounded up while Tom and I panted behind her.

"I'll leave the door open boys," she shouted.

"Someone likes being young again!" I yelled at the steps above us.

"She's faster than everyone now," Tom struggled to catch his breath. When we reached the ramp that led into the rocket, the door opened. I could hear Violet whooping it up inside. She ran towards us.

"Just as I thought, fully integrated antimatter systems," she said excitedly. "Jake, I think that we could really fire this thing up."

"Don't get too excited just yet. I need to look at the defense systems first," I replied.

Tom wandered around. "Is there room for everyone?"

"I'll take you through," said Violet, grasping Tom's arm and pulling him forward. "It's going to be tight, but we can definitely get everyone on board."

The spaceship's interior was a mix of whites, blues and grays blended together harmoniously. A thick layer of dust coated all the surfaces, which became less obvious as Violet switched on the soft blue lighting. I looked up at the ceiling. Rings of blue lights encircled the room. I wondered if it was some kind of new centrifugal system. I turned around. Quantum consoles with slender seats were positioned under large portholes. A more complex main quantum console was central to the command room, surrounded by a half moon pattern of ten seats. Violet put her hand on my arm. "They have some sleeping quarters on the next deck, a kitchen and the smallest particle accelerator that you can imagine." I nodded. Tom waved at the quantums and they glowed with lines of purple data dancing across the screens.

"The rooms are spinning circles within the rocket," he said, as the engineering plans appeared. "They provide centrifugal force and align themselves constantly to the rocket's position."

I sat down at the ship's main control quantum and began to check the systems. A compressed force field could be activated around the rocket, and small antimatter blasts could be fired. These would create shock waves around the rocket so should be used sparingly. Better not let Julia see those! I leaned forward on the quantum, put my head in my hands, closed my eyes and concentrated. Winds blew across the Martian surface. Red dust swirled around the green algae. No one was visible... but I had a feeling, a sense that all was not as deserted as it appeared. How to be sure. I sighed. Stranded on Mars waiting for a rescue, or stranded on Earth waiting for a rescue. What was our best option?

As if in answer to my question, I felt, rather than heard a loud banging sound and vibrations ran through my body. My mind instantly flicked back to Earth and the roof above Site R. My heart beat faster at what I saw. The gathering of thousands of Citons! They had found us. Hundreds of their bubble machines and other strange contraptions were trying to break through the force field. How had they found us so quickly? My mind raced to the cavern roof again. Almost imperceptible, fresh cracks in the ground appeared where they had parted to admit the helicopters. Tom and Violet came running through the doors to where I sat, shaking.

"What was that?" asked Tom, looking scared.

"They're here," I sighed.

"The Citons?" asked Tom.

"How?" asked Violet, "How did they find us so quickly?"

"They searched for any recent disturbances to the soil in the whole of North America."

"Clever," she nodded. "Very clever."

"What can we do?" said Tom quickly.

"Don't worry," I answered, and put my hand on his shoulder to calm him. "The force field will hold. Our decision has been made for us. I had hoped to stay here for a while, but as the entire Citon army is banging above our heads, it might be wise to leave sooner rather than later."

"I'm with you on that one," said Violet, nodding her head.

"Violet, take Tom back up to the command center and bring everyone down here. I'll start a systems check and decide on a plan of action."

"Are you sure they can't break through?" said Tom, still looking frightened.

"Positive," I replied. "Now go."

Tom and Violet scuttled out of the door. I could hear them racing down the stairs. I was shocked at how quickly we had been found, and realized it wouldn't be wise to underestimate the Citons, even though they had weakened since being on Earth. My hands flew over the quantum systems, my fingers automatically programing the nano codes. I closed my eyes again and let my senses guide me through. I heard the enraged battering of the cavern roof dimly above my head. Citons, in massive gel filled exoskeleton suits, clicked furiously at one another. I ignored the anger that I sensed, and concentrated on the quantum. The lights became brighter and I felt a low hum. Screens and crystals flickered and glowed. A soft voice spoke gently over the rocket's com system.

"Systems start up initialized. Please stand by for antimatter count down."

I opened my eyes. The force field swayed, but held. I pictured Dad's face and breathed deeply. The lens was pulling at my mind. I tipped my head back as the cosmos came racing towards me. I felt pulled through white and blue tunnels of light. My head swam and spun. Then I saw what it wanted me to see. The fractal was open. It had cracked and separated into two pieces of perfect white symmetry. I could see nothing else, but it had to mean something. Was it possible that a rescue was underway? The cavern shook again and the cosmos receded from view.

"Antimatter injections complete," the soft voice whispered. "Systems are nominal for go."

I saw myself, my younger self, sitting at my school desk just a few months ago, chewing my pencil, doodling on my Pid Pad and now, at the control console of a rocket to Mars. I shook my head in disbelief. More bangs and vibrations rattled through the ship. I heard a clattering on the stairs. Violet appeared first.

"They're pretty scared. You'd better have a plan."

Seffie and Sookie came next, staring at my face searching for answers. Julia followed, brandishing two massive machine guns. "If they get in, it's prawn stir fry tonight," she shouted angrily, waving the guns in front of me. Will helped Emily through the door. They both looked terrified.

"I brought your dog for luck," Emily said quietly, on the verge of tears, and put Kiki on the floor.

"Thanks," I said smiling as Kiki bounded over to me. Tom came in with Chin. They were both supporting Odo. The sweat dripped off Tom's face. He and Chin had carried Odo all the way up the steps.

"We didn't pack a lot," panted Tom. "A lot of the stuff got left behind. I thought it was more important to get here fast."

I nodded. "The rocket has some provisions on board. If we use them wisely we should be okay."

Will groaned, "Not the powdered food again."

"So are we blasting off for Mars?" Julia asked, holding her guns tightly.

The ground shook, the force field swayed and then held again. "They are going to bombard us continually with everything that they have," I replied, and then added, "the fractal has opened."

Violet clapped her hands. "They got the message from SETI. Are they on their way for us?"

"First of all, I can't see any rescue ship, secondly, I don't know who they are and how long they will take to get here and thirdly..." a loud bang shook the rocket again. "I'm persuaded that it might be an idea to check out Mars." Tom slammed the door shut, and it sealed automatically.

"All systems are nominal, do you wish to start count down sequence?" the com voice whispered.

"Yes," Violet and I shouted, as another bang vibrated through the chamber.

"Okay," I said. My fingers moved quickly through the air, directing the quantum.

"Find a chair and strap yourselves in. The G force is going to pin us to our seats on takeoff." The rocket shook again. "Then we'll experience zero gravity until we pull out of Earth's orbit and I can switch the centrifugal systems back on."

"What are they doing up there?" asked Violet, quickly fastening her seat straps.

"Nuclear fission lasers," I replied without hesitating. "It will take them a while, and even then it's doubtful that they will cut through, but..."

"Best not to take any chances," said Violet, her eyebrows raised.

"Agreed," I smiled and then lowered my voice. "Can you take over the antimatter blasters here in case we need to shoot our way out? I know Julia would love to do it but, she's a bit trigger happy and I don't want to fire unless it's necessary."

"Understood," Violet smiled reassuringly. "I think we're ready."

I looked around, Julia was clutching her gun. Tom's face was grim. Emily and Will had their eyes closed, while Odo, Sookie, Seffie and Chin looked at me expectantly.

Will opened an eye, "I haven't got a clue how you're going to fly a rocket to Mars, and you know I don't need the details, so just go." The rocket shook violently.

"May I suggest we make that now," breathed Will, his knuckles white from grasping the arm rest.

I moved my hands elegantly through the air and the countdown sequence began. The lights dimmed and everyone was silent. I could hear Emily breathing and Julia shuffling with her gun. The rocket began to vibrate violently. I leaned forward and looked through the lens. Above me the Citons were working. The whole airspace was covered in Citon bubbles and machinery. They would soon move towards us if we launched, therefore the element of surprise was everything. I had to lift off with maximum antimatter thrust, and time the opening of the force field at the exact second that the rocket tip reached the cavern ceiling.

"No one say anything," I commanded, as the sequence neared its conclusion.

"It's not exactly a chit chat moment," Will shouted, from behind me.

I felt the lift and went for maximum velocity. My fingers raced across the console. The rocket shot up at a crazy speed just in time to trigger the force field release. The Citons fell through the roof of the helicopter cavern nearby, while we blasted through thousands of bubbles. Massive shock waves sent the Citons spinning around beneath us. I felt a collective scream go through the lens, and I shuddered. Behind me I could hear Julia, Tom, and Will throwing up. Emily had passed out. Backpacks began to swirl and rise towards the ceiling as we reached the upper atmosphere. I looked around, chunks of vomit floated by my face encircling the room. I waved them out of my field of vision.

"Is everyone alright?" I shouted, clinging to my seat straps.

Will looked at me pitifully through all of the floating puke. "It was never like this in Star Wars!"

Violet began to undo her straps.

"Stay where you are," I commanded. "The droids have begun to take formation. I need you to help me." I spun around in my chair. The rocket slowed. We were hurtling through the vastness of Space. Images of our trip to Moonbase came back to me; Julia crying and asking about the whirly thing, Mom drinking lemonade and Dad watching the news.

"Here they come," I shouted at Violet urgently.

I could see her quantum brain processing all probabilities, and disregarding her human emotions. A swarm of small robotic machines equipped with nuclear lasers streamed towards us. Violet lined up for the blast, and the rocket shook and dipped. It righted itself and shot forward. I could see another crowd chasing us. Violet swung around, lined up the blast and fired again. We plummeted through Space a second time and shot forward again gathering speed. We were now thousands of kilometers, from Earth travelling at an unimaginable velocity, pushing through the fabric of Space. Blackness and flashes of starlight whizzed past the portholes like a meteor shower.

Violet breathed, "I think we've lost them now, or they've decided not to give chase."

We waited, tense and ready for another swarm to appear. Finally Violet relaxed. "We've shaken them. At this rate of acceleration unless they contain antimatter, they can't catch up with us."

"I agree," I replied in relief. "The fact that we've shaken them gives me hope that the other two rockets were able to do the same."

I sensed the lens expanding my mind and I saw the hundreds of dead and injured Citons. The side of the mountain at Site R was ripped open revealing the Future Project in all its glory. Collapsed bubbles and machinery lay wrecked inside and on the mountain slopes. Shocked and enraged, Citons walked slowly among the carnage helping one another. Emergency aircraft began to arrive with mobile medical care for the many wounded. My mind flicked back again and I switched on the gravity systems. The room reached an ambient temperature and I sank back into my seat.

"That's gross," I could hear Julia saying behind me.

"You don't look too sweet yourself," replied Will.

Sookie and Seffie undid their straps and immediately ran to Emily. They sprinkled water on her pale face and she blinked quickly, her eyes gradually focusing on me.

"We made it Emily," cried Seffie triumphantly. "We're on our way to Mars."

"Is that true Jake?" said Emily, holding her hand out. I unbuckled my safety harness and knelt down next to her.

"We should be there very soon," I said elated, squeezing her long, slender fingers.

"Great," sighed Will. "On the plus side no aliens, on the minus side, no air, food or water!"

"Let's get cleaned up," said Tom. "It stinks of puke in here."

"Not wanting to be a whiner," groaned Will again. "But is getting down as bad as getting up?"

"It should be a lot less traumatic," I said, in a voice more confident than I felt. Odo struggled over to where I knelt, and put his hand on my shoulder, "Good job Jake." I patted his hand, and took a drink of water that Seffie offered to me. Everyone started moving around, now spraying their suits and the floors.

"How long to Mars?" asked Violet peering at the controls.

"A few hours," I replied, "and then hopefully we'll find what we're looking for."

"Hopefully," repeated Violet. "Because, there's no going back now! Either way for better or worse, we are stuck on Mars until we're rescued or..." We looked at one another.

I swallowed. "Let's hope that the open fractal is a sign of a rescue mission."

"But they will be flying to Earth," Violet sighed. "Unless, we can divert them."

"We'll have to set up a beacon, figure something out when we get to Mars," I speculated. "Perhaps I can use the lens to let them know where we are."

"Whoever they are," said Violet thoughtfully.

I turned around and busied myself at the controls. Chin prepared food in the small dining area, while Tom, Will, Emily and Julia took turbo showers in the rocket's steam rooms.

Julia came through and flicked a dry towel at me, "Your turn stinky."

I laughed, "I haven't had a shower since 2,000 and..."

"You won't believe how good it feels," she continued, and I took the towel from her.

She was right. I looked in the mirror afterwards and rubbed away the steam with the wet towel. I was shocked at my reflection. I had aged so much. The beginnings of a beard covered my chin and around my mouth. All the baby fat on my face had disappeared. It was leaner, more angular. My hair hung to my shoulders in long blonde waves. Most surprising was the lens. It seemed to have dissolved right into my eyeball, the blue veins barely visible now! I pulled down my lower eyelid and began to examine it more closely. Then came a loud knock at the door and I hastily grabbed my towel.

"You might want to take a look outside," shouted Violet.

I exited the steam room, my hair still wet and ran to one of the port windows. I tightened the towel around my waist. We had coasted into orbit. There, right in front of me, so close I could see the tiniest details, was a picture that I'd thought I would only see in school text books or on film: Mars.

263

Chapter Twelve

STARSHIP INFINITY

"We are just an advanced breed of monkeys on a minor planet of a very average star. But we can understand the universe. That makes us something special."
Stephen Hawking

We orbited Mars for three days, during which time we took a closer look at the surface. It had changed over the centuries. The red planet was now speckled with patches of green, and the South Pole had a large area of grey blue water. I zoomed in and out above the surface with the lens, but apart from dust blowing over the rocky plains, everything was quiet. The terraforming of Mars had not been fully completed. I wondered if the Citons had thought to resettle the human species here before the great alien war. After all, we needed water to survive which Mars had, but we didn't need to actually live within it. Perhaps, I just wanted to believe that some good existed in those amazing aquatic creatures.

The domes of the settlement were surrounded by a plasma window, similar to the one at Site R. This reassured me, as I reckoned someone had to have been alive inside to turn it on. As much as I searched though, there were no signs of life on the surface.

The oxygen levels were too low to walk around comfortably. We would need to take some canisters with us and keep breathing it every few minutes or so. The temperature was hovering at a freezing minus ten degrees C, and I was worried how we would manage with Odo. He had spent the last few days lying down. Will was convinced it was because I'd told him he was over a thousand years old. He said that was enough to make anyone feel queasy!

I checked our orbital position. The quantum confirmed that we would land in two hours. To the west of the domes lay a clear strip, obviously designated for that purpose. What I found puzzling was that I couldn't see any other ships scattered around the deserted hangers. It would be a three-mile walk from the landing field to the first dome. Perhaps there we would find some answers. I sighed and examined my eye in the bathroom mirror. I had tried now for two nights running to remove the lens, but despite mine and Violet's best efforts, it seemed to have molded itself to my eyeball and wouldn't come loose. Violet sat on my bed waiting for me. I opened the door and flopped down next to her.

"Can you still feel it?" Violet asked, scrutinizing my face.

"No not at all," I replied. "In fact, I can barely even see it now."

"How do you feel?" She knelt down, peering into my face with a small flashlight and holding my eyelid open. Her brow furrowed as she strained to see further inside.

"Fine, apart from the fact it's a bit freaky that it won't come out."

"Can you still look around the galaxy? See the fractal?"

"Yes," I murmured, "better than ever. It doesn't seem to take any time at all now. The dizziness and time adjustments have gone, everything seems to happen almost instantaneously as I think about it."

Violet leaned back and lowered the torch, rocking on her haunches. "I think the tentacles of whatever that thing is have embedded themselves so deeply into your neural connections, that to yank it out now might harm you."

"So, how were we able to take it out of the Citons eye so easily?" I asked.

Violet shrugged her shoulders. "No idea. Perhaps you have a unique match with it. Either way, as long as it's not causing any problems, why worry about it?"

"I'm not worried," I said. "I'd just like to be able to take the thing out."

Violet stood up. "Let's concentrate on finding out what's in those domes. One problem at a time!"

"You don't think that the others are alive do you?" I asked.

She looked unusually serious, "I'm not sure," she sighed "it worries me that you can't see anything down there. But hey, one moment I'm a little old white haired lady and then I wake up as a twenty something knockout, so anything is possible."

I smiled at her. "You were always a knockout!"

She waved her hand at me, laughing. "Join my cue of admirers will you?"

Julia came in, saw me sitting on the bed laughing, and looked at us both with raised eyebrows

"Having fun?" she said, with her hands on her hips.

I ignored her comment and asked, "Is everyone almost ready?"

"Yes," she sighed. "But Seffie and Sookie are discussing staying behind with Odo. They think he's just too old and frail to go walking around in minus temperatures."

Violet looked concerned. "Is he worse?"

"Not really," Julia sat down. "It's just that it doesn't make sense to try and drag him through the cold. You know, being a thousand years old and all!"

"I agree," I said glancing at them both. "He's better off staying here until we've checked out the domes and decided what next."

Julia looked at me uncertainly. "You're sure you can land this ship?"

I put my hand over hers. They were rough and dry. Gone were the beautiful pink manicured nails and soft creamy skin. It said a lot for how much she had changed, that she didn't complain about it.

"I know it's hard for you to believe. I find it hard to believe myself sometimes, but I can, and I will bring this ship down safely on Mars."

Julia shook her head. "I would never have thought it possible if someone had told me a few months ago that my brother would fly me to Mars."

"You find that unbelievable," said Violet pointing at herself.

Julia laughed. "You're right, and may I say you are going to have a hard time explaining that one to Henley." She got up and added, "When you're finished with the eye exam, we're outside waiting."

As the door closed, Violet sighed. "She's right of course; if by some miracle the others are alive, it's going to be one huge shock for Henley."

"Think you've got problems," I commented. "Try, hey Mom and Dad, I fly spaceships and view the galaxy with an alien contact lens."

She slapped my arm and chuckled. "You're right. I don't know who is going to have the most explaining to do." We hauled ourselves up off the bed.

"Let's land this rocket, and find out what's happening inside those domes," I said, feeling suddenly optimistic.

Tom, Will and Julia were at the viewing station on the main deck.

"What are those huge mirrors for?" asked Julia.

"So you can do your lipstick on a cloudy day," replied Will. Julia punched his arm.

"Actually Julia, they've been placed in orbit to create an autocatalytic effect," said Tom authoritatively. Julia looked at him blankly.

"What Tom is trying to explain," Will interrupted, "is that the surface is being heated by the mirrors which releases lots of carbon dioxide. That melts the ice and allows even more carbon dioxide to escape, thus creating an atmosphere via a greenhouse effect." Julia rolled her eyes at me.

"Okay, still preferring the lipstick explanation!"

"It's amazing that Mars is now habitable in such a short space of time," said Tom, resting against the porthole.

"Still looks like a desert to me," Will sighed.

"At least there are no Citons down there," said Emily joining us.

"Are you sure about that?" shouted Julia, holding her gun up.

"No water equals no bad fishies," Will shouted back.

Emily giggled. I could tell that she was happier already. Seffie on the other hand looked at me sadly. Things had changed between us since the revelation that she was a quantum. In many ways it made no difference, but if felt odd to think that she was a machine. Strangely enough, it was easier to accept Mrs. Henley as Violet and as a real person than it was to see Seffie as anything other than an intelligent conscious computer. Perhaps if I had known her when she was human it would have been different. I couldn't help feeling that even a machine that contained a human could never truly be a human. Seffie must have realized all of this. It was much to her credit that she showed no ill feelings towards Emily whom I clearly liked. Who was I kidding? I more than liked her! I always had. At school, I never dreamt that I would ever have a chance to date her, but now? I felt so confused. Maybe it was all in my imagination, maybe Seffie didn't care at all. I gazed at her dimpled open face and had to remind myself that it was built that way in order to look the most appealing and trustworthy to humans. I remembered Dad's words from so long ago, 'never be seduced by the illusion of software,' and then Odo telling us, 'if you can't tell the difference between a human and a machine then the machine is equal to a human.' Who was right? And what had Seffie looked like in real life? Although she might argue with me that this was her real life, Violet seemed happy as quantum. She had been old and like me, seemed to have a unique ability to adapt to something that would terrify most people. How would I feel now if I was suddenly transferred to a quantum? I touched my cheek lightly with my fingertips. How strange to wake up in a new body, still you, but with a machine face

All of this passed through my mind as Seffie said, "We would like to stay on the ship with Odo."

I gazed at her intently. "Are you sure?"

She returned my gaze steadily. "Odo is too frail to be walking long distances with an oxygen mask. Not long ago, we told you that we would go with you to SETI and no further. Through necessity we evacuated our bunker, and then even our planet. We have followed you to Mars Jake, and you still can't tell us what we will find, or how we will even live. You need to complete this part of the journey yourself." She paused and sighed wearily. "Come back when you have figured out what we are supposed to do."

"Don't be so hard on Jake," Julia appeared over my shoulder.

"If it wasn't for him you'd still be living in that underground hole, hiding from the Citons."

I heard Will coughing behind me. "As opposed to living in a hole on Mars, freezing cold with no food or water. Oh, not that that's so important to you guys..."

"The Citons weren't hunting us," replied Seffie angrily.

"Seffie," Sookie left Odo and put her hand on Seffie's arm. "We can still live here, it's not as pleasant as being on Earth, but as long as everyone is safe then surely we should be grateful to Jake."

"You didn't even want to go to SETI," Seffie was shouting now. "We had to twist your arm to get you there, and now you're telling me to be happy that we're going to be stranded on Mars."

"We are not stranded," yelled Julia.

"It's getting to be a regular fireworks show now," said Will, raising his eyebrows.

Tom got up and waved his hands at everyone. "Just stop arguing. Firstly, our parents could be here, and secondly, we could be rescued at any time."

"Can't we just land?" shouted Violet above everyone. "Am I the only one who is even just a bit excited about setting foot on another planet?"

"Let's kiss and make up," said Will, puckering up his lips. Julia pretended to punch him and Sookie laughed. The tension was broken. "Come on Flash Gordon," continued Will looking at me. "Strut your stuff with the landing sequence."

"It's unbelievable," said Tom, as I took the control chair. "We are the ones with the enhanced intelligence yet you get to fly the ship!"

"How could our parents have known that a superior eye structure would have been a better choice of gene enhancement to select," Will laughed.

"That was a total fluke," I replied. "It was well documented on the quantum that out of the billions of humans on Earth, only a few could wear the Citon lens."

"Yet not only have you worn it, you've used it, mastered it and increased its power. Don't underestimate what that takes," Will smiled at me. "It's pretty impressive to say the least."

"When you've finished sucking up to Jake, can I have some help here?" Violet shouted, bending over the quantum.

Will shook his head. "She's even more demanding as a quantum than as an old lady, don't you think?"

Tom looked around, "Is everyone strapped in?"

"More to the point," asked Will. "Does everyone have a sick bag as I've yet to have either a good takeoff or landing that didn't involve lots of puke!"

"Jake, please try to bring the ship in slowly," yelled Julia, from her seat. "Because I'm the one that gets sick the most."

"I'll do my best," I yelled back, and set to work on the controls. We approached the Martian atmosphere slowly, weaving in and out of the orbital mirrors.

"Here we go," I cried out to everyone as we began to hurtle downwards.

"Let's rock this baby," shouted Violet.

"Please tell me she's not driving," screamed Will from his seat.

"I'm in charge, don't worry," I shouted back at him as our speed increased.

Our entrance into the Martian atmosphere was for the most part smooth. As the thin clouds parted, I slowed the ship and began our decent. No storms or swirling dust clouds obscured our view. The red desert, visible to everyone through the small windows, was touched now with patches of green. We flew over the deserted domes and came to a landing strip. The ship began to automatically brake, and dipped lower. We touched down softly, and quickly came to a complete stop.

"That's it, we're here," said Emily quietly.

"What now?" asked Julia, unbuckling her straps.

"Now we pack up our equipment and go," answered Violet. "It's a short walk over to the first dome, and we can take a look inside." Julia stood up and reached for her gun.

"Here we go," said Will, raising his eyebrows. "Maybe you'll find a Martian bunny to fire at."

"Can you imagine a Martian bunny?" asked Emily happily. "Red, with a pink, fluffy tail perhaps."

"It will be red alright, when Julia's finished with it!" replied Will raising his eyebrows.

"Okay," panted Tom dragging equipment behind him. "I've got some small tanks here with enough oxygen for everyone." He began to pass them around. "We'll need to get into some of these space suits," he kicked a pile of bags on the floor. "The climate isn't completely terraformed to Earth's atmosphere. The pressure is still too low for human survival, so we'll need a bit more protection than our smart suits can offer."

"Great," Julia sighed, pulling a suit out of the bag. "Really, I have to wear this thing, really?"

Even Will looked doubtful. "Er, well at least it's a nice shade of blue and the helmet is quite funky." He stuck it on his head at a jaunty angle.

"Not exactly the outfit that I had planned to wear for my first visit to another planet, not that I ever thought I'd visit another planet," she added. Will coughed.

"Hey Julia, what kind of candy do Martians like?"

"Mars Bars," she replied instantly, and they hi-fived each other. Tom groaned. I just laughed.

"You had to have seen that one coming." He shrugged his shoulders somewhat contemptuously.

"Are you sure you want to stay?" I turned to Seffie and Sookie.

"Yes," Sookie smiled at me and Seffie nodded.

"What about you Chin?"

Chin appeared uncertain, and then looked at Sookie. "I should stay," he said slowly.

"You should go," croaked Odo, from the back of the room where he was strapped to the medical bed. "I'll do just fine with the girls, and if we need you, we can signal with a flare flash."

Will smiled mischievously at Chin, "The more the merrier!"

"Just go Chin," said Seffie gently "We'll be fine here. Come back when you've seen inside the domes."

Chin picked up one of the spacesuits. "I'm coming with you then."

As everyone loaded up the equipment, I sat on Odo's bed.

"Look after them and bring them back safely," he said solemnly.

"I will," I replied, and patted his old, wrinkled hand.

I stood up and walked over to the porthole, fascinated by the red desert that stretched out beneath us. My mind wandered through the lens. Site R was deserted now. The huge gap that we created when we escaped was left open and exposed to the sky. The Citons had left nothing behind. No machinery or debris indicated anything had happened recently. The waves crashed against the western seaboard and I searched for the sad and smiling face of our Citon friend. I was shocked when a different face appeared. A cruel looking older man, with the same dolphin like features, but a much harder expression. My heart began to pound and I tried to look away. I sensed pure hatred through the lens, and its ugliness was overwhelming

"Don't go, listen to me." His voice boomed around my brain. "We know that you and your companions have evaded our droids for now. If you are able to find and offer us the cure for the Micro Virus, we are prepared to leave Earth and look for another planet."

"No," I said automatically and defiantly. "No," I repeated and I felt a massive scream of rage go through me as I spoke. My mind raced away, frantic to escape, and sped out into the Cosmos. I saw it then. The swarm had activated as soon as we had touched down on the Martian soil. How could I have been so blind? Why didn't I realize that if the Citons couldn't leave Earth, then neither could we. I was wide eyed with horror as I stared at the robotic particles of death. Sensing my brain activity, the micro virus turned in my direction. The cleansing chips were mining for iron on a remote moon. Replicating into thousands of chips every hour, they were light years away in a distant galactic spiral arm. A swarm began to form and race towards me Their program was humming in anticipation of the destruction that they would wreak upon us all. I quickly calculated that it would take a day, maybe less, for the deadly virus to reach Mars. My body shook with fright and I grasped the window to steady myself.

"Are you alright?" Emily put her hand on my shoulder. "Jake, are you alright?" She looked at me in alarm, and I fought back the tears behind my eyes. I felt numb. All this way for nothing.

"Yes, just that the lens is bothering me a bit," I replied, rubbing my eye. "Is everyone ready?"

"Yes," she answered, still looking concerned.

"Let's go then," I said in my best pretend upbeat voice.

Will was already at the door joking. "Shall we send Kiki out first, one small step for a dog, one huge woof for canine kind?"

Julia sighed impatiently. "Just get out, ok? Hundreds, perhaps thousands of people with all sorts of dogs, bots and kids have already been here."

Violet pushed past him and opened the hatch. A freezing cold blast of air barely registered before our space suits provided warmth. I put my helmet on and tightened it. The tube on the oxygen pack hung down in front of me. After taking a few breaths of the thin Martian air, I sucked on it. Everyone else was doing the same. Violet was the first out, followed by Tom, Will, Emily, Julia and lastly Chin. I looked behind me and waved at Seffie and Sookie then slammed the hatch shut. There was an eerie silence as we stood in contemplation, surveying the Martian landscape. I began to walk. Kiki followed behind me.

"This way," I said in a hollow voice, waving everyone forward. There was no point in telling them about the Micro Virus. I didn't want them to panic and I needed time to think. Hiding was obviously not an option. Those things could swarm though the tiniest hole and swim up your nostril. You would be infected without even knowing. We wouldn't even see them in the air. One day, I thought, or two if we were lucky.

Violet caught up with me. "You're setting quite a pace here Jake, is there anything wrong?"

I looked at Violet. "Walk faster," I said. We strode ahead more quickly than before, and we were soon far enough from the others that they couldn't hear us.

"Violet, the Micro Virus that wiped out humanity was activated in space as soon as we landed." She slowed and stared at me incredulously.

"No keep walking," I whispered.

"How?" she whispered glancing back over her shoulder, half running to keep up with me.

"It sensed living intelligence and now it's on its way to Mars."

"When will it get here?" she asked grimly.

"Today, perhaps the day after, if we are lucky" I replied.

"But there's no escaping it," she said agitated. "Even the Citons couldn't master the mutated form."

"Don't you think I know that," I whispered fiercely. "I've more than likely brought us all to a death trap."

"No, don't even think that Jake. The Citons would have killed us if they'd caught us, you had no choice." Violet stopped as Tom began to catch up. "Don't tell the others yet," she whispered quickly before he approached us.

"What's the big hurry," said Tom panting. "Can we slow down?"

"I'm eager to get us all inside," I answered out of breath. "It's freezing."

"It's not that cold," replied Tom. "Just slow down will you!" Violet and I eased off on our pace, and soon everyone was walking together. The red soil beneath our feet began to show patches of green.

"Try not to step on the vegetation," I said. "it's producing oxygen."

"Hey," screamed Will suddenly. "Look, crap, the ship is gone." We all turned at the same time and scanned the horizon.

"It's disappeared," whispered Emily horrified, her oxygen tube in her hand. "Where is it Jake?"

I was confused as to where the rocket could have gone, and cast my mind around frantically. An underground chamber. Of course, the landing strip collapsed to a docking area beneath the surface. Probably in the hope of getting intelligent life below ground quickly, and so avoid triggering the virus. Other ships lay beneath the surface covered in red dust.

"They're okay," I said quickly. "Beneath the surface is a subterranean landing site. We should have stayed on board and exited via the underground system. I was distracted by our landing and didn't pick up on it."

"Are we able to find them again?" Julia asked frowning.

"Yes," I said calmly. "Let's concentrate on getting into the first dome to explore. We can make our way back to the underground system afterwards."

"Are you sure?" asked Emily still looking shocked.

"I'm sure," I said reassuringly. We trudged through the dust concentrating mostly on our breathing.

"What now?" asked Will, as we finally stood outside the giant dome. "There doesn't appear to be a doorbell."

Tom circled the side of the black, dull, brick structure.. It towered above us hundreds of feet high. I ran my hands over the smooth surface.

"There's a squiggle on the wall over here," shouted Julia.

Tom and I raced over to where she stood. "It's a double helix sign," he said, rubbing a gloved hand over the dusty tiles.

"What does that mean?" Julia asked, as we all crowded around.

"It's the sign that represents DNA, the code of human life," Tom replied.

I looked thoughtfully at the solid wall and at my gloved hand. "The dome is DNA activated," I replied. "That's the entrance code."

"So how does it work then?" asked Julia impatiently before sucking on her oxygen tube.

"I'm just going to spit on the dome surface," I said.

"Really high tech," Will laughed, as I spat on the dark tiles. The exact spot where my saliva landed began to open up. Will stopped laughing and stared at the wall.

"Unbelievable," whispered Tom in shock. I touched the shimmering surface where a large hole in the plasma window had begun to form. I pulled it apart with my hands. The wall melted away.

"Quick squeeze through," I said. "This won't stay open long." We all pushed through and stood inside. I turned around. The hole had closed behind us. It was impossible to tell where we had entered. I looked around at a huge empty circle. Heavy carbon floors and walls, no doors, no furniture, no quantums, nothing!

"What now?" asked Violet, looking around cautiously?

"More of the same I'm afraid," I replied and spat on the floor. Everyone gasped as a staircase appeared in the floor where my saliva landed.

"I would like to caution anyone against dribbling or even blowing their nose at this point," whispered Will.

"That's amazing," gasped Tom awestruck.

"Let's go down the stairs."

"After you," waved Will. I cautiously put my foot out and feeling firm ground beneath me, began to descend. Kiki scampered down the steps beside me. My smart suit began to activate to a still warmer temperature.

"What's the reading down here?" I shouted to Violet behind me.

"I'm thinking -17 degrees C and dropping," she shouted back.

"It's so cold and dark," Emily's teeth chattered. "I can't see anything."

"Is it some kind of storage facility?" asked Tom. I strained to make out the shapes in the dim light. They were the shape of...

Emily let out a piercing scream. "They're coffins!"

"Shut up Emily, they're not," Julia said angrily.

"Can we spit and get out of here," said Will, turning around in a panic.

"Calm down," I said loudly. I got out my flashlight and shone it around. Emily was right. It looked like a room filled with hundreds of coffins. I breathed deeply and walked over to the nearest one. It was some kind of see through, graphene like material that I couldn't identify. I leaned over it, my breath making a small cloud in the cold atmosphere. A face was suddenly visible inside. I jumped back in shock.

"What is it Jake?" asked Tom. Will, Emily and Julia were clinging to him.

"Suspended animation," replied Violet, who was rubbing at another container with Chin.

"You mean it's full of frozen people?" said Julia wonderingly. "Why would they do that?"

I leaned back against the coffin-like structure and ran my hands through my frosty hair. "To escape the Micro Virus," I said softly. "They landed and transferred here immediately. Once frozen the virus wouldn't attack them. It couldn't pick up any life signals. They were safe."

"But the virus is gone now," said Emily. "Why haven't they begun to defrost?"

There was a silence and Violet spoke first. "Because the virus hasn't gone," she said quietly.

"What do you mean?" asked Emily in a horrified voice.

"I mean, any sign of life outside Earth's atmosphere will eventually activate it," replied Violet.

"How eventually?" whispered Will.

"Soon, not immediately but soon," said Violet sadly.

"So we have to go into suspended animation as well?" asked Tom calmly.

"You're joking right," shouted Will angrily. "We talked about the risks Tom, and here with no one to monitor the systems it would be insane to freeze ourselves. There has to be something else that we can do, right Jake?" He appealed to me.

"I'm not sure," I said uncertainly.

"Then look in that lens of yours," said Will breathing heavily, "and find an answer."

"I need some time," I said shaking my head. My stomach was churning over in knots. We were running out of options.

"I'm guessing we don't have much time," replied Tom perceptively.

"If we did go for the deep freeze option, who is going to let us out?" shouted Will.

"We don't know," said Tom before I could speak. "That's the whole point. Everyone is trapped by the virus. You, me, the Citons..."

"They're not frozen," shouted Will.

"They have figured out a partial answer to stop the trigger on Earth," I said quietly. "But even they are unable to get back into space because of the virus."

"We could lie here for centuries, forever," whispered Emily in despair.

I wandered along the rows of containers, my mind whirling. Could I find an answer? All these people had failed. They had chosen suspended animation in the hope that someday, at some point in the future, help would arrive and restore them to their life again. I brushed against the frozen coffins. Face after face appeared as the surfaces lit up. I stopped suddenly and blinked back tears.

"Mom?" I whispered. She lay in the graphene coffin, her hair spread around her shoulders. There was more grey in it now, but the lines on her face were barely visible on her frozen white skin. Her hands were folded in her gloves and the tubes in her system lay unseen beneath her suit. I knew who would be lying next to her and as I moved along. I could hear Julia sobbing behind me. We held one another as we looked at Dad. His hair was pushed back off his face and he was clean-shaven. He looked as if a gentle shake would wake him up. I stared at him, wishing the lens could somehow penetrate his mind. Had he been paid to betray us? I had to know.

"All this way," Julia cried. "All the hope we had, to end up like this!"

She shook with emotion and I hugged her tightly. As we wandered down the line of containers. Adam, Ruby, Previn, Jim, Faith, Peter, Bronwyn, Alex and little Maya, all of our family and friends lay still in their dreamless sleep. Violet pushed past us and embraced the container where Henley lay. I wondered what he would think if he could see the tall, beautiful redhead, weeping directly above him. Tom and Will, grim and silent, stood by their parents. Tom held his head in his hands. Tears ran down Emily's cheeks, her face contorted in a silent terrible grief.

"They're not dead Emily," I said, softly putting my hand on her arm. "They're just sleeping."

"Can we wake them now?" she asked, wiping her face with the back of her sleeve.

"No," said Will before I could speak. "No one is to touch any of them. The reanimation process is an extremely delicate procedure and we can't possibly revive them without expert help. It's not like defrosting a chicken dinner in a microwave you know."

"Jake, could you do it through the lens?" Emily pleaded with me.

I shook my head. "I'm not sure Emily. I would really need to spend some time thinking it through."

"Well let's go and find the ship then you can work it out," she continued through her tears.

"We don't have time," said Violet harshly, her voice cracked with emotion. "We have to find containers for ourselves."

Will looked at her incredulously, "I've told you no, Violet."

"The Micro Virus is headed our way Will, we have to," she insisted.

"Where is it?" asked Tom brusquely.

"Out in space," I answered. "Our flight to Mars triggered the chips. That's how it picked up on us, and now it's on its way here to kill us."

Will stood looking at me with his mouth open, "We just can't catch a break," he finally said. Emily covered her face with her hands.

"Can't you do something Jake?" Julia shook me urgently by the shoulders. "Come on, you always seem to think of something."

"Not this time Julia. This is beyond any powers of the galactic lens. The Citons have been unable to completely deactivate the virus after centuries of experiments. There just isn't enough time. Violet is right, we have to look for containers and hope there are enough. Once frozen the Micro Virus will sense no signs of life and leave."

"But who will save us Jake?" asked Julia urgently "What will happen?"

"There's no answer to that question," replied Violet unhappily. "Emily's right, we could lie here for months or centuries, who knows when someone will come and help us."

"No, I'm not doing it," said Will. "Knowing our luck, I'll open my eyes and find a big fish in a spacesuit looking right back at me."

"What about them?" asked Julia, questioning me and motioning to Violet and Chin. "Can't they survive the virus? I mean they don't have flesh and blood."

"It still destroys quantum systems Julia," replied Violet drily. "Even my new body can't beat the virus, which sucks because I've become quite partial to it!"

I looked at Dad sadly. I was so close to him. Inches away after all this time and still I couldn't talk to him and now perhaps never would.

"I've had enough," said Julia angrily. "I'm sick of running and hiding. I'm with Will on this one. No way am I strapping myself into a living death without an end in sight. We might never be defrosted, never." We all stared at one another and Will stepped closer to Julia.

"I'll take my chances in the freezer," said Violet finally. "I'm a survivor and I'll get through this like everything else."

"We can't freeze some and not others," I argued.

"Why not?" asked Violet. "Everyone should decide their own destiny and it appears to me that this is mine." She swung around. "The statistics in my data bank for this virus are not good. One hundred percent fatal. That's not the kind of odds you should mess with."

"I agree," said Tom. He looked at Will "I don't think we have a choice."

"I strongly disagree," Will shouted "Let's just stop and think about millennium man back in the spaceship. How come he's still alive?" Violet was silent, blinking as she considered logical answers to Will's question.

"We still have some time," I said. "Let's find our ship first and tell Seffie and Sookie what we've found." I ran my hand over Mom's and Dad's containers and began to walk down the rows and rows of holding equipment. Slowly everyone followed. As we reached the end of the suspension laboratory, I saw the empty containers open and waiting for us. To my horror I counted only four.

Julia gasped behind me. "There aren't enough."

"Well that solves that problem then," said Will. "We either decide who stays and gets to be chicken tonight, or we draw straws."

"I'm staying," I said immediately.

"So will I," said Violet bravely. She put her hands on Emily's shoulders. "One day I want you to tell Henley how much I loved him."

"No," replied Emily her voice cracking. "You'll tell him yourself."

"Okay, stop the heroics and crying right now," said Will, putting his hands in the air. "It's like a bad romance movie in here. Jake, let's find the ship first and give you an hour to come up with a plan."

"He's told you he can't," said Violet irritably. "So we'd better face reality and decide what to do."

"I know Jake can find a way," Emily took my arm, her face shining with confidence. "I just know he can."

I felt the weight of all their hope upon me. "Let's get out of here," I said despondently.

We wove our way in silence through vast chambers and corridors. Quantum systems were visible in the pipes and nanotubes lining the walls. Live bacteria coexisted in a symbiotic relationship with the mainframe, powering up a whole network. The system could thus remain operational for many centuries to come. Everyone followed me, lost in thought. I sensed the ship out in front of us, and sure enough, after thirty minutes or so of picking our way through the freezing underground maze, we found it. My heart jumped when I saw where it was parked, right next to our very own Time Train. It was the rear section, which had broken away during our disastrous landing. It still shimmered silver, in the dim light.

"We've come full circle," whispered Violet. "Here we are, back again at the train."

"They managed to use the antimatter to propel themselves to Mars," said Tom to himself.

"Can we still use it?" asked Will suddenly.

"Where are you planning on going?" said Emily shocked.

"Another time zone that doesn't have a Micro Virus, killer fish aliens and powdered food!" replied Will.

"What and leave our parents here?"

"It's not like they're going anywhere Emily. As we could be the only humans left, it won't do them much good if we are frozen right next to them."

"Can't we go back in it Jake?" pleaded Julia. "Can't we find a way with the lens to go back home?" She looked so desperate. My stomach lurched. For all of the amazing courage and fortitude that she had shown, I wished with all my heart I could take her to Paris, where she could admire floaty designer dresses on a runway all day long.

I shook my head sadly. "I've told you before Julia, it can't be done. I think the very laws of the universe forbid it."

The space ship door activated and the steps lowered. Seffie appeared. "Have you found what you were looking for?" she shouted.

"If you mean frozen parents and a killer virus only hours away, then yes," shouted Will back up the stairs. Seffie turned and walked back into the ship. "It's okay, I know you don't do sympathy very well," Will shouted again after her. "A little, oh that's a pity, would not be asking too much though," he grumbled.

I scrambled quickly up the steps and followed Seffie back into the ship.

"How's Odo?" I asked, resting my hand across my churning stomach.

"He's sleeping," she replied calmly.

"Help the others," I said abruptly. "I need to gather my thoughts."

Back in my room, I lay on the bed and shut my eyes. Time was running out. I reached with my mind through the lens and into the cosmos. I concentrated with everything in me and let out the primeval cry of every human in distress since language began. "Help." My body shook and my teeth chattered. Suddenly a calm feeling flooded through me. I saw the open fractal and heard a voice, quiet at first then louder and clearer.

"We hear you Jake, we are coming."

"Who are you," I asked, wonder and awe filling my senses.

"We are the descendants of Starship One," came back the voice strong and clear. "Our Starship Infinity has been travelling towards you since we first received your message. You don't have much time, so do exactly as we tell you."

"Anything," I whispered in relief.

"The entity known to you as Micro Virus is ahead of us, and may reach you before we do. We need you to go to your Time Train and perform what is called a drop sequence. This will drop you out of time and thus ensure your safety until we land on Mars."

"How do I perform this drop sequence," I asked.

"We are transmitting to you now," the voice replied gently. I clutched my head. It was so loud. The knowledge appeared in my brain. I didn't know how, but suddenly I knew what to do.

"Do you have your instructions?" the voice asked.

"Yes,"

"Go now and hurry."

I leapt to my feet and ran through to the command deck. As usual so many questions were unanswered. Violet had her arms around Emily and Julia, trying to comfort them.

"Heard any voices? Had any ideas?" asked Will hopefully.

"I know what to do," I replied. "Let's go. We need to hurry."

"Where?" questioned Violet. "What's your plan?"

"We need to drop out of time," I said, hurriedly helping Odo to his feet.

"Er, that sounds a bit drastic," said Will appearing uneasy.

"Oh yeah, and death by a robotic virus is a better alternative?" said Julia.

"You're right," replied Will. "It's a hard choice and thinking about it, I'm all for dropping out of time whatever that means."

"Quickly," I said, "we need to get on the Time Train."

Everyone clattered down the steps of the spaceship. Chin and I helped Odo between us. Violet arrived first at the train, she had the door open in seconds with her quantum systems. A strange feeling shot through me as I raced down the corridor towards the rear Q Room. I was a different person from the Jake that had walked down these corridors only a few months ago, and yet I was still me.

"What's the plan, how do you know what to do?" asked Tom out of breath behind me.

"The fractal has opened, a rescue mission is underway, and they've sent instructions for us."

"Who's they?" asked Tom, grabbing my arm, as I frantically waved at the quantum.

"The descendants of Starship One. They downloaded a new program into my brain via the lens."

Tom just stared at me, still clutching my arm. "Hey, where is the lens? You're not wearing it."

"It's disappeared into my eye," I said quietly. I shook his hand off my arm.

"How do you know it's humans that have sent these commands?" He stood in front of me blocking my access to the quantum."

"I just know," I said looking at him directly.

"It's okay Tom" said Will gently. "He's always acted in everyone's best interests before, let's trust him now."

Tom continued to stand in front of the quantum, and Violet put her hand on Tom's arm. "It's my belief that Jake has some special ability, perhaps triggered or enhanced by the lens. He's been able to use it in a way that I don't even think the Citons thought possible. He can save us Tom."

"Just get out of the way Tom will you," Will shoved his brother to one side, and Violet stepped deftly between them.

I fell on the quantum and started working furiously, blocking out the shouting in the background. "Is the door sealed?" I called out to no one in particular.

"Everything is ready," Seffie spoke softly behind me.

"Are we going to feel all that freaky spinning and whirling?" asked Julia.

"I'm afraid so," I replied frantically programing the quantum.

"Let's lie on the floor then," I heard Emily say.

Chin and Sookie lay down next to Odo, holding the old man tenderly. I felt a whirring in my head and my mind looked out. The swarm was entering the upper Martian atmosphere.

"Are you okay?" asked Violet, noticing my terrified expression.

"The virus is breaking through. It's here," I replied breathlessly.

Tom and Will stopped arguing, and Will pulled Tom to the floor. "Ready when you are," he shouted cheerfully and stuck his thumbs up at me.

I started the drop down sequence. The information flowed from my brain to my fingertips without conscious thought. My mind raced through the controls and I felt a free falling sensation, the sort of thing that I'd had in the past, when Dad suddenly drove the car down a really steep hill. I heard the screaming behind me and then suddenly we were released and floating around the room.

"Turn on the gravity," shouted Tom, trying to hang onto the quantum console.

"There is no gravity," I replied calmly. "There can be no gravity outside of time." I reached down and caught Kiki as he floated by.

Julia, Violet and Emily held on to one another. "I actually don't feel sick," said Julia surprised. Everything glowed, shimmered and spun inside the room.

"Where are we?" asked Seffie drifting past me.

"Nowhere in particular," I replied relaxing on my back. "We technically don't exist."

"Er, well I'm talking so I must exist," said Will, holding onto Tom.

"More to the point Jake, how long will we be floating like this?" Julia asked, waving her arms around and kicking her legs, swimming through the chamber.

"Not long," I replied. "Not that long has any meaning right now. Just relax and sleep. They are on their way, and we're finally safe."

We drifted this way through time and space. Once everyone stopped struggling and flailing around, we all settled into a comfortable, floating dreamlike state. Now and again I looked at the quantum. The clock had stopped. I don't know how long we stayed that way. It could have been minutes, it could have been years or even centuries. A quiet grinding noise eventually alerted me to the fact that we were reentering the time line. Gradually, we began to sink back to the ground. Odo snored and Sookie sighed. The lights returned to a normal hue, and the shimmering glow on the walls and floor faded.

"What's happening?" said Emily, sitting up on the floor and rubbing her eyes.

"We've landed," replied Violet, brushing the creases from her suit.

"We never took off so how can we have landed," yawned Will.

"I mean we've landed back in a time line," said Violet, stretching out her arms.

"So this is it," Julia stood up straight. "What do we do now?" she looked at me expectantly.

Everyone quietly gathered at the main console where I stood. "Now we will find our destiny," I said calmly.

"Man, that's deep," said Will, gazing at me open-mouthed.

"But true," sighed Seffie softly. The feeling of movement had completely stopped now, and not a sound could be heard.

"Is everyone ready?" I asked, taking a deep breath.

"For what?" whispered Emily, looking frightened.

"To go outside," I said. "They're waiting."

"You're scaring us Jake," Julia said, her hands clutching her gun.

"There's no need to be scared," I replied. "They want to meet us, they just don't want to burst through the doors and alarm everyone."

I could see them in my mind's eye, in the place where they had sent all their information. Humans and quantums, standing side by side. I understood now what the human genome project and DARPA had been doing at Moonbase so long ago. The scientists had taken their baby, Nostradamus, to Moonbase. The supercomputer, itself, had sent me the warning based on possible outcomes of future scenarios. Given the entanglement of time, it couldn't be certain of all events. Dad had hacked into Nostradamus at Site R and realized that a hostile, alien takeover of Earth was one among many possibilities. He had been bribed to say nothing and make the trip. The traitor wasn't my father! The traitor was still an outcome for my future, still waiting for me. My heart sank as I looked at Tom... what would he do to me? Henley had taken the gun for an all too human reason. He was scared.

As for the human genome project, they were following the recommendations of the famous physicist Stephen Hawking. He had argued that artificial intelligence could take over the world, and so genetically engineered humans had been made fantastically intelligent in order to keep up with the quantum life that they had created. Tweakies were cavemen compared to these beings. They were advanced way beyond our comprehension and yet, as I looked at the group gathered outside the train, my heart soared. I believed in the nobility of the human spirit. A force that had compelled these strangers to reach out across a galaxy of 100,000 light years to rescue five children, four quantums and one old man.

My memory went back to a time long ago, when Dad had said that we would have a welcoming committee upon our arrival in the future, like those when a time capsule is opened. His words had proved strangely prophetic. If and when he awoke, I would tell him that... and many other things. The shimmering golden spaceship that they had come in shone bright on the Martian sands. The intertwined circles embedded with a laser stretched out beyond the Martian atmosphere, far into space. I estimated that it must weigh at least a million tons. Captured behind this immense vehicle and propelling it through the galaxy was an artificially created, massive black hole!

"You're sure they're human?" asked Emily anxiously.

I nodded. "Humans and quantums, evolved from Starship One's Human Genome Project."

"Like us?"

I shook my head at Sookie. "No, these quantums are not downloaded people. They have their own consciousness and their own thoughts, which have formed independently. They are true, living, artificial intelligence; machines who in every sense pass the Turing test."

"Did they come through the fractal?" asked Violet.

"Yes, from the nearby Galaxy Andromeda," I replied. "Humans now live on various planets in that region of space. They have been aided by technology acquired from one of its native species, the Andromedans."

"These Andromedans, they're not like the Citons are they?" asked Emily nervously.

"No they are..." I paused, and strange new images flooded my brain. "Invisible gas-like molecules. A highly evolved, peaceful, extragalactic, intelligent life form... consciousness in its purest design. They don't live or interact with people. The Andromedans moved on long ago. No human has ever met them."

"What about the Micro Virus?" asked Will.

"Contained in the Martian upper atmosphere," I replied. "It's been paralyzed but will be unleashed again after we leave in order to keep the Citons on Earth."

"But it's our Earth," said Tom fiercely. "We should get everyone together to fight the Citons and take it back."

I put my hand on Tom's shoulder gently "There's no need to Tom. You didn't always live in the house where you were born and it's the same with Earth. It's where we grew up, and as such we will always treasure it but there are other beautiful places to live. One day we will go back, but not now. It's not important." He looked for an instant as if he would say something else, but then closed his mouth again.

"Ready?" I faced everyone.

"Has anybody got a hairbrush?" asked Julia, smoothing down some stray pieces of blond hair around her face.

"Don't worry Julia, you look fabulous," smiled Will. "Er, but could you put the gun down now?" Julia smiled back at Will, and unexpectedly leaned her head on his shoulder affectionately. Then she reached out her hand and pulled Tom towards her.

"Don't think I'm getting soft," she warned them, "but after 1500 years, give or take a year or two, people can grow on you."

Will laughed and ran his fingers through his hair, "It's okay to say you like me Julia. I'm a good looking dude that's for sure!" Julia rolled her eyes at me and shook her head. Will continued, "It's going to be a bit tricky to work out where to take you for our first date, given the lack of venues! But, please feel free to bring your gun! There's nothing I like better than a strong girl to protect me!"

"He just never shuts up," said Julia laughing and clamping her hand over Will's mouth.

Odo chuckled and wrapped his arms around Seffie and Sookie. "We're ready to go."

Violet and Chin linked arms, and I gently took Emily's hand. Kiki wagged his tail.

"This is where the real future begins."

I keyed in the sequence on the exit panel and the door slid open.